As the Dandelion Blooms

Ellen Pearson

BLOOMING DANDELION BOOKS

Praise for *As the Dandelion Blooms*

As the Dandelion Blooms is a fictional story that many of us can identify with. Whether you've been through trauma and its effects on family, or know someone who has, you will appreciate the layered dynamics between sisters, mothers, and daughters. You will also root for the mysterious writer of the letters that are central to the story. Ellen Pearson has written about realistic characters who show their humanity, as they navigate grief, family, and finding peace with the past. I recommend *As the Dandelion Blooms,* whether you're looking for a good story, or trying to find your own peace of mind.

–Julie Monetta

As the Dandelion Blooms is a book about the psychological long-term effects of childhood sexual abuse. Yet, despite the dark subject matter it is an engaging and hope filled story with an unexpected mystery woven in. Clues sprinkled throughout the narrative entice the reader to keep turning the pages right to the surprise twist at the end. It is a compelling story.

–K.S.

Table of Contents

To my daughter Rose, may you bloom every day
in all of your beauty and complexity.
Forever yours, Mom

Acknowledgements

First, I want to thank every woman and man who has experienced trauma—whether remembered clearly or discovered later in life. To those who shared their stories and inspired me to write healing words over the last four years—thank you. Deep gratitude to Dr. Bessel van der Kolk, whose book *The Body Keeps the Score* opened my eyes to the lasting imprint of trauma.

Although I love to write, and I do call myself a writer, I have never actually written a fiction novel before. And, truthfully, because I never had time to read a lot of books, I truly didn't know what I didn't know. Then a lovely friend at church named Tawnya introduced me to her step daughter Lara Helmling, an editor out of Chicago with Forest City Publications who might take a look at my book. I quickly found out that this book turned out to be a "novella" at a mere 90 pages. Lara offered to help me edit my book, and, well, here is the finished product over 300 pages later! I didn't know so many basics of writing! Lara taught me. I was so insecure about the quality of my work! Lara made me feel worthy. I felt knocked down after our sessions and wondered if I was just wasting her time. Lara raised me up. I felt alone in my journey many times, Lara became my friend. I truly don't think my dream of becoming a published author would have ever come to fruition without Lara. She held my hand and kept me moving forward. There aren't enough words to express my gratitude for you, Lara, and your influence and friendship has meant everything to me.

I am lucky to have a beautiful young artist in my life that I love as much as a daughter. My partner's daughter, Ava Kostia, in the midst of her crazy busy life, created the image you see on the cover of this book. Thank you, Ava, for wanting to be a part of this journey with me and sharing your talent with all of us!

And that partner of mine is Steven Pinkham, who has put up with my frustrations, expenditures, and many shortcomings and still stood by and supported me, beginning with staying by my side on that very first weekend, four years ago, when a beautiful friend shared her beach house with me so I could have total peace and quiet and time to sketch out my book idea. Steve has been by my side through all this time. Thank you for being there through thick and thin.

To my sister Nancy who was my catalyst in the beginning and has been a support to me until the end. She was my editor until I found Lara! She gave me the beginning encouragement that I needed to take on this journey.

To my daughter Rose, who keeps the lifeline with me open. She truly embodies the attributes of the dandelion, spiritually resilient and strong, living her life in a reverence of allowing transformation when it calls on her and letting go when needed, always connected to the Earth and Spirit, and forever open to healing. I am so blessed for her love and support.

To a beautiful friend, who would like to remain unnamed, thank you for being my biggest cheerleader and kick in the pants over all these years. Whenever I started to slide, you had a way of pulling me back to my feet and giving me the strength and inspiration I needed to keep going. This has been our pattern for a lifetime, and I feel so blessed to have a friend like you. You are a true catalyst of success to every life you come into contact with.

In closing, I would like to say that I am the luckiest gal in the world to have so many amazing friends in my life who inspire me and love me and give me the inspiration to want to help others in their healing journey. I couldn't possibly name all of you, that would be another book! You are all my lifelines!

Chapter 1

Michelle struggled to get out of bed. It didn't help that it was cold and rainy. It didn't help that her mother's funeral was yesterday. The thought caused a heavy lump to form in her stomach. She pushed it away as soon as it entered. Instead, she listened to the droplets of rain tapping the window panes. She shivered despite the down comforter wrapped around her. She glanced at the clock. The brightly lit '6:30' shouted that it was time to get up. The school bus would arrive in one hour. She sighed. The events of the last few days had pushed her to her limits, emotionally and physically. She felt weary in every muscle. "Just stay in bed. What would it hurt?" she thought. At the same time, she was compelled by a penetrating sense of responsibility to her sleeping children to get up. Grabbing the edge of the bedside table, she pulled herself to sit on the edge of the bed. "No, just do this." She slid off. Bare feet hit the cold floor. She winced. She quickly slipped on her warm fuzzy socks. Cold drafts were common in the old house. Somewhere between a cape cod and a traditional design, the two story home was built in the 1950's. People back then were accustomed to drafts, and they weren't energy conscious. She hated that part of having an old house. Yet she loved her home, if for no other reason than it was hers. It was a house of its time, an answer to the post-World War II era and the explosion of the population with the Baby Boom. She sometimes would think about the families that might have lived here, whether they were cramped into the tiny three bedrooms or they overflowed into the finished basement, which had now become her art room.

She began her morning ritual, thankful that some things just happen without even needing to think about it. She walked into her master bathroom. There was nothing master about it; it was just another bath that happened to be off of the bedroom. She picked up the toothpaste and her toothbrush and readied the apparatus as if it would jump start her day. She would wait to actually brush until she was sure the girls were out of bed. With a toothbrush in hand and a camouflage of confidence, she dragged her stiff body out into the hall. She was greeted by a stream of sunshine to the left side of her body through the window at the end of the hall and illuminated the stairs which led to their cozy living space below. She walked toward the remainder of the bedrooms and the one bath that the girls shared on her right.

"Come on, little rugrats, hop on out of bed! Time for school! Jaimee, Janine, Jessie! Let's go. The world awaits you!"

The girls grumbled as they crawled out of bed.

Michelle retreated to her bathroom, turned on the water and began brushing her teeth in one smooth motion. Jaimee sidled up to Michelle and put on her pouty face. "C'mon, Mom, do we have to? We should be able to take a day off because of the funeral."

Michelle rolled her eyes. She had expected this. Although Jaimee loved all the after school activities and fun with her friends, she hated school itself. Michelle rinsed and tapped her toothbrush on the side of the sink. "The funeral was on the weekend. No special treatment for us. Life goes on, and Grandma would want you to go to school, make something of yourself so you don't embarrass her. So hop to it!"

Jaimee groaned and left the bathroom. Michelle held onto the sink to steady herself. The weekend had left her so weak, physically and emotionally.

Michelle came out of the bathroom and headed toward the girls' rooms. Exhaustion and grief weighed on her. It was hard to lift each foot to place it in front of the other. Reaching the doorway of her younger daughters, her attention fell on the full length mirror. Her middle daughter Janine stood in front of it, posing as if she were a model.

Michelle's heart skipped a beat.

Her eyes locked with Janine's in the mirror's reflection.

"What in the heck am I looking at?"

Janine glared at her mother in the mirror without turning around, daring her to battle. "What?"

Michelle steeled herself against the anger and despair rising in her. These struggles with her middle daughter had been increasing over the past months. Michelle didn't think she had it in her this morning to deal with it, but she knew she had to.

Jessie snickered from her side of the girls' room.

"Where did you get that—what is it, a skirt? Or an oversized headband?"

Janine looked down at her outfit and shrugged. "Of course it's a skirt."

Michelle bristled. She could feel the nerve endings in her entire body tightening. "I didn't buy you that tiny piece of fabric. And you certainly don't have a job at 13. Where did you get it?"

"I borrowed it."

"From who?"

Janine turned and faced her mother head on. "Does it matter?"

As Michelle came face to face with her rebellious middle child, she could see Janine was wearing heavy makeup on her eyes and bright pink lipstick. She tried to hide her panic. She wasn't up for this. She knew from experience her daughter would have the last word. As far as Janine was concerned, she had nothing to lose in battling her mother. Michelle knew Janine had everything to lose—her future. Michelle mustered up the energy to respond as she knew she needed to. "Yes, it matters. I want to know who is loaning their clothing out to you and making you look like a tramp? And why is she even allowed to wear clothing that barely covers her butt?" She put her hands on her hips, mostly to keep her from toppling over from the weakness she felt in her body. "And are you wearing makeup?"

Janine pulled back her shoulders to strengthen her stance. "It's Debbie's skirt. Her mother bought it for her, unlike you who won't even buy me the clothes I need."

"Oh, honey, you have all the clothes you need. This?" She pointed her finger and swirled it in the air down her daughter's body. "This is not happening. Take it off now. And take off that make up. You're too young for it."

"Ugghh!!" Janine rolled her eyes. "You can't stop me. I'll just put it back on when I get to school."

"Not if I take it away from you."

"All my friends have makeup, Mom. I can borrow somebody's, just like I borrowed this skirt." She turned and started unzipping the skirt.

She bit her lip gently and sighed. Michelle recognized the time to retreat. At least she had won the battle of the skirt. She raised her voice so all the girls could hear her. "I'm going to make pancakes. If you don't get down there in ten minutes, you'll carry a granola bar out the door with you."

Michelle made her way down the stairs. The scuffed hardwood stairs gave way to the living room where life and love occurred. She wondered about that life and love, kids running up and down the stairs, from the living room to their bedrooms, making forts and pretending to be campers in the wild. Before they were 13 going on 40, they would wrestle and play 'kick the balloon,' the only rough and tumble game Shawn allowed in the house. She imagined the families that came before them doing the same, chasing the oversized dog back and forth between rooms, hours and hours of homework, dance contests with their girlfriends. As they got older, the Barbie dolls and GI Joe guys were replaced with walls plastered with pictures of their favorite celebrities and record players blasting their favorite songs. The foyer made a perfect spot to set up the camera for prom pictures as the girls came down the stairs in their ballroom dresses.

She entered the kitchen. Like most homes in the 1950's, her kitchen was small and square, leaving a narrow path between the stove, fridge, and round table. She padded over to the coffee pot first, flipped on the switch, then took out a bowl to start a batch of buttermilk pancakes. Her mother always made a hot breakfast for Lisa and her for as long as she could remember. Michelle carried on this tradition, maybe as a way to carry her mom with her. Maybe she did it so that the mornings would begin with promise.

There was nothing more important to her than her girls learning to live in the promise of each new day. She had them early in her marriage, beginning at age 23 and every two years like clockwork afterward. She had worried from the beginning that she was too young to raise them right and that the world would destroy their youthful dreams because they were biracial. Now, with womanhood looming for all three girls Michelle could see hints of the lovely young women they were becoming. With Jaimee age 15, Janine age 13 and Jessie age 11, all three were determined to achieve their dreams, and each of their dreams was so unique.

Jessie was always the first one to the table. "Yay! I love pancakes!"

Michelle smiled. "You love everything. I could serve you dirt and you would love it."

Jessie smirked. "Well, I don't think I would like dirt. Hey Mom?"

Michelle turned to Jessie. "Yesss…"

"What's it like to die?"

Michelle's heart caught in her throat. This was the last thing she was expecting–and the last thing she wanted to deal with right now. "No one knows, Jessie. That's the thing about death: once people die and know what it's like, they never come back to tell us."

"Mom!" Janine poked her head through the door. "Jaimee won't let me wear her leopard print scarf! You said when you bought it that she had to share!"

Michelle shook her head and smiled to herself. The women they would be one day weren't here quite yet. The teenage angst and sisterly competition ruled most of their time together. Plus it was a welcome interruption from the conversation with Jessie she did not want to have. "Jaimee, I did say that you had to share the scarf." The coffee pot chirped, letting her know it was ready. She poured herself a cup.

Janine took her place at the table.

Jessie followed. "Can I have some coffee?"

Michelle placed a plate of hot pancakes in front of each of them. "Absolutely not. When you're 16 you can start drinking coffee."

Jessie poked her fork into the first one. "Angie's mom lets her drink coffee."

"Good for Angie."

Janine scoffed. "What do you think? I can't have it so why should you? I'll get coffee before you will."

Jessie stuck her tongue out, showing Janine her mouthful of chewed food.

Janine did the same back to her.

Jaimee was still standing by the door, arms crossed. "Ewww. You're disgusting."

Michelle pointed at Jaimee's seat with her spatula. "Sit. You don't have a lot of time. And give that scarf to your sister."

Jaimee flopped into her seat. "Mom, I am going to wear it today, so it isn't available for sharing."

Janine bellowed through a mouthful of pancakes. "You didn't decide to wear it until I reached for it, and besides you wore it Friday!"

"It doesn't matter. It is meant to be shared except when I am already wearing it, and I am wearing it today."

Michelle intervened, "So, I am pretty sure that sharing means taking turns. And communicating when you plan to wear the scarf. I suggest you two make out a calendar and claim your days ahead of time. In the meantime, two days in a row is not sharing; give the scarf to Janine."

"God," exclaimed Jaimee, "You always side with Janine. She's your little favorite love child!"

"I can assure you that none of you are my love child. I despise you all equally and drag my butt out of bed every morning to make you this amazing breakfast just to make myself happy, even though I could find bliss in sleeping an extra hour in my warm soft bed. But, no bliss, just being an every day mother to three children who love and appreciate everything I say and do."

"Ugh. God, Mom, you are so deranged." Jaimee begrudgingly removed the scarf and handed it to Janine. "It's too old for you and you look ridiculous in it but here it is, lovechild. Maybe you could wrap it around your hips and wear it as a skirt."

Janine scrunched up her face and leered at Jaimee. She grabbed the scarf and tucked it around her neck. "Well at least I don't look like the wicked sister of Cleopatra who stuck her finger in a light socket."

"What? You're crazy. They didn't even have light sockets in the days of Cleopatra."

Michelle smiled. "I just so enjoy seeing the love between my girls." She grabbed three lunch sacks from the refrigerator. "Okay, time is up. The bus is coming. Jaimee, did you finish that assignment on whatever it was–the penguins?"

Jaimee moaned, "Mom, it isn't due until Friday. I have all week."

"Oh no you don't, girl. I want that report done by tomorrow night so we can check it over and make sure it is done right. No child of mine is going to get bad grades in school. You have to prove to the world that you deserve the best; success isn't going to be handed to you on a silver platter."

As Michelle declared that last phrase, Jaimee was mouthing the words with her eyes rolled up, looking at her mother.

"Whatever."

The three girls grabbed their coats and ran out the door.

Jaimee yelled back, "Don't forget, I have dance practice after school. 5:30 pick up!"

"Be on the watch for Dad in case it's him. I have to make a trip out to Grandma's house to meet Aunt Amy and Uncle Mike. I'm not sure if I'll be back in time."

"Okay, see you later!" Jaimee called back as she disappeared behind the bus door.

The room was suddenly silent, as it was each day when the girls left for school. She called it her sweet silence. Every day, she looked forward to this moment. Even though she loved the crazy, chattering, fighting, playful and not so playful banter that filled the walls in the mornings and all the other times of the day and night, she also loved the moment right after the girls stormed out the door for school. It was her little gift of sanity in a world of uncontrolled mayhem.

This morning it wasn't as sweet. The silence felt more like a dark cloud, descending upon her and weighing her down. She turned to pour herself another cup of coffee, hoping the bittersweet flavor would help.

She heard the back screen door creak open. Her heart lifted. Shawn was home.

He walked through the door, taking off his work boots. "Good morning, my beautiful wife!" He strolled over to kiss Michelle on the cheek.

Michelle smiled and leaned into his kiss. The shroud of darkness that was settling on her lifted for the moment. She knew it would be back. She recognized it was the grief of losing Mom, waiting in the wings until nothing else would distract her from it. It was as if grief was a child who refused to share her attention with anyone else.

Michelle loved that one kiss from Shawn could have the power to help her fight back the descending grief. It was as if he had a direct connection with Michelle's emotions. He clutched her body to his and held her close. She could feel the embrace give way to a submission of her tense muscles into his strong body.

"I'm so sorry I couldn't be here last night."

After a few peaceful moments in his arms, she felt a flood of pent up emotions rising to the surface. She wasn't ready for them. She pushed at his chest to break away. "It's okay, I understand. You have to keep those college kids safe. Was it a quiet night?"

Shawn smiled. He gently slid his hands down her arms as she pulled away. He squeezed her wrists lightly before she left his arms. "It was. How did you sleep?"

She shrugged. "Could've been better." She pulled from his embrace and turned her body toward the coffee maker, redirecting the conversation. "That bedroom is so cold! We need to fix that thermostat!"

"You mean 'I' have to fix that thermostat?!"

"Yes, you do."

"Ohhh, all right." He reached past her and grabbed a pancake off the plate.

"Hey, get outta there. Grab a plate for those and use a fork. I'll get you some coffee."

She poured a cup of coffee while Shawn heaped some pancakes on top of the plate. She set the coffee on the table and pulled up a chair to join him. "I had another lovely interlude with our rebel daughter this morning."

Shawn swallowed his first bite of food and sipped his coffee to wash it down. "Oh, God. What was it about this time?"

Michelle just held her coffee cup in her hands and turned it back and forth in her hands. "Apparently she borrowed a super short skirt from her friend Debbie. I wouldn't let her wear it. She of course was pissed. And then, she was wearing make-up. She is 13 years old!"

"Wow. Kids these days. They are growing way old before their time."

Michelle prepared to dig her heels in. Most of the time she felt like she was the only one who disciplined the girls in this house. "Well, it is more than that, don't you agree? It's not just the accelerated passing of time. It's our daughter making a statement to us that she is not going to live in our world, under our rules. She has another agenda. I don't know what road she is turning down, and frankly, it scares me."

Shawn popped a bite of pancake into his mouth. "And on the other hand, it is just a short skirt."

"And make-up."

"And make-up. Maybe not the earth coming to an end. It's hard to choose what battles to fight with her."

Michelle sat up a little straighter in her chair and could feel her body become tense. "If we let these small things go at this stage in the game, then what will be next? I'm afraid I am losing my little girl. That thought scares me so much. When do we take a hard stance and when do we let it ride? Doesn't it scare you wondering what the boys are thinking when they see our daughter in a short skirt like that?"

Shawn bristled. "No, because I would murder any boy with thoughts like that."

"You may not have the chance. We don't know what she is doing, what signals she is giving off when she leaves this house. She's already growing away from us, Shawn. We have a very short window to figure out what is happening with her. I don't want to lose her like my mother lost me." She grasped her forehead, rubbing her temples against the headache that was sure to follow this discussion.

Shawn scraped the last of the maple syrup off his plate. "That won't happen. We won't let it."

Michelle took a sip of her coffee and fidgeted in her chair, trying to shake off the guilt that once again hung over her like a heavy fog. "I have to drive over to Mom's house today. I'm going to meet with Amy and Mike before they leave town. We need to go over the last of the belongings before the estate company comes. If I'm not back before 5:30 can you pick up Jaimee from dance class?"

"Absolutely. I'm on it."

The two sat in silence for a few moments.

Shawn stood and put his plate in the sink. As he turned toward the door, he leaned over and gave Michelle a soft kiss. "Well, I need to go get some shut eye and you should get on the road then. Be careful on those roads. I love you."

She turned into him and returned it with another, reaching up and caressing his cheek. "Me too."

Chapter 2

The hot, humid air weighed on Michelle's shoulders as she slouched on the edge of her mother's bed. Her mother would never lay there again. That thought, combined with the smell of old wood and dust-filled carpet, made her chest tighten. She wondered how long it had been since her mother had deep-cleaned the house. It might have been a decade or more. Every summer the 1930's Cape Cod home allowed all sorts of bugs in through the cracks in the windows and doors. Michelle saw evidence of it in every corner, particularly in the dormer windows. Here on the first floor, her mother's bedroom got the most sun in the morning, but it also got the most rain beating against the windows. Signs of water damage along the windowsill alarmed Michelle at the possibility of mold. Looking up, Michelle saw more water damage on the ceiling. She frowned. Above this room was her sister Lisa and her childhood room. There was no reason for water damage there. Michelle sighed. It might be more difficult to sell this house than they thought if these things weren't remedied.

The worst strike against the house was the lack of central air. No one would want a house like this, with upstairs rooms that became stifling in the summer, without it. She had tried to get her mother to install central air for years, but she never would. It seemed that this year she again didn't get around to it, and now Michelle and her siblings would pay the price. She was paying now. She wiped sweat from her face and pulled the crepe material of her dress away from her body, trying to get it to stop sticking to her. It returned to its clinging position the minute she let go. It was just like her mother to refuse to make the living environment more comfortable. She never took Michelle's input. The clinging of her clothes reminded her of the lifelong struggles she had with her mother, not to mention Lisa whom she hadn't spoken to in years. It was just sticky.

The doorbell rang. She sighed, pulling herself to stand beside the bed. Aching muscles caused her to groan. She felt so weak that she wondered if her legs would support her. She touched the walls as she walked through the house to the side door. As she entered the small kitchen, the scent of old spices and stale baked goods filled her nostrils. Looking ahead to the door, she could just make out the form of Mother's neighbor Mrs. Burk through the weathered glass.

Michelle opened the door.

Mrs. Burk smiled when she saw Michelle, her face barely visible over the sprays of flowers in her arms. "Michelle, is it really you? My, it has been so many years! You look beautiful!"

"Mrs. Burk..." Michelle struggled to get the name out. "Well, thanks. Are these the flowers from the funeral?"

"Yes, yes. I saved them for you from the funeral." Mrs. Burk thrust the large bouquet into Michelle's arms.

Michelle sneezed.

"Oh, bless you!"

"Thank you." Michelle turned to get the offending objects that were tickling her nose out of her arms. She set them on the counter behind her. "Why do you have them?"

Mrs. Burk scurried into the kitchen behind Michelle. "I actually work part-time for the funeral home. That's why you didn't see me at the funeral. I was working in the back. Here, let me get them some fresh water." She scooped the flowers off the counter and started running water. "I know your mother had a vase under the sink. Let me see." She crouched down and opened the cabinet door.

Michelle looked heavenward, praying for patience. This isn't what she needed right now.

Mrs. Burk fluffed the flowers in the new vase. "There. Doesn't that look nice?" She beamed at Michelle, brushing past her. "Here, let's put these on the table."

Michelle bristled. "I thought all the flowers had gone to the gravesite."

Mrs. Burk's expression dropped. "We did bring most of the flowers to the gravesite, as I am sure you saw, but I wanted to make sure there were a few here in the house, for, you know, the family. To take home. In case anyone showed up here." She forced a new smile. "And here you are! I'm so glad you are here! I haven't seen you in so long."

Michelle didn't return Mrs. Burk's smile.

A pregnant silence fell between the women as they stood there for what seemed like a moment of eternity.

"So, do you still live next door, Mrs. Burk?"

Michelle turned toward the door and gazed out the dirty window towards the house next door. Her eyes moved to the glass pane in the neighboring house's screen door. The glass was much newer than the rest of the door though both showed signs of age now. She knew why the glass was newer. In her mind she could hear the gunshots. Two distinct sounds. Bang! Bang! Michelle let her book drop from her hands and ran to the window. She couldn't see anything, and there were no more shots. Somewhere, her mother was yelling. Crying. In the distance, sirens. The sound drew closer until two officers emerged from a police car. They approached the door with guns drawn. They knocked and spoke, but she couldn't hear what they were saying. Horror overcame her as she saw her father burst through the side door, breaking the glass. He ran to the backyard and jumped to climb the chain fence. His shirt was splotched with red. What was that? she thought. The officers pursued him. She watched as they tackled him before he could scale the fence. They threw him onto the grass and handcuffed him. They dragged him to the car.

Mrs. Burk was still talking.

"I have kept tabs on Karen for years. Not that she talked much about her life. She had become quite a recluse, as I am sure you know. I haven't seen anyone over here visiting in a very long time. The house has fallen into some disrepair. So sad." She looked around the kitchen.

Michelle's gaze followed hers, scanning the dull formica counters and cabinet doors that wouldn't stay closed. "How can I help you, Mrs. Burk?"

"Oh, please, call me Evelyn. I'm here to help you! I was always here for your mother. Well, as much as I could be. I baked her cookies now and then. To care for her. She was so alone." Mrs. Burk smiled again. "Oh, these flowers are so beautiful. Karen deserves them."

She could feel the flushing of her skin as she tried to dismiss the guilt Mrs. Burk was trying to instill on her.

"I always told her to share the cookies with her family. I hope she did….when she saw you?"

Michelle focused on the flowers, stroking the pedals. "I hadn't seen her in several years."

"Well, you traveled around for so long. And then when you settled closeby, well, you had a family of your own to care for." Mrs. Burk hummed an indiscernible tune, twittering like a little bird. "It's understandable. Children grow away from their parents. In more ways than one. It's just the way of the world. I saw in the obituary you are still with Shawn and you had three girls? Are they here? I'd love to meet them."

"No, I mean, yes, we are still married and we have three girls. We brought the girls home last night. They are back at school."

"Oh, darn, I'm sorry to have missed them. I think I saw your sister Tracy at the service, but of course I was just peeking in from the back. I didn't see Lisa anywhere. She has never been seen since she left after high school. Is she still around?"

Michelle could sense the anticipation in Mrs. Burk's probing tone. She no doubt wanted the latest gossip to share with the breakfast crowd at Burger King. Michelle now had to decide how much to tell her.

Lisa had been a rebel for as long as Michelle could remember. She had never wanted to do anything that they did as a family in their earlier years, which put tremendous pressure on Michelle to be the 'good child,' the present child, the child that might be the successful one in the family, especially after Tracy had moved on and Michelle and Lisa were the only ones left at home. It hadn't exactly gone as planned….

Michelle leaned against the counter. She was so tired, but she didn't want to sit down and give Mrs. Burk an invitation to stay. "She's been estranged from the family since high school, Mrs. Burk. I don't know why she wasn't here, she lives near me but I never see her or talk to her."

Mrs. Burk's hand fluttered to her heart. "I'm so sorry to hear that. I have asked Karen about Lisa over the years and she just wouldn't talk about her. I wondered if anything happened between them?"

Michelle locked eyes with her unsolicited guest. "Mrs. Burk, this isn't really something I want to talk about, nor do I think my mother would want us to, particularly on the day after her funeral. Could we talk about something else?"

Mrs. Burk took a step back. "Oh, of course. Well, I have seen Tracy here a few times. She was a good daughter. Well, of course, as you were, I am sure. Will Tracy be here today? I'd love to see her, too."

Michelle felt the muscles in her body tense almost to the point of cramping. She felt nauseated. "I don't think so. I'm just here to meet Amy and Mike and make one last check before we have the movers come and pack it all up."

"You look like you need to sit down. Here, sit beside me." Mrs. Burk sat at the kitchen table, patting the seat next to her.

Michelle obeyed. She was too tired to argue, even though it meant a longer visit with Mrs. Burk.

Mrs. Burk squealed. "So Amy and Mike are coming? Wow, I don't know if I would even recognize them, it's been so long! They never lived in this house, did they? Living with their dad and stepmother, they hardly ever came around when you were growing up, as I remember."

"Yeah, well, they are about ten years older than the three of us. I guess Tracy knew them a little better but not really Lisa and I growing up." Michelle paused, trying to think of a way out of this conversation. When none presented itself, she continued. "But, yeah, holidays and reunions…They should be here any minute."

"So tell me about you. Where are you living now? Last I knew you went to college in Buffalo, and then next thing we knew you got married and I don't think I ever saw you again. I hope you at least kept in touch with your mother by phone, since you hardly ever visited."

"We moved around a lot in our marriage. Shawn's job had us moving to different security positions. We came to visit when we could."

"Well, it couldn't have been an easy life, being a biracial couple in the late 70's. I mean, Shawn is a very handsome man that I recall, and Karen liked him very much. But it must have been challenging. Not everyone was ready for the blacks to 'come over to our side of the fence,' so to speak."

Michelle stood up. She felt as if she were suffocating. Michelle crossed her arms, as if she were daring this woman to continue.

Mrs. Burk cleared her throat. "Of course, that is not what I thought. I was very open to the changes. I am just acknowledging that I am sure it was a challenge for you."

Michelle nodded. Mrs. Burk was making things challenging at this very moment. The irony was not lost on her. "As it continues to be…" Outside she heard two car doors closing in quick succession. Her heart leaped at the welcome interruption. "Oh, this must be Amy and Mike now."

As Amy and Mike walked into the kitchen, Michelle happily retreated into the corner of the room nearest the hallway exit. She eyed her mother's bedroom at the end of the hall. Turning her attention back to the others, she said, "Hey, Amy and Mike, you remember Mrs. Burk from next door. Mrs. Burk, you remember my sister and brother, Amy and Mike."

Amy spoke first. "Hello, Mrs. Burk. Yes, I remember you! It's been many years but I think we did meet once in mom's backyard. How are you?"

"Oh, call me Evelyn, please. Mrs. Burk was my mother, as the old saying goes! I just stopped by to drop off flowers from the funeral. It is so great to see Karen's children that I haven't seen in so many years! You look so much like your mother! And Mike, what a handsome man! I can see your mother's eyes, right there looking at me!"

Mike leaned forward and extended his hand to shake Evelyn's. "Thank you, Evelyn. It's so nice to see you. And thank you so much for looking over our mother these years."

"It was my pleasure. I mean, somebody had to. She was so alone…It was hard to watch her draw into herself over the years. It's hard when your children all move away, never to return. Not your fault of course. It's the world we live in. I know Tracy would come home now and then to visit. I'd see them sitting out on the back porch having coffee and snacks." Looking at Amy, she added, "I don't remember seeing you back there, but it's been so many years."

Mike took a step back. He glanced over at Michelle with raised eyebrows as if to ask, 'How long has this conversation been going on?'

Michelle obliged with a tight smile. "Well, I am going to retreat to mom's bedroom and leave you three to catch up. Mike, Amy, I'll see you shortly." She gestured to Mrs. Burk with a timid wave of her hand.

Mike mouthed the word, 'Traitor.'

Michelle stifled a laugh. "Mrs. Burk, it was great to see you again. Thanks again for the flowers." She slowly backed out of their vision, as if she could disappear into the aging wallpaper.

Michelle walked into the bedroom. The awkward irritation she felt in the kitchen gave way to a heavy knot in her stomach. She tried to pinpoint the emotion. Was it sadness? Guilt? Anger? Despair?

It was despair. She knew that mom was gone, placed in the earth and in her resting spot. She hoped her mother was finally at rest from the demons that surrounded her. And yet, the feeling of unrest in this room was very much alive. It was not an electric energy; it was more like a low buzzing, a long drawn out sadness. It weighed on her, much like the way she had often felt in her mother's presence. The only difference was the anxiety that had accompanied her was gone, leaving her only with the heaviness of her mother's despair.

Michelle couldn't help but feel that the bedroom was a mirror for her mother's inner world. It was small and dimly lit. The walls were dull tan with only one window, covered with heavy drapes. Michelle wondered if the original color was tan or if the paint had faded over the years. A tall silk Ficus tree in a bamboo planter sat in the corner next to the dresser. The leaves were covered with a thick layer of dust. The afternoon heat had permeated the room. Michelle looked up to see if she could turn on a fan to get the air moving. As with many old homes, there was no ceiling light or fan. There was a slight background scent of mildew mixed with eau de toilette cologne. She knew it wouldn't be long until the heat and the smell got to her.

She moved to the dresser to see what her mother had left there. Even after all this time, her mother was still a mystery to her. The dresser was covered with a pearl cotton crochet table runner, slightly yellowing from its years of service. Atop this sat a Blessed Virgin Mary statue wrapped in rosary beads and a hand mirror that Michelle remembered playing with in her early years. It was her favorite prop when she would act out the story of Snow White. Michelle picked up the mirror, contemplating the much older reflection that stared back at her. Who was she now? The Wicked Queen or Snow White? Had she abandoned her mother as Mrs. Burk insinuated or were her mother and she both victims of time and circumstances?

"Find anything you want to take with you?"

Michelle whipped around.

Mike stood in the entryway. He was a very distinguished gentleman, ten years older than her at the age of 48. His age was beginning to show in a sprinkle of gray hair among his jet black base. He wore it short and styled perfectly, not a hair out of place, just like his life. He had looked so handsome in his funeral attire, a black pinstripe suit with white shirt and gold tie. He was controlled and cordial at all times. Even his eulogy had been perfect. "Gold is the color of hope," he had said. "Hope bears all of our sadness, and it will be the source of our inspiration to keep on living with mom in our hearts." It was perfect though inauthentic. He hadn't known her. Hell, neither had she. How could he keep a woman in his heart that he never knew to begin with? Today, even his jeans were designer, and did not sport a wrinkle.

Michelle set the mirror down. "Not much here. She lived a pretty simple life, especially in the years after Harry died."

"What about the mirror?" Mike asked.

"Well, maybe." She picked up the mirror again. "This might be an interesting canvas for an art project. Maybe a small epigram about finding the beauty within."

"Maybe one of your art students could do something with it."

Michelle shrugged, noncommittal.

"How did the reunion go with Mrs. Burk?" Michelle asked with a sly smile.

"Wow, she is a trip. Talk about passive-aggressive. Why don't you say what you really feel, Evelyn?"

The siblings laughed.

It had been a long time since she had laughed with her brother.

Mike sat on the bed and looked up at her. "Tell me what's going on with Tracy. I saw her at the funeral, but she didn't come to the gravesite."

He said it in the way that only he could–with a tone that was both empathetic and neutral.

Michelle fiddled with the handle of the mirror. "Truth be told, I don't know. Tracy and I aren't really talking these days. Ever since her husband died. I couldn't make the funeral. Maybe I should have made myself go. I don't know." Michelle sighed and rubbed her brow. "I did the best I could."

Mike patted the bed next to him. "Sit down. It's been a long day."

Michelle obeyed. "I apologized so many times, but it made no difference. You know, Tracy was always my best friend. I used to share everything with her. We would talk on the phone for hours. When Tracy's husband passed away, it was right after our youngest Jessie was born. I had bad postpartum depression."

Mike shook his head. "You never told me."

"I know. I didn't tell anyone. I couldn't handle going to the funeral, as much as I wanted to be there for Tracy. It was a very dark time for me, and before I could even talk to Tracy about it, Lisa convinced her that I chose not to go to the funeral, because I no longer cared about the family. Tracy believed it. I don't understand how she could have believed that of me, especially coming from Lisa."

Mike shook his head. "I didn't know that Lisa was even in the picture. I thought Lisa took off right after high school and never looked back."

"She did, but she kept her claws in Tracy. She even took Tracy and Scott on vacation."

"Classic move. She bought Tracy's loyalty."

"But she only talked to Tracy or did anything nice for her when she wanted something. After that vacation, Lisa roped Tracy into babysitting her kids for a year every day after school. Lisa was just manipulating her. Tracy couldn't see it. But she and I talked every day. Every day. Yet when this happened and I couldn't go to the funeral, she believed Lisa." Michelle's eyes welled up with tears. "After everything we had shared, how could she believe that about me? But she did. How I wish I could just talk to her..."

Mike gently patted Michelle's back. Instinctively she began to pull away. She stopped herself and hoped he hadn't noticed.

Mike pulled back a little.

Apparently he had noticed. Michelle was frustrated with herself. He was being kind, and it was a simple gesture that she didn't want to recoil from. It was just difficult for her to receive human touch, unless it was from Shawn. She had been that way as long as she could remember. She hadn't received much affection from anyone in her life, certainly not from Mike whom she rarely saw over the years. She did yearn for her sister Tracy to touch her, hug her, laugh with her once again.

As if he had read her mind, Mike said, "When the time is right, you and Tracy will find each other again."

Michelle wiped a tear from her eye. "I hope so."

"I see Lisa didn't care to show up yesterday. My God, it was our mother's funeral. Is there that much hatred in her? What did mom ever do to her that was so horrible?"

Michelle stood up and walked over to the closet. "I don't know, and I don't care. That woman lives in the same town as me, our children go to school together, and yet we never speak to or see each other. She's just a stranger to us. And frankly, from the things she has done to me, I actually prefer it that way." She started looking through the clothes in the closet.

"So y'all left me without the knife!"

Michelle turned her head and jumped.

Amy's tiny form filled the doorway.

"What knife?" asked Michelle.

Amy joined Michelle by the closet. "The one needed to cut through the tension in that kitchen! Wow, what planet did that lady come from?"

The three siblings laughed, but then the ladies turned their attention to the task at hand. Mike sat on the bed and watched.

Michelle could not imagine Amy wanting anything in her mother's closet. Her mother was a size 14-16 and Amy couldn't be bigger than a size 0. Amy was even more Michelle's senior, the first born and two years older than Mike, yet Michelle had to admit Amy looked and acted younger than she. Plus as long as Michelle had known her, Amy had always dressed with classic elegance. Today she wore a light sage green empire waist dress with a chiffon skirt, flowing around her flawless body, and effortlessly announcing her status in the fashion world. There was no dressing down for Amy. She was always on stage no matter where she was.

"Michelle, do you want any of these clothes? I think they would fit you. What do you think?" Amy held up a paisley design dress in front of her. She swayed back and forth in the small room, pretending the dress was her dance partner. Michelle envied Amy for the way she moved with such grace, her steps light and airy. Amy moved as if she had not a care in the world.

Michelle felt her muscles begin to tense as they had in that kitchen. Her perspective shifted. It was as if she were an outsider, seeing the three of them from afar. She saw three people, two beautiful high society people who were well-dressed and one struggling middle-class woman who needed to lose at least 15 pounds.

Why was it that they were dealt the cards they held? Amy and Mike were so happy in their lives, financially secure, lucky in everything they touched. Pillars of society, secure in who they were. It was like they did not have the same genes that made Michelle and her sisters. The three girls had to grow up in this tiny, little, cramped, smelly, stuffy, loveless shack. Amy and Mike were raised by their father in a large beautiful home and every toy they ever wanted. They had dance classes and t-ball practice with their parents in attendance while Michelle and her other sisters had house keys around their necks and evenings in front of the television. What happened here? Did a fairy come down and sprinkle her pixie dust of happiness and success over Amy and Mike? It was nauseating. At the same time, she felt guilty for even thinking the thought. They were lovely and were always kind to her.

Michelle's attention reverted to Amy and her dance partner. She set aside her unfair judgments. She may not be able to control the hand she was dealt, but she could control how she responded to it. She would not be petty. "Very pretty, but not my style, really."

Amy put the dress back and held out a red shawl, heavy wool with fringe around the edges.

"Wow, this would certainly keep you warm in these northern winters."

"Um...red is not my color. Oh LAWD no!" exclaimed Michelle. "Besides I know a better way to keep warm; I'll just come to Florida and spend my winters with you!"

"Ha ha! You are welcome anytime. And in that case," she said, pulling out a sleeveless mock turtleneck top, "you will probably need something like this!"

"You know Mom would never be caught dead wearing a sleeveless top in public. Showing skin is the work of the devil, mind you! Oh, LAWD, where is the jacket to go with this?" Michelle flipped through the clothes in the back of the closet.

They all laughed. Amy and she searched until they found a jacket to match the top.

Amy drew her perfectly manicured fingers through her beautiful long red shiny hair which Michelle was pretty sure was the result of a standing appointment at the beauty salon. Her lean, athletic body was a window to her wardrobe of designer clothes, her mansion in Sanibel Island, her perfect husband, perfect children, perfect pets.

Michelle did not feel worthy of sleeping on her curb. She wondered if accepting her lighthearted invitation was easy for Amy, because Amy knew that Michelle would never make the trip to Florida. Michelle just could never be comfortable trying to integrate into Amy's perfect world. Besides, there was no money in the budget for such a trip. No, there would not be a visit to Florida any time soon.

Michelle tried on the jacket. It was way too small to even get her arms through. They both laughed as Michelle removed the jacket. She attempted to hang it back up. It fell off the hanger to the floor. As Michelle bent over to pick up the jacket, she felt something hard. She bent down further. It appeared to be an old wooden box. She pulled it out and carried it over to the bed.

Amy was beside her. "What on earth is that?"

"I'm not sure. It looks like Mom's old jewelry box. But why would it be in the back of her closet?" She set it on the dresser and fumbled with the clasp to open it. She lifted the lid. Her stomach lurched as memories began to flow.

Swallowing the tears that came unbidden to her eyes, she focused on the happy memories the pieces produced. She was determined to remember the positive today. She reached in and pulled out a pair of pearl droplet earrings that were clasped together. "Oh my gosh, I remember these. She wore these every day while we were growing up. Even when she was scrambling to get breakfast on the table for us before school, wearing just a ratty house dress, she had these beautiful pearl earrings on. It was like mom was living in a make believe world of riches and glamor."

Amy took the earrings in her hands. She held them up to the small light on the wall, rolling them in her fingers. "I doubt they are real."

"It doesn't matter. They were real to her." Michelle could sense the distance growing between them as Amy became less a sister interested in the memory of her mother and more a stranger who cared about the difference between real and fake pearls. She brushed off her irritation. The fact was that they were strangers who lived in very different worlds who just happened to share some of the same genetic code. She picked up a necklace with a leather rope and a wooden carved elephant dangling from it. "I remember this," Michelle reminisced. "She wore it to my high school graduation. Mom and Harry waited by the front doors of the high school for me after the ceremony. Mom was dressed in an animal print dress, tea length to show the least amount of skin in public, of course."

Amy giggled. "Oh, of course!"

"She was so excited, she swung me around in a circle when I reached the door. I was so embarrassed, but I loved it." Michelle held the necklace up to her throat and twirled in a circle as she remembered doing that day. It was a simpler time, when life was carefree. "She wore a cotton scarf around her shoulders, and this beautiful carved elephant necklace. I remember telling her she looked beautiful! Just like she came back from an African Safari! Mom blushed and said, 'Well, you just take that diploma and make something of your life or I will feed you to the lions!' Ha ha!"

Mike chuckled. "I can't see her saying that."

"She did." Michelle smiled at the memory. There were too few of them.

Amy smiled with her and added, "I wish I could have been there to hear that come out of her! I remember you used to always draw an elephant's trunk when you were younger."

"Yes," answered Michelle. "It was my way of starting the flow of my design and opening my imagination." Looking at the necklace and its memory, she wondered if she had been influenced by this necklace in her art pieces. The thought crossed her mind that there might be countless other unconscious influences like this, and they might not all be good. Still, she knew without a doubt that she wanted them. She wanted these influences, these connections with her mother. All that day, and for years before, she hadn't wanted anything that had to do with her mother. But now she knew she wanted this old costume jewelry. "Amy, do you mind if I keep this?" Somehow, the mere act of asking made her feel uncertain. What would Amy think, that she wanted this old worthless jewelry? Her mind searched for a compelling reason that Amy would accept. She spoke quickly, "The box is so old, I think it might be an antique. I'd like to check it over and see if I can find out its history."

"That old thing? Sure, take it but don't get your hopes up. Just looks like an old box to me. Although someone handcrafted it so it deserves a home." Amy shrugged, handing the pearl earrings to Michelle. "Here, these won't really match my collection."

Michelle placed the earrings in the box, ran her fingers softly along the jewelry, then up the sides of the top and gently closed it.

Mike stood. "We're going to have an estate seller come and sell the house and its contents. Is there anything else you want to take home?"

Michelle took one last look around the room. "No, I think I'm good."

Amy held her arms out to Michelle, inviting a hug. "Not the best of circumstances, Michelle, but it was so good to see you again. Give my love to your beautiful family."

Michelle obliged. "Ditto. Let's not wait so long to see each other again.

Amy pulled away and gave Michelle a final squeeze.

Somehow Michelle felt like she was being abandoned. The thought of being left alone in her mother's house overwhelmed her with dread.

"Mike and I are headed to the airport for our flights, so take those flowers home for yourself."

Michelle blinked back tears and shrugged. "Let's leave them for the estate sellers."

Mike reached down and squeezed Michelle's hand, and pulled her into a hug. "Don't be a stranger." I know you come to Pennsylvania for those artist retreat weekends now and again. Look us up. Kristie would love to see you and Shawn and the girls."

Michelle pulled back gently from the hug. "Send my love as well."

As Mike and Amy left together, Michelle sat back down on the bed again. She felt so drained. She tried to take a deep breath, but the still humid air was suddenly stifling again, and the lingering scent of eau de toilette was suffocating. Placing her hand on the mattress beneath her, she imagined her mother sleeping all those nights alone after Harry's death.

"Well, then, I guess this is it." Swallowing a lump in her throat, she stood up, picked up the jewelry box and mirror, and walked away, leaving the world she knew as a child behind forever.

Chapter 3

Michelle walked in the door of her house to the smell of hamburger cooking. She walked into the kitchen where Jaimee had started frying the meat for dinner. She gave her a short hug from the side. "Thank you, honey. How was dance class?"

"Terrible! It was a really hard practice, and I was so exhausted from the weekend. I should have taken today off. My muscles are so sore."

Michelle could see that Jaimee was no worse for wear. She suspected Jaimee's dramatic response was an attempt to gain her sympathy and get out of her homework. She knew better than to say anything. "So sorry, honey. What are we making?"

"Goulash, what else? That's all I know how to make."

"Oh, yum, goulash it is." She relieved Jaimee of the spatula in her hand. "Here, let me take over this. Why don't you jump on that penguin report while I finish this up?"

Jaimee groaned. "Fine."

"Before you stomp off, where are dad and the girls?"

Jaimee turned with her hand on her hips. "Dad went back to bed for a few hours. Janine and Jessie are upstairs. Working on some very essential white collar world preparation, I imagine. Anything else?"

"I am sure they are. No, thank you. I'll call when dinner's ready."

Later that evening, after dinner had been orchestrated, dishes washed and homework completed, laundry hung up, and one long cup of tea sipped while sitting up in bed, Michelle set the empty teacup on the bedside stand and reached over to turn off the light. She sat in the dark, with just a small light coming under the bathroom door from a soft night light on the wall. She listened to the silence. At least on the outside of her head. Inside, so many thoughts were making noise. She feared they would keep her awake all night like a rock and roll band playing in the next room. Screams. Gunshots. Sirens. But exhaustion overcame the thoughts and she succumbed to slumber, as unpeaceful and intruding as it was.

Morning came way too soon, and Michelle pulled herself out of bed for the next day's adventure. She could feel her body fighting her as she got the girls ready for their daily morning breakfast ritual.

Jessie squealed with delight at her favorite breakfast–scrambled eggs and grits. "You make the best grits, mom!"

Michelle grinned back. "Well, of course I do. It's a mother's job to make the best grits anywhere."

Jaimee looked up from her breakfast. "Will you be able to pick me up at 5:30 tonight from dance class?"

"Yes, are you sure you can handle the class tonight?"

"Well, I have to. Competition is coming up this weekend. I have to be ready."

"As you always are. You make me proud. Can't wait to see you perform." She turned toward Janine and Jessie. "How about you girls? More grits?"

Jessie held her plate out for more.

Janine declined. "I'm watching my weight."

"Janine, you don't have a weight problem. You are perfect just the way you are. Where is this coming from?" Michelle couldn't help but think there was more to this refusal than grits and weight. Why was she so antagonistic lately? It seemed that nothing she did for Janine was ever good enough.

Janine shrugged. "Well, I need to work to stay this way; perfection can change at any moment. Besides, since you won't buy me new clothes, I have to figure out how to stay small enough to keep wearing my old ones or to stay the same size as Debbie so I can borrow her clothes."

Michelle gave a big sigh. She didn't remember throwing these digs at her mother when she was the middle child. Of course, she didn't remember much conversation with her mother at all. "As long as it isn't that short skirt. Okay team, it is time to roll. Lunches, coats, and out the door!"

Jessie took one last gulp of grits and ran over to give her mother a big hug. "Bye Mom, I love you!"

"Love you too, love you all!! Have the best day!" she yelled as they scrambled out the door.

She cleared the table and started a new pan of eggs in preparation for Shawn to walk through the door. She poured a cup of coffee and was just turning around to set it on the table when he stepped inside. "Good morning! I have hot coffee ready for you."

"Oh, my savior! Thank you! It was a long night; I hardly got to even drink my coffee." He leaned over to kiss Michelle. "Is it a good morning? You were sure keeping busy last night when I left; I didn't think you wanted to be disturbed." He watched her as she turned to attend to the eggs cooking on the stove, and scooped grits onto a plate.

"I'm not sure how good it is yet. I'm still feeling a little numb from yesterday."

Shawn sat down at the table. He opened his arms to accept the breakfast being set in front of him. "Anything you want to talk about?"

Michelle sat down. She folded her hands in front of her. Was she ready to talk about it? She sighed. "I think so."

She took a long sip of her coffee. "Stay here, I will be right back. I want to show you this old jewelry box I found in my mom's closet."

Shawn smiled, and grabbed her hand gently.

"I'll see you in a few." As she walked away, he grabbed a spoon and dove into his grits.

She padded down the hall to the cupboard where she stashed the antique box the night before. Her mind drifted to the events of the last twenty four hours. Seeing Amy and Mike again, the striking differences in their lives. Mrs. Burk. The jewelry box. The cupboard door creaked as she opened it. The smallness of the jewelry box and silver mirror struck her, made more trivial in appearance by all the many, larger items surrounding them. Reaching up, she retrieved the box. 'Gosh, there wasn't much in her world,' Michelle thought.

She brought the box into the kitchen. She set it on the table, gently as a mother's first cradling of her newborn baby. She ran her fingers along the top edge as she had done countless times as a child before opening it.

Shawn looked at the box and at Michelle. "Well, let's see what we've got here." He pushed his plate away to give Michelle and the old box his undivided attention.

The hinges creaked slightly as the top was lifted up. The first thing she saw was the pair of pearl earrings. Michelle felt a whir of emotions. Her breath caught in her chest, as if a spirit had entered and left her with a momentary paralysis. She shook off the feeling and picked them up. Lost in thought, she held them in her hands for a minute, as if she could conjure her mother back to life through her memories. She then held the earrings up to her ears.

"Pearls? Are they real?"

"No," answered Michelle. She smiled. "But they were real to her." She looked up, as if watching a scene unfold in front of her. "I remember Mom in the kitchen, making pancakes, playing referee to Lisa and myself as we fought over clothes and art supplies and whose turn it was to use the electric typewriter, and whose turn it was to help with the dishes, and which one of us stepped over the line in our bedroom and made a mess, and who pulled whose hair, and why one of us deserved more allowance than the other. All the while wearing these glamorous earrings! Sometimes I feel like I am walking in her shoes."

Shawn grinned. "Or wearing her earrings."

She smiled in recognition of how much some things never change. She thought about the banter in the kitchen this morning with her own daughters. She put the earrings on. Sitting beside Shawn, she held her ears in her fingertips, gently rubbing them.

She lifted up a faux ruby necklace and bracelet set. "Do you remember this set?" She gently rubbed over the smooth stones, and her fingers got caught on the slightly lifted prongs. "Mom wore this set on the day of Jaimee's baptism. At the time, I thought Mom was a little overdressed for a baptism, and I told her as much."

"She was proud of you, and of Jaimee."

"I know." Michelle shook her head. "I feel bad about that. Why couldn't I just let it be? I mean, she never had the chance to dress up for our wedding since we were married by a justice of the peace. And then I made that comment about her outfit. I knew it was wrong the minute I said it. But I didn't apologize." She stopped and swallowed hard. "She looked beautiful in this set."

"I remember her wearing it. Your mother was beautiful that day. You got that beauty from her." He scooted his chair close to Michelle, leaned over and kissed her softly on the cheek.

Michelle smiled, feeling a little flushed. She held up another piece, a rhinestone brooch in the shape of a dog. "I used to play dress up with a pair of Mom's ruby colored high heel shoes that I never saw her wear. I pretended that I was Dorothy of Kansas and this brooch was my little dog Toto."

Shawn laughed. "You still watch that movie every year."

"I've always loved *The Wizard of Oz.* I used to pretend I lived on a ranch with a real Aunt Em, and my guardian angels were Scarecrow, the Cowardly Lion and the Tinman." She clasped the brooch in her hand and looked up toward the sky. "I imagined that they protected me through all the harsh realities of the world."

"What harsh realities?"

"Mostly fears. Fear of speaking in public. I could never do a verbal report in class; just being in that spotlight made me feel naked. I would beg my teachers not to make me stand up in front of that class. Most times they would see my fear and not make me do it. But sometimes, well, I just had to do it even as frightened as I was."

"That's a pretty common fear."

She thought for a moment. "And fear of talking to boys."

"What? Fear of talking to boys?! Not the way you came after me!"

Michelle giggled. "That was later on. In high school I was scared to death. Whenever I was in the boys' world, I was fine, like when I was scorekeeping at the soccer games and needed to talk to them about the scores and lineup, even one to one. But to talk to that same boy after the game about anything personal, no way! I couldn't even muster the nerve to look at them or say hello in the hallway."

Shawn sighed. "I'm certainly glad you got past that by the time you met me."

Michelle snorted. "Yeah, because you would never have said 'boo' to me if I hadn't talked to you first."

"Not true."

"True." She gave Shawn the look, that look that says, 'I'm right and you know it. Give up now while you're ahead.'

Shawn widened his eyes, feigning innocence.

"Anyway, I was also afraid of Halloween. I couldn't understand why people would want to have fun with that unknown dark side of the universe. Did they not know they could be pulled into another realm over which they had no control? I didn't want to think about or do anything that might stir up the other side. It was hard enough to live on this side of the universe. I didn't want that dark side coming in too close to me...nope, not a fan. I get through it for the girls, but it is not by choice."

Shawn nodded, more serious now. "You know, all your fears have to do with being seen...and with losing control...to someone or something more powerful than you."

Michelle thought about that. He was right. She had spent most of her life feeling like she had almost no command over her life. But here, with that little brooch dog in her hand, it didn't matter, if just for a moment. She didn't need control, because she felt embraced in love, caressed, and playful. She was safe. She closed her eyes, and clicked her heels together three times, and whispered, "There's no place like home."

She suddenly felt the yearning that Dorothy experienced when she clicked her own heels together. All she wanted to do was to be home again, but it wasn't the home she grew up in. It was a home she had never had, except in her imagination. Just a few hours ago, Michelle had walked out of the only home she had known as a child for one of the last times. Yet it had never been the safe place she needed. Her mom tried to make their house a home, a safe place for them, but in truth she had failed. The shroud of dark despair covered her again. She shivered from the slight chill hovering in the air. Did she have that home now, the one she had always dreamed of? She didn't feel it was true, but she had no factual reason to feel that way. In their early married years, she hadn't been sure where tomorrow would take them as Shawn's jobs had moved them around every few years. Yet for the last five years, they had been grounded, secure, raising their kids in this house, in this neighborhood, in the same schools. It was safe and secure, a good place. So why did she not feel safe and secure? She shook her head to clear these dark thoughts and gently placed the brooch back into the jewelry box.

Shawn yawned. "I think my body is ready to get some rest. He leaned over, placed his hand on her lower back, and whispered into her ear, "There's no place like bed. You are welcome to join me. "

Michelle grinned. She leaned in to Shawn and gave him a kiss. "Too much to do in my day."

Shawn gave her back a light squeeze and walked away.

Michelle turned her attention back to the jewelry box. 'What do you want to tell me?' she thought.

She removed each piece of jewelry gingerly, as if each would break and might cause her to lose a piece of her world. She placed them on the kitchen table. She turned the box over, looking to see if there was an inscription or company name stamped into the bottom. She saw nothing by the naked eye. She slightly rubbed her fingers along the wood in hopes of feeling a number or letters burned into the casing. As she rubbed the wood lightly and traveled along the bottom edge, she stopped at a small rough spot. As she pressed a little harder, it felt like a small hinge. She turned the box around to see it closer and noticed a hinge on each side of the box near the bottom edge. She ran her finger up along what appeared to be an opening in the wood. Here it would seem the back and sides come together. However, halfway up the back, there was a break in the wood, appearing like the back was made of two pieces of wood.

"That's strange," she thought. "Why would they make the back out of two pieces of wood instead of one?"

She noticed a tiny piece of fabric sticking out at the very edge of the bottom piece of wood. Her heart skipped a beat. What could this be? Is this a trap door leading to a mysterious treasure? She startled from a shiver traveling up her arms into her shoulders, feeling the thrill of possibilities of the unknown. She reached over and very carefully, with just the tips of her fingers, felt the rough edging of the fabric. She pulled ever so gently. The backside of the jewelry box opened up. Inside were several small white envelopes, tightly fitted into the small hidden capsule of the box. She stared at the envelopes. She reached in and pulled out the envelopes. Her hands trembled as she held them in front of her.

Michelle looked around the room as if wondering if someone was watching. She hesitated. Guilt overcame her. These were her mother's most private possessions. Yet her mother was gone. The letters were one of the few things she had left, possibly knowing a part of her mother she had never seen. They might be nothing personal at all, but then why would they be hidden?

Michelle shuffled through the envelopes. Each envelope was numbered. Numbers one through eight. Maybe she shouldn't look inside, to preserve her mother's privacy.

"I might need to make some extra coffee for this." She remembered that she used the last of the coffee with this current pot. She decided she needed to put these envelopes in a safe place while she went to the store. Maybe the distance would allow for more clarity as to whether she should cross this line. Would this start her down a path that she could not return from? Would this close a gap that had existed between her and her mother or just widen it? She clearly wasn't ready for this just yet.

Michelle stood up and walked to the hall pantry. She grabbed an empty shoe box that she had kept for the next time she had bits of stuff with nowhere to put it. Michelle saved shoe boxes as they were the perfect size to keep all sorts of things that just didn't fit anywhere else. It was like having separate little treasure boxes that gave her a nice surprise when she opened them later. This particular box was from a pair of stylish Chelsea boots that she had recently purchased for Janine. 'I don't buy her clothes,' she thought, 'but I just bought her new shoes last week.'

She brought the shoebox back to the kitchen table. Turning over the jewelry box and gently closing the now empty compartment, she smoothed the edges with her hand. She wanted to make sure nothing was disrupted or out of place, almost as if thanking it for the mysterious gift. She placed the letters in the empty shoebox, allowing them to breathe and stretch out in their new and spacious home after who knows how many years of being cramped in that small secret space.

She stood up, intending to place the shoebox back into the hall closet, but in a sweeping moment became overwhelmed with a trembling fear. She could feel her breaths becoming more shallow and faster. She felt a twitch in her chest. Her heart pounded in her ears and her knees weakened. She wanted no part of this. The letters had been hidden, and maybe there was a very good reason for that. What if they held secrets about her mother she didn't want to know?

"I can't do this," she said out loud. She abruptly grabbed the box and shoved it into the kitchen wastebasket, not caring that the wet coffee grounds and breakfast waste would soak into the cardboard. Tears rolled down her face. She couldn't take any more pain. She grabbed her purse and car keys and bolted out the door to go to the store.

Chapter 4

The year was 1975. Young Michelle sat cross legged under the sage green and mustard yellow granny square crocheted afghan that provided a backdrop to several used tissues laying in a disheveled pile around her. She had been awake for hours, but she still didn't have the energy to get out of bed.

Her mother called up the stairs, "Michelle, are you up? I'm making pancakes. Twenty minutes!"

"All right!" She yelled back, but she knew her words were empty. She had no intention of getting up just yet. She stared at the small desk at the foot of her bed. Her typewriter called to her to write, to unburden her heart. She knew she needed to let this heaviness out, but she wasn't sure how to form the words. She wasn't sure she wanted to invite her feelings to the surface.

She gulped. Her arm felt heavy as she reached over and pushed the play button on the cassette player next to her bed. With a weak voice, she sang along with Neil Diamond from the song she had recorded off of the radio the day before. Her voice cracked from the dryness in her mouth and the lump lodged deep in her throat.

"I am," I said
To no one there
And no one heard at all
Not even the chair
"I am," I cried
"I am," said I

And I am lost, and I can't even say why[1]

She had played it over and over in these last few hours, in between bouts of tears. She flopped over and curled up in a ball, sobbing as silently as possible. What was she crying for? She didn't know. It just overcame her and she needed to find some way to get it out. Maybe if she put it into words, she might understand why. Her chest felt a little lighter after the tears, but still her body was weighed down with heartache. She had to release it.

She pushed aside the heavy blanket of tissues and tears and rolled to the edge of the bed. She stood up, wobbly at first. Her legs could barely hold her from being cramped under her body for so long.

She sat at the desk, grateful for the quiet morning. Her sister was at a sleepover with her best friend as usual. The large flowered wallpaper that framed the desk spoke to her with splashes of bright colors. Big blossoms of yellow and orange, green and red. It was almost as if they were jumping off the wall and into the air around her. A moment of girlish joy replaced the tears as she gazed upon her pictures of David Cassidy. This month's centerfold from *Tiger Beat* magazine. She heard his voice singing in her head. " I think I love you. Isn't that what life is made of? Though it worries me to say; I've never felt this way.."[2]

"I love you too, David." The tears returned. If only he loved her. If only she could talk to him about the torturous sadness she felt.

She reached onto the shelf beneath her electric typewriter and grabbed her prized box of antique stationery. Mr. Brandson from next door had given it to her. It was cream colored with edging that resembled the vines of a rose bush. The freshness of the paper had faded over the years.

The day he had given it to her was a happy memory. They were sitting in his backyard as they did every Saturday afternoon. He had two canvases set up on easels.

Mr. Branson gestured toward them. "Now, today I am going to expand your art interest out of the world of animals. They are beautiful, especially the elephants you draw so much, but there are other areas of beauty that need your talent to allow others to see and enjoy it." He pointed to a beautiful rose bush growing alongside the back porch. "Look at this rose bush. Did you know that the rose is the state flower of New York?"

Michelle gazed at the flower bush and shook her head. "Really? These are really pretty, but I never thought of them as being that important!"

"Well, it is. And it is one of the oldest flowers in the world. Fossils from roses date back 35 million years."

"Really? Fossils of roses? I thought fossils were just of animals."

"Nope. All kinds of plant life, too. And in Germany, there is a living rose that is 1,000 years old today."

"Wow!" exclaimed Michelle. This is what she loved about spending time with Mr. Branson—he always had such amazing facts. She never thought that one flower could have so much to it beyond just its beauty. She could hardly imagine a flower that was actually 1,000 years old!

"Yeah, and you think I'm old!"

Michelle giggled. "You're not so old, Mr. Brandson!"

Mr. Brandson smiled. "And each rose color has a different meaning." He reached forward and gently cradled a red rose in his hand. "When I asked Mrs. Brandson to marry me, I gave her red roses, like these. Red is the color of love."

Michelle placed her hands over her heart. "Oh, that is so romantic."

Mr. Brandson's hand moved to the pink rose beside it. "But now, when I present roses to Mrs. Brandson, I cut pink roses. They are the color that represents grace and elegance, which describes the woman she has grown to be. Not everyone deserves pink roses, you know. You have to earn it!" He leaned into Michelle's ear. "But sometimes I add in a red rose just to remind her how much I love her."

Michelle smiled and giggled. "She's lucky."

Mr. Brandson leaned back in his chair. "No, I am the lucky one! So, today, I think we will work on drawing yellow roses, because yellow is the color of friendship. And we are definitely friends! Now, to inspire you, I want to give you a gift. Give me a moment." He stood up and disappeared into the house.

Michelle felt the energy buzzing through her body like a bee as she sat in the momentary quiet and anticipation. A gift? She felt a shivering sensation. As she sat waiting, she turned her thoughts to the love between Mr and Mrs. Branson. She imagined the day when a handsome man presented her with red roses, asking her to marry him. Her heart quickened.

The sound of the sliding glass door interrupted her reverie.

Mr. Brandson offered her a box.

Michelle studied the plain 8 ½ by 11 box. It was the kind of box she saw in the school office. 'Typing paper?' she thought. It didn't look very exciting. She glanced up at him. He was beaming at her as if he was giving her something truly amazing. She held her tongue like her mother told her to do when she was about to be a big mouth, waiting for him to show her what was inside.

He opened it with a flourish. "This is for you," he said with pride.

She peeked into the box. There was paper inside, but it wasn't plain typing paper. It was faded and slightly wrinkled. It was beautiful stationary, with roses designed to be climbing along the edges on a vine. She reached out to gently touch the vine; it looked so real she could almost feel the prickers that guarded these beautiful blooms.

She gasped. "Oh, that is so beautiful!"

"And very old. Not a thousand years old like that rose in Germany! But as old as me. My mother gave it to me when I was a young man. She told me it was the perfect paper to write a love letter. I never used it, mainly because I met Mrs. Brandson right out of high school and we have never been apart. We live in our own love letters every day."

Michelle gazed upon the paper as she ran her fingers along the edges, as if she could feel the pedals under her fingertips. The paper had a rough, raised texture. It even felt fancy.

"I want you to have it. It will remind you of this day, the day you brought roses into your art."

Michelle smiled. "Thank you. I will cherish it."

"Well, better if you use it!"

"I will!"

"Okay, good. You're welcome. Now let's turn our attention to roses."

A familiar cold sensation engulfed her body, pushing out the warmth of the memory. Tears welled up in her eyes again.

She took out a piece of the antique stationery and fed it into the typewriter.

"I woke up crying again this morning. Please, I would like to know—why do I cry?"

Chapter 5

Why Do I Cry?

It was afternoon by the time she returned. The shopping was completed, dinner was planned, her tomato sauce was beginning its several hours of simmering, and a new pot of coffee was on the burner. Michelle was a firm believer in letting the flavors simmer into her sauce for hours to release the best flavor of each ingredient.

She sat at the table. She couldn't stop thinking about the envelopes from her mother's jewelry box that were now sitting in the trash. She wanted to read them, or at least face her ambivalence over opening them, but she couldn't bring herself to do it. She felt like a coward.

There was a knock at the backdoor. She stood and turned. Through the sheer curtain over the window, she glimpsed a sheriff's uniform. Her heart leaped into her throat. She quickly stood up and with wobbly knees made it to the door. The last time a sheriff showed up at her door was when Shawn's father died in a car accident. She couldn't handle something happening to one of the girls. She felt nauseated. She opened the door. Looking past the sheriff to the car in the driveway, Michelle immediately saw the silhouette of her daughter Janine sitting in the back seat of the sheriff's car. Her heart sank while pounding ferociously. She knew the girls were safe, but she also knew she was too late to stop Janine from going down the path she had feared would engulf her.

The sheriff began to talk. "Ma'am, my name is Officer Kowalski with the Sheriff's Department." He looked Michelle up and down, no doubt noticing the difference in skin tone between Michelle and the girl sitting in his car. Michelle had been to this rodeo many times. "Is this young woman your daughter Janine?"

Michelle nodded, pushing through the wave of nausea and shock overcoming her entire body.

"I wonder if we can talk."

Michelle scanned the officer's body and landed on his badge and name tag. "Of course, Officer Kowalski. Come in. Is Janine under arrest?"

Officer Kowalski didn't answer her. "I just need a few minutes of your time."

She glanced once more toward the car and looked at Janine. She had her head bowed down and refused to look at her mother. "Something tells me I'd better get my husband."

"Yes, if he is here."

Michelle turned and quickly ran up the stairs, fumbling and tripping before she made the final step. She finally reached the top of the stairs and ran into the bedroom. "Shawn," she whispered as she shook him awake.

He opened his eyes slowly and grumbled, "What is it?"

"An officer from the sheriff's department is here, and he has Janine in the back seat of his car. I don't know what it's about. Get dressed and meet us downstairs!"

He rolled out of bed and on his feet in one fluid motion.

Michelle hurried back downstairs. There was a quickening in her body. Fear of the total unknown. Her body trembled from all the possibilities this could be. She could barely feel anything in her legs as they carried her back into the kitchen. "Please sit," she offered. She sat on the other side of the table from Officer Kowalski.

Shawn entered, locking eyes with Michelle for a moment.

Officer Kowalski turned around to greet Shawn. Michelle could see the sheriff now processing the source of Janine's skin coloring.

Shawn reached his hand out to the sheriff. "Hi, I'm Shawn, Janine's dad. Is she okay?"

"Yes, she is fine. We caught her and her friends before any damage was done."

Shawn took his place at the table.

Michelle tried to keep her hands from trembling as she addressed Officer Kowalski. "What's going on?"

"I am one of a group of officers that patrol your daughter's school. It's hard to imagine that kids this age are getting into trouble, but we deal with it every day. We have been watching your daughter's group of friends for a few weeks now. They have been skipping school, jumping into the cars of some of the older students that have their permits, and they drive off to who knows where. We have followed them a few times. Once they walked into the department store and were there for about an hour. Pretty sure they were shoplifting, but we don't have jurisdiction to stop them there. One afternoon they were partying in the Forest Hill Graveyard. I believe there was alcohol involved. We arrived near the end and they ran away, but the bottles remained."

Shawn pushed back on his chair to balance on its back legs, then came back to ground level. This was something he had done throughout his entire life whenever he was nervous or agitated. He reached up and rolled his hand over his balding head.

Michelle just could not believe what she was hearing. "Alcohol?!" she challenged him. My daughter doesn't drink alcohol! She's 13! I won't even let her drink coffee!"

Officer Kowalski cleared his throat. "Today, we caught the kids at the statue in the park, with open paint cans. We caught them just before they started pouring paint all over it. We handcuffed them and told them they were under arrest for vandalism. Put each of them in a separate car. We would like to give them another chance. I suspect from your reaction that you were not aware of any of this behavior."

Michelle shook her head. "She has been quite rebellious lately, but mostly in the way she talks to us. Always challenging us. It's been hard to tell if she is walking down a dangerous path or just exercising her ability to make her own decisions. Coming into her own, you know."

Officer Kowalski listened intently. He looked at Shawn who was just listening to Michelle and nodding his head in agreement.

Michelle continued. "But we never thought it was anything this serious!"

"Some things change from innocent to criminal in an instant. It's scary letting your child out into this world today with all the pressures on them. I have a daughter about Janine's age. She's 14 actually. My wife and I struggle with her every day. Which is probably why I did not take your daughter to jail. I don't necessarily believe juvenile hall is the place to turn them on the right path. Hate to put you on the hot seat, but it is going to take a lot of work on your part. The first step is just knowing what is happening. If you don't know, then you can't deal with it. If it's okay with you, I'd like to bring her in and leave her to talk it out with you. But just know that the next officer may not give her leniency. Especially with, and I hate to say this but it is reality, racial profiling. Next time it may be a real arrest."

Michelle reached over and took Shawn's hand in hers. She gave a heaving sigh as if to inhale the energy needed to face this next even tougher battle and exhale the fear paralyzing her. "Okay, well, thank you for making the choice you did. We will deal with this fully."

Shawn stood up as Officer Kowalski stood and shook his hand. "Thank you so much. I just don't know what to say, except that she is from a good family and very loved, and she obviously is taking that for granted."

Officer Kowalski pursed his lips. "I'd like to think that she is just confused. Lots of messages out there; she just needs help sifting through them and finding the right ones. And she might make a few more mistakes before she learns what she needs to."

Michelle stood up to join them. "Can you tell me who the other kids were?"

"I'm sorry I can't since they're also juveniles. Same goes for your daughter. Nobody will know about this. I think Janine would be a good place to start in finding out. I've told Janine the same thing I've told you. I've put a bit of the fear of God in her, so she might be a little more humble and ready to talk to you."

"Yes, thank you again so much."

Officer Kowalski nodded as he walked out the door. Michelle and Shawn watched as he retrieved Janine from the back seat of the car. He assisted her as she struggled to crawl out of the tight space with handcuffs on. Tears streamed down Michelle's face at the sight of her child in handcuffs. A deep sob escaped. Shawn placed his hand on her shoulder. She turned and saw that the tears were streaming down his face, too.

Michelle turned back to the scene outside her door. Janine reached her feet, and the officer spoke a few words to her with his hand gently on her shoulder. Michelle studied her face. Janine looked much more like a scared little girl instead of the rebellious teen that faced her this morning. He turned Janine away from him and removed the handcuffs.

She walked to the door and ushered Janine into the house. Shawn grasped Janine's trembling body into her arms and held her tight. Then he leaned over and placed his arms around them both. Michelle wiped her tears from her eyes, readying herself for the conversation that was about to occur. No words were needed in this moment, although Michelle could write a book describing all the emotions and fears that flooded her.

Michelle pointed to the kitchen chair. Janine obediently sat. Michelle and Shawn sat down at the table with her.

Michelle broke the silence. "Well, where should we start?"

Janine's head was down. "I don't know," she mumbled.

Michelle could feel her muscles tighten. She knew there were a few ways this conversation could go. "Well, I don't know either. How about with how long you have been skipping school? And why has the school not called me? And who are these 'friends' you have been hanging out with? Where do you go when you are not at school? Are you shoplifting? Have you been drinking? Where did you get the paint cans? And do you have any idea what happens to your life, and to our lives, when you get yourself arrested? Then we could go into, What have we done so wrong that is sending you down this path? Oh, and how about...Why? Just why?"

Shawn reached over and placed his hand on Michelle's arm. "Before we get into all of that, maybe we should start out with confirming that we love you more than anyone will on this earth, and nothing that you do will change that love."

"I haven't been skipping school completely. Just a few classes now and then. It was just in fun...It was fun. Exciting."

Michelle laughed. It was a curt sound with no humor in it. "Exciting? Was it exciting when the officer pushed you into the back of that police car? Do you know what he said to us? He said next time it will be an arrest mostly because of racial profiling. You are presumed guilty just because of your skin color."

Janine slapped her hand onto the table. She looked straight into her mother's eyes. "Oh my God, here we go again. Look, I am sorry that my skin coloring is such an embarrassment to you! I wish you had married some white man so you could have white children and be proud of them! So you wouldn't have to worry about them being arrested and ruining your precious reputation and your art career! This is who I am and I can't change it!"

Michelle bristled. There was a familiarity in this conversation. Michelle remembered having similar feelings about her mother when she married Shawn. Even though her mother never said as much, Michelle assumed that marrying a man of color was an embarrassment to her mother. Maybe that is what drove a wedge between them? Maybe that is what kept her from visiting more often?

Marrying a man of color. Michelle wondered what Janine would think if she knew Shawn wasn't the first man of color she fell in love with.

In her mind, she was suddenly with Daniel, her first and only love in high school. Daniel was one of the few African American boys in her class. They met in science class, and their chemistry was undeniable.

"Why do you want to be with me?" he would ask her over and over.

Michelle was always willing to open her heart to Daniel. "Because you make me feel beautiful."

"Well, that's not me. You *are* beautiful."

She would shiver every time he leaned over and kissed her.

But their love was not meant to last. That shiver of excitement turned to gut-wrenching fear as they walked down the hall. Their bodies would tighten as they heard the snickering of their schoolmates.

"Hey, there goes Chocolate and Vanilla! Do you actually taste like that?"

One day Daniel tried to stand up for Michelle and a fight broke out. Daniel ended up in the hospital. His parents moved him out of the school, and he never spoke to her again.

She could still feel the devastation just thinking about it. The heavy feeling in her chest. Hard to swallow. Numbness in her arms and legs. Self-hatred that she wasn't good enough for either race. Caught in between colors. Heart aching so bad she could do nothing but cry. She never got over that heartbreak and never dated anyone until she met Shawn.

When Michelle gave birth to her girls, she gazed upon their exquisite, beautiful brown skin. She couldn't believe that love made these beautiful beings. But she couldn't help but feel bitterness, too. Such beautiful girls, made from her own flesh, each one their own miracle. Yet they were also a reminder of what her life with Daniel might have given her sooner, if the opportunity had not been ripped from the two of them. All because of racial prejudice. And now, it was Janine that felt this prejudice from her own mother. She looked at her daughter. She was exquisite. And she was made with tremendous love. How could she possibly be embarrassed by that?

Michelle recognized Janine's accusation as her own self-hatred. A sense of urgency crept through her body. She couldn't let this continue for Janine the way it had for her. She swallowed hard to suppress those familiar feelings from overcoming her. "Okay, now stop right there. This family is about love, not color. Marry another man? You won't witness greater love between two people than your father and me. And embarrassed by your color? You are my flesh and blood, dear child. Racial profiling is something we take very seriously; it is not a matter of embarrassment. It is a matter of fear for your rights in this country. Fear of watching my daughter sit in a hard, cold jail cell for no good reason. I pray for you and fear for you every single solitary day when you leave this house and get on that bus! You are my life. What happens to you, I feel. Someday you will understand that.

But for now, we need to get back to the issue at hand, which is not your color but your behavior, that put you in the back of that police car today. Were you really going to pour paint on that statue? Don't you know that this is against the law? It's called vandalism. Destruction of property."

"We just didn't think we would get caught." Janine looked from her mother to her father. "I guess I screwed up on that one."

Shawn reached out to hold Janine's hand across the table. His voice was gentle but direct. "Honey, you screwed up on a lot more than that. We have got some unraveling to do. Let's start by just getting some facts clear. Do you know why the school has not been letting us know when you skip out?"

Janine shrugged. "Maybe because I changed our phone numbers so they couldn't get a hold of you."

"And how did you do that?!"

"I wrote a note and signed your name."

Michelle felt like screaming. She stood and poured herself a cup of coffee. She leaned against the counter and gulped it, scowling at Janine.

Shawn squeezed Janine's hand. "Okay, so tomorrow you and Mom and I will go to school and get the correct numbers reinstated. I hope you understand the seriousness of this. If something happened to you, if you were having a seizure or something, they need to be able to get a hold of us."

Janine nodded. She looked at Michelle for confirmation.

"We'll drive you to school in the morning and we will go straight to the office. What happens after that, maybe you can shed some light on how I am supposed to know any time of the day or night where you are? When I put you on the schoolbus in the morning, what happens after that? How do I not sit in worry all day long for your safety? Any ideas? Maybe I should put you under house arrest and do homeschooling."

Janine pushed her chair back so she could turn towards her mother. "Mom, you are always so intense! Always thinking things are worse than they are! Now you want to imprison me and cut me off from all of my friends? Are you going to lock my windows too so I can't jump out and slip into a getaway car?"

"If I have to. Keep talking, I am getting lots of ideas."

Shawn jumped into the conversation. "Okay, so we are not going to solve all this in one afternoon. It's been a very difficult day so let's attempt to retreat, take a breather, deal with step one tomorrow and take it one step at a time. In the meantime, you need to go to your room and think about the very close call you had today. And how you being arrested could affect everyone in this house, including your sisters, who are innocent bystanders."

Janine stood up and began to walk past her mother.

"Stop there." Michelle spoke as Janine turned back towards her. "And no phone calls."

"I was supposed to call Alison."

"Nope."

Janine shook her head and headed towards the doorway. "Oh hell."

Michelle called after her. "Don't say hell."

Janine glared back at her mother and walked out of the kitchen to the stairway. Michelle took a sip of her coffee and almost fell into the chair at the table. She looked at Shawn. "That went well."

Shawn sported a forced grin. "Painful as it was. She did get one thing from her mother–passion."

"Passion? Is that what you call it?"

"Passion can go both ways. You are passionately angry and you're scared–not sayin' that's a bad thing–and she is passionately defending herself. What bothers me is that she's ashamed of her skin color. We need to change that. But first, we need to get this skipping school thing straightened out. We gotta get her turned around to make the right choices in a world of bad ones."

Michelle could feel the tension in her body lessen a little. Shawn was her rock; he was the voice of reason that grounded her anxiety. "Okay, so where do we start?"

"First a little time and distance. Let her have this evening to reflect on what just happened. Then tomorrow morning, we can bring her into school to straighten out the phone number thing and the skipping school. And find out just how much skipping has occurred. Maybe we are on the cusp of this or maybe we are drowning in it. Since I'm off tonight, I can go with you.

Michelle nodded. "Then what? I think we need to ground her so she has to come straight home after school."

"Well, let's see what the extent of this is first. Then we'll have a better idea of how long to ground her for. Let's see what tomorrow brings." Shawn placed a comforting hand on Michelle's back. "Let it go for now. We'll get through this. We always do." He stood up to throw a crumpled napkin in the garbage. He stopped short.

Michelle winced. She knew he had discovered the shoebox. It was hard to miss, sticking straight up out of the garbage can. In the back of her mind, she wondered if she had done that on purpose.

"What is this?"

Michelle tried to sound casual. "A shoebox."

Shawn scuffed. "Well, obviously." He shook the box. "It's not empty and it doesn't feel like shoes."

"Nope, not shoes."

Shawn stared at her. His expression was an invitation to share.

After a long pause, she looked up and sighed. "Letters. Before this all started, I was taking a closer look at Mom's jewelry box. I wanted to see if there was a designer's name or year on the bottom of it, to see if it was really an antique, and I found a hinged compartment in the back of it."

"Really? That's cool." Shawn returned to the table and sat down, setting the shoebox on the table.

Michelle's body tightened.

He leaned back in his chair. "That's right out of a mystery novel. Don't tell me–love letters from WWII or letters that your mother kept from her high school sweetheart?"

"I don't know. I didn't look. There's a series of envelopes, all numbered one through eight."

"Why didn't you read them?"

Michelle shrugged. " I felt guilty for even finding them. Obviously they were very private for my mother to have hidden them in there. Or maybe they aren't even hers. Maybe she didn't know they were in there either." She looked into Shawn's face for his reaction.

Shawn's brow was furrowed, but he said nothing.

Her stomach churned. "I felt if I opened them I might be crossing a line. They were private. Or finding out a bunch of secrets. I don't know. I put them in the shoebox, but I decided I don't want to know what's inside."

Shawn leaned forward, placing his arms crossed in front of him on the table. "Secrets, huh? Secrets are like the devil, you know. They need to be confronted or they will control you. Secrets have caused so much distress over the years in your family."

Michelle knew he was waiting for her reaction. She gave him none.

"Maybe it's time."

"Time for what?"

"Well, obviously your mother felt these letters were important enough to keep. Maybe it's time to open the vault. Maybe it will help you, to free you from those chains that have been strangling you."

Tears welled up in her eyes. "And now our own daughter seems to be struggling from her own secrets."

"Exactly."

"Damn, you're right. I gotta break this cycle. We need to teach her to talk about things." She pulled the box over to her. "I am just going to go for it and see what's in there."

"Absolutely, I think you should."

Michelle stared at the top of the box, hands poised to open the lid.

"Do you want me to be there when you open them or is this something you need to do by yourself?"

Michelle knew he was prompting her, trying to give her courage. She looked into his eyes. "Thank you for giving me that choice. I think I would like to do this alone. But if there's something in there that—well, I know where you are if I need you."

Shawn stood up and kissed Michelle gently on the forehead. "Okay, then, I'll go grab a few more short winks and a shower. Smells like a great sauce brewing for that chicken parmesan."

As he began to walk away, Michelle grabbed his hand and pulled him back. "Hey, you do know that the color thing isn't a thing, right?"

Shawn squeezed her hand. "I know that if it was, we wouldn't be here today, together. You are an amazing mother, her one and only mother, and someday she will learn that love isn't dependent on being the right color." He touched her eyes gently. "Love doesn't come from here." He pointed to her heart. "It comes from here."

Michelle gently giggled. "Thank you, Professor Jackson. Go to sleep!"

Shawn left the room, leaving Michelle alone. Waves of dread that she had been holding back in front of Janine and Shawn overwhelmed her. She took a deep breath, releasing as much of it as she could with her exhale. She focused her attention on her next task: the letters. "Well, here goes nothing." Walking down the back hall, she retrieved the shoebox. She brought it out to the living room and set it on the coffee table. She sat down and just looked at it. The shroud of guilt clenched her heart. Thoughts continued to swirl in her mind of how she was betraying her mother. "No," she said aloud. "No more secrets." She opened the box and removed the envelopes.

Inside the first envelope were two pieces of paper. One was a beautiful piece of stationery with antique edging that resembled the vines of a rose bush. It was cream colored, faded, and had a wrinkled texture. The other was a plain white paper. Both were typed. She was drawn to the antique writing paper. It looked like a letter, but it wasn't addressed to anyone in particular. She began to read.

I woke up crying again this morning. Please, I would like to know–why do I cry? I can't for the life of me tell you what is wrong. All I know is that this feeling of heavy sadness is overwhelming. I cry; therefore, I live. That seems to be my mantra lately. The taste of the salt of my tears sustains my life. But is this what should be life sustaining? Is this what God has planned for my life? I see so many people around me, smiling, laughing, loving. But it is like they are out in this free space, and I am in a little enclosed fishbowl, trapped, looking out at them but unable to feel their joy or touch their existence. Am I even alive?

Michelle tore her eyes from the page as the heaviness of the author's despair overcame her. She could relate. She had awoken many times over the years with her face moist from tears, warmth from the droplets rolling down her cheeks, heaviness in her chest. Each breath would give way to sobs as she tried to stifle the sound so her husband would not hear her. She didn't want him to think it was his fault. It had nothing to do with him. It had nothing to do with anything in particular. It just was. It would just come, overpowering her without rhyme or reason.

More importantly than all of this, she had to know, was this written by her mother? She continued.

The only physical sensation I have right now is the warmth of my tears. I feel frozen in my existence. People talk to me, and I answer, but it isn't reality. It is like a scene unfolding in a dark play. I want to know. Is this sadness? I don't know that I am feeling sad. I feel nothing actually. Is it despair? I have everything I need to survive. I have a family, a home, a bed to lay my head. I have my art. I have food to eat. Maybe if I could figure out why I cry, then I could figure out how to make it stop. And I want to make it stop. How do I make it stop??????

Michelle sat back in her chair. She agreed, sometimes you just have no answer for why the tears begin or how to make them stop.

She couldn't help but wonder, who is this writer? What has brought this person to this state of sadness? The more she read, the more it seemed likely that these could be her mother's words. She closed her eyes. Her thoughts took her back to her old room in her mother's house. She must have been around nine years old. Michelle could hear her crying behind the closed door of her mother's room. The same room Michelle was in just this day. The young girl in her memory recognized that her mother crying was a common occurrence. She shivered.

A young Michelle tiptoed to her mother's bedroom and slowly pushed the bedroom door open. The hinges creaked as she crept over the threshold. She found her mother sitting on the edge of her bed with her face buried in her hands. Her shoulders hunched forward as if trying to protect herself from the crushing sadness. She let a breath out and held it, as if afraid to breathe in again to bring on the next wave of sobs.

Michelle tiptoed over to her and placed her hand on her thigh. "Mom, are you okay?"

Mom turned. She stared at Michelle with sunken eyes.

Michelle froze. The air was heavy. They both struggled to take a breath.

Mom reached up to hold Michelle's small face in her hands, caressing it as if she were a fragile and precious rose petal. "I am now." She pulled her daughter into a tight hug, then gently pushed Michelle away with trembling arms.

"Now you stop worrying about me. Go find your sister and have some fun."

Michelle's mind brought her back to the present. She inhaled sharply. Did she cause her mother's sadness?

Michelle opened the plain paper and began to read.

Do not be afraid of the tears. They are yours. Whether wanted or not, they belong to you. They are a symbol of your feelings. Yes, you are a living, feeling person! You are alive! Your tears are a testimonial to this. You have many pent-up feelings that you may or may not recognize, but the universe knows that you cannot keep these feelings locked up inside. You must release them. So the universe begins the flow. At the exact time that it is needed. It may be in the middle of the night. In the warmth of a bath. While driving in a car. When you least expect it but need it the most. Trust the universe. Do not desire to prevent the tears from flowing. Do not wish to be rid of them. Do not think that they are an enemy to you. Your tears are one of your greatest assets. They will help you see more clearly after they fall and loosen the tightness your body feels. Notice how your body feels a sense of relief and a higher sense of self appreciation and energy after the tears flow. You shed the judgments of this world, and you begin to feel your strength. The universe has got you. The universe will make your tears flow, and the universe will stop them at the right time. All you need to do is let them flow and trust in that which you cannot see. Because it sees you. It is one with you. It protects you. It loves you. It knows your worthiness, your strength. And it serves to restore you. Beginning with the warmth of your tears.

Michelle leaned back into the couch. She thought about the day's events. The struggle with Janine. Her rebellion. The sheriff. Seeing her beautiful daughter in handcuffs at such a young age. What road was this leading down? The heaviness weighed on her as she gave way to the devastation of the events of this day and the challenge her daughter had brought to their table. Did she have the strength for this fight? The fears of what this could mean to Janne's future. Sitting today in her mother's bedroom, revealing the very place where she had witnessed her mother's tears as a child. Now Mom was gone, and she would never again have the chance to close the distance the years had put between them.

Somehow, the events of the last few days were leading her to question herself more than ever before. Was it the years that put distance between them? Or was it her shortcomings as a daughter? Her inability, or unwillingness, to maintain a relationship with her mother all these years. Her oldest daughter, Jaimee, and the struggle to help her understand the seriousness of proving her worth in a white collar world. Then this thing with Janine.

The events of the day began to close in on her, like a huge thundercloud descending from the sky and wrapping her body. She felt moisture from the heavy cloud about her, until she realized the moisture was from her own tears. She let them flow.

Chapter 6

I am so afraid. All the time.

It was later in the afternoon, and Michelle knew that Shawn would be waking from his slumber. She allowed the couch to support her body, heavy with turbulent thoughts. Thoughts of Janine and what transpired earlier. Thoughts about the letter and the feelings it stirred up in her, as well as the questions it brought. Her emotions welled up as she thought about it, and she attempted to fight back a tear.

Shawn came down the stairs. His distinguished balding scalp revealed the effects of years of hard work, stress, and the unwanted advancing of time. His pajama bottoms gave way to the tiniest bulge of his stomach which served as a trophy to the cooking they enjoyed doing together. He stopped at the bottom of the steps, yawned and stretched.

Michelle looked up from her thoughts. "How was your sleep?" she asked.

Shawn quietly gazed at Michelle. "Well, the second half was kind of rocky. Thinking about Janine."

Michelle nodded. "Me too."

"You were just wiping a tear from your face. Are you okay?"

Michelle reflected for a moment. "I think so. I opened the first envelope. It's a letter."

Shawn began to walk toward Michelle. "To whom?"

Michelle shrugged. "Doesn't say. It doesn't even say who the writer is. It just has a question and an answer."

Shawn sat on the couch to be closer to Michelle and settled into the conversation. "What do you mean, an answer? What was the question?"

"The question was, how does this person who is writing the letter stop the tears from flowing?"

"Oh, that's heavy."

Michelle sipped on her coffee and then looked up, catching Shawn's eyes. "This person was very sad. He or she could not stop the tears from falling. They sounded isolated from their world. My heart went out to them. I just wanted to hug this person. I know the mental anguish of tears that sometimes don't seem to want to stop. I need to know if this is somebody that I knew?"

"Do you think they could be your mother's letters? They were in her jewelry box."

"Yes, but did she even know about them? If this was my mother, then when did she feel this way? When was this letter written? Who caused these tears in her? Who dried these tears? Who wrote this beautiful answer to her?"

She could feel her body tightening as her anxiety climbed. She cleared her throat and fidgeted on the couch, trying to stop the escalation of emotion in her body. She rubbed her forehead with her right hand as if to massage an impending headache. "I hadn't reached out to her in so many years. Did I cause this? And now she's gone. If this was because of me, there is no way to ever make amends." Another hot tear rolled down her cheek.

Shawn reached out to lovingly hold Michelle's arm. "Whooaaa! Slow down there, girl! Don't jump on a train that has no way of stopping. I can assure you that your mother was given plenty of chances to be a part of your life, and she was not able to do so for whatever reason. But you were not the demon in her life. You barely saw her for over 20 years except for an occasional family visit."

Michelle softened. "I know that, intellectually. But my heart feels differently."

She quivered as she felt Shawn's hand move lovingly down her arm, to hold Michelle's hand in his. "How so?"

Michelle loved the warmth of his touch. "When I went off to college, I never looked back. I don't know why. Mom didn't do anything to make me want to get away from her. It's just that once I was out of that house, I didn't want to look back. I wanted a better life, I guess. My own life."

Shawn caressed her back with his other hand. "You know, all college kids feel that way. I remember feeling that way a little, too. It's kind of a rite of passage, isn't it?"

Michelle shrugged. "To basically never speak to your parents again after you go to school? I didn't even come home for most holidays, even missed a few Christmases. I called her once in a while, but being so far from home, it was easier to just stay at college. And then, over time, it just didn't seem natural to be home. You and I even got married by a justice of the peace. We didn't even give her the joy of attending our wedding. Visits home were just the few obligations–the girls' christenings, some Christmases as they were growing up. Then we started using an alternate day for those few Christmas visits so we could be home on Christmas Day. I just wasn't there for my mother. Tracy was the hands-on daughter, and I let her take that role. I didn't know her. I didn't know what she felt. What made her laugh. What made her cry."

"Why do you think you never wanted to look back? Was it really for a better life or to leave something behind?"

Michelle thought for a minute. "I'm not sure. Maybe a little of both. Mom always had a sense of sadness about her. Sometimes it was suffocating. And with Lisa being such a rebel and me always feeling like I had to make up for her crazy behavior, I just had to get out of there. I still remember Mom saying that day I left for college, "I'll never see you again." I said, "Stop it, Mom, of course you will." Now, as I see my daughters getting older, I know how much I want them to always be in my life, and I feel more guilty every day that I denied my mother the one thing that mothers want most: having her child in her life." Tears rolled down her face. "And now, there is no undoing the pain I must have caused her."

Shawn reached over to pull her close to him. "Michelle, your mother loved you, and that kind of love forgives all. She knew you loved her. She knew that you were struggling as well. She loved you enough to give you that space. And you became an amazing artist. You took after her. That was how you reached out to her. Hanging your art in her house was like being able to have a conversation between you every day. We all show love in different ways. She was so proud of you."

Michelle allowed herself to be comforted by Shawn's embrace for a long moment, then she sat upright. She fidgeted with the letters in front of her. "After the question and all of that sadness, there was an answer. Someone answered her letter. About the tears being beneficial to the person. Releasing their feelings, keeping them alive. And there was something about the universe. The universe brings their tears and how the universe will take away their tears. The answer says that the universe protects them, loves them. My question is, what are they talking about? The universe?"

Shawn shook his head. "Hmmm, I don't know. I imagine it could be other people in the world who watch over you. Family. Friends. Angels. Or maybe it's God. Or Buddah. Allah. The Brahman in Hinduism. Maybe it's the Sun and Earth. And moon. And sky."

Michelle giggled. "Anything else?" She thought about her struggles through the years with finding anything or anyone to believe in. With the feelings of exclusion she'd had with her family, it was hard to imagine anyone watching over her. Surely she would have felt it. She would have been happier, more carefree. "So the universe is universal. It is what it is to the believer."

Shawn nodded. "Yeah, I guess. We all need something to believe in."

Michelle inhaled slowly and forced her breath out, sighing deeply. "I just wish I knew what I believed in sometimes."

Shawn leaned into her ear. She could feel his warm breath upon her. "Well, I know what I believe in....you." He kissed her ear. She shivered, allowing a smile to come to her face.

Shawn leaned back. " So what about the other envelopes? Are they all letters like this one?"

"I don't know. I want to open them in chronological order. I have no idea what is in the others, but I hope they'll give me a clue as to who this is."

Shawn took her hand in his. "Be careful with that heart of yours." He placed her hand over his heart. It belongs to me, you know."

Michelle pulled their joined hands to her face and kissed Shawn's. "Okay." She let go of Shawn and sighed. "I have some cleaning to do and then I'll need to pick up Jaimee. What do you have planned for the rest of the day?"

Shawn stood up and gave a big stretch. "I think I need a shower to wake up, and then maybe help you make that Chicken Parmesan?"

Michelle smiled. "Ooh, I would never turn that offer away! Maybe you could entertain the other rugrats until we get home."

"Sure thing. I'm gonna check on Janine as well. See if she wants to come down and help with dinner." He stood up and headed up the stairs.

She waited for him to leave, then looked over the first letter again. She sat in silence for a few moments. Under her breath, she could hear herself whispering, "Mom, if this is you, please know that if I caused any of these tears to flow, I never intended to do so. If you were suffering, I didn't know. In the future, when I cry, I will feel you. When I wipe my tears dry, I will be wiping your tears. One thing I am sure of is that too much time has passed, and for that I am truly sorry. I'm sorry I didn't come back home. I just wish I could see you one more time. Hold you, wipe your tears." A deep sob escaped her chest, followed by another and another.

"Mom?"

Michelle looked up to see Janine peeking around the corner. She blew her nose and sniffled to stop the tears. She was so exhausted from sobbing that she didn't notice her daughter coming down the stairs. She could barely react. "Janine." She forced herself to scoot over on the couch and patted the seat next to her to invite Janine to come and sit.

Janine walked over to the couch and flopped down.

Michelle felt so weak she almost fell into Janine as the couch cushions gave way to Janine. She steadied herself with her hand. "What a day, huh?"

She could feel Janine's breath become heavy as she started to cry. "Mom, I didn't mean to make you so sad."

She reached around Janine's shoulders and pulled her close. Michelle recognized the parallel to the times when she saw her mother crying as a young girl. "Oh, honey, these tears were not caused by you. Don't you even think for a minute that you did this to me."

Janine looked up at her mother for answers. Her eyes welled up with tears of her own. "Then why are you crying so hard?"

Michelle took a deep breath. "Well, I just learned an interesting fact about crying. That it isn't necessarily a bad thing. It can be cleansing. It can release your pent up fears and stress. Bring you closer to this "universe" that watches over us. I was reading about it in this letter here, and then the universe just started the flow."

"The Universe? What does that mean?"

Michelle picked up the answer letter. "I'm wondering that myself. I think it might be God. But I'm not sure. Listen to this, '*The universe has got you. The universe will make your tears flow, and the universe will stop them at the right time. All you need to do is let them flow and trust in that which you cannot see. Because it sees you. It is one with you. It protects you. It loves you. It knows your worthiness, your strength. And it serves to restore you. Beginning with the warmth of your tears.*'"

Janine reached for the letter, reading it. "That's beautiful. Where did you get it?"

"Well, that's an interesting story. I found this old jewelry box in the bottom of my mother's closet. I brought it home and was looking through each piece of jewelry and thought of so many memories of Grandma that I had forgotten about."

"Wow! That sounds cool! I want to see it. I mean, if you want to share it with me." Janine looked down.

Michelle could see Janine's shame in her slumped shoulders. "I would love to share that with you. Right now I know you have a chicken parmesan experience with Dad and Jessie, but in the next few days, yes. Let's sit down and go through it."

"Were the letters in with the jewelry?"

"They were actually in a hinged compartment."

"A secret compartment? That is so cool! Maybe they're worth something, like you could sell them on ebay."

Michelle smiled. It felt good to see through Janine's eyes for once, the innocence of a child whose first thought is of treasure hunts. "I doubt that. It's just Grandma."

"What if Grandma was really a spy?"

Michelle laughed. Teen girls were such an anomaly. In one moment, so grown up and in the next, dreaming of pirates and spies. "I love the way you think! You never know. We will definitely check that out. This one is a letter of sorts, not addressed to anyone in particular. It's on a sad topic, something that I think we all struggle with in this life at one point or another. The letter asks a question, 'Why do I cry?' and then there is an answer. It had a pretty powerful effect on me."

Janine nodded. "Who wrote the letters? Are they Grandma's?"

"I just don't know. That's a mystery so far. I suppose I will find out as I read more."

Janine bounced up and down on the couch. "Oh, I love mysteries!"

Michelle picked up the letter and placed it on top of the answer which was already in Janine's hands. "Well, would you like to try and help me figure this mystery out? I mean you're going to find yourself with extra time on your hands...grounding isn't always the worst that can happen. It can lead you into adventure."

Janine's body deflated. "Oh, mom, am I really gonna be grounded? For how long?"

Michelle felt anger rise at the audacity of the question. Closing her eyes, she took a breath before responding. She knew that to come at Janine now like a ton of bricks would ruin this precious time with her. Yet she still had to address it. Choosing a softer tone of voice, Michelle said, "Let's think about this. You came home in a police car. You skipped school to vandalize a statue at the park. What do you think?"

Janine sighed. "I know. I'm grounded."

"Right. You really didn't leave us a lot of choice there, my sweet girl."

"But how long?" Janine whined.

"I'm not sure. We need to meet with the counselor tomorrow and talk through this. See what she recommends. But you know, if there are no consequences to our actions, we never learn the lesson. Truth be told, I didn't make the best choices all the time either when I was your age. But we all need to grow and learn. And grow we will. All of us."

"Life is too hard."

Michelle gave her a tight hug. "It is sometimes. But life is good, too, especially when we have each other." Michelle couldn't remember the last time she had a conversation like this with any of her daughters, least of all Janine, her sullen rebel. Yet here they were. What was making the difference? Was it the letters?

Janine wriggled away from her mom. "Can I read the letter?"

"Of course." Michelle felt a momentary sadness to see the moment end. Desperate to preserve the connection they just had, she held the envelope out to Janine. "Here, take a gander at this first envelope, and then why don't you go help Dad with dinner? Maybe after dinner we can talk about the letter and the answer."

"Okay. Can I take it upstairs?"

"Sure, but keep them in the envelope. We don't want to lose them in this great mystery."

"Okay." Janine gently folded the letters and tucked them into the envelope, stood up, and walked over to the stairs. She stopped, turned and looked at Michelle. "Are you going to tell my sisters about the letters?"

Michelle wracked her brain, trying to figure out what Janine was thinking. She might be wanting this to be just hers to know, or she might be eager to tell her sisters. It was so hard to tell. "What do you want to do?"

"Maybe we don't have to tell them right away?"

Michelle nodded. "Yeah, let's have this be our adventure. That'll be so fun."

Janine grinned from ear to ear. She lifted the letter up to wave to her mother and disappeared up the steps.

Michelle stared at the empty space on the steps where Janine had just been. "Well, that might just have been a baby step."

Chapter 7

Michelle stared at her typewriter. She had to do the assignment for Mrs. Foley for fifth period English class. She fidgeted. She had been sitting for so long that her legs hurt. She had to get this done.

She read the assignment sheet for the tenth time. "In discussing our current book, *The Red Badge of Courage,* Henry Fleming found himself coming face to face with his greatest fear in the charge of the 304th regiment. Like Henry, we all have fears. What fears do you have? When those fears are descending upon you as Henry was experiencing, how do you face those fears? Do you retreat like Henry did? Or do you face them head on?"

Fears. Yes, she knew about fear. Racing heart. Impending doom, afraid to look ahead and see something she cannot control. Sometimes fear is painful. Panic caused a tightening in her body that hurt. Suddenly she just wanted to run away.

She reached up and stretched her arms toward the ceiling. She brought them down and scowled at the typewriter, wringing her hands as if they were going to conjure up the answer to this challenge. "Nope. Got nothing," she exclaimed aloud. She sighed.

She grabbed a piece of looseleaf paper and pencil. "Okay," she directed herself, "just write. What are my fears?" She began to make a list.

Spiders.

"Oh, yes, spiders."

Bees.

Cockroaches.

Bugs.

"Swallowing bugs." She shivered at the thought.

Tripping and falling.

Falling down stairs.

Falling on my butt.

Falling in front of my friends.

People laughing at me.

Getting out of bed.

Getting into bed.

Closing my eyes.

Darkness.

Opening my eyes.

Darkness.

Sounds in the night.

Shadows in the night.

Fear of facing my fears.

Fear of being chicken.

Fear of being like Henry.

She read the list over and over. An uneasiness crept over her. The room seemed so silent and yet full of an energy; an unwanted energy. A dull tingling sensation encased her. An impending sense that she was not alone. Like the boogeyman was sneaking up behind her.

She took a quick glance to the side and behind her.

Nothing there.

"Ugghh, of course not."

She pulled out the box of rose writing paper and fed it into the typewriter.

Chapter 8

"*I am so afraid. All the time.*"

Feeling a little more energized, Michelle picked up envelope number two, and turned it around and around in her hands, until she finally stopped and opened it, retrieving two more pages, one on antique stationery, one on plain paper, both typed. She opened the antique stationary and began to read.

I am so afraid. All the time. If I knew what it was that I was afraid of, it would help me cope. I mean, sure I know a lot of things that I am afraid of–I am afraid of spiders. Those big, furry gray and black ones. I am afraid of bees, especially the big fat yellowjackets. I am afraid of tripping and falling in front of people. I am afraid of swallowing a bug in my sleep. I am afraid of sleep. I am afraid of falling out of bed. I'm afraid of getting into bed. I always check between the sheets. I am afraid to turn out the lights. I am afraid to close my eyes. I am afraid that when I come face to face with what I fear, it will be a force that I will not be able to overcome. Again.

Michelle looked up and took a deep breath. Fears. She could certainly understand that. She too had many fears. Bees and spiders, of course; who isn't afraid of those? There were so many times that she herself woke up in the middle of the night, fearful of the dark, the quiet, wondering what might be behind her. She smiled slightly, remembering as a child when she and her sister Lisa would hide under the covers to avoid the 'boogeyman.' Lisa eventually grew out of that fear, but Michelle's fears continued. Their bedroom was upstairs in the attic of a cape cod house, dark and chillingly quiet, a perfect setting for a ghost to appear out of the depths of the hallway outside their door.

She remembered lying in bed, terrified, knowing her sister was beside her but afraid to speak. Somewhere deep inside, she believed she would alert the evil lurking in her room and it would attack. Each and every time, at some point, her fear of not reaching out to her sister overwhelmed her fear of speaking. The conversation was always the same.

Young Michelle forced a soft whisper. "Lisa. Are you there?"

"Where else would I be? Scaredy cat." Inevitably, Lisa turned toward the wall to attempt to ignore her sister's nightly fears. "Go to sleep."

Michelle could feel a chill in her body, even under the two comforters draping over her. "I heard a sound. In the hallway. I peeked out, and I saw a shadow."

Michelle waited for a response, but there was none. She pulled the covers just slightly down enough to reveal her eyes, but they could only stare forward in fear. She didn't dare blink. "Lisa!"

Lisa flopped over to face Michelle. "What?!"

"Do you see anything?"

Lisa picked up her head and looked into the hallway. She fell back and sighed. "Nope. I don't see anything. I hate it when you do this. It spooks me!"

The two lay in silence for a long stretch. Michelle lay frozen in her bed, her ears perked and listening for any sound other than her sister's breathing.

Lisa peeked over the top of her covers. "Do you want me to turn on the light?"

Michelle wanted the lights on more than anything, but turning on the light was a sign of her defeat. It meant that once again she was caving into her fears. She sighed. "Yes, please."

Lisa huffed as she stretched to turn on the light. "Okay, big sister. You're supposed to be my protector, you know. Not the other way around."

The memory ended there, likely because she always fell asleep once the lights were on. Michelle smiled as she remembered the simple, innocent intimacy of sisters. They accepted each other just as they were, even with all the arguments, the fights, and the differences between them.

As she got older, those fears lingered. She remained uneasy when she was alone in the house, or even when she crawled into bed by herself. A nightlight helped to lessen some of that uneasiness. At least until she fell asleep. However, when she awoke in the middle of the night, it almost made the anxiety worse. The nightlight created an eerie glow amidst the shadows that made her more uneasy than the dark. It seemed that the light was calling all the creaking noises in the night to come to life; the wood floors expanding and contracting to the changing northeast weather, the pilot of the fireplace kicking on, the wind outside beating against the windows, ready to infiltrate her home like a thief in the night.

Shawn working the night shift was tough. She wished that Shawn was there in bed with her every night, so she need only turn over and there he would be, protecting her from the big, bad shadows and noises in the room. But now she needed to face these fears alone. She loved the nights that Shawn didn't have to work. It was so irrational. She was a grown woman, and she was still afraid of the dark.

Of course there were other fears she faced that were more reasonable. She feared for the safety and happiness of her children. She feared that they would not be able to see how much a mother loves her children, and that they would grow away from her over time like she did with her mother. This afternoon with Janine had made that fear grow stronger. She feared that they might grow away from each other as her siblings did. Some days, she feared being able to pay the bills and if she would have enough money for next week's groceries.

As a developing artist, she feared that she wasn't good enough to show her work. She remembered her first art exhibit. Her mentor and friend, Marilyn, tried to help her through this first show.

Marilyn stood with her hands on her hips, giving Michelle that stern look she was famous for. "What are you afraid of? Your art is amazing!"

Michelle gazed at her abstract art. She reached up and softly touched the textured surface. "What if my art doesn't truly express my soul?" She depended on her art to be her voice, the articulation of her inner world. She sighed. "At the same time, I'm afraid that my art will indeed express my soul!"

Marilyn sighed. "So....you want the world to know what is inside this amazing, creative soul, but afraid that it won't be good enough once they see it? Honey, you have a message to put out there, and the viewers will love the message."

Michelle shrugged and tilted her head as she gazed upon her work. "Maybe." She stepped back and tried to get a different view, listening for the canvas to speak to her.

"How will they know the message? How will they see what I am trying to say? Sometimes I wonder if I even see it."

Michelle shivered as her mind returned to the present. She felt so disassociated lately, reaching out to her art to help her frame the pieces of her life together as wife, mother, friend, artist, teacher, sister, daughter. What if the frame is never closed? What if she is never able to feel whole? Completed like a piece of art? Accomplished as a woman works to achieve completion in her life? Accepted? Worthy? Happy? Loved? Yes, she lived every day in fear that these would never materialize and she may be left as a fragmented, insufficient, unnoticed smudge on the map of life. She took a deep breath. She shook her head and shoulders as if to dismiss the cloud hanging above her.

Hoping to distract herself from this dark and endless spiral, she opened the next letter. It was the answer to the last one. Perhaps it would be her answer, too.

Experiencing fear is a part of growth. You are growing, not just in years but in knowledge, in strength, in experience. One of the greatest ways to overcome fear is to develop the strength to face it. Knowing how to do that can be tricky, but know that in the darkest, most fearful times, you are not alone. You belong to the universe, and the universe is with you. It is the buzzing energy inside your soul that speaks to you and propels you forward. It is in your breath, which anchors you in the present moment....So breathe. It is in the practice of positivity in the face of uncertainty. Remember that as you flow positivity out into the world, the universe will help it flow back to you. As you keep others safe from their fears, the universe will keep you safe from your fears.

Ask the universe to show you the meaning of your fears. Meditate to speak to the guardians of your soul. Reach out to that which gives you peace and ask it, "How can I face my fear? What am I really afraid of? Failure? Physical harm? The unknown? How is this fear rooted in my mind? If the fear is of something real and tangible, I may not be able to change it. But what can I do to change my view and my response to this fear?"

Michelle laid the paper down on the couch next to her. It was as if she was afraid of the paper itself. Or at least the words on it. "What am I afraid of? Is it real or tangible?" Such a deep question. "What makes me afraid? As a child it was being alone. The dark. The shadows. Not being accepted at school. Not knowing exactly who I was. Today, pushing 40, I'm still afraid of being alone. The dark. The shadows. Not being accepted in this world. Not knowing exactly who I am.

She could feel that familiar tingling of her skin as if it were trying to keep her tightening muscles at bay.

She shook her head. 'All these years of supposed growth and maturity, and yet these same fears still follow me.' Maybe the reason she stayed away from her mother all these years is that she sensed she felt as lonely, as fearful as her, and she didn't know how to talk to her about these fears. Maybe she feared acknowledging the absence of a close relationship with her mother, one she longed for but was never able to experience. Maybe she lives in fear that history will repeat itself with her own daughters. So can she change this pattern? Can she truly change her response to these fears? Can she teach her daughters how to be strong, how to face their fears, how to be brave enough to give love fully and accept love without doubts?" She picked the paper back up and continued reading.

Bring another into your universe to talk about your fears, such as a therapist, pastor, teacher or friend, someone you trust to confide in. Plan ways that you can distract yourself from the fear. Know that the universe holds you in the palm of its hands; it gives you the strength and resilience to face any fear, it keeps you surrounded with love and acceptance, and confidence and perseverance, and most of all, it helps you breathe.

Fear wants you to feel alone. As you reach out to your universe, you gain strength, and the hold of fear weakens. No matter what the cause of your fear is, you can overcome and triumph over its hold on you. Do not cower, stand tall!

Michelle sat back, absorbing the words she just read. Were these her mother's letters? She had never viewed her mother as a fearful woman, at least in her younger years. As Michelle grew older, she saw signs that her mother was withdrawing from the world. Was this a way she chose to deal with her fears, by isolating herself? Was she running away from something? The letter mentioned that she feared she would not be able to overcome this "force" again. Michelle wondered if she was there when her mom was dealing with these fears, this "force." She wished so much that her mother could have talked to her about her feelings and her fears. Michelle couldn't help but think that if her mother had shared more with her, maybe they would have a closer relationship. Any relationship at all. Maybe if her mother had talked to her more, she would feel a little more confident in talking to her own daughters about their feelings. She hoped it wasn't too late to begin with the girls. She was good at talking to Shawn about her feelings, but she realized that this cannot be enough. She needs to be the mother, the teacher, that her mother wanted to be, but couldn't.

She thought about the few visits they made to her mother through the years. Christmas six years ago. Not Christmas exactly, but a visit the week before. Visits around Christmas helped curb the guilt that they would not be there on the holiday.

In the living room of Mom's house, Michelle was watching the girls play a game of SORRY. Michelle noticed the absence of her mother and went into the kitchen to find her. She found her sitting at the table in a trance-like state, staring into the back hallway. "Mom, what are you doing in here?" She could see her lips moving, but could not hear any words coming from her. "Mom?" Mom turned slowly toward Michelle. She reached up to wipe a tear that had forced its way out, beginning to roll down her cheek. "Oh, I just needed a minute." Her voice was weak and soft.

Michelle sat down next to her. "You were far away. Do you want to talk about it?"

Mom took Michelle's hand in hers and squeezed it gently. "No, at this age, some things are better left alone."

"Like what?"

Mom averted her gaze. "Oh...fears. Pains. Dreams never realized." She shrugged. "At my age it's all the same." She turned back toward Michelle and forced a smile.

Michelle caught the distance in Mom's eyes. She wondered where the mother of her childhood was. What changed her? She wanted to say, "Mom, I love you. How can I help?" She wanted Mom to respond by sharing all those hopes, dreams, and disappointments. Yet she felt frozen in place. She struggled for something, anything, to say. "The girls want you to join in the next round." The minute she said it, she felt a wave of disappointment wash over her. She knew with those few words, she had ensured that the moment had passed, the opportunity lost.

Mom stood up. "Of course."

Coming back to the present moment, Michelle sighed. The heaviness in her chest denied her attempt to take a deep breath. She had the letters to thank for it. At least she felt something, even if it was pain. For so long, she'd felt numb whenever she thought of her mother. If only her mom had been willing to open up. If only she had been brave enough to ask. Now she would never have the chance. Her heart sank and tears came to her eyes.

She knew that she should share the letters with her siblings, but for now she just wanted to keep them all to herself, along with the connection they gave her to the mother she felt she had lost long before her death. She smiled. She remembered Janine's words to her just a little while earlier. "Maybe we don't have to tell them right away?" Was Janine also searching for a way to connect with her that Michelle yearned for with her own mom?

She would not let history repeat itself. She pulled the couch pillow into her chest and laid her head down on the arm of the couch.

Michelle opened her eyes. She could hear Shawn's voice in the kitchen, instructing Janine and Jessie. The smell of his famous red sauce wafted over her. It must be near dinner time. She must have drifted off to sleep.

In one fluid motion, she sprung to a seated position and grabbed her phone to check the time. Crap, she thought. It was 5:15. If she didn't leave now, she'd be late picking up Jaimee from dance class. She jumped up off the couch. Michelle put on her jacket and zipped it up as she walked toward the kitchen door.

The savory scent of the chicken parmesan filled her senses. Before her mind's eye, a vision of a small town in Italy took form. She could imagine the windows frosted up by the contrast between the warm food cooking inside and the cold outside air pressing against the panes. Someday she wanted to go to Italy and experience it for herself. Shawn and she would stroll an Italian strada where stone buildings on either side would give way to the smells of breads baking in large brick ovens. Sauces simmering on the stoves. Garlic and basil filling the air so heavy you could almost see it lingering in front of you. Meanwhile a windowpane framed the scene of pasta being rolled through an old fashioned pasta maker and being dried in long stands on a drying rack.

She entered the kitchen. The view of the girls sitting on the counter beside the stove, swinging their legs and talking to their dad warmed her heart. Even if she never got to Italy, she knew she had everything she could possibly want right here. At least, she would have it as long as she was able to keep her relationship with her girls and Shawn strong. She was realizing more and more that this was the key to everything.

Shawn looked up from the sauce. "Hey, sleeping beauty."

She smiled and gave him a quick kiss. She followed with a squeeze for each of the girls. "I am heading out to pick up Jaimee."

Janine and Jessie spoke in unison. "Bye Mom!"

As she exited the house, she pulled the door closed tight. Michelle could feel the chill in the air. She pulled her jacket around her neck and climbed into the car. She drove to the school and parked outside of the gymnasium entrance. She sat in the cool mist after a day of April showers, which were now subsiding and giving way to a light fog that was creeping towards her in the distance ahead. She allowed herself to be mesmerized by the fog, letting her thoughts wander. Jaimee, her oldest. She was so proud of Jaimee. Committed to her dance and so talented. Even outside of school practices, Jaimee had begun organizing extra sessions with her team, including 5k runs to increase her stamina and overall strength. As a result, she often earned solos. It was such a joy to watch her. Yet she still worried…about her academics, her future career. Being a dancer wasn't going to give her the foundation she needed to be successful.

She thought back, as she did so many times, to the day when this beautiful baby was given life. She remembered the pain of labor melting away as the doctor placed her into Michelle's arms. Oh, the life that stretched before her and the dreams she had for Jaimee!

Those dreams became complicated in ways Michelle had never anticipated on that innocent day. In addition to the pressure of raising a strong young woman, they had faced the challenges of raising a biracial child in a world that judged her by the color of her skin. She feared that being female and biracial would be two strikes against her. Michelle felt a growing pressure to make her hopes and dreams for Jaimee come true. She'd had many conversations with Shawn about it.

Every time they talked about it, Shawn took the same position. "Why can't we just let Jaimee follow her heart and be the woman she wants to be instead of the woman you want her to be?"

"I want her to be the woman she wants to be. I admire her for her creativity and her strength and her commitment to something she believes in. But I'm so afraid that outside forces will push her down and keep her from her hopes and dreams."

"Are you sure that these hopes and dreams you speak of are Jaimee's and not yours?"

Even now, remembering this conversation, Michelle rolled her eyes just as she did that day. She recalled answering, "I just wish that Jaimee would put more effort into her academics. This world will become more and more cruel to her as she gets older. Children from mixed races need to prove themselves more than most kids. I wish Jaimee would listen to me more often. It seems that everything I say falls on deaf ears. I do have the best of intentions."

"I know you do. Let's just believe in her path. It's hers, not ours. We should be grateful for the amazing young woman she is becoming."

To add to all these fears, she now had to contend with Janine and this rebellious behavior. It put the biracial fear right smack in her face again. She didn't expect this to be an issue so soon with Janine. She was hoping she would figure out how to deal with all these issues with Jaimee so by the time it started with Janine she would be an expert. "Oh, Lawd," she thought, "Nothing is happening the way I expected."

She had to remind herself, in these moments when her fears threatened to overwhelm her, that it wasn't all bad with the girls. Despite the morning argument over the scarf, Jaimee really was a good big sister to Janine and Jessie. Yes, she had many things to be grateful for.

The passenger door swung open, jostling Michelle out of her reverie.

Jaimee jumped into the seat. "Hi, Mom! Oh, MAN, what a practice! I am exhausted!"

"Hi, honey," answered Michelle. "Exhausted is good; that means you are working hard and becoming a winning dance team!"

"I sure hope so....first competition of the season a week from Saturday, so we shall see!"

"Well Dad and I have a nice dinner prepared to restore your energy so you can get started on that report this evening."

"Oh, Mom! Really? Can't I just have a night off? It's not due until Friday!"

"You had the whole weekend off, and waiting until the last minute will never get you the grades you need to succeed."

"I had my grandmother's funeral this weekend. It was hardly a weekend off."

"The grandmother you saw only a handful of times your entire life? I noticed you were not so affected by the funeral that you couldn't play your video games all weekend."

"I needed some distraction from my overwhelming sadness."

"Not funny. Let's just stop there. I hope this is not a precursor of the day I am gone!"

"Mom," Jaimee reached out and touched Michelle on the leg. "Don't even joke about that. You do not have permission to leave us–ever!"

Michelle smiled at Jaimee. "Okay, but if you don't get working on that penguin report it might be you leaving this earth!"

"Hahaha. You know that I am an A student, GPA 3.7. You always say I am well rounded. I am hardly a goof off."

"I know that, and I am so proud of all you do. But these high school years are going to fly by, and a 3.7 GPA will not show your true potential to the white collar world. I want you to break out of the mold society puts you in and show them you are as good as, or better than, the competition."

"Yes, yes, again.....Mom, you worry too much. I'm 15, you know. I don't really feel like I am pushed into any "mold," but whatever. I wish you could back off a little, but I know that's not gonna happen." Jaimee stared out the window, pouting.

They sat in stifling silence. It was a familiar feeling. Lately all her conversations with her daughters seemed to end with this awkward discomfort. She just wished they could understand how much she loved them. She wanted only the best for them, but somehow it was coming across as nagging or demanding or...something. Was she pushing too hard? Was Jaimee on the brink of rebelling, too? She wondered how she could get her message across to this beautiful young woman sitting beside her without alienating her further.

Jaimee turned toward her mom. "So what amazing meal have you prepared to stimulate my brain cells for this evening's study session?"

Michelle smiled wide, squeezing Jaimee's knee.

Jaimee yelped. "Hey, that tickles!"

Michelle laughed. This was the difference between Jaimee's and Janine's personalities. Jaimee was more like Shawn in that she took things as they came and got over little slights more easily. Janine was more like Michelle—she got stuck in her own emotions and stubbornly clung to what she saw as past wrongs. It was food for thought.

"SO?" Jaimee said.

"So what?"

"So what's for dinner?!"

"Oh. Right." Michelle shook her head at herself, getting lost in her own thoughts in the middle of a conversation. "Chicken Parmesan with spaghetti, and garlic bread. One of your favorites."

"Oh, yum....you're always thinking of me, Mom. I am sure that chicken parmesan will indeed help me break out of my mold and surge me into that white collar world."

Michelle laughed again. "Well, I wish chicken parmesan had that kind of power. I'm glad you're thinking along those lines, for sure."

As the car came to a stop in the driveway, Jaimee jumped out and ran to the back door, shouting over her shoulder. "I'll go help!"

The screen door slammed, leaving Michelle alone with her thoughts. She could hear the faint sound of the girls' chatter. Unbidden, a burning fear arose from her gut. The happy, innocent sounds of her daughters was a stark contrast. Would they be safe? Happy? Successful? They had no idea the forces that existed in the world to keep them from success. She wanted a better life for all of them. She feared that it would never happen if she didn't make it so. It was a thin line between encouraging and controlling. She feared crossing that line and losing them forever. The last thing she wanted to do was to alienate them. All she knew of her mother for the last 20 years was resentment and awkward silences. The thought that such a thing would happen between any of her girls and her was her worst nightmare. She sighed, pushing the unanswerable out of her mind. She opened the car door and went inside.

Chapter 9

Shawn let out a huge burp. "That was delicious."

Michelle rolled her eyes. "Seriously? At least say 'excuse me.'"

He pulled himself up to his full height and straightened his shoulders. The corners of his university sweatshirt grew taut against his muscles and his full belly. "Excuuuuuse me," Shawn said.

The girls giggled.

"Shawn, you're supposed to set a good example." Michelle tried to sound upset.

Shawn made a face at her.

Michelle couldn't stop from laughing. She had always marveled at how he could say and do outrageous things without a hint of malice or rebellion.

He grabbed Jessie around the neck and gave her a nuggie. "C'mon, kid, let's go get that art project done."

Jessie's hair clip got caught on his sleeve and fell on the floor. Her curls spilled out around her face, like a cork released from a bottle of champagne. "Ow! Hey!"

Shawn let her go.

She reached down to get it.

Jaime got to it first. She picked it up, gathered Jesse's hair together into a ponytail, and put the holder back in. "There you go," she said.

"Thanks." Jessie poked her dad in the stomach. "Gotcha!"

Shawn fell back a step. "Ooouuuuch!"

"That's what you get! C'mon, let's get started. I've got a great idea!" She skipped ahead of him to the back room.

Head bent over the sink full of dishes, Michelle allowed herself to smile. Maybe Jessie would take after her. She loved art just like Michelle always had.

Jaimee slipped her plate into the soapy water and gave her mom a kiss on the cheek. "I'm going to do my homework."

"Sounds good."

As Jaimee left the kitchen, she swung around the corner of the doorway.

Michelle groaned. "I hate it when she does that," she said.

Janine leaned against the counter and crossed her arms. "You probably did it as a kid, too."

"I'm sure I did, but back then I didn't have to clean the smudges off the paint."

"You know you love it."

Michelle laughed. "You're probably right. Better than having a perfect home and no girls."

"Mmm-hmm." Janine moved to the kitchen table and sat.

Michelle's eyes followed her. Being honest with herself, she had to admit Janine was becoming more and more of a mystery. Janine was wearing her favorite sweater, a short black pullover. It was the plainest sweater in Michelle's eyes, but for some reason Janine loved it.

Janine spoke without raising her gaze. "So I read the letter."

"Yeah?" Michelle sat at the table and gave Janine her full attention. "What did you think?"

"At first it made me sad. It sounded like this person spent a lot of time crying. And they were trapped. Felt like they were in a fishbowl while the whole world went on without them."

Michelle didn't try to hide her surprise. "Wow, that's interesting. You picked up on the person feeling trapped while I picked up on just the heavy sadness and not knowing why they were sad. Sometimes I feel sad and overwhelmed, too. I wonder why you picked up on the feeling of entrapment?"

Janine came to the table and sat down across from her mother. "Sometimes I feel trapped."

"Trapped? Like the fishbowl from the letter? Someone your age has the whole world ahead of them! You should be like a sponge, soaking up all the world's experiences. Why would you feel trapped?"

Janine thought for a moment before speaking. Michelle could see that she was searching for just the right words. "Yes, the whole world is before me. But I can't get to it. I feel trapped by all these rules that I have to follow that keep me from doing what I want to do."

Michelle sighed. "I never thought of that. But you're right. You are 13. On one hand, there are no limitations to what you can achieve. On the other hand, you do have rules holding you back."

"The world tells me, don't do this, don't do that. You can't go there. You can't hang out with that person. You have to do your homework. You can't wear that skirt." She gave a small smile as she locked on Michelle's eyes. "It's like I am on the brink of being an adult, but something is trying to hold me back from doing so."

"Do you mean I am holding you back?"

"Not necessarily you. Well, yes you. It's your job, I know. But school. Laws. Society. Life. Life, the way it's set up."

Michelle thought for a moment. "This is a hard age to be. I get it. So what do you do about all these rules? How do you manage?"

Janine hesitated, then forced a timid laugh as she cocked her head playfully back and forth. " I fight with you. I break the rules." She became serious again. "And sometimes I cry."

Michelle reached out to hold Janine's hand. She shook her head in acknowledgement. "So, maybe we can work on this where we can. Maybe you and I can work on some compromising when we don't agree on an issue. Society's rules just cannot be broken, but we can talk about our frustrations from them and how we feel about them. I want you to know that I am always here and will listen. As we grow older, we all have to follow those same rules, so I just might understand your frustration. Man, it is hard to stop at a red light when absolutely NOBODY is coming from both ways! And you have to get home because you have to pee so bad!"

Janine laughed.

Michelle felt a comforting warmth in her body. "Don't be afraid to talk to me, okay? I'll try to work on being a better listener."

Janine nodded her head.

Michelle wiped a small tear from her own face. "And crying....well, does it release the tension like the letter says?"

Janine thought for a moment. "Yes, I think it does."

"Well, okay, then don't be afraid to let them flow. Feel the cleansing and you will feel stronger to face your challenges."

"You sound like a counselor."

"Oh, Lawd no! Counselor, no! Just a mother and a student of life who is learning herself. We never stop learning. So you see? There's something we have in common. We're both still learning." Michelle knocked on the table and pointed to Janine. "Stay right there! I'm gonna grab the second letter." She hustled into the living room and retrieved the second letter. She brought it in and handed the envelope to Janine. "Do you want to read this while I put these dishes away?"

Janine nodded, reaching for the envelope. She opened the envelope. She removed the two pages inside. One, the faded rose stationary, and the other a plain white paper. She began to read while Michelle tried to put the dishes away as quietly as possible.

Janine began reading. "*I am afraid of swallowing a bug in my sleep. I am afraid of sleep.*" She snickered. "Afraid of swallowing a bug in their sleep? We talked about this in science class. That's a myth. We do not swallow any bugs in our sleep, but we do swallow lots of bug parts in the food we eat every day."

Michelle laughed. "Oh, that's encouraging! Glad you clarified that! Now I'm afraid to eat!"

Janine giggled. She continued reading. "This person is afraid of sleep, afraid of the dark. I sometimes get a little afraid of the dark. I like that you keep a nightlight on in your room because it glows a little into our room at night. It's comforting."

Michelle's heart warmed with the sound of her sweet laugh. "I agree. That's why I keep it on at night. I have always been afraid of the dark, even when I was your age. I used to ask Aunt Lisa to turn the light on. It felt like a security blanket to keep me safe through the night. It drove her crazy!"

Janine smiled. She continued to read. "This person's fears start out mostly about things–bugs, spiders, bees, until they get to less tangible things, like being afraid of the dark, afraid of sleep, afraid of closing their eyes."

"Tangible?" Michelle asked. She had never heard Janine use adult vocabulary like that.

"Yeah. You know, things you can touch."

"Okay."

"It's funny she's afraid of closing her eyes. I feel like that sometimes. I get all these images in my head that I can't get rid of. They don't let me sleep."

Michelle felt a tightening in her body. She couldn't identify where it came from. Maybe it was her recognition of the same issue. "What kind of images?"

"Oh, images of the day. People I talked to all day, people I wanted to talk to but didn't, so I think about what the conversation would have been. Songs going through my head."

Michelle listened and nodded her head gently in agreement. "Hmmm. I hear you. I sometimes have that same problem. It's like your body wants to sleep, but your mind is still awake from everything in your day. And your life."

"What kinds of things?"

Michelle drew a long breath. "Well, I have a recurring nightmare. It keeps coming back to me and sometimes it won't let me sleep."

Janine set the letter down on the table and gave her mom her full attention. "What happens in it?"

Michelle hesitated for a moment. Truth was, this was probably as good a time as any to talk about this. She drew another deep breath. The moment she decided to tell the story, a familiar emptiness overtook her. "In the dream I am about your age." She glanced to see whether Janine was interested.

Janine's eyes locked on hers.

She continued. "I am in Aunt Lisa's and my room at Grandma's house. I hear yelling and my mother screaming out and our back door slamming. Grandpa was traveling for work so he wasn't home." She wrung her hands together. "A few minutes later, there were two gunshots. Mom was crying back in our kitchen. I heard sirens. I see...a man...being dragged out of the neighbor's yard in handcuffs. I see images of yellow crime scene tape." Tears welled up in her eyes.

Janine reached up and wiped the tears from her face.

"Wow, what a horrible nightmare."

"Truth is, it isn't a nightmare. It really happened. It's a memory that won't let me go."

"You mean this really happened?" Janine's body leapt forward with anticipation. "Oh, my heart is pounding right now! Were you a witness to a murder?"

Michelle could feel a warm tear rolling down her face. "Murder. Wow, I haven't heard it described like that in a long time. No, I wasn't a witness. I was just looking out my bedroom window. I just saw the aftermath. And I was just a confused young girl who wasn't sure how to put the pieces of what I heard and saw together. I remember this sickening pit in my stomach that made me want to throw up. I was too frozen in fear to even get to the bathroom to vomit."

Janine shook her head and shuddered. "I can't even imagine. Who was the man being led away in handcuffs?"

Michelle gazed toward the kitchen door, and then back at Janine. "My father."

"What? Your father? You said Grandpa was away on business."

Michelle tried to ignore the cold sensation wrapping her body. "He was." She turned to face Janine. "Okay, I know I've never told you this before…and now that I'm telling you I'm going to need to tell your sisters. But please let me do that. Your grandpa was my stepfather. He married Grandma when us girls were young. That doesn't change that he was your grandpa–he was! He loved you like no other." She stopped and smiled. "He was the best stepfather a girl could ever want." She glanced at Janine to see her reaction. "And the best grandpa."

Janine's mouth had fallen open. Michelle saw a softness in Janine's eyes she couldn't remember ever seeing. "So you had another father?"

"Biological, yes. I don't remember much about him." She hesitated for a moment, then forced out the words that had been haunting her. "Except that he shot our neighbors, Mr. and Mrs. Brandson, and today, he's still rotting in prison. Or he could be dead for all I know." Michelle deliberately shook her head as if to rid herself of the memory. She blinked back more tears.

Janine's mouth opened to speak but initially nothing came out.

The clock on the wall was ticking. Michelle thought it was strange that she could hear it so clearly.

Janine said, "Do you want to know?"

Michelle just shook her head no. "He killed two people. I don't want to know."

"Was he arguing with Grandma in the kitchen? Why?"

"Yes. And I don't know. Mom never talked about it again. In fact, Mom barely talked at all after that. Mr. and Mrs. Branson were the sweetest people. Mr. Branson knew that I liked art and he would sit in the backyard and draw with me all afternoon. He taught me the basics of art that I still use today." She gazed upward, seeing him in her mind's eye. "I still miss him to this day." She looked back, surprised to see a tear in Janine's eye. "Well, anyways, that is a scene that has never left me and keeps me awake at night. You don't forget something like that."

Janine just shook her head. "No, I'm sure. Mom, I'm so sorry..."

Michelle felt so many emotions. The imprisonment of the memory. The fear. The sick feeling in her stomach. The devastation. The painful emptiness in her heart from the loss of her mother as she knew her. But in between them was a sense of relief that she was able to share this with her daughter. She pointed to the letter that was still in Janine's hands. "What else is in this letter?"

Janine nodded her head in agreement. She glanced back at the letter. "*...afraid that when I come face to face with what I fear, it will be a force that I will not be able to overcome. Again.*" She looked up at her mom. "What is this 'force?'"

"I don't know. I can't tell if it is something to be feared or just fear itself. Another mystery! Go on to the answer, and let me know what jumps out at you."

Janine picked up the plain paper and began to read, mumbling the words, bringing up ones that struck her. "Ugghh, fear is a part of growing. Growing is hard sometimes."

Michelle nodded, and couldn't help adding, "And being grown is also hard."

Janine continued. "You are not alone. Breathe." She mumbled the words again. She looked up. "Breathe. Mrs. Foley in school always tells us that before our tests. She says, 'Be silent and gather your thoughts. Breathe. And begin.' We all think it's kinda weird." She snickered.

Michelle asked, "I can see how it seems weird, but does it work?"

Janine considered this. "Yes. You know, I guess it does work. It helps calm the anxiety we are feeling."

"Sounds like good advice then."

"Guess so." Janine continued reading. "'The positivity you flow into the world will flow back to you.' Do they mean like a boomerang?"

"Yeah, I think so. That's one concept of the universe, right? I think it's kind of like karma. What flows out will come back around. Or like the golden rule. Treat others the way you would want to be treated."

Janine nodded. "Meditate. Do you meditate, Mom?"

"You know, I try, but again, just like when I try to sleep, it is hard to clear my head." She could feel that cold sensation creeping back into her body, the one from her dreams. It was the same when she tried to meditate. Bile filled her mouth. She shook her body like a rehearsed dance move, pushing away the memory that was determined to creep in. She swallowed hard and took a deep breath, forcing her stomach to settle. "I hear it takes a lot of practice. I'd like to work on it."

Janine nodded. "Hmm, I'd like to try it."

"Maybe we could try it together."

Janine nodded. "Maybe."

Michelle feared the idea, but there was something positive in it, too. She desperately wanted to protect herself from the memory she didn't want to recall. But, on the other side, a ray of hope? Could this be a way to connect with the stranger in front of her? She smiled and nodded her head. "I'd like that."

Michelle's mind wandered back to a day when she sat outside with Mr. Branson as a young girl. He was just finishing up the meditation session which he did every morning in his backyard. Michelle wondered what this thing called meditation was about.

"Why do you do that? Get all quiet and close your eyes, like you're sleeping?" she asked.

Mr. Brandson smiled. He took one last deep breath in, deep breath out, before turning to her. "It's called meditation. I do it to ground myself, to put me in touch with a part of me that nobody knows. To allow myself to be guided by something bigger than myself."

"That sounds like a lot! I don't think I could ever do that!"

Mr. Brandson laughed. "But you already do, in a way."

"What do you mean?"

Mr. Brandson pointed to an art project they were working on together. "I mean that. Meditation is a lot like art. Your art grounds you. It puts you in touch with a part of you that nobody knows, sometimes not even you. You learn about yourself through your artwork. And when you do your art, you are guided by something bigger than yourself. You just have to be open to letting it do its magic."

She wished it could be that simple. He always had a way of knowing just what to say.

Michelle's mind returned to the present. She gave Janine a little hug. "I don't know how good I can be, but I can try if you want to."

Janine smiled and nodded. "Okay, let's do that. This universe sounds like a great healer. This line here is pretty heavy. 'Fear wants you to be alone. As we share with others, the hold of fear weakens.' Maybe that's what is meant by this 'force.' Fear is an enemy that can be fought, and weakened. Kind of like Darth Vader in the Star Wars movies Dad loves to watch. "

Michelle smiled. "You are smart beyond your years! That's a great way to look at it." She hesitated. "Do you have fears?"

"I guess so. I guess I never actually thought about my fears." She hesitated. She set the letter down on the table. "At least until lately."

"What do you mean?"

Janine sat for a moment in silence and Michelle could see her facial expression tensing. "Sometimes I am afraid at school."

"At school? What's going on at school?"

"It's hard for me to feel like I fit in. There's so much pressure to prove myself to fit in. It doesn't come so easy like it does to Jaimee. It's hard walking in her footsteps. I feel pressured to do what I need to be to be popular."

Michelle fought the urge to scream. No, she thought. She wanted to tell her, no, she never needs to prove herself to anyone! She needs to believe in herself and be who she is and not what others want her to be. She remembered this feeling from when she was Janine's age. Having an amazing sister like Tracy that everyone loved in school put so much pressure on her! She remembered never feeling like she was able to live up to Tracy's popularity. Of course she knows the truth now, that she had nothing to prove. But it took many years to learn that lesson and it caused years of pushing down her jealousy and lack of self worth. She reached out to Janine and held her hand.

"In what way?"

Janine looked up at Michelle with watery eyes. "Well, skipping school for one. That's what the popular kids do. If I want to belong I have to go along with it."

Michelle was now getting a deeper understanding of what was happening at school. It almost gave her a sense of relief to know so they could talk about it. She nodded her head.

"And if you don't, you will be unpopular?"

"Yes."

"Teased?"

"Yes."

"Without a friend?"

Janine swallowed, before catching her breath again. "Yes."

Michelle just nodded her head for a moment. "You know what? I understand. This may seem strange to you, but I have struggled with this myself. It happens to everyone. It can be a sports thing, a money thing, getting good grades in school which makes others feel insecure and lash out. It can be a racial thing. Just know, you are not the only one who feels this way. Like an outsider wanting to fit in. It's actually part of growing up. Now that you have said it out loud, do you feel any better?"

Janine thought a minute, and slowly spoke. "Yeah...I think so."

Michelle put her second hand up to Janine's chin and raised her face towards hers. "So, first of all, let me reassure you that there is nothing you need to do to prove yourself to these kids at school. If you give in to them, you only give them power. Don't give in. Be yourself and know what an amazing young woman you are. And come talk to me or Dad if you need strength or advice. That's what we are here for. I know it was, like, hundreds of years ago, but we were just like you once. We understand. Okay?"

Janine smiled. "Okay." She hesitated, then looked up at Michelle. "What about you? What are you afraid of?"

"Well, I could talk all night on this. Just like you, I never really thought about my fears before reading this letter, but wow, I have come to realize I have many fears."

"Even at your age?" Janine gave a smart smirk.

Michelle smirked back. "Yes, even at my old, old age!"

Janine giggled. "Well, you're not old, old. Maybe just old."

"Ha ha. Okay, old." She thought for a few seconds. She lightly rubbed her hands together, feeling the weathered years on her dry, rough skin. "Fears about being the cause of my mother's pain. Fears about who I am and who I am growing to be. Fear of losing you girls as you get older like Grandma lost me. Maybe that's why I am hard on you. I just want to tie you down so you don't get away from me!"

"Do you really think Grandma was in pain?"

"Oh gosh, I hope not. I so hope not. But the truth is, it is a strong possibility.

"Do you think these are really her letters?"

Michelle shrugged. "They were in her jewelry box in her house. She was always very distant, like something was bothering her. You know," she blinked at Janine, "circumstantial evidence."

Janine giggled.

Michelle smiled. She could see how much Janine loved this idea of solving a mystery.

Janine spoke as if she were a detective. "Every investigation has other suspects to consider. We don't want to overlook others if we are fixated on Grandma until we have hard evidence."

Michelle nodded in agreement, playing along with this scenario. "So, do we have any other suspects?"

"No, but what if we give the writer a fictitious name while we investigate?"

Michelle felt a surge of excitement from the inquisitive nature of this conversation. And another adult word. Had she missed her little girl growing up right under her nose? "So kind of like a Jane Doe?"

"Yeah, Jane Doe! But not Jane. That's too close to mine. How about Dosey Doe?"

Michelle laughed. "Good one. But how about Dorothy Doe? Remember in *The Wizard of Oz,* Dorothy had many fears and was looking for answers as well."

Janine held her hand up to Michelle's for a high five. "Dorothy Doe it is!"

Michelle and Janine slapped their hands together.

Janine swung her legs against the chair rails, clunking against them. It was something she had done since she was a toddler when she was excited and happy. Michelle was so thankful for the little girl that was still in there even though she rarely saw it anymore. She was drinking in this feeling of togetherness.

Janine reached out to Michelle and gently touched her arm. "I don't want to lose you either, Mom. Ever."

Michelle could feel her ambivalent heart drowning in a conflict of love and rebellion. Is this the child that very recently challenged her in her own motherhood role, her identity? And now, this rebel child is saying she never wants to lose that mother. Which is it? What will win in the end? Love or rebellion? She placed her hand on Janine's.

"Don't worry. You'll never lose me. You are stuck with me! At least for as long as you will have me."

"Then we will be stuck together forever."

Michelle gazed at her daughter's beautiful face. She could see her resemblance to her father as she smiled. The way her eyes turned up in the corner, the defined cheekbone sitting high on her face, the perfection of her smooth brown skin that called Michelle to reach up and stroke her face gently. "And I will hold you to that! Okay, off to bed. Tomorrow is going to be a big day for you. Close your eyes and think positive thoughts. Think flowers! Ice cream! Puppies!"

"Cute boys?"

Michelle laughed. "Okay, so that's what fills your mind when you're trying to sleep!! Whatever works!"

Janine stood up. She laid the two envelopes and letters on the table in front of her mother. She caressed them with her hands to make sure they were smooth and preserved. She gave Michelle a sideways hug. "Good night Mom, love you"

Michelle hugged back. "Good night, honey, love you too."

With a final little wave, Janine was gone, heading upstairs for bed. Michelle was left alone with her thoughts. Thoughts that always began with a feeling of panic when she was left alone. A fleeting picture of her recurring dream always seemed to want to invade her. A man...being dragged out of the neighbor's yard in handcuffs...images of yellow crime scene tape...the familiar tears welling up in her eyes as every time before. She shivered her body to force away this memory. This silence was filled with the events of the day and her conversation with Janine. This is not the conversation she would have had with any of her daughters before this day. Just yesterday, a door had slammed between Janine and her. She could still feel it shudder with the force of the impact. Now 36 hours later it felt like the door had opened a crack. A little light shone through, like the nightlight from her room that she never knew was soothing to her daughter.

The night was settling in. She could see the darkness closing in from outside of the kitchen window. As always, being alone in the dark sparked a momentary feeling of panic, like someone was behind her. This time of night should have brought her peace, but that hadn't been the case since the day Mr. and Mrs. Brandson were killed. She tried to shake the chills running up her arms, but she couldn't. She whipped around to see what was behind her. Nothing. As always. Yet she still looked. Sighing, she stood up and put on the teapot.

Once the pot began to whistle, Michelle poured herself a cup of chamomile tea and looked at the clock. 10 PM. Walking out to the couch, she passed the stairs and perked an ear toward the girls' rooms, listening for the sounds of giggles or arguing. All was quiet. She sighed. Hopefully, they are actually asleep, she thought. She flopped onto the couch, hearing her mother's voice in her head and her own to the girls as she did so. "Don't flop! You're gonna ruin the couch!" Sometimes it was fun to flop. Today was a day where flopping was necessary.

Shawn walked into the living room, scraping dried flecks of paint off of his arm from his earlier project with Jessie. "Is that an Irish Coffee?"

Michelle laughed. "Even if I craved a real drink I would be too tired to finish it anyways." She rarely drank alcohol; maybe that came with being on the alert every night since Shawn worked the graveyard shift. When she did, she almost never finished one drink. But a nice warm cup of tea, yes, that was calling her name. "I'm so glad you were here tonight. It helps when you're here to share the load. And I can go to sleep knowing I don't have to be on watch."

Shawn smiled. "Except to watch out for me." He reached over to Michelle and dropped flecks of paint in her hair. Michelle dropped her head down to fluff her hair and get the paint out, laughing. "Get out of here! You are worse than a child!"

Shawn gently ran his fingers through Michelle's hair, picking out the flecks of paint. "Just sharing some of that load I shared with your baby girl tonight."

Michelle pushed Shawn back. "What were you working on anyway?"

"A volcano for science class. Don't go back there. It may blow up on you! And she wants it to be a surprise."

Michelle laughed. "Okay, then I will just have to trust that you two won't blow the house up."

Shawn sat down next to Michelle. He gazed at her face, eyes catching tiny flecks of paint in her hair. He smiled. "I could never blow the house up and risk losing my beautiful family or my beautiful wife."

Michelle rolled her eyes. "Yeah, so beautiful."

He reached his arm behind her back and pulled her close to him. "Yes, so beautiful. I know things have been stressful lately, but you don't look a day over 25!"

Michelle forced a smile.

"I'm serious!"

"Thank you, honey. I sure don't feel 25. I feel like the years have taken their toll on my soul." She blinked back tears.

Shawn squeezed her tighter. "So I could hear you and Janine in the kitchen tonight. I don't see any blood stains..."

Michelle laughed. "Actually, Janine walked in on me after I read the first letter this afternoon. I shared it with her. And we had a really nice talk!" Her body perked up with excitement. She turned toward Shawn. "And then, after dinner, I brought her the second letter. It was about fears. She read it and we talked about what thoughts it sparked in her."

It was Shawn's turn for tears to well up in his eyes.

"I am seeing through these first letters that she has her own feelings, and her feelings are as important as her grades, behavior at school or how she acts with her sisters. I know I should have realized it earlier, but...anyway..."

"It's okay. I'm so glad that you are sharing these letters and talking."

"I hate to jump the gun, but we might be making a connection. You didn't hear me say that! I don't want to jinx it!"

"You're not jinxing anything. Run with it."

"It's early, but she is loving the mystery part of these letters and so we are looking at them together as an adventure." She thought for a minute. "I think this might be a good thing."

Shawn nodded in agreement. "And a good thing is a great start." He leaned over and gave Michelle a kiss on her cheek. "You are a wonderful, caring mother and she will learn that." He stood up and ran his hand down her arm until their fingers locked and then let go slowly. "Gonna go finish cleaning up in the art room. I'll see you soon."

Michelle smiled and reveled in the feeling of pure love and contentment without the struggles motherhood had given her earlier in the day. Shawn disappeared to the back of the house. She took a sip of tea. The warm liquid was soothing, easing her emotions. She took a deep breath and let it out as slowly as possible.

Chapter 10

Michelle sat on the edge of the cement ridge in front of her high school. She shivered as the cool September breeze brushed over her body. She watched as couples walked by, holding hands, some with arms wrapped around their partners' waists, sometimes kissing. She looked down, studying her worn sneakers. She felt so empty, so alone.

"Hey, Michelle!"

Michelle glanced up. It was her friend Diane.

"Are you gonna meet us at the homecoming game tonight?" She jumped up on the ledge beside Michelle.

Michelle shuffled over on the ledge. She didn't like to share her personal space. Being touched by another person always made her uncomfortable. 'Why do you have to be so close that you have to touch me?' she would think. It made her feel on edge. When someone gets that close you never know what their intentions are. This was a hard feeling to deal with when she was dating Daniel last year in ninth grade. She was never one hundred percent sure that he truly loved her. And, with what ended up happening between the two of them, she was certain that he did not feel towards her as deeply as she felt towards him. Or they might still be together. It was just hard to trust what getting so close to someone can trick you into. "Who's going?"

"Everybody. Me, John, Lacey, Bobby."

"All couples. Really, I don't want to be a 5th wheel. I think I'm just gonna stay home."

Diane softly pushed Michelle with the toe of her sneaker, forcing Michelle to rock back and forth. "Awww...come on. We don't care about that. And besides, you won't meet anyone for yourself if you don't come out of that cocoon you live in."

"I don't live in a cocoon."

"Yeah? What do you call it? You never want to do anything. I want to see you laugh. And smile. Jump up and down with excitement! What better time to do that than at a football game - a homecoming football game at that while we are crushing Thompsonville!"

"I'll see. I'll call you later." She jumped off of the ledge and started the long walk up the hill to her home.

Diane called after. "We're going at 6:30 to get good seats! Please come!"

Later that evening, Michelle looked at the selection of clothes she laid out on the bed. 'Yes,' she thought, 'the blue checkered bell bottoms. Well, no, maybe my favorite white painter pants. Oh, heck no, not on those bleachers. I could wear my white sweater with these checked pants.' She stopped. She felt weary. Drained. It was just too much. She couldn't pretend that everything was okay. Besides, she couldn't bear to watch all the flirting, teasing and banter. Just reminders of what she didn't have. What she had lost and probably would never have again. She drew a deep breath. She headed downstairs and picked up the phone, dialing Diane's number.

"Hello?" Diane answered in her usual chipper voice.

"Hi! Yeah, hey, I'm just not feeling well."

"I think I'm gonna just stay in tonight."

"Oh c'mon! It's homecoming." Diane sounded genuinely upset.

"I know. I know. Next time, huh?"

"Hey, you know that what happened to you and Daniel was not your fault. You deserve to find happiness again."

Michelle bristled. 'Please don't bring that up again,' she thought. She didn't want to relive this over and over.

"I know that, Diane. Just not tonight. I don't feel like it."

Diane gave a long sigh on the phone. "Okay, well if you change your mind, you know where to find us."

"Okay, call me tomorrow. Have fun. Bye."

She walked upstairs. She sat at her typewriter, and pulled out a piece of her rose stationery.

Chapter 11

*H*ow *do I feel love?*

Feeling a new surge of emotional strength, she decided to go back to the box of envelopes and read letter number three. The box sat patiently on the living room table, waiting for her to open it, almost as if it was bursting with revelation. She wondered what the next letter would divulge to her. She took a few more slow sips of the peaceful nectar, snuggled into her recliner chair, and looked at the shoebox sitting in front of her. She reached over, lifting the box gently and placing it on her lap. She ran her fingers along the top of the box before opening it slowly and glanced at the series of envelopes tucked neatly inside. She pulled out the top envelope with the number "3" in the corner, opened it and pulled out the two letters. She opened letter number one.

How do I feel love? Everyone says we should use the words 'I feel' to describe our thoughts or sensations. But I can't use those words. I don't 'feel.' I just exist. And because I have no feelings, how can I ever love or be loved? Because love is a feeling. What is it inside of me that makes me so less worthy of love than the world around me? I see people every day, hugging each other, exchanging glances, touching, pressing their lips together, and saying those words that I long to hear ("I love you"). I feel like I am just walking through the motions of life and observing from the outside. Why can't I step into the circle? Am I unclean? Am I unworthy? Undeserving? What makes a human being worthy of love? Is it a gift that is given to them, or does it have to be earned? If so, how do I earn it? I don't want to feel empty. I don't want to just exist. I want to feel loved again.

Michelle set the letter into her lap and drew a sharp breath. She felt a heavy sense of sadness. She put her head back. Love. What is this love that the writer longs for? Love means different things to so many people. But it sounds like this person feels empty inside, wanting to feel the touch of another human being, and yet doesn't feel worthy of that desire.

She remembered a conversation with her older sister Tracy. They had been best friends until their falling out. She was fresh out of college, during which time she was unable to feel a closeness with any other person. Now here she was, a new graduate at 21, with what was described as the whole world at her feet. Except she didn't feel like the world was on her side. She felt so alone. She remembered visiting Tracy, who was in a successful career, married and pregnant, reminding Michelle again of what she did not have in her life.

"Why do so many of my friends have people in their lives that they love and have a relationship with, but I feel so alone? I feel like I have no family except for you. And nobody to love me. What's wrong with me?"

Tracy challenged her. "You and Lisa are the ones who never really came back to the family. I know the two of you have had issues, but I don't know why you left Mom by herself. She would be a great source of that love you desire."

" I don't feel worthy of that love. And...I need a different kind of love."

"What? Friendship love? Romantic love? What is it that you need?"

Michelle wasn't sure how to answer. She had tried to develop relationships in college, but it seemed none of them worked out. Whenever she dated anybody, it never felt right. It was so hard to get close to anybody. It was as if she was afraid of love. What was she afraid of? Fear of letting someone new in and being vulnerable to the pain that relationships can cause? Fear of exposing herself to someone and finding out she doesn't meet their expectations? She wondered why it had to be so hard.

"Maybe I never really learned how to love. Maybe Mom failed me there."

"Or maybe you never put in the effort to learn."

Michelle bristled, feeling attacked by that statement.

Tracy was silent.

From experience, she knew that Tracy was giving her space to think about it.

"Maybe Mom was there for me. Maybe I pushed her away as I was growing up. Or maybe she tried but just wasn't good at it. I don't know." Michelle paused. "Is love something you learn?"

Tracy shrugged her shoulders. "I don't know. Love is lots of things. I think love is something you feel. Something unexpected. Like a surprise sitting in a tiny box with a big bow. Love is feeling complete. Love is being open to the gifts that come your way. Love is sharing. Sometimes love hurts. And, yeah, I guess it can be something you learn."

Michelle shook her head as she moved out of the memory. Tracy was no longer sitting next to her. She felt so alone, sitting by herself in the recliner. Just herself and these letters. She reached for the second letter and read the response.

Words can be very powerful. Unloved...Unclean...Unworthy....Undeserving....these are crushing words. However, notice when you remove the prefix from these words, what you are left with: Loved...Clean...Worthy...Deserving... These are words that have the power to make you feel again. When you are loved, and clean, and worthy, and deserving, your heart blossoms like a flower and you feel. You feel the warmth of the sunshine and the coolness of the light breeze sweeping across your soul. You allow the buzzing bee to gather its nourishment from your pedals. You sip gently the moist dew of the early morning. The emptiness goes away. So the question becomes, who has the power to remove the prefix from these words? Who has the power to change you from unfeeling and empty to fulfilled and loved? This, child of the universe, is your journey. It is your choice. It is your challenge. You have the power to invite the journey to begin. Those other human beings that are able to experience love have been able to open up their hearts and accept it. Love is not earned. It is given to you by grace, and you need only accept it.

She shivered as that conversation with Tracy jumped back into her head. She remembered so clearly how Tracy had taken her hands in hers. She could feel Tracy's smooth, silky skin. They felt so good on Michelle's skin, dry and cracked from constantly washing paints off of her skin.

Tracy said, "You have your whole life ahead of you and you will always have me. Some people have absolutely nobody in their life. If you can open up to the world around you, you can learn to be open to the love it brings your way."

She came back to the present time, nodding. Of course, other fears of love had arisen through the years, especially her fears surrounding her children. She loved them so much, more than life itself. She had thought many times, would she receive the love she needed from her three daughters? She was giving her entire life to them. But in the end, as she found out with her own mother, it was up to them to reach out in love to her. Would they open the circle and allow her in? Or would they move away like she did from her mother and rarely keep in touch?

She wished that she could have connected with her mother more, the way Tracy did. She wondered, did her mother also need to feel this love? How can she teach this love to her daughters when she never learned it from her own mother? She cringed at the thought of losing her daughters. This was indeed her greatest fear. She continued to read.

Accepting love is not easy for everyone. There are some necessary steps in this journey. First, educate yourself with new vocabulary. Take the negative words and make them positive. As you think about and speak these words, you will be able to begin picturing them. Second, as you picture these words, place yourself within them. Imagine what you would feel and be if these words were a description of who you are. Speak of the words you want to be in a daily mantra. "I am loved. I am clean. I am worthy. I am deserving." Third, as the universe brings you opportunities to feel love, open your heart to receive them, know that you have the power to reach within and show the world that you are ready to accept them. There may be parts of you that you cannot open to the world. That is okay. Open what you can. Begin. Take the first steps in your journey, and know that no true journey happens quickly. Know that you are loved. Know that you are worthy to be loved. Feel....as the universe provides you with experiences and you open your heart to them.

Michelle felt overwhelmed, weighed down with heaviness in her heart. For such a simple answer, this was a tall order. She had spent her life not knowing whether she deserved to feel loved, even in her own marriage. She had no idea why Shawn chose to stay with her all these years, as she certainly pushed away a lot of his love. Why did she push him away when all he wanted to do was love her? She was starting to have some clarity as she read these letters. If these were her mother's letters, then is it possible that her mother also never learned to feel worthy of love? She folded the letters and gently returned it to the shoebox in front of her. She carried it to the back entranceway and placed it on the shelf.

As she climbed the stairs to her daughter's rooms, she felt her heart racing and a sense of urgency to get to them. She softly knocked on Jaimee's door. "Are you awake, Jaimee?"

Jaimee turned over in her bed and lifted her head up. She was groggy from being almost asleep. "Mmmm." She yawned, opening her eyes halfway. "Mom?"

"Yeah, it's me."

"Everything okay?"

Michelle walked over and sat on the bed next to her daughter. "Yup, everything is fine. I just wanted to come in and look at your beautiful face in the moonlight."

Jamiee crinkled up her forehead and turned her head sideways. "Uhhh, what?"

Michelle reached up and stroked Jaimee's hair. Jaimee pulled away just ever so slightly. After a moment, she relaxed the tension in her neck. Her head relaxed back. She allowed her mother to touch her lovingly. "That feels good."

Michelle spoke ever so softly. "My beautiful daughter. Someday, some boy is going to fall deeply in love with you, because you are so beautiful and you are so loveable, and so deserving of being loved."

Jaimee giggled. "Yeah, and then he will steal me away and you will never see me again, right?"

"No!" exclaimed Michelle. "You ought to know me better than that, dear, I would hunt you down and drag you home by your heels!"

"Okay, now you sound like my mother. I was worried for a second there…"

Michelle and Jaimee sat in silence for a few more seconds. Michelle bent down and kissed Jaimee softly on the forehead. "Just don't ever forget, you are loved right this very minute and you will always be worthy of being loved, wherever you go."

Jaimee looked at her mom, puzzled. "Okaaayy…."

Michelle got up and headed to the door. "Good night, my little rugrat." She slowly closed the door behind her. She moved to Janine and Jessie's door and opened it. They appeared to be in peaceful slumber. She walked over to Jessie and gently sat on her bed. She gave her a soft kiss on her cheek, whispering, "You are loved. You are worthy of being loved." Jessie's body shook from the touch of her mother's lips on her cheek. She stretched and turned over in bed without waking up. Michelle stood up and walked over to Janine's bed and sat beside her. Janine stirred in bed and turned over to look at her mother's face. She gave a weak smile. Michelle reached over and caressed Janine's face.

Michelle gazed upon the beautiful daughter that she was raising. She was so filled with emotion. Seeing two sides of this child today was weighing on her heart. She sighed, desperate to release these feelings.

Janine lowered her eyes. "I'm sorry about today."

Michelle could feel her shoulders give way to the tiniest yet real sense of relief. She let her hand land on her daughter's shoulder. "We made it through. Tomorrow will not be fun, but we will make it through that, too. In the space between today and tomorrow, know that you are loved. And I mean by a great big mama heart!"

Janine smiled and turned back onto her side. "Thank you. Good night Mama."

Michelle got undressed and slid into bed. She was so glad that Shawn would be at home to sleep tonight. She loved these occasional nights when his schedule would give him two nights off during the week. Michelle got to have him in bed beside her for two nights in a row. She just slept better; it was as if he lifted the shroud of worry off of her and allowed her to feel weightless, comforted, carefree. She lay in bed and thought about the last letter. She was more determined than ever to teach her daughters that they are worthy of being loved. She always thought that she showed them through her care of them, being a supportive mother, feeding them, driving them to school and all their activities, all the tangible things that a mother does for her child. All the things that her mother did for her. But now she wondered...was it enough? What about the intangible things? Feelings? Confidence? Self worth?

It seemed clear to her that there had been a lack of these things in her life. And whose responsibility is it to teach a young woman growing up about these things? Of course the mother. But when would this occur? She didn't really learn these things from her mother when she was growing up. Once she was out of the house, Michelle never looked back, never giving her mother the opportunity. Her heart twinged with regret. She'd been so bitter toward her mom. It was only with hindsight that she could see the truth. How could her mother have taught her how to love herself when she didn't know? Michelle closed her eyes. She stated, "I am worthy of being loved. I am clean. I am deserving. I am loved." She repeated these phrases in her mind, over and over.

She was lying on her side when felt the cool breeze on her back as Shawn slipped into the bed next to her. She shivered slightly but then felt his warm body next to hers. His tight muscles, warmth, and scent of rapture. The feel of desire. His familiar arm came across her body, following his hand that paved the way across her side, causing another shiver, this time of excitement, across her stomach, his finger circling her belly button, causing her lower pelvis to contract in pleasure, then across the other side of her abdomen, stroking her side up and down for which she responded with a series of shivers. His top leg came to her body and nestled between her legs.

She wanted to turn and melt into his muscular arms, but as always, she hesitated. The same unbidden thought entered her mind. Am I worthy of his love? She knew that Shawn loved her dearly, as evidenced by the many years of their marriage that he has stood beside her. But is it the kind of love that draws a burning fire deep in his soul? She wondered if he shivered at the feel of her touch as she did to his. She wanted to reach out to him, to make him quiver with excitement, but it was as if she was pinned down by an outside force, unable to make the move. Fear and insecurity stopped her.

He gently brought his leg around and pulled her over onto her back. This is where she always felt so vulnerable. Does he want this as badly as she does? No matter the answer, she was grateful he persisted despite her hesitation. She felt his hand start at the knee of her outer leg, and gently but intentionally move up to her hip while softly kissing her on her neck. He decisively pulled her hip towards him so her face was in his chest.

Oh, the scent of his body was enough to draw her into a trance of sexual ecstasy. But something deep inside her shouted, "No! Don't touch me!" She moved her head so her face hid into the pillow. Shawn abided, moved back an inch, knowing that she was not ready.

Every time they came together in a sensual manner, she had this hesitation. Twenty plus years has taught him to give her the time she needs. She was never taught this! She, like the woman in the letters, did not feel worthy. "Oh Mother," she thought, "I don't blame you. Now I know you didn't have what you needed to teach me."

As Shawn held her tightly but gently, showing her that he was willing to wait, she closed her eyes, and repeated in her mind, "I am worthy. I am deserving. I am clean. I am loved."

Shawn, as if he heard the words going through her mind, whispered into her ear, "You are so beautiful. You are so sexy. I love to touch you. This is all I thought about all night. Holding you, loving you." After a few moments, Shawn slid his hand along her back side, and ignited the fire inside.

Chapter 12

Michelle enjoyed the warmth of the water as she showered. She could hear Janine and Jessie shrieking with delight as they bounced on the bed trying to wake their dad up from his slumber. "Come on, dad!" they shouted, "You get to make us breakfast today!" Then she heard the loud bang and many giggles as the three of them toppled out of bed onto the floor.

"Okay, okay!" surrendered Shawn. How about we make mom breakfast before school? Go get dressed and meet me in the Chef's quarters!"

"I wanna fry the bacon!" she heard Jessie yell! Followed by Janine, chiding, "You are just a baby! You can't even reach the stove!" Their voices fell lower and muffled as Michelle turned off the water and the three of them exited their bedroom. "I can to reach the stove! And I don't burn it like you do!!"

Michelle wrapped herself in a towel and came out to sit on the bed. She sat in bliss as she enjoyed the quiet. She looked back and ran her hand along the sheets. She remembered Shawn's words from the night before. "You are so beautiful. You are so sexy. I love to touch you. This is all I thought about all day as well. Holding you, loving you. It was beautiful."

She took a deep breath in, then let out a loud sigh. "Okay, let's do this day."

Michelle could hear the bacon cooking as she stumbled down the stairs. She was led into the kitchen by the mesmerizing aroma.

"Wait, mom! We're not ready for you yet!!" yelled Janine. "Go into the living room and wait. Dad, do you have the coffee ready yet? Maybe she could have a cup of coffee?"

"Coffee?" asked Michelle. "That would be amazing!"

Shawn came over to her and softly touched his hand to her backside, and whispered, "I'll bring you coffee. You go sit and relax. You had a workout last night." Smiling, he gently pushed her forward as she walked into the living room and sat down.

"What smells so good?" Michelle asked as she moved into the living room. "Bacon?" Michelle listened to the chatter in the kitchen. She could hear Jessie exclaiming, "Dad, she is burning the bacon! ?" Just like I said she would!"

"Nope. The bacon is not burning. It's just fine. Are you pouring the orange juice?" Shawn came to the living room and handed Michelle a cup of coffee. He bent over and touched his lips to hers, and softly they pushed her lips open while the tip of his tongue slowly explored her upper palate and her tongue. As he pulled back, she squeezed his upper arm. Oh, his muscles were so tight and smooth! No other words were needed; last night was amazing and they were both enjoying the afterglow of the love they shared.

"So," Shawn exclaimed as he pushed away from her. "Today after we take Janine to school, the day is yours. I will pick them up from school and the girls and I have an adventure to embark on, and you are not invited!"

Michelle stood up and followed Shawn into the kitchen. "Oh, that sounds wonderful! How did I get so lucky?" Shawn winked at her. She felt flushed with a surge of the memory of the love from last night.

The girls stirred with excitement. "What's the adventure, Dad?"

Jaimee turned from the sink where she was drying her wet hands with the kitchen towel. "And why are you taking Janine to school?"

Shawn held his arms out as Jessie raced to his side. "It's a surprise. I will not divulge until we are in the car on our way. But I am sure you all agree that mom can use some time to herself today. And we are just having a conference with Janine's teacher."

Jaimee started a teasing dance back and forth. "Oh....oh...Janine's in trouble...la la la la la.."

"That is a top secret mission that we could tell you about, but then we'd have to kill you."

Jaimee laughed, "Oh, yeah, she's in trouble!"

Janine sneered at her big sister, "Well, you would know!"

Jessie jumped up and down and asked, "But what do we wear?"

Shawn answered, "Something between a ballgown and your bathing suit. So give that some thought while you are at school today. Is breakfast ready?"

Janine announced, "The bacon is done!" Jaimee followed, "French toast is cooked!" Jessie called out, "I'm pouring the orange juice!" The four busied themselves with setting the table as Michelle sat down with her coffee. She took a sip, willing the caffeine to give her the energy to face this day and the meeting with Janine's counselor. "We can do this", she tried to convince herself.

As Jaimee and Jessie jumped onto the bus, Jaimee was saying to Jessie, "Very soon I will get my driver's permit and I can drive us all to school!"

Michelle rolled her eyes. "One crisis at a time, please!" She turned to Shawn. "How did we get so old?"

Shawn laughed. "Speak for yourself, dear."

Michelle turned to Janine. "Well, let's get this over with. Come on, jump in the car." Janine trudged in front of Michelle and walked out the door and to the car without saying a word. Michelle glanced over at Shawn.

He winked. "Off to the firing squad we go." He held his arm out behind Michelle's back to usher her out the door.

Michelle cringed as they entered the administration wing of the school. This was the area to be feared when she was in high school. Being called to the office would trigger a wave of emotions and a sense of urgency wondering which tiny, little insignificant breaking of a rule she was going to get reprimanded for that day. She wasn't called up often, but every time was etched in her brain along with the anxiety and fear of being a kid facing that kind of authority and possible punishment. She looked over at her young daughter. Janine was dressed in her most conservative outfit. No short skirt today, Michelle thought with a wry smile. What Michelle loved most was Janine's straight shoulders and purposeful walk. Janine was facing the moment. It made Michelle proud, despite the fact that they were there for all the wrong reasons.

Shawn pulled back the heavy door and held it while Janine and Michelle entered the counselor's office. Michelle heard the door swing shut behind Shawn. A young woman sporting a business-like skirt and blazer was sitting behind the desk. She stood up as they entered and extended her hand to Michelle.

"Good morning, my name is Lillie Witzell. I am the counselor for Janine's grade." She quickly looked toward Janine. "Hi, Janine, come over and sit, honey." She pointed to the middle of three seats. "Right here, between your parents."

Janine turned her head away from Mrs. Witzell. She rolled her eyes slightly so only Michelle could see.

Michelle tried not to laugh. It was almost an oxymoron, a contradiction that the situation that had one day earlier separated these two women now gave way to a shared emotion.

The woman turned back toward Shawn and Michelle. "So you must be Janine's parents, Mr. and Mrs. Jackson. It's great to meet you. I did receive your message last night, and I have been in contact with Officer Kowalski."

Michelle cleared her throat in an attempt to prime her body for this conversation and to muster up the strength that seemed to be evading her. "Yes and it is nice to meet you, although I wish it wasn't under these circumstances. I want to start out by saying that we had no idea that Janine was skipping school. That's not your fault, I guess, as she told us that she had changed our contact information so you couldn't alert us."

Mrs. Witzell looked at Janine. "Is this true, Janine?"

Janine fidgeted with her backpack in her lap. "Yes."

"Do you understand how dangerous that could be? If something bad happened to you at school we would have no way to contact your parents. Just for example, what if you fainted at school and had to go to the hospital?"

Janine squirmed in her seat. "Yes, I know."

Mrs. Witzell continued, "And nobody was there to give them your allergies, and they gave you the wrong medication and you died from a severe reaction? Do you see how serious this could be?"

Janine looked over at her dad. Her eyes shouted, 'Help me here!'

Shawn shook his head in agreement. "We did talk about this yesterday. I think she understands the seriousness of this now. Right, Janine?"

Janine nodded her head. "Yes, I do."

Mrs. Witzell leaned forward to ease into the meat of the conversation. "Okay, so let's start with first things first. Let's get that contact information corrected." She pulled up her clipboard that was already prepared with a contact information sheet to hand to Shawn. "Dad, do you want to fill this out?"

Shawn reached out for the clipboard. "Sure."

Michelle crossed her legs to disguise her nervousness, as Shawn responded obediently. She felt as if they were musicians being directed by a prominent conductor in a Carnegie

Hall concert, afraid to make any mistakes. She imagined the concert hall being so quiet you could hear a pin drop and Shawn and Michelle were second and third violins, sitting poised and ready for the nod of their feared leader.

"Now," Mrs. Witzell continued on with confidence. "What we would have been reporting to you, if we had the correct information here, was that we have had eight instances of Janine skipping class, usually the last two classes of the day, in the last two months."

Michelle frowned. "So she skipped eight days?"

"Well, no. It was two classes each time, so four days."

Shawn chimed in. "In the last two months."

"That's right."

"What were those classes?"

"Music and Study Hall."

Michelle and Shawn exchanged a look. Janine caught it and looked from one to the other of her parents. Michelle didn't dare say anything, but this was a lot less serious than she had thought...minus Officer Kowalski.

Mrs. Witzell turned her attention to Janine. "Janine, do you want to tell your parents who you have been with and where you have been going? Because I can tell them who you have been with and Officer Kowalski can tell us where you have been, but it would show a lot more responsibility and possibly earn some leniency on your consequences if you are willing to own up to the details."

Smart woman, Michelle thought. She was guiding the parents as well with bringing up the consequences. Mrs. Witzell undoubtedly knew that Shawn and she had absolutely no idea what the consequences should be.

Janine let a period of silence fall. Mrs. Witzell spoke. "Janine?"

"I don't want to get anybody into trouble."

"Oh, you don't have to worry about that, Janine. Nothing you are going to say is news to me. I can assure you that I will be having this same conversation with them. Now it is up to you to own up to your actions. You will not get past this until you own it."

Janine fidgeted in her chair.

Shawn reached over and put his hand on Janine's shoulder. "It's okay, Janine. Just tell the truth. The truth will never hurt you as much as lies or secrets will."

Janine audibly gulped. "We just thought it would be fun to run off and party a little in the park. One day we went to the store and I think the older kids stole some items." She turned to her mother, "But I didn't! I didn't steal anything!"

Michelle nodded her head gently. "It's okay. Just tell us what happened."

"We mostly went to the park and just hung out. Then Greg dropped us back at the school so we could catch the bus home."

Michelle could feel a sudden tightening in her body. A sensation of needles stabbing into her chest. "Greg? Greg who?" She only knew one Greg in Janine's world.

"Greg Easton. He recently got his permit. He drove us."

Michelle's heart sank under the weight of the needle sensation. She felt like her world had just been ripped out from under her. "Wait a minute. Greg Easton–as in your cousin, Greg Easton?"

Janine shrugged. "Yeah, I guess so."

Michelle covered her mouth in disbelief and to stifle whatever words might spill out next. She turned her head away so Janine would not see the horror on her face that she felt in her heart. She could physically feel a knife being turned in her back, and she struggled for a breath. It was bad enough that she had to face her sister Lisa's torture over the years, but now Lisa's own son had gripped her daughter with his claws.

She turned back to catch Shawn's eyes locked with hers. He had this great power of speaking with his eyes. She could tell exactly what they were saying to her. 'Hold it together.' She swallowed hard and fought back the urge to scream.

Mrs. Witzell broke the tension. "Oh, Greg is your cousin! I wondered how you knew this boy since he is two years older than you and in the high school building."

Janine looked up at Mrs. Witzell. "I don't really know him as a cousin. But my friend knows him pretty well."

"And that would be…?"

Janine reached up and rubbed her forehead. "Alison Park."

Mrs. Witzell nodded her head in agreement. "Mmm-hmmm. And there was a fourth."

"His name is Bryan. I don't know his last name. He went on the last few runs with us. He is a friend of Greg's. Please, I don't want them to know I gave you their names."

Shawn placed his hand on Janine's lap. "Honey, we have to know who they are so their parents can be made aware."

Janine turned to Michelle, her eyes wide. Her body tensed up in pensive anticipation. "Mom, are you going to call Aunt Lisa about this?"

Michelle was speechless. Still processing.

Mrs. Witzell jumped in the conversation before Michelle could speak. "I'd prefer you didn't call her, Mrs. Jackson. We have our own protocols, and we know how to best handle these things."

Michelle looked first at her daughter and then to Mrs. Witzell. "That's fine. I don't really speak to my sister." She looked back at Janine. "The officer said there were empty alcohol bottles that day in the cemetery after you all ran away."

Janine straightened up and fidgeted with her backpack on her lap. "I swear to you, Mom, those bottles were there before we got there. We were just jumping on and off the tombstones. People go in there at night and drink all the time. There are always bottles in there."

Michelle wondered with another surge of anxiety how Janine was able to say "always." How many times had she been there with these high school kids? With Greg?

Mrs. Witzell leaned in to Janine. "Do you understand, Janine, that jumping on and off tombstones where someone's loved one is laid to rest is not only disrespectful but a form of vandalism itself. Do you know what vandalism is, Janine?"

Janine looked down as she spoke. "Yes. It is ruining someone's property."

"And disrespecting it, such as jumping on the tombstones of those laid to rest. The painting incident in the park is much more serious, and if those officers had not followed you and stopped you, you would be sitting in a juvenile detention hall this morning. Do you understand that?"

Janine nodded her head. "Yes. I do now. I didn't know that yesterday."

There was an eerie silence in the room. Michelle felt the same intimidation of sitting in the principal's office in middle school for talking too much in class.

"Mrs. Witzell, I don't know what to say right in this moment. This is a new experience for us. I don't know if I should be apologizing for my child, or yelling at her, or accepting her attempts to sound innocent in all of this, or put her over my knee and spank her. Which, by the way, I have never done. But maybe that was my mistake. Can you guide us on what the next step should be?"

Mrs. Witzell began to stand up. "Yes, I can. The very next step is to get Janine back into the classroom so she doesn't miss any more school than she has. Then you and I can talk about consequences." She looked at Janine. "And there will be consequences, Janine. When you do something wrong, you have to pay the price. You understand that, don't you?"

Janine spoke in a timid voice. "Yes."

"And do you understand that Officer Kowalski has informed me that the next occurrence of this will end with you being arrested and sent to juvenile hall?"

"Yes." Janine's lip quivered. She swiped at her eye where a tear had escaped.

"Okay then, why don't you run out of here and get to class, and when you get home from school today your parents will discuss the consequences with you."

Janine looked to her dad and then to her mom and stood up to walk out.

Shawn took her arm gently. "Do you have anything to say to Mrs. Witzell?"

Janine looked back at her. "I'm sorry."

Shawn squeezed her arm as if to say "More."

She obliged. "Thank you."

She turned to Michelle, forced a grin that seemed to represent half apology and half relief and turned to walk out of the office.

Mrs. Witzell grabbed a pink slip from her desk. She handed it to Janine. "Here, this is for the late arrival to class. I am here to talk anytime you need to."

Janine looked down at the pink slip and then walked out of the room.

Michelle got up and moved over next to Shawn. "Okay, I take it the next step is up to us. Tell us what we need to do."

"Well, first of all," Mrs. Witzell began as she sat back down in her chair. "Don't beat yourselves up. Janine is a good student. Before this incident she has never had any behavioral issues and I think we can get this turned around. Skipping school is an act of rebellion that is quite normal in this age group. We want to catch it now before it becomes more serious."

Michelle leaned into the conversation. "Like pouring paint all over a statue in the park? That is true vandalism. I'd say it has gone further than an act of rebellion."

"It wasn't meant to destroy. For them it was just in fun, and right now they are learning what limits they can push. We do need to show them that there are consequences so that they can think about them next time they want to do this again."

Shawn crossed his legs and shifted in his seat. "Do you have any suggestions on the consequences? We were thinking about grounding her but didn't know how serious this is and what amount of time is appropriate. We wanted to wait to talk to you."

"And I am glad you did so. I do have a suggestion, and I would hope all the parents would do the same. It's totally up to you, of course. I can only suggest. In experiences of this nature, I would recommend going strong enough that it will make an impact on their freedom but not so strong that it makes them rebel even more."

Shawn looked confused. "What do you mean, specifically? Strong enough but not so strong...? Like grounding or loss of TV privileges...?"

"Yes, something like that. Grounded long enough to get her attention but not so long that she gets weary. In this age group, three weeks is usually sufficient. Taking away TV, computer, or video game privileges for one week can be beneficial, but of course that's at your discretion."

Michelle and Shawn sat in contemplation for what seemed like an eternity. Finally, Michelle stood up. Shawn followed.

Michelle said, "Thank you, Mrs. Witzell. We will talk about this. I trust that you will let us know if anything else comes up with Janine. And, I am sorry this happened."

Mrs. Witzell stood and leaned her hand over the desk to offer a good-bye gesture. "Of course. And one thing I try to leave with all parents. This is the age of rebellion. It's what they do. They are not criminals. They need consequences so they can learn the right choices to make in this world. But they need your love more than anything. So many kids don't have that. I can see that Janine has that. Of these four kids, statistically I will only see two sets of parents coming to follow through. I'm glad you were one of them, for Janine's sake. It's going to be okay."

Outside in the car, Michelle slumped forward and held her head in her hands. "I was hoping that yesterday was all a dream. But I guess it's not."

Shawn looked over at her from behind the steering wheel. "No. But it may not be as bad as we feared. We will do this together."

Michelle sat upright and took a deep breath, mustering strength from within. "Yeah."

"What do you think about three weeks of grounding and one week of TV privileges?"

"Well, I think three weeks is a good timeframe. I think she should lose her TV for the whole three weeks as well, but if one week is what she recommends, then we can go with that." She paused, thinking. "Yeah, I guess I agree with Mrs. Witzel's recommendation."

Shawn reached over and squeezed her hand. "Are you okay with this Greg Easton thing?"

Michelle tightened up her body at the sound of his name. "I can't believe that son of Lisa's is influencing our daughter! And don't talk to his parents about it? I just want to go over there and ring their necks! Both her and her son! I'll bet she is one of the two parents Mrs. Witzell won't hear from!"

"We'll talk to Janine together after our outing this afternoon."

"And what might this outing be?" Michelle inquired.

Shawn put his finger up to his lips. "Top secret."

<h1 style="text-align:center">Chapter 13</h1>

After school, the girls rushed into the house, brimming with excitement. They fell over each other running up the stairs to get changed for their top secret mission. After a rumbling of chatter and activity, they appeared back into the kitchen, ready for their journey.

Shawn was waiting for them in an old suit coat and hat that made him look like a train conductor. He blew a whistle. "All aboard!" he yelled out.

The girls pushed past him out the door.

Michelle smiled from ear to ear. They were growing into beautiful, unique young women. Jaimee was dressed in black stirrup leggings, high-heeled wedge sandals in a trendy animal print, and a tunic designed with the bold image of a jaguar. She completed the ensemble with a thick gold necklace and matching hoop earrings that dangled almost to her shoulder. She was always the one to go out on the ledge and be the trend setter. Janine sported a pair of jeans with a tank top and midriff overlay, cowboy boots, and a western hat. An avid book reader, she loved to pick a scene out of one of the books she was reading and play one of the characters. Michelle wondered which character she was emulating today. Jessie, ever the princess, was dressed in a pair of capri leggings and a flowing chiffon tunic with her favorite white sandals. She was the one with a flair for the romantic era of flowers, lace, and all things girly. All of that combined with her confident love for life, not knowing or caring what it might throw at her.

"Bye, Mom!" the girls yelled as they piled into the rusted Oldsmobile.

"Goodbye, my girls! Have fun!" Michelle yelled and waved. She caught Shawn's eye and tapped her heart with one finger in a silent gesture of appreciation for the time alone.

Shawn nodded his head and yelled, "Okay, everybody into the time machine!"

"Oh, Lawd." Michelle laughed. "I don't even want to know."

As they drove away, Michelle went back into the house. She poured herself another cup of coffee and sat down to think. Her mind immediately returned to the letters. At this point, she needed to share this with someone. But who? Mike and Amy were so far away, and their lives were wrapped up in their own perfect world that never really included Mom. After Mom remarried, they almost never came back to visit. Mom was more of a biological connection to them than a living, breathing human being. They had their stepmother who really shaped and created their world. Tracy was someone Michelle would love to talk to, but she had not spoken to Michelle since the whole funeral fiasco. She had Lisa to thank for that, too. Michelle wished she could explain why she could not make it to the funeral and how much she missed both Tracy and her husband Jack. She wished Tracy could feel the pain in her heart and the longing to have her older sister back in her life again. But Tracy had rejected Michelle's attempts too many times. Then there was Lisa. She was right here in town, but they had been estranged for so many years. Lisa spent so much time alienating the family against Michelle that she didn't think of her as a sister anymore. She was a stranger.

Michelle sighed. She had to tell someone about these letters, about their mother's suffering. It had to be family, because who else could understand or even care a little bit about all this? Of all of them, Lisa was the best choice. Lisa was the one that was there while they were growing up. Maybe Lisa would have some details that could help her better understand what had been happening to Mom, or maybe when all this was happening. She had not spoken to Lisa in many years, but she decided she needed to make an attempt. She pulled the phone book out of the kitchen drawer, looked up her sister's number, and dialed the phone.

"Hello?" Lisa answered on the other end of the line.

Every muscle in her body tensed. She hadn't been ready to hear her sister's voice, a sound she used to cherish. Now she braced for the inevitable conflict. She felt nauseated, lightheaded. She wondered if Lisa could sense this reaction through the phone line. Shaking her head, she struggled to regain her composure. She forced herself to sound upbeat. "Hey, Lisa. It's Michelle."

Lisa didn't respond.

Michelle waited.

The silence was deafening.

Michelle's stomach was in knots and her heart was in her throat, but she had come this far. There was no turning back. She took a deep breath and dove in. "I wonder if we can talk. I have discovered kind of a mystery and I think you might be able to help me figure it out."

Michelle paused for a response.

Lisa was still mute.

Her continued reticence was disappointing. Nevertheless, Michelle took it as a positive sign that Lisa hadn't hung up on her. She pressed on. "It's about Mom."

"Mom?" Lisa answered. "I haven't spoken to Mom since I graduated from college. I am not the one who knows anything about her, nor do I care."

Michelle took a deep breath and sighed. "I know you haven't seen her in a long time. But you may have some info in those last years you were there that might help. Can I see you for a few minutes? Can we meet for a cup of coffee? Here, your place, Jane's coffee shop?" She could feel the tension right through the telephone line. "It's really important."

"Like when?" asked Lisa.

"Now? Today? One hour? Whenever is good for you."

Another moment of silence passed that seemed like an eternity.

"One hour. Jane's coffee shop."

"Okay, than...." Michelle began. She heard the phone click on the other end.

She hung up the phone. Just like old times, she thought.

Michelle sat at the corner table of Jane's coffee shop, sipping her coffee. She wondered why coffee made in a coffee shop always tasted so much better than what she made at home. Was it the beans? For the price they charged, it ought to be premium. Maybe the water they used? She didn't filter her water at home. They had tried for awhile, but with three girls and Shawn, they just went through those filters way too quickly for what they cost. Maybe it was the beautiful ceramic mug that Jane served her coffee in. It sure did feel smooth and warm in her hand as she caressed the outside of the cup. Just a touch of luxury. Her momentary bliss was interrupted when Lisa came from behind and abruptly sat down. The two just looked at each other, the distance still and cold between them.

Michelle broke the silence. "Hello to you, too."

Lisa rolled her eyes slightly. "Hi, so what is this mystery you had for me? What about Mom?"

"First of all, we missed you at the funeral. Mike and Amy came up, clear from Sanibel Island and Hartford, Connecticut. "

"I had no desire to go to a funeral and say goodbye to someone I have not talked to in over a decade. Was Tracy there?"

"Yes, at the funeral only. I didn't get a chance to speak to her. Doubt that she would have if I tried, thanks to you."

"You're the one who deserted her at her husband's funeral. That was none of my doing."

"It was also none of your business. You took psychology courses in college, didn't you? Do you know what one of the hardest things to do is when you are severely depressed? Attend a funeral where everyone is grieving. Even if I could get my body out of that dark room that I laid in for months, I certainly could not sit through a funeral without having a breakdown. It wasn't a choice."

"We all have choices, Mickey.... so I thought this was about Mom. I'm kinda in a hurry."

Mickey. Michelle hadn't heard that nickname in many years. They never made it to Disneyland, but the two girls would put on their mouse ears that they bought for a dime each at a neighborhood garage sale and called each other Mickey and Minnie.

"Well, can I ask you how the kids are?"

Lisa gave an inpatient sigh. "The boys are fine. Growing teens. I am sure Jaimee sees Greg in school. He says they don't talk."

Michelle thought, well, he certainly talks to Janine. She swallowed the urge to confront Lisa about Greg and his influence on her middle child.

Lisa continued. "Soccer, basketball, life is pretty busy. Keith is growing tall like his dad; very busy, into everything." She paused. "The girls are doing well?"

"Oh, yeah. Jaimee is on the dance team and they expect to have a pretty successful season. Janine is an avid reader. She loves a good mystery. I'm hoping she will be a writer someday. We'll see. And Jessie just loves to cook. Anything! I wish I was more of a cook so that I could teach her more."

"Okay, good. So what is the reason we are here?"

Michelle took a deep breath, pushing past her disappointment that she could not even carry on a conversation with the sister she grew up with. They had shared a bedroom. Played music and danced and shared their dreams. Now, it was just a flashback of a seemingly make believe world. "Well, I took an old jewelry box home from Mom's house after the funeral. The next day, I was looking on the bottom of it to see if I could find a manufacturer, and I discovered a secret compartment in the bottom. It had eight envelopes stuffed in it. Each envelope had two letters, one with a question, and one with an answer."

"Questions and answers. She was developing a concept for a TV game show? Nope, she never shared that with me. Are we done?"

"No! Listen. The questions are not just an ordinary question. They are a search for an answer to a brokenness that the writer was feeling. I've only gotten through the first three letters, but one was about tears, what causes her tears and how does she keep the tears from falling? One was about being afraid; she was terrified of something but doesn't really get specific. And the third one was about feeling love. She felt that she was unworthy of being loved. I think these letters were written by Mom."

Lisa held Michelle's gaze. She rubbed her right wrist. What makes you think that?" asked Lisa.

Michelle narrowed her eyes. Rubbing her wrist was Lisa's tell that she was uncomfortable, that she felt unsafe. Even after all these years, Michelle knew the meanings of every movement her sister made. Lisa was holding something back.

"Well, they were kept away in a secret compartment in her jewelry box. And then—and here's the kicker—there is an answer to the letters. She was writing to someone and they were writing back to her. Beautiful, healing letters. What I want to know is, when did she write these letters? Was it when she was a child? Was it when she was raising us? Was this when she was with our dad before the divorce?"

"Fucking asshole…" interjected Lisa.

"Yes, he was. So could he be the one who made her feel so bad? Or did she end up with the asshole because of the feelings of unworthiness that she had from when she was younger? Or was this when she was with Harry? I always saw him as such a good man and a good stepdad to us. Was this later in life after we left? Did we abandon her? For sure we were never there to give her the love she needed later in life as a mother. And then someone wrote these beautiful healing letters." Michelle paused. "I just have so many questions."

The two sisters sat in silence while Lisa just looked at Michelle, clearly uninterested. Finally, Lisa broke the silence. "And you want–what from me? "

"I'm not sure. Just to jar your memory I guess. Wondering if you saw anything different about Mom after I went away to college. Or if you remember anything that I don't from when we were younger. I'm not quite sure."

Lisa started to get up from the table. "Okay, well, nothing on the tip of my tongue. I'll let you know if something comes to mind. And if anything more specific comes up, you apparently know my number. I thought I made my number unlisted, but I guess not." She turned to leave.

"Wait! Aren't you concerned? Intrigued? Emotional about this on any level?"

Lisa stopped and turned to face Michelle again. "Look, as I said, I left the house after college and never looked back. I'm just not interested. She was probably a child. Every child cries, has fears, feels unworthy of love at some point in their life."

"A child? Mom couldn't have written them when she was a kid–the paper isn't aged enough for the letters to be that old. Definitely older stationery, but not from mom's childhood years. Maybe as a young adult? She was not a child."

After a few moments of silence, Lisa offered, "Maybe give Tracy a call?" She tapped the table. " I gotta go."

Michelle gaped at Lisa.

Lisa forced a smile. "Hey, enjoy your coffee. It looks yummy. See 'ya around."

Michelle was certain her face was saying what she couldn't put into words.

Lisa sighed. "Hey, whoever wrote these letters was obviously hurting. I understand your desire to find out who this is. I hope you find what you're looking for."

Tears sprung to Michelle's eyes. She heard a hint of the love they had once shared in Lisa's voice. She blinked them away. "Thank you," she managed.

Michelle's stomach clenched as Lisa turned and walked out the door of the coffee shop.

Back at home, Michelle finished up the dishes in the kitchen. After drying her hands, she stopped. For the thousandth time that day, her thoughts returned to the conversation with Lisa. It was hard to believe they were sisters with how different they were from one another. Michelle's earliest memories with Lisa were so sweet, so innocent. Two giggling girls rolling down hills in the backyard and squabbling over their favorite toys. But that all changed when Lisa was five. Michelle never understood why. Since that year, Lisa had become more and more withdrawn. By the time Michelle went to middle school, it felt like they were not sisters at all; just two strangers growing up together.

She sighed. 'Heck,' she thought, 'I'm lucky that she even agreed to meet with me at all.'

She wished she could just be happy with that. She leaned her head in her hands on the counter. Reaching up to her ears, she twirled her mom's faux pearl earrings between her fingers. "Mom, maybe you can tell me," she said, "Did Lisa and I truly come from the same DNA? The same uterus? The same mother?" Of course, there was no response. There never would be real answers.

Her mom was gone. Forever. Even though Michelle had lost any emotional closeness to her mother years ago, she felt empty without her. Why had they grown apart in the first place? She didn't know, and now the only person who could tell her why was gone. She felt cold. The pit in her stomach returned. She realized it was the hole left by the departure of the people she loved growing up. It was a hole that would never be filled. She wanted so much to feel whole, but she wasn't even sure what that would feel like. She sighed and walked over to the couch. Once she was in her comfy spot, she covered herself with a soft blanket and closed her eyes.

The back door burst open, and the three girls and Shawn bounded in, talking a mile a minute.

Groggily, she opened her eyes. She pushed herself to a seated position.

"Mom!"

She rubbed her face to wake up. She could hear them racing through the kitchen to the living room. The pitter patter of little feet had become a thundering herd of elephants now that they were older.

"Hi, Mom!" shouted Jessie. "We are back from our adventure!!!"

Michelle sat up on the couch. "Well, did you have an amazing time?"

"Yes we did," shouted Janine. "We went in the time machine and drove up a big HUGE mountain."

Shawn interjected quietly, "Just a little cliff."

"We were entering the time of Shakespeare. We collected swords–"

Shawn interjected, "Little sticks."

Janine threw him a questioning glance.

"Okay, medium sticks"

"And we had a sword fight!"

Shawn interjected, "Several feet away so the sticks never touched their bodies."

Jaimee added in, "I was the best. I made Janine fall backwards off the mountain!"

Shawn quickly responded. "A tiny one foot step off a rock ledge to the soft grass below."

"Anyways, she died but dad said we had to give her another life because she is his favorite."

"I did not say that!" defended Shawn.

Michelle stated, "Oh, yes, the favorite love child. This sounds familiar. Well, has anyone worked up an appetite for dinner?"

All three girls shouted, "Me! Me!"

Jessie added, "Mom, can I help you make dinner?"

Michelle smiled. My little chef, she thought. "Well, of course you can. Go change your clothes and meet me in the kitchen. The rest of you, get cleaned up. Dinner in 30 minutes!"

"Okay!" The girls shouted as they ran upstairs.

Shawn turned to go up the stairs and asked, "So I have time for a shower? All that swordfighting made me sweat."

Michelle laughed, "Go on, Henry, the banquet will not start without the king."

Michelle turned around, surprised to see that Jessie had already returned with changed clothes. She liked to think of her as the baby, but the reality was that she was 11 years old and was quickly turning into a young woman. There were definitely moments when she would still crawl up on her mama's lap after a long day for an evening cuddle, but most of the time, she was just quiet, watching and listening and learning from her older sisters just how to develop and maneuver in this crazy world. The thought of that made Michelle inwardly cringe. She thought, 'I cannot let Jessie learn just through watching her big sisters. I have to put the effort into guiding her to be the woman she desires to be.'

She smiled at her youngest. "So, what shall tonight's creation consist of? Something deserving of a Shakespearian feast? To feed hungry sword fighters?"

Jessie thought for a moment, and then uttered, "Ummm....ummm... peanut butter and jelly sandwiches!"

"What?" asked Michelle. "Are you serious?"

"Yes! Peanut butter and jelly sandwiches!"

Michelle took a deep breath and let out a big sigh and said, "OKAY! Peanut Butter and Jelly Sandwiches it is!" She walked to the pantry and pulled out the peanut butter and bread, handing them to Jessie. "So, in keeping with the Shakespearean Banquet, there must be other things on the table. You know, a banquet is a large meal served to many people that has a variety of food offerings, one item usually being the featured dish. That would, of course, be our lovely tray of piled high peanut butter and jelly sandwiches. So what do you think we could have as our royal side dishes?"

Jessie took the items to the counter and pulled out a butter knife. "Side dishes? I don't know." She opened the fridge and fetched all the jelly they had. "Grape, strawberry...where's the raspberry? Janine hates grape and strawberry. Oh, there it is!" She gathered all three jars in her arms and carefully maneuvered over to the counter.

"Here, let me help." Michelle hurried to grab two from her arms, picturing them shattering on the floor.

"Thanks." Jessie sat the last one down.

"So, side dishes," continued Michelle, taking a pencil and paper in hand, "Let's make a list of ideas and then decide what we want to make and we can write out a menu for the royal banquet....befitting of every royal swordfighter, of course."

"Okay!" shouted Jessie, jumping up and down with excitement. She flopped into a kitchen chair.

Michelle sat beside her. "So, I am thinking of the foods they had available back then. Natural foods, no potato chips or anything like that. Meat, vegetables, fruits. How about ....broccoli?"

Jessie looked at her mom for a moment. She frowned and made the thumbs down sign.

Michelle continued, "Okay, no broccoli. I guess that leaves out brussel sprouts and cabbage. How about applesauce?"

"Ooh, applesauce is good!" exclaimed Jessie with delight.

"And I think if I lived in the days of Shakespeare, my favorite dish would be......"

Jessie pulled in closer.

"Macaroni and cheese!"

"Yes!" shouted Jessie. "But with bacon because dad says they ate a lot of bacon back then."

"Macaroni and cheese with bacon! Stupendous! See how good you are at this?" Michelle held up her hand for a high five.

Jessie came over and returned it. "Yes!"

Michelle continued, "Okay, so by order of the royal chef, Jessie, we have peanut butter and jelly sandwiches, applesauce, and baked macaroni and cheese with bacon. Does that sound good to you?"

"Yes, that sounds perfect!"

"Okay," Michelle continued, "So now to divide up the responsibilities between the royal chef..." She pointed to Jessie. "And her royal assistant (that would be me!) what can I help you with, my honorable, executive chef?"

Jessie looked around the kitchen. "Hmmmm......you can make the macaroni and cheese, I will fry the bacon. You can spoon the applesauce into bowls, and then we can make the sandwiches together."

"Sounds like a great plan!" Michelle announced.

Jessie clumsily picked up the tongs to flip the bacon and Michelle put the water on for the macaroni. The sounds of bacon sizzling and pans clanging was like a symphony to her ears.

Jessie turned to Michelle. "Mom? What does it feel like to die?"

Michelle folded her arms in front of her. She could feel that sense of cold wrap around her as she felt earlier in the day. The hole in her heart was so intense it was physically painful. This was a question she had wrestled with herself. She had never really come up with an answer, but here was the challenge right in front of her. She took a big breath and blew it out, trying to muster up the words to answer Jessie. "Whew. That's a big question. To tell you the truth, I don't really know. I don't think anyone knows the answer to that question. I'd like to think it's like going to bed, closing your eyes, and being done with the day. But then when you open your eyes, you are not really in your body."

"Not in your body? Then where are you?"

"Well, hopefully you are in Heaven."

"What's that like?"

Michelle leaned in to Jessie and put her arm around her shoulders. "I don't know, but....well, have you heard the expression 'I wish I could have been a fly on the wall'?"

Jessie nodded. "Yeah, you can listen in on conversations because you are so small nobody sees you."

"Yes. I think Heaven might be like that. You are still with the people you love, listening to them and loving them. They can't see you or hear you, but they can feel you and they know you will always be there with them."

"Do you think Grandma is still here like that?"

Michelle pulled Jessie into a tight hug and then released her. "I think Grandma would be flipping this bacon if she could! And, yes, she is here. I can feel her. Can you?"

Jessie closed her eyes. She folded her arms in front of her as if she were hugging herself. "Yes, I think I can feel her, too."

"So when you feel her, you can talk to her. You can tell her you love her. I think she would love to hear that."

Jessie smiled, still with eyes closed, and whispered, "I love you, Grandma."

Michelle whispered into Jessie's ear. "And one more thing. Never close your eyes when standing in front of sizzling bacon!"

Jessie giggled. She reached up with the tongs to turn the sizzling bacon.

Yes, she will be a great chef, Michelle thought, but if I have anything to do with it, it will be in her own time working toward her own goals and blooming as the universe has laid out for her.

Chapter 14

I can never measure up

    With homecoming over, Michelle's sophomore year was settling in like the cold of winter descending upon her. She was struggling to keep her grades up. It just seemed like nothing was going right. Mostly because it was hard for her to concentrate on her studies when she felt like she was sitting in the front row of a romance movie unfolding in front of her. Diane and John sat across from her in science lab, giggling and touching each other playfully.

"You guys are gonna get in trouble when Mr. Evans sees you."

Diane smiled and leaned forward toward Michelle. "Then you'd better keep watch and warn me if he is coming over!"

Michelle just shook her head. Her lab partner Lexi nudged her. "Come on, get your head back in the game here. I'm not going to get another B just because you can't keep up. I can't believe I got stuck with a deadbeat wallflower like you."

Michelle bristled back at Lexi. "Deadbeat wallflower? Tell me—how do you really feel about me?"

Lexi threw Michelle a sour face. "You don't want to know."

Diane jumped into the conversation. "Hey, leave her alone. Not everybody is as perfect as you." She laughed and added, "Thank God."

Lexi leered at Diane. "I'm not perfect, but I'm damn close." She looked at Michelle. "But this one? Worse than a wallflower. A dull, dandelion weed in the middle of a beautiful green meadow. Something my dad would spray weed killer on."

Michelle could feel her heart sink in her chest. She blinked her eyes, fighting back a tear.

Diane reached over and tapped on the table in front of them and then pointed to her. "Do not let this T-Rex get to you. She will never know how amazing you are. Someday, this whole world will know what's inside of that protective shell."

They all jumped slightly as the bell rang.

Diane said, "Oh, saved by the bell!" She turned to Lexi. "Time for your feeding! Go chomp on a few more people. It's such a delightful quality of yours."

Lexi smirked at Diane and then to Michelle. She picked up her books and walked out of the lab.

John gathered his books. "Come on, Michelle, come to lunch with us. Forget about Lexi. She isn't worth it."

Michelle wished she could take John's advice, but she couldn't. That evening, she sat at her desk, staring dully into space, hot tears in her eyes. She looked at the big flowers on the wall. 'When is it time for me to come down off that wall?' she thought.

She pulled her rose stationery out of her drawer and rolled it into the typewriter.

I can never measure up.....

After dinner, Shawn and Michelle sat with Janine in her room while Jessie and Jaimee cleaned the royal table.

Shawn began to talk. "First of all, we both want you to know that we are proud of you for telling us what we needed to know today in Mrs. Witchel's office. That couldn't have been easy for you."

"No, it wasn't." Janine answered in a low tone. She pushed past a crack in her voice. "I guess this is my talk about consequences."

Michelle leaned forward and rested her arms on her lap. "Yes, it is. We talked it over with Mrs. Witzell, and she is recommending the same consequence for all of you kids who were involved in this. She recommends three weeks grounding and one week without TV privileges."

Janine looked startled. "What? Three weeks grounding and no TV? That is a very harsh punishment, not a consequence!"

"Janine, do you know the difference between a punishment and a consequence?"

"Well, not exactly, but a punishment seems more harsh and this is harsh!"

Michelle cleared her throat to continue. "Well, you are right in that a punishment can be harsh. It is meant to inflict pain on someone whether they deserve it or not. A consequence is a result of your behavior and meant to help you grow past bad decisions."

Shawn reached forward to touch Janine's arm. "Our goal is not to make you feel punished, but to help you see the seriousness of what you did so you won't be tempted to do it again."

Janine sniffled a little and swiped at her nose. "I know, but three weeks is so long. My friends won't know me after so long."

Michelle gulped to keep from laughing. She glanced at Shawn. He was rubbing his jaw. He was trying to keep from laughing, too. Michelle cleared her throat. "Believe me, child of mine, you are unforgettable! They will still know you! And , I suspect Alison will be grounded also, so no loss there."

The three sat in silence for a few moments. The tension in the air was palpable. They had never had to do a grounding before with any of the girls. This was the first pretty serious event they had encountered so far. And of course it would be with their rebellious Janine. Always trying to stretch the boundaries. That's partly what Michelle loved about her. She was vivacious! She will be a winner for sure in life. The events that brought them to this discussion flitted through her mind. If she doesn't end up in jail first, she thought.

Shawn leaned back into his chair again. "All understood?"

Janine nodded her head. "Okay, yeah. I get it. And I am really sorry."

Michelle began to stand up. "Thank you for saying that. I believe you mean it. So, I was about to dive into another letter. Would you like to join me? We can check it out together."

Janine perked up from her slouched body. "Sure!"

Michelle smiled. This made her happy. The past several months have been difficult for Michelle and her troubled daughter. Perhaps this was a way to connect with her on a different level. Maybe they will grow together on this journey. Maybe Janine will grow personally as well. She sure could use any help in growing these young women into adults.

Shawn accepted his hint to make himself scarce. "Okay, well, you young ladies go to work on your mystery and I will go see how the other two warriors are tending to their wounds from the big sword fight this afternoon." He looked at Janine and touched her shoulder. "Love you, girl. Now and always."

Janine looked up at him. "Love you too, Dad."

The three proceeded down the stairs, and Michelle walked over to the hall closet, pulling out the shoebox of envelopes. "Let's go back upstairs to my room. We can have some privacy."

Janine smiled. "Sure. We'll call it the mystery room!"

As they walked through the living room to the stairs, Shawn was already in his slouched position on the couch while Jaimee and Jessie knelt on the floor with pillows in front of the TV.

Jaimee looked up at Michelle and Janine as they walked by.

"So, are you grounded for life?"

Janine sneered at Jaimee. "No, I am not grounded for life." She glared at Shawn for help.

Shawn sat up straight and grabbed the remote off the coffee table and handed it to Jaimee.

"Jaimee, this is no such thing as life imprisonment in this house. Janine can tell you when she is ready. But just remember, some day you might need a little understanding from your sister. So how about if you back off for now?"

"Whatever." Jaimee grabbed the remote and began clicking. Jessie bounced in her place when her favorite show appeared. "Stop!" She pounced on her pillow and pointed to the TV screen. "Clifford!"!"

Jaimee furrowed her brow and turned toward Jessie. "Oh, heck! We are not babies anymore! Let's find 90210."

Shawn covered his face with his pillow on the couch and grunted.

Michelle and Janine went back upstairs to Michelle's bedroom. She sat on the bed and Janine flopped beside her.

"So, I read the third letter last night. It was about opening yourself up to love. Remember when I came into your room last night to kiss you goodnight and tell you that you are loved and deserving of love?"

Janine nodded. "Yeah."

"Well the letters were saying that we shouldn't be afraid to feel loved. And to believe that we deserve love. We should never use words like "unloved, unclean, unworthy." We should turn those words around and say, "I am loved. I am clean. I am worthy." The idea is to use the right vocabulary to tell your mind what to think."

"Tell your mind? Like talking to yourself?"

"Yes, kind of like a mantra. Words you say over and over to change your mindset. It can help you think more positively, or get through an uneasy situation. This letter suggests a mantra: 'I am loved. I am clean. I am worthy.'" She closed her eyes and breathed audibly, expanding her chest. "You know, Mr. Branson taught me about meditation. First you take a deep breath, because that helps you start to relax your body so your mind can assimilate the words." She took another breath and blew the air out slowly. "I am loved. I am clean. I am worthy." She opened her eyes and turned to Janine. "I can feel the difference. I feel more positive, like a small surge of positive energy."

Janine closed her eyes. She took a breath and blew the air out slowly. "I am loved. I am clean. I am worthy." She opened her eyes.

Michelle nodded. "Yeah, just like that. It almost seems like a mini-meditation we can do daily. I'm gonna try doing this every day, too. We all need reminders of these things."

Janine nodded. "Sounds like good words to live by."

Michelle reached into the shoebox and took out letter number three and its answer. She handed them to Janine. "Here, take these with you tonight. Maybe you can read them before you go to bed."

"Okay." Janine accepted the letters and set them beside her on the bed, pushing them away from the edge so they wouldn't fall, smoothing them with her hand as if they were her most prized possessions. When she was satisfied that they were safe, she said, "So what's behind door number four?"

Michelle smiled. "I don't know. Let's see!" She took out letter number four and its answer. She opened the first letter and began to read aloud.

I can never measure up. I'm not even sure what I am supposed to measure up to, or how or by whom the bar got set, but I know I am never good enough. Why must I be judged in everything I say or do? I can never meet the world's standards. So why even try? I have felt inadequate for as long as I can remember, so how can I go through life even thinking for a minute that the world will see me as successful? Beautiful? Because they don't. No boy looks at me the way they do the other girls. My teachers don't tell me that I am full of potential. I don't have a lot of friends. I probably don't even deserve the life that others have.

Am I destined to be a nobody?

A follower?

A wallflower?

A single dandelion weed in the midst of a beautiful green field?

Should I just stop trying to fit in? I feel so stupid. Everyone is laughing at me behind my back. If they look close enough, I'm afraid they will see my tail between my legs. Retreating. Defeated. A disappointment. Is there any reason for me to go on? If I left this world, would anyone notice that I am gone?

Michelle wiped a tear from her eye. "Oh, mother," she said out loud. "You were hurting so much."

Janine softly responded. "You mean Dorothy Doe, don't you?"

Michelle locked eyes with Janine, then smiled. She perused the letter again. She muttered, "*no boy looks at me.....my teachers don't tell me....* This is a girl or a young woman who is in school, maybe middle to high school? Old enough to be a girl hoping to have a boy look at her, and needing some encouragement in school. Well, this is a clue."

She felt a little bit of a relief. Maybe her mother's sadness over the years wasn't because of their strained relationship. Maybe her mom wrote these letters way back in high school. Could they be that old? Michelle didn't see why not. Her mom had never talked much about her high school years.

Actually, she didn't talk much to her girls about their own high school years either. She never was a hands-on mother. She did everything a mother was expected to do; cooked their meals and packed lunches, spent her days while they were in school doing laundry, cleaning, trying to rid the house of the lingering odors of Harry's cigars. But there were things she never did as well. She had never learned to drive so she couldn't help them get to their events. The girls always walked.

Her mother never came to school activities like football games, musicals, concerts, parent teacher conferences. Harry was always working so he couldn't help, but they lived close to the school. Mom could have walked with them, but she never did. In fact, that day of Michelle's graduation may have been the first time she ever walked into the school building. She didn't mind not going out, not driving. She always was a homebody. She never talked to the girls about how to act in school, how to look their best, how to have confidence, how to talk to a boy.

"Maybe Dorothy felt ignored." Michelle wondered if Mom was distant with the three of them because she didn't think she was important to them.

Janine took the letter from her mother's hands and studied it. "This young woman felt like a throw away–like a weed. That had to have taken away any self-confidence she should have had."

Michelle closed her eyes and then opened them slowly. "Yes, I know that fear of not being good enough." She had spent her lifetime in fear that she was not as good as everyone else.

Janine looked at her mother and asked, "In what way?"

Michelle cleared her throat. "While starting my art business, I second guessed myself constantly. I destroyed so many of my own paintings before I even finished them, because I thought they were sub par."

"Sub par?"

"That means not as good as other artists. I feared so much having my art critiqued. I always expected the worst." She looked down in self reflection. It occurred to her that her mom had felt inadequate, too. Mom may never have learned how to bloom. The question now was had Michelle herself learned how to bloom? Was it possible this was why she pushed her daughters so hard, compensating for her own feelings of inadequacy? She brought her attention back to Janine. "Dorothy Doe was really suffering."

Janine nodded, and looked as if she had an understanding of what the writer was going through. After all, this person could even be her age. "I feel a little like Dorothy sometimes. Wondering why I don't have a boyfriend yet. Why I am not as popular as some of the kids. What my teachers think of me. Sometimes I feel like I'm not as good as everyone else. What makes some kids popular and some destined to be a wallflower, a weed, like Dorothy Doe feels? Is is destiny? Is it luck? Is it money?"

Michelle answered, "I know a lot of wallflowers who grew up to be amazing adults. Maybe a wallflower is just a late bloomer."

Janine nodded her head. "But I don't think that's what would have made Dorothy feel better in the moment."

Michelle smiled. "I believe you are correct. Just know that you are a beautiful young woman, and you need only the right person in your life to make you feel that way. And that person will come. Faith is believing without seeing. It's a hard concept to develop."

"Yeah, I guess."

Michelle reached out to Janine and gave her a hug. "You are amazing. You will get there." She released the hug and held Janine out at arm's length. "Some things, a mother just knows."

Janine smiled and nodded, agreeing in obedience.

Michelle released her hold. "Shall we see what the second letter says?"

Janine reached for the envelope. "Sure. Can I read it?"

"Absolutely" said Michelle as she handed the envelope to Janine.

Janine opened the second letter and began to read.

Though you may think of it as a common weed, a single dandelion in the midst of a beautiful green field manifests one of the highest forms of beauty in this universe. Each flower head of the dandelion is actually a collection of thousands of small ray flowers. As the head of a dandelion flower opens, each yellow tubular spike is actually a separate flower, a separate creation of the universe.

Janine looked up at Michelle. "Ooh, I see a research paper coming on." Michelle smiled. Janine looked back at the paper and continued to read.

How, then, can the dandelion be compared to a disappointment, when it holds so much more complexity than most flowers? If you are a dandelion, then you need only see yourself for the beauty and the complexity that you possess. As the universe created the seemingly simple dandelion as a complicated structure, know that it made you as a symphony of beauty, of success, of strength, of wit, of so many beautiful attributes that are uniquely yours. You will bloom in all your splendor when it is your time. Do not feel less successful than someone who has achieved their goals. Those are not your goals. Their time is not your time. Your talents need only to be given the time and opportunity to blossom like the dandelion. Do not rush it. But do keep working at it, and have faith that the universe knows the time and the circumstance. It knows the boy you dream of, the recognition you desire, the love you seek, the touch you quench for, and the talent inside of you. She looked up at her mom, hesitated, and then continued on. *Keep developing your true inner beauty and know that your time to shine is near. Just know that your true success will not fit anyone else's definition but yours. Your goals. Your work. Your success.*

"Wow." Janine set the letter down on the bed beside her and smoothed it out with her hand." Just wow. I just want to shake that Dorothy and tell her to hang in there. Her time to bloom is near."

Michelle reached out and placed her hands on top of Janine's as she held the letter in place on the bed. "As a mother, I want to do this with my children just about every day. Sending you out into the big world, I just want to say it'll be all right. You will bloom in your time."

Janine sat back and pulled her hands out from under Michelle's. "Really? I don't ever hear you say that. All I hear is, your skirt is too short. Take that make up off. Share with your sisters."

Michelle smiled. "Well, yes, same thing!" She chuckled. "If you read between the lines, that is. It's my job to help mold you into what the world expects, teach you right from wrong, and prepare you for the tough moments." She hesitated. "But in the end, what I'm really saying is, it'll be all right. You're gonna be just fine."

"Hmmm. Well that's good to know."

" I guess I forget to spell that out. I should work on that!"

Janine laughed. "And I'll have to listen a little more closely next time!"

Michelle patted Janine on the leg. "Well, Miss Blooming Dandelion, it has been a very long day! Shall we turn in? I think your sisters are way ahead of you. Unless they were able to agree on a TV show which I doubt."

"Yes, good night mom." She stood up and leaned into her mother and kissed her on the cheek. "Love you."

"Love you too," Michelle answered as she returned the kiss to her daughter, then sat and watched her walk away. She drew a deep breath, then stood up and turned out her bedroom light.

Chapter 15

1973 would haunt Michelle's dreams forever, although it would be a long time before she really knew why. She was thirteen years old, impressionable, and innocently convinced the world was at her fingertips and she could be and do anything. She was a sponge, soaking up every bit of knowledge that she could to prepare herself for this wide world that laid out in front of her. She especially enjoyed her time spent with her neighbor, Mr. Brandson. He was an artist and was always opening her mind up to so many forms of art. She envisioned many afternoons spent sitting at his easels, painting and drawing, using acrylics and watercolors, pressing flowers, sculpting. His back porch was a safe haven for her, a place where his impromptu art lessons ushered her into a world where she truly belonged. It helped her escape from things in this world that scared her, and she even felt it helped her escape from things unknown. Which was a weird feeling at her age. What things unknown? She didn't know; it was just a feeling that something or someone was out there. Maybe like the boogeyman. Yes, that had to be it.

Years later, she would recognize this day as one like no other. In the moment, Michelle had no idea what awaited, and she stepped out into the beautiful warm sunshine, hurrying as best she could while carefully cradling her art palette and canvas in both arms. She walked across the grass, humming the melody of a song she just heard on the radio. Life was promising.

She had no idea that the day would end in tragedy.

She turned the corner to Mr. Brandson's backyard. The porch was empty. Knowing he would be out in a moment, Michelle began setting up her canvas.

The quiet scratch of the screen door announced Mr. Brandson's arrival. "Okay Mother, I will put my hat on if we venture into the sun."

Michelle snickered as she heard this familiar conversation. Mr. Brandson was balding a little on top of his head and needed to protect his scalp from skin cancer.

"Why do you call your wife 'mother'?" she asked.

"I often call her Mother because she is always doting over me like a mother over her child."

Michelle giggled. She called out past him, "Don't worry, Mrs. B, I'll make sure he wears a hat!"

Mr. Brandson scoffed. "Oh, two on one. And siding with the missus. You know where your bread's buttered. You might just have earned yourself an extra piece of cake today!" He walked over and sat down next to Michelle. "Paints, I see. Okay, what's your pleasure today?"

Michelle sat back in her chair and cocked her head up towards Mr. Brandson. "Abstract?"

Mr. Brandson laughed out loud. "I could have guessed! What is it that draws you to the abstract style of painting lately?"

Michelle held her paint pallet in her left arm and used her right middle finger to gently trace around the different colors on her plate. "Oh, I don't know. It helps me to bring out a blank area in my mind by giving it color. It's like there is something that I can't picture in my mind, but then the colors give me something to bring it life." She looked back to Mr. Branson. "But it's abstract, of course, so you never really get to clearly see the picture. I guess I'm hoping some day the picture will come through. Until then, I guess I'll just keep working on it."

"Hmmm..." Mr. Branson nodded his head. He pulled out his paints and a blank canvas from his pile on the porch, setting the canvas on his easel. "Okay, so let's get started."

Both Michelle and her teacher began laying images on their canvases. Mr. Brandson said, "So, of course what you will end up with is not a specific design, but by using images–shapes, strokes, colors, curves, straight lines, textures–you can bring out the message which represents a design."

Michelle moistened her canvas with a log, curved stroke of red. "When will I know when my message is completed?"

"Well, that is a very personal decision. Only you will know when the message is completed. You will feel it. And the thing about abstract art is, maybe the message is never completed. Sometimes an artist completes a piece earlier in time, and then goes back five years later and is ready to add another layer, based on what is happening in their life."

Michelle started patting the brush back onto the red curve, making a raised texture in the line. "Sounds a little like writing a journal. It's never finished."

Mr. Branson had just completed painting a yellow circle on his canvas, and looked at Michelle. "Yes, except the written word in a journal is true to what the writer is experiencing. And clearer to the reader. An abstract painting, however, is interpreted differently by everyone who looks at it."

"Why is that?"

"Because the painting draws out the individual's interpretation based on what their life experiences have been. So, looking at that red line over there, a soldier may go back to the battlefield and remember injuries that caused a lot of blood loss. A young woman may look at that and think of red roses that her husband picked for her."

Michelle felt a giddiness inside of her. "Like the ones you gave Mrs. Branson when you asked her to marry you?"

"Like those exactly!" Mr. Brandson chortled. "I know you are just beginning, but what does that red line represent to you so far? Remember, it may change as time goes on."

Michelle looked intently at the design. "Well, the curved line kind of reminds me of someone running their fingers along a body. A leg or arm or something."

Mr. Branson nodded. "I can see that. A body is not a straight line. It has curves in it. And why the texture?"

Michelle became more solemn. "It feels rough."

Mr. Brandson looked from Michelle's face to her canvas. "What do you mean, 'It feels rough'?"

Michelle hesitated for a moment, trying to reach back into her memory to search for the answer. "Well, my father had very rough hands, you know. He was a hard worker." She glanced up at Mr. Brandson. He was studying her face, the same way he always did when she talked about her father. She blinked several times then turned back to her canvas.

Mr. Brandson asked, "What does that have to do with this image?"

She stopped midstroke. "When my father ran his fingers up and down my legs, it would feel rough." She reached up with her paintbrush and drew a small blue tear shape dripping off of the red curve. "Sometimes it hurt. This is a sad tear."

Mr. Branson sat straight back in his chair. He folded his left arm across his stomach and supported his right below while he rubbed his forehead. "Michelle, are you sad now?"

Michelle continued to fill in the blue tear with paint. "Not now because I'm with you. I'm safe here."

He lowered his hand and scooted his chair a little closer to Michelle. "Who else makes you feel safe?"

"Mrs. Brandson!" she exclaimed with a smile.

"Mrs. Brandson!" Mr. Brandson spoke extra loud.

In a moment Mrs. Brandson appeared at the door, listening with her arms crossed. Michelle smiled at her. Mr. and Mrs. Brandson both smiled back.

"Who else helps you feel safe?"

"Umm my mother. My dad."

Mr. Brandson interrupted. "Stepdad?"

"Well, sure but he's my dad. I know he's not my real dad, but he's my heart dad, as mom says."

"And what about your real dad?"

Michelle stopped. Her mind went blank.

Mr. Brandson pressed on. "Your real dad? Does he make you feel safe?"

Michelle swung her legs back and forth under the table, hoping to dispel the nervous feeling that threatened to overwhelm her. "Well, we don't see him much anymore."

"Did he make you feel safe when you were with him?"

A lump formed in Michelle's throat. "I was mostly scared."

"Scared of what?"

"Of his rough hands. They hurt."

Mr. Brandson leaned forward and touched Michelle gently on her leg, to which she startled. He pulled his hand back quickly. "I'm sorry. Did your dad touch you on your legs?"

Michelle looked down at her legs. "Yes."

"Like, around your knees?"

Michelle's eyes moved up her leg. "Higher."

"Your thighs?"

"Yes. But higher."

Mr. Brandson swallowed hard. "Between your legs?"

Michelle looked into Mr. Brandson's eyes. "Yes. But that's okay, isn't it? He said it was okay. As long as I didn't tell anybody." Michelle's hands flew to her mouth, covering it. "Oh, I shouldn't have told you!"

Mr. Brandson looked away and covered the quiver in his chin as he choked back a tear.

Mrs. Brandson slid the door open and knelt in front of Michelle. She took Michelle's hands in hers and held her eyes in a firm gaze. Michelle was transfixed by the softness, the kindness, in Mrs. Brandson's eyes. Mrs. Brandson spoke more gently than she'd ever heard anyone speak before. "First of all, I want you to know that you are a beautiful girl, and I hope you know that. I also want you to know that it is never okay for anyone to touch you in a place that hurts you. Or to keep it a secret. You need to be able to talk to someone you trust. And I hope you know you can trust us in everything, sweetie."

Michelle's heart pounded in her chest. She felt like she had a pit in stomach. "Oh, I do trust you. Did I do something wrong? I didn't mean to!"

Mr. Brandson fell forward in his chair to give Michelle a big hug. Mrs. Brandson joined him. In their warm enveloping embrace, Michelle felt so safe, so secure, like nothing bad could ever happen to her again.

Mr. Brandson's deep voice resonated in her ears. "No, you have done nothing wrong! Talking about how you feel is never wrong. Let's get back to the canvas, and see what else your art has to reveal."

Later that day, Michelle was sitting upstairs in her room. The evening hours were quickly descending on the house, and the sunshine through the window in her bedroom was quickly fading, leaving shadows where it shone brightly earlier in the day. Michelle heard a car screech into the driveway, and the door slam shut. She looked out to see that it was her father's car. This wasn't her day with him. She was in no hurry to see him as her heartdad was out of town. She always felt better when her heartdad was there. She didn't know why. Just a feeling. After a minute she could hear the rumbling of voices and could tell that her mom was very angry. For the second time that day, her heart was in her throat. She ran to the top of the stairs and called down, "Mom?"

She waited with a heaviness in her heart. Every moment that passed felt like a year.

Finally, her mother yelled, "Don't come down here! Everything's fine! Just stay upstairs!"

Michelle stiffened with fear. Her mother had never scolded in this tone of voice before. She obediently scurried back to her bed and sat and waited. She could not hear the conversation, just the angry yelling. Folding her hands in front of her, she prayed, "Please, God, make it alright."

After a very short wait, and more yelling, she could clearly hear her mother yell out, "No, stop!" Then she heard the kitchen door slam.

Next her mother's voice echoed from the kitchen. She strained to hear every word. "Hello? 911?" her mother said, "My ex-husband is out of control! I don't know what he's going to do. And he has a gun! .... Yes, yes, please come right away. My address is 226 Chestnut Street. But he's headed for my neighbors' house at 228 Chestnut. Please come right away. I'm afraid my neighbors are in danger."

She could hear her mother crying out from the kitchen.

Michelle sat frozen on her bed. That was the Brandsons' address. What should she do? Her mother told her to stay put, but what was happening? Did the Brandsons need help? Why did her dad have a gun?

For several long minutes, there was an eerie silence. Deep in her soul, Michelle knew something was happening. She didn't know what to do. She drew her knees into her chest and waited, the sound of her breath her only comfort against the pounding in her ears.

There were sirens in the distance.

She heard a loud pop, like a firecracker or a quarter stick of dynamite, but not quite that loud. Mrs. Brandson screamed. Then another pop.

Her mother screeched, "No! No! No! Oh please God."

She jumped up and screamed. "What's happening?!!"

She ran to the top of the stairs and yelled for her mother. Her mother was screaming, crying. She ran down the stairs, headed for the kitchen. At the bottom, she was met by her sister Tracy. Tracy grabbed her, pulling her to sit on the second step with her. She held Michelle tight to her body. Michelle screamed, "What is it? What's happening?" She peered out the front picture window. She could make out the flashing blue and red lights of a police car and she saw dark figures moving around, but the sun had set. In the gloomy light of the evening, she couldn't make out what any of them were doing.

Tracy stood Michelle up. She spoke in a low tone, almost a whisper but with forceful direction. "We need to go upstairs. Mom will tell us when we can be out there. It's not safe right now."

"What's not safe?" bridled Michelle.

"I'm not sure. I know as much as you do. Come on, let's get upstairs."

The two girls dragged each other upstairs. Michelle could not feel any function in her legs, thinking if Tracy let go she would flop down the stairs. Once they reached the doorway of the bedroom, Michelle ran to her window. Darkness was quickly approaching. All sounds were muffled because of the location of her window, but she could see the Brandsons' home across the driveway. "Something's happening at the Brandsons!" she yelled.

"Stay away from the window!" Tracy shouted.

Michelle moved back to her bed, listening as hard as she could. The policemen were yelling. They were angry. She had to see what was going on. She ran back to the window, pushing the curtain back just enough to peer out. She plastered herself to the wall.

"Get back, Michelle!"

"I'm not in front of the window! I'm off to the side! I have to see. I have to see what's happening." She saw a figure run from the house to the backyard with several policemen behind him. They caught him and threw him to the ground. In just a few seconds, they had him handcuffed and they were dragging him to the front, putting him in the back of the police car. "That's Dad! They're arresting Dad!" Michelle turned to her sister. "Did he shoot the Brandsons?! I've got to go see the Brandsons!" She ran to the door.

Tracy caught her as she turned. "You're not going anywhere. It's not safe! Besides, they won't let you anywhere near there. You need to stay here. I'll stay with you. We need to let the policemen work."

"But the Brandsons! What if they're dead?!" She sobbed, wiping the tears streaming down her face with the sleeve of her shirt.

"We don't know that. Shot doesn't mean dead. Maybe he missed! We need to wait to see what happened. Take some deep breaths."

Michelle attempted to take deep breaths but could only come up with jagged grunts. She looked back out the window, despite Tracy trying to keep her away. Another car of officers were laying out crime scene tape as neighbors were beginning to congregate. She could see the yellow under the moonlight.

It was a picture she would never be able to get out of her head. She tried to close her eyes to erase the picture but she couldn't erase it. She collapsed onto the bed.

Tracy and Michelle were at home for several hours while their mother was at the police station giving a statement. She tried to make sense of what happened but could not. Lisa was at her friend's house for a sleepover, so Michelle had to face the demons of the night herself. At least Tracy was there and willing to sleep in Lisa's bed for the night so she wasn't totally alone. But she was such a sound sleeper. How could she sleep after what just happened? Where was mom? What was taking so long?

She climbed out of bed, still fully dressed from the evening, and sat down at the typewriter and scrolled in the piece of rose stationery..

Don't Touch Me.....

Chapter 16

D*on't Touch Me*

Michelle was almost glad to have the girls leaving in the morning for school. She loved spending time with them, but the day before had been very intense. By the time the morning rolled around, she was just ready for some quiet time to collect herself. Spring was approaching, and Mother Nature provided them with just a tease of what they had been dreaming of all winter...beautiful sunshine and temps in the 40's. Of course this is a temperature that would make other parts of the country cry, but in New York, 40's and sunshine was a welcome visitor. Michelle poured a cup of coffee and this time put it into a thermal mug, pulled down the shoebox from the closet and retrieved envelope number five. She wrapped herself in a thick quilt and walked outside to the front porch to sink into the wicker rocker. She rocked for a minute, then took a few big sips of hot coffee, and allowed it to warm her from the inside out. When she felt ready, Michelle opened the envelope and read the first letter.

Don't touch me. Not that way. Don't let your fingers creep along my side and pull across my stomach, pulling me closer to your body. Don't lay next to me in the bed and tell me that it is okay. Because I am confused. I'm uncomfortable. And I am too afraid to tell you so. I'm too afraid to tell you that your fingers are large and rough and hurt me when they move between my legs. And when they touch me in that place, it makes me sick to my stomach. I want to tell somebody but you kept saying not to, and now I don't know what is okay and what is not. All I know is, it doesn't feel okay. And all I can think is, don't touch me. I hold my breath, I close my eyes, but I can still feel you. Don't......

Michelle could hear and feel herself gasp for breath. She couldn't believe what she was reading! Her mother was molested! Sexually assaulted! She never would have thought this; Mom never divulged any clues to this that Michelle could remember. *Don't touch me....* Those words did ring familiar to Michelle, though. Maybe there were conversations, about the girls not letting anyone touch them. Maybe her mother did try to warn the girls by teaching this to them. Michelle could remember many nights when Shawn would crawl into the bed beside her and come close behind her and spoon to her body, placing his strong arm over her side. Michelle would close her eyes, stiffen her body momentarily, and think "Don't touch me". She always felt so guilty for thinking this since she trusted Shawn so implicitly. Where else would she have gotten these words?

She thought about her mother. Her own mother was a victim. She was sickened at the thought of it. She wondered if this was the reason for her emotional detachment in the later years when she seemed to be staring off into space on those few visits. Michelle had wondered if there were ghosts in the house; maybe they were demons of another kind. Memories that she could not get rid of that tortured her years later. Maybe with the kids gone and after Harry died, all she had was time to relive these memories, this pain. Oh, how Michelle wished that her mother would have shared this with her! She looked at the second letter. And this person knew about it, she thought. This person might have some knowledge as to who did this to her mother. Is this a friend? A clergy? A relative? Did our grandmother know about this? Is this person even alive now? Her feeling of anxiety increased as she contemplated these questions.

She took another sip of her coffee and opened the response letter.

First, my precious child of the universe, writing this out was the right thing to do! Never keep something like this bottled up inside. Being violated in this way will in no way define who you are or what you deserve. Know that in this moment, you are safe. I know that hurtful experiences can try to stay with you and haunt you, but the key to surviving this is to acknowledge that it happened, deny any thoughts of blaming yourself, and move forward knowing that you are not defined by what happens to you. You have been violated, which is never what anyone asks for or deserves. And never where you need to be stuck. You can move past the violation. You are safely enfolded in the arms of the universe at this very moment.

You do not have to go through this alone! When someone attempts to violate you, get as far away from that perpetrator as you can, and surround yourself with a safe zone. A trusted parent, sibling, friend, teacher, clergy, counselor. Talk to them. Do not be afraid. You are not the one who wronged. You are the one who WAS wronged. Tell yourself that this was not okay! Tell the world that this is not okay! Never be afraid to tell all who will listen. This is not okay! Stand tall and know that you are so much stronger than this. You are a warrior. You will conquer this enemy!

Know, in your heart, that you will go through your life being loved much more than you will be hurt. You need to keep your eyes open and your soul accepting of the love. You are not broken to the point that you cannot find the right love in your life. The universe cannot prevent people from hurting you, but it does give you the resources you need to move past it.

Michelle didn't even stop to think. She jumped out of the wicker chair, ran into the house and immediately grabbed for the phone book off the kitchen counter. "I have to tell Lisa," she thought. As she started to find the page with Lisa's number, she stopped. "No," she thought. "She won't meet with me again. I have to go talk to her in person." She was still in her morning, lounging clothes but that didn't matter. She picked up the letters from setting them on the kitchen counter, took one last big gulp of her coffee as if it gave her the confidence she needed, grabbed her purse and car keys and ran out the door.

Lisa lived on the other side of the small town. Her home was in a newer neighborhood, much more expensive and maintained than Michelle's old Colonial on the lower middle class side of town. "She must have done well selling that house in California" Michelle thought. She pulled into the driveway that was edged by a well manicured lawn without a weed to be seen. Walking up the sidewalk to the stained glass door, she felt queasy and her legs felt as if they were going to give out on her. She could feel her pulse racing. She rang the doorbell and stepped back when she heard the very large dog barking on the other side or the door. She could see the silhouette of Lisa's body inside pulling the dog back away from the door. Lisa opened the door and just looked at Michelle for a long moment, then broke the silence. "Really? Are we best friends now? Don't tell me. You're dropping in for a cup of coffee."

Michelle forced a smile. "Why, I would love a cup but only if you have some brewed. Don't go out of your way for me." She took a step toward the door. Lisa stepped back.

"Well then, make yourself at home. To what do I owe the pleasure?"

Michelle held up the two letters. "This. We need to talk! Something terrible happened and I need to know if you can help me figure this out." Michelle walked into the entranceway as the dog sat a few feet away, slowly growling. "But can you call the cannibal off first?"

Lisa turned toward the dog and nudged him to the basement door, "Come on, Prince, go downstairs for a few minutes. Good boy."

"Thank you," said Michelle.

The two looked at each other for a few moments. Michelle thought that Lisa looked just like she did in their younger years, still had maintained that very young appearance despite the many years that had brought challenges, marriage, divorce and remarriage, and children into her life. Michelle never felt that she faired as well; she figured having money helped Lisa to maintain her youthful appearance.

"Come into the kitchen," Lisa directed. She led Michelle to the kitchen and poured her a cup of coffee. The kitchen was not like her encounters with Lisa in recent years, few as they were. Whereas Lisa was usually uninviting and cold, this kitchen gave a feeling of warmth and welcoming. The padded chairs were not only comfortable to sit in, but were aesthetically pleasing with the colors of autumn.... The walls were pale orange with tan trim, slightly darker than the beige appliances, almost framing them. The backsplash had a pattern of pineapples in gold on a background that resembled wheat swaying in the field. It was homey, inviting. She thought, how opposite of the woman who actually lives this kitchen.

Michelle sat at the kitchen table. "Lisa, I am pretty sure that mom was a victim of sexual assault."

Lisa sat down across from Michelle. "What?"

"Sexual assault. This letter..." She opened it and gave it to Lisa. "...describes it."

Lisa took the first letter in her hand and read it quietly. She placed it down on the table. "Okay."

"Okay?" questioned Michelle. "Is that all you can say?"

Lisa shrugged her shoulders. "What else do you want me to say?"

"I want you to be upset. I want you to be incensed! I want you to not believe what you are reading! I want your hands to shake like mine did! Do you have any feelings at all?"

"Not about this I don't. Hey, don't get me wrong. If she was assaulted, that is a terrible thing. But it must have been many years ago, and she is dead now. What good does it do to dredge it all up? It's over; it's done."

Michelle grabbed the letter into her hand. "Well, not for me, this isn't done. I just have a need to know what happened to her."

"Well, that's pretty clear," Lisa stated. "Somebody touched her. She didn't like it."

Michelle took in a sharp breath and blew it out to try to keep control of her emotions. "That's a pretty insensitive response."

Lisa shook her head. "Not insensitive, but real. Look, Mickey, I left that house after my two years of college and never looked back. Mom and Harry were dead to me from then on. I'm just not interested in going on a wild goose chase to see why our mother was molested or who did it. Now, was there anything else you needed?"

Michelle took a sip of coffee and wrapped her hands around the warm cup. "Yes. I just need you to think back when we were living in the house. Do you remember anything she said to us about being touched? Any signs that would show that she had this experience? Any comments she made about anyone in her life that could have done this to her? "

Lisa just shook her head and then added, "I'm sorry. Nothing. I wiped out any memories a long time ago."

The two women sat in silence until Michelle took one more sip of her coffee and then stood up. "Okay, then. I guess this was a mistake. Sorry to have bothered you."

As she turned to leave, she noticed a picture of Lisa and Tracy and their kids on a cruise from the year before. She gently rubbed her hand over the frame. "Oh, yes, the infamous cruise when you invited everyone but my family."

Lisa just looked at her, and quietly waited for the next comment.

"Do you have any idea the pain you caused me? Being left out of a family trip for no good reason, feeling like an outcast?"

"Mickey, we have been over this. I wanted to spare you from having to admit that you didn't have the money for the cruise. "

"And that is supposed to make me feel better?"

Lisa shrugged. "I don't know what you want me to tell you. It was what it was."

"Well, it sucked." Michelle headed toward the stained glass door. "If anything comes to mind, please let me know. I just need to know."

Lisa gently nodded her head and closed the door behind Michelle.

Michelle still enjoyed tucking in the girls with a hug and a sweet reminder of how much she loved them. She believed the girls enjoyed it, too, even though the older two now rolled their eyes at her and said they were too big. It was their 'goodnights.' Jaimee had started calling it that when she was three. Janine had picked it up instantly, at the tender age of one, and it had stuck.

Tonight would be different. She needed to talk to them. Standing at the bottom of the stairs, she called up the girls. "Family meeting! Now! Please." She moved to her place in the living room, her signal to the girls that they needed to sit with her and listen.

Within a minute, it sounded like a herd of elephants bounding down the stairs, along with a rumbling vibration in the room of this aged house. It felt as if its bones were creaking with every step. Michelle smiled to herself despite the heavy feelings in her heart. The girls had so much energy. Separately, it was energizing but together it was like holding onto a live wire. Jaimee was the first to enter the room, leading the way for her sisters. She appeared so grown up, carrying herself as the confident woman she was growing into. Michelle could see already that Jaimee would be a great leader in whatever she chose to do. She had just returned from a vigorous dance practice and was still wearing her leotard, but her exhaustion was unnoticeable and her resolve palpable. She knew, as all the girls did, that Michelle did not utter the words 'family meeting' lightly. She strode to the couch across from Michelle's recliner and sat. She made a small but determinate scoot over when Jessie came bounding in and flopped onto the couch beside her.

Jaimee threw her arm around Jesse and rubbed her arms gently. "Come on, my princess girlfriend. Keep me company."

Jessie giggled. She snuggled into Jaimee's arms, curling herself into a ball of pink fleece. She, unlike her sisters, was already wearing her pajamas, complete with the image of a brunette princess bedecked with a sparkly fuschia crown. Her fluffy pink slippers completed the ensemble.

Janine was the last to enter, fashioned in a pair of white leggings with an oversized tie dyed sweatshirt. Her most recent mystery novel dangled from her hand. "What's up, Mom? I hope this is better than the book you're tearing me away from."

Michelle smirked and rolled her eyes. "Well, I'm glad you brought it along to fall back on in case I bore you to death."

"In which case, I would be dead and I wouldn't need the book anymore. But I can bequeath it to you." She plopped down on the floor cross-legged next to the coffee table and set her book in front of her.

Now that they were all assembled, Michelle felt nervous. Michelle cleared her throat. She needed to form the right words to begin this conversation. Just go for it, she thought. "So I need to ask you…" She paused, shifting her eyes from one girl to the next. Jaimee's face was serious; Janine raised both brows. Jessie pulled herself upright, swinging her legs over the edge of the couch.

Jaimee said, "Go ahead, Mom. It's okay."

Michelle took a deep breath. "Have any of you been touched by a boy, by a man, by a teacher, by anyone, that made you feel uncomfortable?"

The three girls exchanged glances. It was the kind of communication that only sisters fully understand. They could say more to each other with that one look than Michelle could in talking at them for half an hour.

Michelle loved that they had that. She hoped against hope they would never lose it. With a twinge of sadness in her heart, she remembered the days when she and her sisters had been that way with each other. She missed it. More than she cared to admit.

Jaimee gave a short squeeze to Jessie's shoulders. She uttered a short laugh. "Nooo."

"What kind of touching?" asked Janine.

"Well…" Michelle swallowed hard. This was hard to talk about. From the expressions on Janine's and Jaimee's faces, she could see they were worried. She held back a wince. She needed to say this, no matter how hard it was. "Maybe like…touching your back. Or giving you a back rub that you don't want or that feels uncomfortable. Touching between your legs."

Jessie cringed. "Oh, gross!" She pulled her body into Jaimee's comforting embrace.

Jaimee gave her another reassuring squeeze.

Michelle continued, talking fast to get the words out without thinking about them too much. "Pulling you uncomfortably close to their body. Touching your breast area. Kissing you when you don't want to. Telling you that you are sexy when it doesn't feel right."

Jaimee placed her hand up into the air like she was stopping traffic. "Moooom! Stop!! We GET it!" She adjusted her position on the couch, keeping Jessie in tow, who was happy to be along for the ride.

"Good. Okay. Well?" Michelle looked from one to the other, catching each of their eyes. She examined their faces, searching for any clue of discomfort with her words or recognition of her examples. She did not see anything although she sensed a bit of annoyance, which was probably with the idea that she would even broach such a subject. After all, they were growing into women, and this was not an unknown topic, at least to Janine and Jaimee. Still, it was not a topic they expected to come from their mother. And Jessie needed to hear it. Michelle knew Jessie was almost at the age when girls were likely to be targeted if they were not already. "Jessie? Janine? Jaimee?" She called each of their names, summoning them to an answer.

Jaimee looked down at her baby sister and gave her a soft nudge. "Jessie, how about you? Tell Mama."

Jessie just shook her head. "No, Mama. None of that."

Jaimee moved her eyes and locked them on Michelle. "Ditto. Nothing of the sort. But God help the person that tries."

Michelle couldn't help but grin at her headstrong and, frankly, scary daughter. She smiled, looking into Jaimee's eyes with adoration and respect.

"Good. I feel sorry for anyone who messes with you." She looked to Janine.

Janine straightened her legs and leaned back against the TV stand. "No, Mom, not here." She looked at Jaimee and smiled. "And I know the best body guard if I need one."

The girls leaned forward across the coffee table for a high five.

"Oh, yeah!" exclaimed Jaimee. As they sat back, Jaimee's eyes narrowed, her gaze returning to Michelle. "Why are you asking us this? We know what a pervert is."

Michelle held Jaimee's gaze without wavering. Her body felt so tight. She hated that word. Pervert. So violating. So invasive. The thought of someone like that touching her daughters made her sick to her stomach. And more than a little bit homicidal. Jaimee came by her pugnacious spirit honestly. She nodded her head. "I know you do."

Jaimee put her arms around Jessie again. "We are not going to let someone like that touch us."

"Exactly," Janine said.

"Yeah, right!" added Jessie.

"Just hear me out on this, okay? First of all, it doesn't need to be a pervert that touches you inappropriately. In fact, many times it is someone you know and trust. A friend. A teacher. A babysitter. Me or Dad even. We can't even touch you in that way."

Jessie squirmed a little under Jaimee's hold. "You and Dad would never do that."

Michelle stopped and gave a soft smile to Jessie.

"No, we would not. But you need to know that no one, not even a parent, can touch a child like that. That's just a rule in life and you need to know that. Not a parent, not anybody."

Jessie nodded her head.

"I just need you to know that it is NEVER okay for anyone to touch you or talk to you in a way that makes you uncomfortable. Second, if it happens to someone, it can never be their fault! You may never ever ever blame yourself, do you understand?"

The girls nodded their heads in unison.

"And third, you need to know that no matter what that person threatens you with to keep you quiet, you must always tell someone! No matter if it seems to you like it's no big deal, you need to say something to someone safe. Me, Dad, a trusted friend, a teacher, the police. It is the right thing to tell someone. It is the *only* thing to tell someone. Even if it means that person gets in trouble, even if you think that person is nice and just made a mistake. You *must* tell someone safe." She waited for a response. The bored look on Jaimee's and Janine's faces revealed that this was not news to them. "And fourth, you need to remember that you are always loved by myself and Dad, and there is nothing that you cannot tell us. Being touched in that way is a violation, and it is a crime. It is never okay. And we will always be here for you to help you."

The girls traded another of those telling glances.

"Hey, got that?"

"Yes!" The girls responded in unison, this time with a strong hint of boredom and irritation.

"Okay. Okay, good." She couldn't care less that they were bored or irritated. In her mind, that was a good sign. It meant they got it. Michelle could feel some of the tension draining from her body, tension she had not realized was there. She was so relieved she got through it. "Don't ever forget this!" Michelle stood up, signaling for the girls to get up to go to bed. "Okay, off with you. I'll be up for goodnights in a few minutes, little girlies."

Jaimee stood up and pulled Jessie behind her. "Mom, really? We're too old for tucking in."

"I know," Michelle said. She grabbed Jaimee in a gentle headlock. "Humor me."

Jaimee squealed. "Hey! Inappropriate, Mom!

Michelle laughed. "Ha ha ha." Leave it to Jaimee to turn the seriousness of their talk into a moment of levity. She let Jaimee go, but Jaimee did not let go of her. Jaimee threw her arms around her mom's in a big hug, resting her head on Michelle's shoulder. It still surprised Michelle that Jaimee was now the same height as her.

Jaimee whispered, "Don't worry, Mom. We're okay. Really. And I've always got my eyes on my sisters."

Tears sprang to Michelle's eyes. "I know you do. I'm counting on it." She reached out to reel Jessie into the hug. "I'll see you in a few, Miss Princess."

Jessie hugged her mom back. "Okay, love you, Mom."

"Love you, too."

Jaimie and Jessie headed up the stairs while Janine lagged behind. When the girls were upstairs, she plunked down on the couch.

Michelle longed for the day that the girls stopped bouncing on her furniture like a troop of baboons.

Janine folded her arms in front of her, turning her laser focus on Michelle. "Letter number 5, I take it?"

Michelle moved over to the couch and sat beside her. "Oh, it was a doozy!"

Janine raised her brows in anticipation. "Tell me."

"Well, the writer was apparently touched by someone. The letter began with, 'Don't Touch Me.' It never talks about who or when, but this was someone who was touched in private places."

"I kinda figured it was something like that."

"I feel like this was an earlier time than the other letters. The writer seems younger. Maybe the letters got out of order." She reached into her pocket and pulled out the letter. "Here, let me read this to you.

Janine cozied up to Michelle's side.

Michelle held the letter so she could see it, too. '*Don't touch me. Not that way. Don't let your fingers creep along my side and pull across my stomach, pulling me closer to your body. Don't lay next to me in the bed and tell me that it is okay. Because I am confused. I'm uncomfortable. And I am too afraid to tell you so. I'm too afraid to tell you that your fingers are large and rough and hurt me when they move between my legs. And when they touch me in that place, it makes me sick to my stomach. I want to tell somebody but you kept saying not to, and now I don't know what is okay and what is not. All I know is, it doesn't feel okay.*

And all I can think is, don't touch me. I hold my breath, I close my eyes, but I can still feel you. Don't......'" She got a catch in her throat. Tears came to her eyes. She looked at Janine. "Is this too hard for you?"

Janine sat silently for a moment, then shrugged her shoulders. "Mom, I'm 13. I read young adult books. The world is full of this."

Michelle sighed. Her girls were growing into knowledgeable, mature women. It made her proud and sad. It was a broken world, one she could not protect them from. She sniffled back the tears. "So you're not bothered by this?"

"Of course, I am bothered by this. This person is being molested. But I am putting it into context. This is Dorothy Doe. It's not personal."

Michelle wiped a tear from her eye. "What if this turns out to be Grandma?"

Janine bristled back as if to ward off a demon. "Oh. Nope. This isn't...Not going there. And you shouldn't either. This is a fictitious person right now. We can't let our emotions cloud the research."

Once again, Michelle was amazed at Janine's propensity for a logical approach to life.

The two sat in an uncomfortable silence.

Janine spoke first. "I assume the answer letter is pretty much what you shared with us tonight, right?"

"Yes, it was. I hope it wasn't too lame. But it meant alot to me to tell you all."

Janine nodded her head. "Then it was the right thing to do. I mean, it wasn't anything we didn't already know. We get this all the time in school. But it felt good to hear from you that you will always be on our side."

Michelle put her arm around Janine and hugged her tight. "Always."

"It was good. Thank you, Mom." Janine rose and headed for the stairs. "See you in a few for goodnights?"

"Yep. Be there shortly."

Michelle remained still, reviewing the girls' reactions in her mind. Had she been too heavy handed? Had she said enough that it would sink in? Had they been honest with her? It was impossible to know for sure. Her mind drifted to the past, the days when she and her sisters might have had the same talk with their mother. It was a talk that never happened. Perhaps her mother had been inhibited by generational expectations. Or was it too painful for her mom to talk about? She would never know.

She shook off her thoughts, rising quickly and heading to the closet where she had hidden the shoebox. She stopped in front of the closed door. She folded the letter along the original creases. Opening the door, she took down the box, gingerly tucking the letter into place and closing the top. She ran her fingers around the edges, whispering, "I love you, Mom."

Chapter 17

M ichelle straightened the rug. She couldn't help but smile each time she saw it: 'Leave reality at the door and enter the place of imagination.' It was Wednesday, art class day. Crossing the threshold into her art studio, she reviewed which youngsters would be in attendance. They were Jessie's age, between ten to twelve years old, in the midst of their transition from youth and adolescence. Many times Jessie would join them. It was an exciting time for them: they were beginning to express themselves more deeply through their creations. She scanned the room, making sure everything was ready. In view were a myriad of materials–paints, dried flowers, buttons, and ribbons. The canvases, easels, and art stools stood ready.

It was still morning, but after school this room would be abuzz with children's energy and innocence. She loved seeing what they could create with the medium of the day. Sometimes Jaimee would stop in and be the "teacher's assistant" if there was no dance rehearsal after school.

The sound of the bus's engine interrupted her thoughts. Michelle reentered the kitchen, announcing loudly, "One block away, let's get a move on!"

The kitchen bustled with energy as the girls scrambled around each other, grabbing their lunches and backpacks.

"Jessie, I'll see you after school for art class?"

"Yup, see you then, Mom!"

Michelle smiled and gave her littlest rugrat a gentle hug, and whispered in her ear, "I might serve peanut butter and jelly sandwiches."

Jessie giggled. "Oh, yay! My favorite!"

The rumble of the engine grew louder, announcing its impending arrival.

"Jaimee, any chance you could join us today to assist me with the little urchins?"

Jaimee groaned. "I'd love to, but I do have a stupid report I have to write after school. 'What would be my Favorite Summer Vacation?'. And you know perfection takes time in the white collar world."

Michelle reached over and placed her hand on Jaimee's arm. "How about you come help me in the art class and then take a little less time with the report? It might not be absolutely perfect, but it will be darn close to perfect, and maybe that's good enough."

Jaimee took a double take at her mother.

"Still good, mind you!! But not everything needs to be perfect. You do need some other experiences in your life as well."

Jaimee stepped back, looking bewildered. "Who are you and what did you do with my mother?"

Michelle felt a tinge of excitement. It had been a long time since she had exchanged this kind of playful banter with Jaimee. It grinned mysteriously. "Wouldn't you like to know? Just don't look in the freezer. And my meat cleaver is missing..." She stroked her chin with a sinister gesture.

Jaimee said, "Good God, Mother." She shook her head and headed for the side door. "Jessie! Standing beside me now, please."

Jessie ran to Jaimee's side, her backpack slung across one shoulder, pulling her to one side from the weight of her books.

"Put that on both shoulders," Jaimee said.

Jessie scowled, struggling to comply.

Jaimee tried to help, but her own backpack inhibited her efforts.

Michelle reached over and placed the second strap around Jessie's flailing arm. She then turned to Janine. "What's on the calendar for today, girl?"

Janine grabbed her lunch in her hands and stuffed it into her backpack. "Track after school, and then Marissa wants to come over for dinner. Is that okay? Her mom can give us a ride here from track practice."

"Sure, that's fine. Make sure it's right home after track. You are still grounded, you know."

Janine rolled her eyes. "Oh, yes, I know."

"I hope she likes peanut butter and jelly!" She turned and winked at Jessie.

Janine looked mortally offended. "We are NOT having PB&J for dinner!"

Jessie giggled.

Michelle gave Janine a mock salute. "Yes, ma'am."

Jessie saluted. "All hail!"

Janine rolled her eyes at Jessie.

Jaimee whispered to Janine, "Maybe her brother will be at track practice. He is sooo cute!"

The girls snickered.

"Hey!" Michelle chimed in, "I heard that! Remember our conversation last night. If that boy tries to kiss you, you know what to do."

Janine cupped her hand beside Jaimee's ear. "Not if I try to kiss him first!"

Michelle bellowed, "Oh, Lawd, girl! You are so audacious! You'll be lucky if I don't enclose you in a bubble until your 21st birthday!"

The bus driver honked at the end of the driveway.

"Go! Go! Go!" Michelle shooed them out the door. "Come on, off to school before I have a stroke listening to you."

As the screen door closed, Jaimee taunted Janine while Jessie ran to keep up. "Don't count on me getting you out of that bubble."

"No bubble is going to hold me."

"Yeah, right. You're not infallible. I killed you in a swordfight last week, remember?"

"You cheated!"

"How did I cheat?"

"I blinked my eyes! You can't stab someone when their eyes are closed!"

"Where in the rulebook does it state....."

Their voices became fainter until they disappeared into the bus.

Michelle sat at the kitchen table, looking at the spotlessly clean kitchen, the results of her morning efforts. It wasn't often that she deep cleaned the kitchen, but today felt like a good day for it. Now she waited for Shawn to come home, knowing it should be any minute. She had a fresh pot of coffee brewing, waiting to welcome him home. He loved to have a cup when he got home, even though he would go to bed shortly afterward. She could never understand how he could do that–it would keep her up for hours. When she heard the large rumble that signaled the end of the brewing process, she got up and poured herself a cup. As if it were calling to him, Shawn came through the door at that moment. He asked, "Do I smell fresh coffee? Is that for me?"

"Michelle smiled. "Hi, yourself!" She looked at the cup in her hands. "Sure! But first, you owe me."

"I owe you?! What do I owe you, my love?"

She set down the cup, walked over to Shawn and melted into his arms like she did every morning, taking in a deep breath of his sweet but peppery scent. It transported her to a time and place that made her feel so comforted, so safe. "A kiss." She pointed to her cheek. "Right here."

"Just there?" He brushed her cheek with his hand. "How about here." He kissed her lips.

"You old dog." She still felt giddy whenever he kissed her. "Okay, you earned it." Michelle handed him the cup, returning to the counter to pour herself a second cup. She grabbed the plate of Danish she had set aside and placed them in front of him.

Shawn sat at the table. "Oh, thank you!"

"Absolutely." Always such a gentleman, she thought. And, a gentle man.

Shawn took a large bite of a cherry danish. "Mmmm my favorite," he muttered. He washed it down with a large slurp of coffee. Powdered sugar hung on his lips.

"You're so elegant, my dear. It's a wonder I don't take you out into public more often."

Shawn stuffed the whole rest of the danish in his mouth and smiled defiantly. After chomping on it a few times with cheeks filled out like a chipmunk, he picked up a napkin and gracefully dabbed the corners of his mouth.

She laughed and sat beside him.

He leaned back and caught her eye. "So, we haven't talked much in a few days."

"Yeah. It's been a whirlwind."

"You were having quite the serious conversation with our daughters last night as I was getting ready for work. Anything about that you want to share with me?"

Michelle took a sip of coffee. "You know those letters I have been reading from my mother's jewelry box?"

"Sure," said Shawn. "You've been pretty bothered by them. I haven't asked you about them. I knew you'd share with me when it was time."

Michelle nodded her head. "And thank you for giving me that space. This last letter...it has been the hardest for me."

He brought his arm forward and took her hand in his. "In what way?"

"I think my mother was abused."

Shawn held her hand tighter. "What? Abused? In what way?"

"The letter is short. But she was touched by someone. Inappropriately. Between her legs. In private areas." Michelle shook her head as if to dispel the image. "She was confused. She wanted to tell someone but didn't know who to tell." Michelle withdrew her hand from his and buried her face in her hands. She could feel the tightening beginning again in her body, just as she felt last night when talking to the girls. Tears fell unbidden from her eyes. "Oh, my gosh, I just feel so helpless. Frozen. Detached. I just don't know what to do. I know there's nothing I can do at this point, but could I have helped her at any time with these memories when she was alive? Could I have been there for her more often? Had a closer relationship with her so she might talk to me about these things?"

Shawn got up and put his arms around Michelle. "Now, you know the answer to that, honey. You can't blame yourself for something that happened many years ago, probably before you were born, and back then women just didn't talk about being abused. There is nothing you could have done. I'm so sorry."

His warmth and sweet scent nearly deafened her to his gentle words. She began to sob. Shawn held her in his arms until she was spent.

Her heart ached even though the tears had stopped. "None of this makes sense."

He sat back down. "What do you mean?"

"There's more," Michelle continued. Her body tightened as she forced the words out. "I went to see Lisa."

"Oh?"

"I thought she may have remembered something, anything, that might give a clue as to what happened to mom. She was there in the house through her first two years of college."

Shawn gave that long, slow nod that he did when he expected bad news. He was not wrong. It was never good news when it came to Lisa. She was sure he remembered each and every time over the years when she had struggled to repair her relationship with her sister, then agonizing when her efforts came up empty. It was as if they had fallen into a dark hole that they could never escape. Shawn had had a front row seat as the sisters grew further apart, their relationship slipping into an impassable chasm.

Shawn spoke, pulling her out of her reverie. "And what did she have to offer?"

Michelle sighed. "As you can guess, nothing. She was very insensitive. Kept saying our family has been dead to her for years and she wants nothing to do with it."

"I'm sorry, Michelle." He sighed. His hands raised up in a surrendering gesture. "Well, that sounds just like her."

Michelle looked at Shawn and reached out for his hand. "The thing is, I feel like Lisa is hiding something."

"I wouldn't be surprised."

They sat in silence for a few minutes. Michelle felt numb yet her thoughts tumbled over one another. One thought kept rising to the surface. She tried to suppress it, as she had for so long, but this time it would not be silenced. She had to tell him. "Can I just say something?"

Shawn gave his hand to Michelle, laying his other hand over hers. "Anything, honey."

"We have never really talked about this, but you know that I sometimes pull away or stiffen up when you first come to me at night."

Shawn's brow furrowed. "It's no big–"

"I know, I know. That's not the point." She swallowed hard. Talking about areas of romance never came easy for her. Especially when it involved being touched. Her hand,, enfolded in his, was beginning to feel clammy. "It's just that…I hope you know that it has never been because of you that I do this. I don't know why I do, at least I never thought I knew, but now I think that Mom must have talked to us growing up even though I don't remember it, or maybe she pulled away from Harry in the kitchen when he hugged her, or ……well, I don't know but I must have gotten this somehow through Mom."

Shawn grinned. "Oh, I thought it was because we have so few nights together, you had to stop and figure out if it was your husband or your boyfriend crawling into bed with you."

Michelle cackled as she pulled her sweaty hand back to her body. "Oh, Lawd! Well, that too!" She leaned into him as they laughed. She stopped suddenly, pausing to look into Shawn's eyes. She could feel a buzzing energy in his gaze that she never wanted to let go. "Please know that I trust you implicitly. I love you to the moon and back. Always."

"I have always known that. And ditto."

Staring into his eyes, and holding his gaze in return, enfolded her in a love that was pure, completely secure, and infinite.

Even the best moments must end. Michelle sighed, breaking their shared gaze. "And so I wanted to teach our girls what could happen to them and that they would not be to blame and that they need to tell someone."

Shawn leaned back in his chair. "I get it. It's a good time to talk to them about sexual assault. They need to know how to respond. And speaking of which, you do know you can always tell me no at any time, right?"

"I would never dream of telling you no. I don't get enough of you as it is!"

Shawn beamed.

The pleasure on his face made her smile. "But yes, I do know. Thank you."

Shawn grabbed his danish and stood. He picked up his cup of coffee, leaned in and kissed Michelle on the forehead. "Thank you for sharing this with me. Thank you for loving me. And thank you for being an amazing mother to our three girls. Now if you want, you may join me upstairs, and if you beat me to the top I may share this danish with you." He taunted her by holding the danish under her nose and then pulling it away.

Michelle smiled, watching Shawn head up the stairs to the bedroom.

<h1 style="text-align:center">Chapter 18</h1>

Help Me Escape

The old colonial home with its large windows drank in rays of the afternoon sun. Michelle felt the warmth of the sun soak into her body, as if the glass from the windows magnified the heat, making her clothes stick against her skin. She grabbed her shirt and flapped it against herself to get some air flow. Walking over to the front bay window in the living room, she cranked open the side to let in the cooling breeze. The fresh air felt so good.

Art class would begin in a few hours. She needed to get ready, but at this moment all she could think about was reading another letter. It seemed like it was getting harder and harder to wait for the next one as each one seemed to deepen the anticipation. What joys or sorrows awaited her, she did not know. All she did know was she had to keep going. She walked through the kitchen and into the hallway. The closet was looming in front of her like a mysterious crypt daring her to step beyond the threshold. What was it guarding? Demons? Secrets? Treasures? She took a deep breath and pulled the door open slowly, burying the rising emotions. She pulled down the shoebox and took out envelope number six. Staring at the envelope, she made her way to the art table. She slid into her chair, unfolded the letter, and began to read:

Please help me escape from this suffering, this sadness, this fear that I live by. My chest is so heavy; it weighs me down so much that some days I can't even get out of bed. It feels like something underneath my body is holding me down, keeping me from being able to get up. What is there to get up for, anyways? Not happiness. Not success. Not life as other people know it. The words of Carly Simon's song just go around and around in my head....

"Suffering was the only thing that made me feel I was alive....thought that's just how much it cost to survive in this world..."

Is this my destiny? How can I escape this feeling that I am locked into? Do I deserve to be happy after allowing the terrible things that have happened to me? If only for a moment, I dream of escaping to a place of love, of being wanted, of feeling whole, no longer a fragmented, broken soul. Where does this place exist?

Michelle closed her eyes against the anguish in those words. They were so hard to read. To know that her mother was in so much pain. The letters were getting harder and harder to read. She wished she had never found them.

Suddenly, she wanted to run away from all of this. She felt the raw emotions of the author as if they were her own. A weakness overcame her, worse than any of those days where she laid in bed with the blinds closed, unable to get up.

Her reaction confused her. Why was it so strong, just from reading a letter that wasn't even hers?

It was a familiar feeling. On those days it was as if she was chained to the bed. Several months passed when she barely saw the light of day. Shawn was her savior, switching to the day shift for several months so he could take care of the girls. Then one day Jessie came in and laid beside her after school, curled against her body. The older girls followed suit. The warmth of their small bodies, their soft breath on her skin, awoke her to the overpowering need to care for them, to be there for them. In the end, no matter how great Shawn was, the girls needed their mom.

Yes, she had been there. She had even missed her brother-in-law's funeral. She looked back at the letter. She could hear the Carly Simon song in her mind. Lisa and she used to sing those words over and over.

Wait a second, she thought. What year did this song come out? She jumped up and rushed to her computer, turning it on. She logged in and looked up "Carly Simon – Haven't Got Time for the Pain."

The answer: 1974.

"What?" she said.

1974? How was that possible? This letter had to have been written during the time when she and Lisa were still living in the house, years after any assault may have happened to Mom. The song wasn't even in Mom's era. "I don't know," Michelle said, continuing to talk to herself aloud. "She must have been listening from the stairway."

What else could it be?

To think her mom's depression lasted that long, so many years of trying to escape the inner pain that was, at its core, inescapable. Michelle swallowed what felt like a large knot in her throat. She knew how long depression could last.

She breathed in long and slow, expelling it in a single rush of air. She pulled out the response letter and began to read.

Suffering is never a destiny. Some experiences make you suffer, yes. These experiences are part of the journey of your life. But you are the conductor of this train. You decide where suffering stops and living your best life begins. This is where a good counselor can be instrumental. You cannot move past the suffering until you see it for what it is. You can't run from something until you know what you are running from. You need to stop blaming yourself for what has happened to you. You need to identify where it is you want to be in your life and lay a plan to infuse your world with the things or the people that can take you there. That is where you will find escape.

What brings a smile to you, even if but for a moment? What brings joy into your life? Think about your interests and what might give you an outlet for your emotions. Consider who in your world you could talk to. Perhaps most importantly, how do you express yourself? Through writing...art...song...physical activity? Sometimes it is good to distract yourself from these thoughts of sadness.

Other times, it is good to focus on what you are grateful for. You might try journaling or meditation. Pray to the Universe to bring you strength. The Universe brings you so many resources to grab ahold of and bring positivity into your life. Spread that positivity with others and it will flow back to you, surrounding you with that which you have shared. You need only look within your soul to find the escape you desire.

The words washed over her, taking her back to the months after Jessie's birth. A weight settled on her heart once again, sinking into her limbs, as the memories engulfed her. Her shoulders slumped. Too heavy to lift, her body became a prison. She could barely breathe.

She quickly drew her shoulders back and straightened her spine. She shook her head in frustration, speaking aloud. "Why is this affecting me so much? This makes no sense."

As she pulled herself back from whatever edge she had just encountered, she recalled her counseling visits that had helped her deal with the irrational fears that had plagued her as long as she could remember. A vision of Shawn's concerned frown flashed before her. For hours, he listened to her cry at the kitchen table, sometimes continuing on into the bedroom so the girls would not hear her. He would get up at the end, when she was too exhausted to move, to get the girls ready to sleep. She would listen from her bed, his quiet voice and their little chirps washing over her. Fortunately, there were many times she was able to dig up the strength to enjoy the girls. Their energy and unconditional love were lifelines that pulled her to safety.

And her art. Her family was the source of her love and support, both given and received, but her art was her passion and her purpose. It is what gave her hope that her life had meaning beyond the everyday. In the end, it was what drove her to pursue the vision of starting her art education business.

She looked down, surprised to see that the letter was still in her hands. It occurred to her that the person who had written the response had felt the anguish of the author, too, and had written to help her. The response author had most certainly thought that her impact ended there. Yet that was only where it had begun. Already, the letters and their responses had touched Michelle and Janine, and by extension Jamie, Jessie and even Shawn. And who knows how many others there had been in the past, or would be in the future?

Her thoughts gave her a sense of clarity that she had never experienced. There was purpose in art, in any type of creation. She could see that her purpose had been born out of her pain, out of the very events that she had tried so hard to avoid and forget. Yet without that purpose, without the struggles even, she would not have had the courage to teach. She would have missed the innocent joy in the faces of the young children in her class as they showed her their art pieces each week. She would have never experienced the hope and promise of knowing that her students could grow into adults who also shared their gifts, healing those who came across their path, building a legacy from Michelle's simple work larger than anything she could have imagined.

The heaviness began to lift, inspiring Michelle to do the one thing she loved to do, especially during stressful times. She rose from her chair, setting the letter aside. Her eyes fell on the open door to her studio. She knew exactly what she wanted to paint. She walked to her art table, pulled out a fresh canvas, and chose a few of her favorite colors and brushes, allowing her heart and soul to guide her hands as her vision took shape on the blank canvas.

"Wow, look at that! Is this your new painting, Miss Michelle? This is cool!" Tommy reached out and touched the canvas. He pulled his finger away, raising a brow at the blue paint on his fingertip. "It's still wet!"

Michelle gently pulled him away with one hand, smiling and shaking her head, using the other hand to take up a brush and smooth out his fingermark. "Yes, it's still wet. Let's leave it for the moment, until it dries." She could barely keep from laughing even as she tried to sound firm. His enthusiasm was infectious, more than making up for the times that it led to spilled paint and other little disasters. She stuck the paintbrush in a newly prepared jar of water and led him to his seat.

He continued to chatter. "Have you been working on this all day? What is it called?"

Tommy's questions tumbled over one another. Michelle doubted he even took a breath between them. Tommy was one of Michelle's favorites. He was a freckle-faced young man with sandy brown hair swept to the side. It was never long enough to stay there, so it continually fell into his face. Time after time, he pushed it out of the way, always with the boyish grin that almost never left his face. Today his thin frame swam in his baggy brown pants and a red and white striped shirt. Michelle gulped back another chuckle. He was a vision straight out of a 'Where's Waldo scene.'

With a whirl of energy, more children began to fill the room, just in time for their weekly art class. Jaimee arrived right behind them, setting her backpack on one of the wicker chairs. "Hi Mom!"

"Hi! Good day?" Michelle came up and gave her a quick hug.

Jaimee squeezed her in return. It seemed there was an extra measure of affection in the hug which Michelle did not understand but soaked in. Perhaps it was the talk they had had last night. In any case, it was like salve in a wound. "Yeah, pretty good." Her eyes landed on the painting. It was an abstract painting, her favorite style, as Mr Brandsen had taught her, helped to give definition to the fragmented pictures in her mind. The background consisted of dark colors and thick stripes, some curving from corner to corner. Lighter strokes seemed to lessen the heaviness of the layers below them, shading them with a sense of light. Three yellow lines interconnected in the middle of the canvas, and a thick blue border seemed to give the edges the definition they needed to be a cohesive image. Spattered about the canvas were multi colored dots of various sizes. "Wow, that's deep. There's a lot of emotion in there. Are you okay, Mom?"

Michelle smiled. "Better than when I started!"

Jaimee half smiled and half frowned. It was a look Michelle had seen on Shawn's face more times than she could count. "You look like your father."

Jessie poked her head out from behind Jaimee. "Hi, mom, I'm here! And Jaimee looks like dad?" She laughed out loud. "That's funny because dad is so ugly!"

Jaimee sneered at Jessie. She turned toward Michelle. "Dad?! He's bald!! Mom, that's not a compliment."

"Of course it is! I don't mean his hair! Your expressions, your kindness, your beautiful smile, and those long eyelashes that are absolutely stunning."

Jaimee rolled her eyes and laughed. "I know, it's fine. You're so funny, Mom."

Jaimee and Michelle corralled the children to their places at the large art table, helping them into their smocks. The room bustled with youthful voices and movement.

Michelle moved in front of her new painting and clapped her hands to get the kids' attention. "Time to get started!"

The children turned to Michelle, their faces beaming. They squirmed in their seats, barely able to contain their excitement.

"Tommy asked me a really good question. He noticed, and I'll bet some of you did, too, that there is a new painting here. I just did this today."

Carol blurted, "You did all of that today?!"

"Yes, I did! I was very busy. It still has some finishing touches to go, but I'm happy with where it is going. Tommy, you asked what it is named. I call it The Great Escape."

Tommy furrowed his brow. "Escape from what?"

"Well, that's what we are going to talk about." Michelle moved to the front of the class. "Today we are going to do something a little different. Usually I pick out one medium and we all work with that material to create our art piece. Today, I have an instruction for you and each of you can choose whatever tool and technique you want to use to fulfill that instruction."

The buzzing began again as the kids murmured to each other.

"Like I can use the small tiles if I want?" asked Becky.

"Yes, you can."

Tommy jumped in. "Pencil sketching?"

"Yes, pencil sketching if you want."

"Watercolor?" asked Jessie, bouncing up and down in her seat.

"Yes, yes, any medium you want. There are so many ways to express yourself. There is oil, watercolor, tiles, clay, words, symbols....the possibilities are endless."

"Wow!"

"Cool!"

The kids chattered excitedly, their eyes moving around the room at the examples that Michelle had set out for them.

"But, remember, I said there is an instruction. This is not a free-for-all. I need your attention. Right here, look at my eyes." She pointed to her eyes with her fingers.

The children knew that was their cue to look at Michelle and quiet down.

"Everyone got my eyes? What color are they?"

"Brown!" the kids yelled out.

"Okay, so you are going to create an image with two important parts. You are going to need to think about this for a bit before you get started. And don't worry if you run short on time because we will continue this next week." She pointed to her painting. "First, you are going to create your own "Great Escape." So before you even begin, I want you to think of one thing that frightens you, something that you sometimes wish to escape from. There may be more than one thing. Like spiders and bees. It can even be something that makes you sad or something that gives you an uncomfortable feeling. Now, I just want you to think about this inside your head. Don't discuss it with your neighbor yet. Quietly think of something right now..."

She stopped for a minute to watch the expressions on their faces. At first, they looked around the room, but then one by one they settled down. Some of them looked at the ceiling, others at their hands. Good, she thought, that's what I wanted. "Your representation of that thing that you want to escape from is the first important part of the project. Now for the second part I want you to think about this: if you could escape from it, what would that safe place look like, feel like? That is what you are going to show in the second half of the project."

She checked their expressions to see if they were following her. They looked confused. Yup, lost them, she thought. "Here's some examples. Say you want to escape from a swarm of bees buzzing toward you. Where would you escape to?"

"I'd run into the house!!" cried Jessie.

"Okay, absolutely, so you could draw a picture of bees, and then maybe you running into the house. Let's do a second example. Say something makes you sad. You don't feel loved. There are times when everyone doesn't feel totally loved, by the way. It's quite normal. How could you escape that feeling?"

The kids just looked at each other.

"Well, what could make you feel better?"

Tommy answered, "If someone showed me that they loved me."

"Yes! If what makes you sad is not feeling loved, then you would escape to a place where you feel love. What makes you feel loved?"

Carol squealed, "A big hug!"

"Yes! Very good. What else?" After a moment of silence, she added, "Does anyone have a pet?"

"Yes!" shouted several of the kids at once.

"I have a dog!"

"My dog is Rusty!"

"Mine is Daisy!"

"I have two cats!"

"My cat died last month."

"I have a cat too. A black one. Her name is Blackie."

"That's bad luck."

"No, it's not. That's just silly superstition."

Michelle snickered and motioned with her hands to grab their attention back. "Okay, okay, back here. Let's have one conversation."

The chatter turned to a low murmur and disappeared as the kids returned their attention to Michelle.

"A pet loves you no matter what, doesn't it?"

The kids all nodded their heads.

"I had a dog growing up and he was my place of love whenever I needed him. So you could draw your pet. You could just write the word LOVE. Words are art, too. What else would be a symbol of love?"

"A heart?" asked Carol.

"Yes, a heart, so you may only need to draw a heart with whatever represents not feeling loved to you."

"Maybe a teardrop?" Becky suggested.

"Exactly! That would definitely work."

Tommy asked, "What are your two parts? You only have one painting."

Michelle smiled. "Great question!" She turned toward her painting. I have put both steps on the same canvas, and you can do that too." She turned to the painting and pointed to the layers. "See the underlayers where I have many dark strokes, thick and heavily layered? That represents the place I want to escape from. Like when I feel sad about something. I call it my dark place. Then you see lighter strokes over this and some designs and curves and brighter colors. These represent the things in my life that help me escape my dark days. These three lines here, for example, are my three girls, the sunshine of my life." She cocked her head, glancing over at Jaimee and then Jessie.

Jessie smiled proudly. "I am sunshine!"

Jaimee smirked Jessie. "Well, since I came first, I am the whole sun. You and Janine are probably just my rays."

Jessie scowled and stuck her tongue out at Jaimee.

"Rays are important, too."

Michelle cleared her throat. "This one blue border is my husband Shawn, who keeps our lives secure. These little dots are all my wonderful art students who bring me joy every Wednesday!"

Carol pointed to one of the dots. "There's me!"

Michelle smiled. "So you see, it only needs to speak to you. It can be very private. You only let people see what you want them to see, or to know what you want them to know. And they might even see something in your art that speaks to them, totally different than what you had in mind to begin with. That's one of my favorite things about art. So, part one: think of something that makes you want to escape. Part two: where or what would help you escape (or where do you escape to)? Got it?"

"Yes!" shouted the kids, jumping in their seats.

"Okay, go to it! If you need assistance, Jaimee or myself are here to help you and give ideas."

Bobby sprung out of his seat. "Yes! Hey, but when is snack time?"

"We'll have snacks in 45 minutes. There will be juice boxes and peanut butter and jelly sandwiches on the table to feed your growing brains!"

As the kids scrambled to gather their favorite art medium, Jaimee looked at her mother. Nodding her head, she said, "Okay, this is pretty cool."

Michelle answered, "Feel free to make one yourself!"

Midway through the art class, Tommy seemed to be in deep thought. Michelle looked at his drawing. "How is it going, Tommy?" He was shading in the figure of a small boy sitting at the top of the stairs in the house with his pencil. There were two people at the bottom of the stairs. One was huge, towering over the other with snaggle teeth and a wide open mouth. The other was much smaller, barely coming up to the knees of the first, and had slumped shoulders. She sat down next to him. "That's a great drawing of a boy. Great features, the body is very well proportioned. You paid attention in that class!"

Tommy looked up at Michelle and then back at the picture. "Thanks."

"Hmm...he looks sad."

He nodded.

Michelle prodded gently. "Do you know why he is so sad?"

Tommy pointed to the two figures at the bottom of the stairs.

"Mom and Dad?"

"Yes."

I know that can be a fearful place, when Mom and Dad have an argument."

Tommy kept his gaze on his drawing. "Not so much an argument. Mostly just Dad yelling at Mom."

Michelle nodded her head. "Oh, I see. That can be even harder, when someone else is sad and you don't know how to help them."

Tommy sniffed. "I get scared sometimes."

Michelle felt a heaviness in her heart. She had been scared, too, when she thought of her own mother's sadness and loneliness. Writing letters to no one in particular, because she had no one to talk to. She wished she could have been there for her.

"I'm sure you do. So, what could make you feel less scared?"

"Well, if my dad stopped yelling and my mom didn't cry so much, I would feel better. Once the crying stops, my body doesn't feel so tight and my stomach settles down."

Michelle leaned in a little closer to Tommy. "That's extra hard. We can't control what other people do, but we can make decisions about how we will react."

"Dad stops after a while and goes away. I don't know where he goes. But Mom keeps crying."

"What helps your mom feel better?"

Tommy looked up at Michelle. "She goes into her room and turns on the TV and watches movies."

"What makes you feel better?"

Tommy shrugged. "Pretty much the same thing. I go into my room and play Nintendo or watch TV."

"So you kind of do the same thing!"

"I guess so." He looked down, deep in thought.

"When your mom finds her safe place, do you ever go into the bedroom and sit with her while she watches her movie?"

"No, when I hear the crying stop I go away."

"Well, you know what? Maybe you sharing your safe space will help both of you feel even better."

Tommy looked up and smiled at Michelle. "I like it! I will try that!"

"So, how could you draw that safe place?"

Tommy thought for a moment. "Mama on the bed watching TV and me next to her."

"Excellent!" proclaimed Michelle. "Go to it!" She walked away, but the conversation stayed stayed with her. She wondered what she could do to help Margaret. Michelle had spent years wishing someone would throw her a lifeline, a girlfriend she could talk to as only women can. Even now she needed a friend, maybe someone to replace that sisterly connection she once felt but had lost over the years. Shawn and the girls were great sources of love and strength, but sometimes she just needed a woman to talk to. Someone who could hear all her thoughts and words–not just the half that she was able to speak articulately, but also the rest of them that were stuck inside her broken heart. They stumble out in half sentences and tears. The safe arms of a loving friend could smooth out the frayed edges of everyday life. Maybe Margaret needed that friendship as well.

As the parents arrived to pick up the children, Michelle instructed everyone to place their art projects in the drying room so they would be ready to finish next week. Michelle watched the door for Tommy's mom to arrive. She knew she had to reach out to her. As if on cue, Tommy's mom walked through the door. She welcomed her as she did every week, but she was nervous this time. Would she want to be friends? Her heart started to race. "Hi, Margaret! How are you?" She winced inwardly at the cracking in her voice.

Margaret did not seem to notice. She was younger than Michelle by about five or six years. Tommy was her one and only. She was slim and put together, a perfect size four, just like Michelle's stepsister Amy. Michelle felt a little self conscious, trying to suck in her stomach a little and pull her shoulders back. Margaret was dressed professionally with straight leg dress slacks, a tailored top in a lighter shade to match, a sporty blazer and two-inch black heels. She could have been any businessperson, except for one thing: an artisan necklace, perhaps that she bought at an art show, hung around her neck. Michelle searched for matching earrings, but she wore only simple gold hoops.

"Hi, Michelle, I'm fine, thanks. How did class go today?"

"Excellent. Tommy has a really good artistic eye."

Margaret's face lit up. "Oh, that's so great!" Tommy ran up and threw his arms around her. She looked down at Tommy. "Miss Michelle says you have a good artistic eye!"

Tommy smiled. "She says I'm getting better every week! I have to say goodbye to everyone. I'll be right back!"

Margaret tousled Tommy's hair before he ran off to talk to his friends. "I loved art when I was Tommy's age. I'm so glad you do this for the kids. Thank you so much."

"I love it. It is the highlight of my week. I would venture to guess that you still love art." She pointed at Margaret's necklace. "Your necklace is exquisite. Is this jasper?"

Margaret reached up and touched her necklace, lightly rubbing it. "Yes, it's been a staple piece of mine. It stands for strength, protection and grounding." She smiled bravely. "It helps me face the day."

"Well, it's beautiful. I can see where Tommy gets his artistic eye from. Does it have earrings as well?"

"It did, at one point. Then when we moved a few years ago, one of the earrings got lost. I was devastated. This is one of a kind jewelry so it isn't easily replaced. But I'm always watching for a set of earrings that will match."

"Yes, I'll bet. I'll keep my eyes open as well. I do work with a lot of unique artists.

"Thank you. I appreciate that."

Michelle nodded. "In the meantime, I have a question for you."

"Sure, what?"

"So we were talking about the things that make us feel good and Tommy mentioned that you love to watch movies. Have you been to that drive-in theater down by the lake?"

"No, can't say that we have. I do love movies, mostly romantic comedies, all kinds except anything violent or too sexual." She giggled nervously. "I guess I'm a bit of a prude."

Michelle chuckled. "That makes two of us! We took the girls down there one night to see some kids movies and it was great fun. But I always thought I'd like to go back to watch an adult movie – PG-13 of course! It's just not Shawn's thing. Would you like to go with me some night?" Margaret's face lit up. "Oh, would I! Yes, anytime! But I would insist on paying admission, since you give so much of yourself to our kids for nothing."

"Oh believe me, I get much more than money out of this class. No one owes me a thing! I should be paying you for the chance to teach them. These kids infuse my soul with energy and love."

"I can see that, but I would love to treat you."

Michelle smiled. "Okay, you can pay but I will bring the Kleenex and the popcorn! I'll call you when I see something playing that we might both like."

Margaret nodded. "Okay, it's a date. Thank you for asking."

Michelle added, "Sure, and if Tommy wants to come spend the evening with Jessie we can make it a night that Shawn is here to watch the kids. They can have their own movie night."

"Sounds good! Thank you!"

Tommy appeared at her side, pulling her toward the door. "C'mon Mom, I've got Karate tonight!"

"Don't you want to show me your art today?"

"Mom, it's not ready! I'll show you next week."

"Oh, okay." She turned to Michelle, giggling. "I guess we need to go."

Michelle chuckled, too, as Tommy ushered his mom out the door.

The room that had been abuzz with the gathering of supplies and parents picking up their little artists a few moments ago was suddenly quiet.

As Jaimee, Jessie, and she finished cleaning up the art table, Janine walked in the door with her friend Marissa. "Hi Mom, we're home! What's for dinner?"

Michelle smiled, "Leftover peanut butter and jelly sandwiches."

Janine and Marissa groaned.

Michelle laughed. "Just kidding!"

Chapter 20

Later that night, Michelle laid in bed, her mind whirling. For once, her thoughts were positive. It seemed like she had been smiling all evening, contemplating all the things that she was grateful for. Shawn, her rock...her three beautiful girls, who kept her moving and shaking, her students, her art. For the first time in a long time, she was grateful for her sisters, for the years that she had with her sister Tracy, and even for her memories with Lisa. She knew without a doubt that she owed this new outlook to the letters, to the emotional challenges they had brought and to the healing they had ushered in. It still pained her to know what her mother had gone through, but it had opened her heart to her mom in new ways. She felt like she knew her just that much more. She was becoming a better mother, a better wife, a better friend, maybe even a better artist.

The peace of sleep began to wash over her like a gentle ocean wave. Her eyelids fluttered. "Universe," she mumbled, "I don't know who or what you are, but thank you for being there for my mom, for me, for all of us who are stuck in this constant cycle of disparity. For giving me the ability to feel again. I feel like I'm in sync again, like I can own my life. I have more confidence in who I am. Thank–"

"Mom!"

Startled, Michelle shot up to a seated position. "What?! What happened?! Janine, why aren't you in bed?" Michelle turned her head to find Janine standing beside her bed, arms crossed, her face in a scowl. Michelle recognized that look. Janine was on the warpath.

"Mom, this ridiculous grounding needs to end! There is a very important dance at school Friday night and nobody can understand why I can't go! Please! I have to go to this dance! This is so unfair!"

Jaimee appeared right behind her. "Oh, no you don't! You always get away with everything, Miss Middle Child! You were grounded for a reason. I have had to do my penance before. I never got a break! YOU need to do the same!"

Adrenaline coursed through Michelle's body. Whatever peace she had been feeling was gone. "Jaimee, it is not your place to decide what Janine's penance should be. Second, you have not been Little Miss Perfect on following your punishments either. You have begged for–and received–plenty of reprieves."

Jaimee glared. "Name one."

Michelle ignored that. "And third, no, Janine. You are grounded for one more week. You will have to miss the dance. We talked about how important it was to follow the consequences we set out."

Janine made her hands into fists, pushed them into her hips and stamped her feet. "But Mom!!!" She turned to look at Jaimee and then back to Michelle. She closed her eyes for a few seconds and took a deep breath then lowered her voice, using a calm even tone. "We have been getting along so well…you know….with the letters and all….and I feel like I have really grown through them. I understand what I did wrong and I hope you know you can trust me more."

Michelle couldn't help but be impressed by Janine's increased presence of mind and self-control. Should she relent? Oh boy, she thought. Where's Shawn when I need him?

Out of the corner of her eye, Michelle saw Jessie shuffle into the room. Michelle inwardly rolled her eyes. The room suddenly seemed very small and claustrophobic. She took a breath to speak. She did not get a chance.

Jaimee grabbed Jessie's hand and pulled her in front of Janine, pushing Janine aside. "And what about these 'letters?' Do you not think that Jessie and I are on to your little private meetings and letter reading? What are these letters about? Why are we being left out?"

Jessie stomped one foot in her place. "Yeah! Why are we being left out?"

Janine pushed Jaimee and Jessie out of the way. "That's none of your business! This is between me and Mom!"

Michelle's mouth went dry. "Hold on, here," she croaked. "Let's calm down so we can talk and not yell at each other."

Jaimee continued. "Talk about trust! Do you not trust us enough to share whatever these letters are?"

Michelle cleared her throat, grabbing water from her bedside table. She held up one finger for silence while she drank. The girls knew the signal and waited, however impatiently. She replaced the water glass and continued. "Jaimee, this has nothing to do with not trusting you. These are my private letters. Janine happened to find me reading one and became interested. It's kind of a mystery and you know Janine likes mysteries. And, wait a minute..." She twisted her body to face Janine. "Why is this dance so important? I thought you didn't like the school dances."

Jaimee piped up. "Because it's a Sadie Hawkins and she wants to ask Jimmy to dance!"

Jessie threw her arms around her torso and moved about the room like she was dancing.

Jaimee giggled. "And maybe get in that kiss she's been dreaming of!" She puckered her lips and kissed into the air.

Janine's eyes narrowed further, which Michelle had not thought possible. "At least I know a boy who will dance with me. Unlike you, ugly duckling."

Jaimee stuck her tongue out at her sister and blew a raspberry.

Janine yelled, "Ew, gross! You spit on me!"

Jessie chimed in with a raspberry of her own.

"Stop ganging up on me!" Janine turned toward Jaimee, pulling back a fist.

Michelle jumped in. "Okay, enough of this! You will absolutely not continue this!" She turned to Janine. "Who is this Jimmy boy we are talking about?'

Janine smiled. Her voice became gentle. "Marissa's brother. He runs track and I see him on the field sometimes." She bent her knee and sat on the bed next to Michelle and began to plead. "Please, Mom, I need this one favor. Please.. please.. please?"

Jaimee interrupted the pleading. "Why are you addressing Janine first again?! See? You're favoring her!"

"Yeah!" Jessie chimed in.

Jaimee continued. "I want to know about these letters! I demand to know why we have been left out! Are they about us? What makes Janine so special that she gets to share them with you? We all like mysteries!"

Jessie added, "Yeah, I like mysteries too!"

Janine sneered at Jaimee. "You wouldn't understand these letters. You have to have compassion. You have to be a deep thinker. They're way beyond you."

Jaimee cocked her head. "Oh, yeah, and you think you do?"

Jessie pressed against Michelle's legs, peering at Janine. "Yeah, you think you do?"

Michelle shook her legs to get Jessie and Janine off. "Okay, STOP! All of you. Just STOP! You are all being ridiculous! I will not hear another word of this!"

The girls stood up and faced Michelle. "Now we have got some issues going on here and all of this is not gonna be resolved tonight. First of all, Janine, Dad and I will talk in the morning about the dance. I know it's the day after tomorrow and there isn't much time, but you could have given us a little more time to think about this. Dad, you and I will talk about this together after school tomorrow. Second, I love each one of you girls equally, and I share some interests individually with each of you. Jaimee, you know I sneak into the gym just to watch your dance rehearsals. You were so mortified when I first did that but now the girls think it is so cool, right?"

Jaimee rolled her eyes. "Yeah, so cool, Mom..."

Michelle continued. "It's weird, I know, but I hope that is a memory you will always share with me. Jessie, are we not always cooking up something special together in the kitchen, just you and me?"

Jessie nodded her head, smiling.

"That's all this was. Janine found me reading the letters and took an interest in them and yes, we have been sharing them." She looked at Janine. "Janine, I think it's time to share with your sisters what these letters are about. Especially now that I am learning how they have helped me. Us. I think we can all learn something special from them. Do you agree that it's time? It has helped you and me so much, maybe it would be good for us all."

Janine looked down and then up at her mom. "I guess."

Michelle reached over and put her hand on Janine's shoulder and gave it a gentle nudge. "Thank you for sharing." She straightened her body on the bed. "Now, are we all good?"

The girls nodded in unison.

"No more fighting?"

The girls glanced at each other.

Jaimee spoke first. "I mean, maybe for tonight, but I'm going to promise anything about tomorrow."

"Yeah, no kidding," Janine said.

It was Michelle's turn to roll her eyes. "Okay, yes, for tonight."

The girls nodded.

Michelle sighed. "Great. All big and little rugrats need to be in bed right now, and give me the night to gather my thoughts. Jaimee and Jessie, I'll figure out the best way to get you caught up. We will share. Sharing is good." She spoke the words as if she were trying to convince herself. The truth was she was not at all certain of how the other two girls would react to the letters. Was Jessie even old enough for the content? She would have to trust the universe in this.

Jaimee gathered up the troops as was always her place as the oldest child. "Okay, let's go back to bed. It's too late to do anything now. Jessie, you have Science Lab tomorrow and that big classroom volcano. You need your sleep."

Jessie followed in line with Jaimee. "Yup, I do. C'mon, Janine." She reached out for Janine's hand and pulled her in line with them. Janine looked back at her mom as they walked toward the door. "Please talk to Dad…"

"I will. I promise."

As the door shut behind them, Michelle sat on her bed, stunned. What was that? It certainly was not the peaceful slumber she had been anticipating. She took a deep breath and flopped onto the pillow, praying sleep would return.

Chapter 21

M ichelle stared at the ceiling. She resisted the urge to glance at the clock. She wondered if she and her sisters had done this to her mother–assailing her with their arguments right before bed, leaving Mom with adrenaline pumping while they returned to sleep. A flicker of grief and guilt flooded her. She had never bothered to take the time to understand what her mom might be going through. Now, she had her own daughters that did the same thing and probably never thought a minute about the effect they had on her. Part of her resented that, but if she was honest she wouldn't have it any other way. She would rather lose sleep than have them sleepless and wracked with anxiety. Her mom had probably been the same. Yet it was worse for her mom, handling everything on her own. Her stepdad was a good father, but he was always working. Michelle thanked the universe every day that she had Shawn.

She needed to talk to Shawn in the morning. Her mind whirled with ways the conversation might go. Should they let her go to the dance? Yes, she had been developing a closer relationship with Janine, and she might even go as far as to say that she was developing some more trust in her. But, on the other hand, a consequence is a consequence. By letting her off of her grounding early, would it totally disregard the lesson she was supposed to be learning? Would she go on to live a life of breaking the rules, disrespecting the law, ending up in jail, ruining her life? She knew what Shawn would say. "Don't catastrophize." Lately, that seemed to be his favorite word.

Michelle sighed and turned over on her side. The older the girls got, the more difficult it was to parent them. The stakes got higher and higher. Or was that catastrophizing, too?

And images of the letters kept floating in her mind. How do I introduce the letters to Jaimee and Jessie? Do we go back to the beginning and re-read each one? Do I create an outline of the subject matters and the beautiful answers? How would they take it? Was Jessie too young? But she couldn't leave her out.

She felt so overwhelmed. She shoved the thoughts from her mind. If she was going to get any sleep at all, she had to stop. She began to purposefully relax her body. She relaxed a foot, then the other, a leg, then the other, working her way up. She could feel it working, but she had to do something with her disobedient mind. She imagined painting, being in her happy place, her studio, paintbrush in hand. She used her favorite color...the subject began to take form. It was Michelle at her daughters' age. The paintbrush flowed over the walls, and the orange and red flowers emerged. She was in her high school bedroom. The paintbrush continued. Someone else was with her. It was Lisa, sitting on the floor, leaning against her bed, facing Michelle.

Her eyes flicked behind her lids. She was in her room. The paintbrush was gone...

Michelle was growing angrier by the minute. "STOP. Just STOP, Lisa!"

Lisa picked up the stuffed elephant from the floor and threw it at Michelle. "No, I won't stop. And I wish you would do something with this damn elephant! It ends up on my side of the room every night! I hate it!"

Michelle raised her hand in the air and caught the elephant, bringing it close to her chest. "If you hate Ella, you hate me."

Lisa rolled her eyes. "You are the primadonna in this house. You always have to be center stage. You get all the attention. You get the best clothes, your needs always come first with Mom...and with Tracy. You won't have it any other way—you want Tracy all to yourself and you think Mom loves you more. Well, let me tell you, she rolls her eyes when you walk away. She thinks you're ridiculous. You drain her. She can't wait for you to go off to college. You whine, whine, whine until you get your way. It's exhausting."

Michelle felt as if she would burst. This is how every day seemed to unfold lately. Her younger sister, always jealous of her, always wanting something more than Michelle had to give. As if Michelle had stolen something from her and she wanted it back. Well, she had nothing to give her. In fact, she needed her. It was just one favor, but Lisa went ballistic, as usual. She could barely keep her own wits about her. "You know what? The only person draining the energy around here is you. You're just a little shit. My life is more complicated because I've lived longer than you."

"*Really? Okay, big sister, next time you call on me to chase the ghosts away in the night, remember that you are the one who has lived longer. You should be protecting me, not the other way around. And by the way, if you move downstairs, who is going to chase your ghosts away?*"

"*I don't ask you to chase any ghosts. I can't help it if I get scared. I have to deal with demons in my life that you can't even imagine. You wouldn't understand. I don't even understand them. But don't worry, I will never again ask you to check the hallway with me.*"

Lisa climbed onto Michelle's bed, catching her gaze and holding it. "I have demons too, Mickey. And nobody is there for me."

Michelle looked away and stared down at her elephant. She hoped the elephant would tell her what to say. After a few uncomfortable moments, Michelle knew what she had to do. Her chin quivered. "Okay, just forget it. You can have Tracy's room. I wish she had never moved out so it wouldn't be an issue. It's just that, well, it's what I saw out this window...I can't get it out of my head. It haunts me. I thought a new setting would help."

Lisa grabbed Michelle's hand, demanding her attention. "Listen, you have to let that go. It was years ago, and you hardly knew them."

Michelle could feel her body tighten up. Every muscle in her body began to burn. She pulled her hand away. "No, YOU hardly knew them. Mr. and Mrs. Branson were a wonderful couple. Mr. Branson taught me so much about art." She blinked a few times, fighting back the tears. "And about life. You could have known that if you weren't always at everybody's houses but ours having sleepovers. Running away from God knows what. And now they're dead. And our father...being arrested like that. You have no idea what I saw." A sob threatened to escape. She stifled it. "Now he is in prison forever. And Mom won't talk about it and I don't think I will ever know what happened."

Lisa softened her voice a little. "Look, we may never know. Hey, I may be younger here but I know you can't let it consume you. You have to go on living. For them."

Michelle felt weak and let her body fall backwards on the bed. She held Ella tight to her chest. She rolled onto her side away from Lisa, away from the world.

Lisa stood up. "If it means that much to you, take the room. I'll get it when you graduate next year. Then we'll both get our turn. She turned to walk out of the room, heading down the hallway towards the stairs. "I'm going to get a soda. Do you want one?"

"*No, it's okay." Michelle answered in a weak voice.*

Lisa walked to the door. "I'll bring you one anyway."

"Lisa?"

Lisa glanced back. "Yeah?"

"Thanks."

"Yeah."

She heard the door gently close. Her whole body felt weak. Suddenly she was immersed in the sounds of that day…gunshots. Two distinct sounds. Bang! Bang! Somewhere, her mother was yelling. Crying. In the distance, sirens. She ran to the window. The police were approaching the Bransons' door with guns drawn. There was knocking at the door and words spoken. Her father bursting out the side door, heading for the backyard. Glass breaking. His shirt splotched with bright red. The officers tackling him before he could scale the fence. Handcuffing him on the grass, dragging him to the car.

Michelle pressed her hands against her eyes, fighting back the tears. "I've got to get away from these memories." She rolled her body up and off the bed. She went to her desk and pulled out her familiar rose stationery and began to type.

Michelle's eyes flew open, whipping her head around to look at the walls. No flowers. She blinked a few times. The sound of typing faded with the present moment. She was sweating and shaking. Thankfully, she could feel the cool early morning air on her arms. What was that? A dream? It felt like…more than a dream. She pushed the thought away.

She looked at the clock at her bedside. 6am. She stretched to loosen her tense muscles as best she could. Pulling the covers back, she lugged her body to the edge of the bed. "Okay, Michelle, let's go. Time to face the piper."

The smell of bacon filled the air, replacing Michelle's anxious thoughts with happy anticipation. Like Shawn would say, "When life gives you lemons, toss them in the trash and make some bacon."

She wanted this morning's breakfast to be special. Her famous baked eggs and bacon graced the table. It was their favorite–English muffins and cheese mixed with scrambled eggs and baked to a golden brown. She waited for the girls, sitting sideways at the kitchen table, bobbing her right leg up and down as it crossed over the left. On the table beside her was a shoebox. And next to that was a small bouquet of dandelions, fresh picked from the front yard. She held another small box in her hands, holding three pieces of paper.

She heard the girls tumble down the stairs like a herd of elephants. Jessie arrived in the doorway first. "Bacon!!!" She screamed at the top of her lungs.

Michelle winced.

Janine was right behind her. "Geez, Jess. It's a little early for that volume."

"I concur," Michelle said, holding back a chuckle.

"Can't a woman be happy about her bacon??"

Jaimee scoffed. "Woman? LOL."

Jessie glared at her. "I am just as much a woman as you!"

"All right!" Michelle interrupted. "C'mon, just sit down and eat. It's your favorite!"

"What is this?" asked Janine. "Mom, it's not Saturday. This is our Saturday tradition." Janine's eyes were glued to the box in the center of the table.

Michelle shifted in her chair, swallowing a lump in her throat. "Well, today we break tradition," she said, her voice a bit higher pitched than usual. She cleared her throat, hoping it would help her speak more evenly. "Today, we have baked eggs and bacon on a schoolday!"

Jessie picked up a piece of bacon and savored the succulent meat. "I'm not going to argue. Bacon's my favorite. I could eat bacon with anything, or just as a meal by itself."

Jaimee chimed in. "And the occasion is?..."

Michelle hesitated a few seconds to watch the other two girls grab bacon off the plate and flop down in their chairs. She pushed the shoebox to the center of the table. "The occasion is, wiping the slate. Opening the gateway to forgiveness and letting your mama grovel a little to apologize for being non-inclusive. The occasion is, the end of secrets. The occasion is, the first day of experiencing a journey that I found totally by accident, that Janine stumbled upon, and that neither of us knew would be a pathway to discovery and growth. And we are ready to share this journey with you."

She looked at Janine, who stared at her with furrowed brow. Michelle studied her face for clues to what she was feeling. She saw ambivalence, maybe a little betrayal and yet a bit of relief, even anticipation for what was to come. "I am ready, and I'd like Janine and I to guide you through this journey." She smiled and grabbed Janine's hand, giving it a squeeze. "Janine, are you ready?"

Janine shrugged and glanced at the box. "Well, we couldn't keep it a secret forever."

She set the small box before them. "This whole letter thing wasn't about secrets anyway. I stumbled onto an unknown. All I did was open my mother's jewelry box. There was a hidden compartment, and the letters were inside."

Jessie's eyes widened. "Whoa, a hidden compartment?"

Jaimee nudged her forcefully in the shoulder. "Shhhh. Let her talk."

"Yes. I had no idea what it could be about. Before bringing it to the world, I needed to know what it was. It could have been hurtful. As a matter of fact, when Janine happened upon me with the first letter, I was crying. Now I know more. This journey has been soulful. It has been sad. And inspiring. For you, we'll see what it will be...maybe it can be whatever you need it to be. And we're not done. And it is getting more intense." Michelle took her small box of three papers and handed each girl a blank piece of paper and a pencil. "Write your name please on this piece of paper, and put it in the box."

The girls picked up the pencils and held their papers in their hands. "Why are we doing this?"

"Just do it. It's a door prize drawing."

The girls glanced at each other, shrugged in anticipation, and started writing their names on the papers.

"I know from last night's impromptu meeting in the wee hours of the night that the two of you want to know what's in the letters, but I want you to realize that it is a journey. It may bring up things you don't expect in your own soul. So do you still want to jump into this journey with Janine and me?"

Jessie looked up at Jaimee, as she always did for direction. Jaimee smiled at Jessie, raised her hand and brushed Jessie's hair back with her long, gentle fingers. She smiled and nodded her head at Jessie. Jaimee answered first. "Yes."

Jessie looked back at Michelle with enthusiasm. "Yes!"

Michelle held the small box out and the girls put their pieces of paper in it.

"Great. Okay, who wants to pick the name of the door prize winner?" Jessie raised her hand. "I do!"

Michelle shook the box gently in her hand and held the box up above Jessie's head. Jessie closed her eyes tight and pulled out a piece of paper. She handed it to Michelle.

Michelle clasped the paper in between her hands, held her hands in a fist, pumping them into the air like they held the heir to a million dollars. She opened her hand. "Drum roll..."

The girls pounded their hands on the table.

She shouted the name with exhilaration. "And the winner is.....Jaimee!"

Jaimee raised her arms in triumph. "Yay!"

"Awww!" squealed the other girls.

"What's my prize?"

Michelle moved the dandelion bouquet in front of Jaimee.

Jaimee crumpled her forehead and gave a confused glance at her mother. "Really? Dandelions?"

Janine's face lit up like the sun as she smiled from ear to ear. "Dandelions! You're lucky!" She exchanged a smile with Michelle. "This is a reminder of the beautiful person we are within. If you don't want them, I'll take them."

Michelle felt a quickening in her heart. It was a good feeling. Janine remembered. She remembered about the dandelion and the meaning of this so-called weed.

Jaimee looked at her sister and rolled her eyes as she shook her head. "Yeah, whatever. Make a note, Mom. We obviously need more weedkiller."

"Janine, would you like to share with your sisters the lesson we learned about the dandelion?"

Janine smiled. "Sure! We all think of the dandelion as an annoying weed. What you don't know is that the dandelion is one of the highest forms of beauty in the world." She picked one of the dandelions out of the vase and gently caressed the yellow bloom of the flower, displaying it to her sisters. "Each flower head of the dandelion is actually a collection of thousands of small ray flowers. As the head of a dandelion flower opens, each yellow tubular spike reveals itself as a separate flower. Like snowflakes, each is a unique creation of the universe." She pulled out one of the many tiny tubular spikes on the flower head. "You see?"

Jessie took in a sharp breath as Janine pulled out the small spike. "That's a flower?" Jessie leaned in, peering more closely at the details of the little blossom.

"Yes. The simple dandelion holds so much more complexity than most flowers. If you are a dandelion, then that means the universe created you full of beauty and complexity. You are not just one being; you are many beautiful beings."

Jaimee shot a sly smile to her sister. "Like having multiple personalities?"

"Well, maybe in your case. But for most people, no, not like that. The simple dandelion is a reminder that the universe made you as a symphony of so many beautiful qualities that are uniquely yours. Nobody is as unique as you."

Jessie folded her hands in front of her. She seemed to drink up every word that Janine was saying. "Wow, that's really beautiful."

Jaimee shrugged. "Yeah, I guess. Is this what these letters are about? Dandelions? Flowers?" She looked to Michelle for an answer.

Michelle nodded. "It is, and so much more. Okay, so finish up your breakfast. The bus will be here soon. Tonight the unveiling of the shoebox letters begins."

While girls turned to their breakfasts, Michelle grabbed her coffee cup and returned to the counter, pouring a fresh cup. A flurry of emotions surged through her. Her skin tingled. In one way, she was excited to begin this journey with Jaimee and Jessie, anticipating how it might affect them. She hoped they would grow individually, and perhaps closer to each other. Her heart begged for a better future for her girls than she had experienced with her sisters. Yet, in another way, she didn't relish revisiting those first letters and the emotions they had dredged up. She had been relieved to put each letter to rest. To bring them out again seemed like a daunting task. It was sure to reopen some of the feelings she had hoped to rebury. In retrospect, repressing them again probably was not one of her best ideas.

She sipped her coffee, staring out the kitchen window, the soft sounds of the girls filtering in behind her. She sighed. There was so much to be excited about. And so much to fear.

The squeaky brakes on the bus broke her reverie. "Okay, up and attem'!" She set her cup down and turned toward the girls. They had already launched themselves from their seats and were nearly to the door. "Lunches are in your backpacks. Love you, love you. Tonight we shall reconvene the dandelion convention."

The girls shuffled into line, wiggling into their backpacks. "Bye mom! Love you too!"

Michelle gave a quick side hug to Jaimee and Jessie as they headed out the door.

Janine stopped short. She looked at Michelle. "Mom, you are going to talk to Dad this morning? About the dance?"

Michelle nodded. "This morning, yes."

"Please, Mom! This is my only chance for this dance! I may never have another moment like this! And I've learned my lesson. Pleeeaase!"

"I'll talk to your dad! That's all I can promise. I love you!"

Janine threw a pleading glance toward Michelle and followed her sisters out the door. "I love you, too. Byeee."

The cool morning breeze was a welcome sensation on her skin as Shawn came through the open kitchen door. She shivered as his soft kiss landed on her cheek. "Good morning Sunshine!"

Michelle felt a flutter in her heart as she felt him leaning over her. "Good morning." She smiled tightly. So much to do this day that she wasn't expecting. Talk to Shawn about Janine. Pull out the letters. Read through them again. Figure out how to introduce them to the girls. How to keep moving forward without changing the dynamic, the feeling that she and Janine had. Would the introduction of the other girls change the connection that she and Janine had developed?

"Big day ahead? You look like you were in deep thought."

"Oh, yes I was. And I am about to lay it all on you! You'll probably wish you had stayed at work. Grab some coffee, dear, and come sit." She patted the chair next to her.

Shawn stepped back and looked at Michelle, seeming to be studying her face, her body language. He turned to grab some coffee. "Oh, boy, why do I feel like I am in trouble?"

Michelle laughed. "If it were that simple! I could whip you into shape a lot faster than today's challenges."

Shawn came back to the table, sat down with his favorite mug and took a sip of coffee. "Okay, lay it on me."

Michelle stretched her arms and brought her hands back to the table and clasped them in front of her. "First, Janine." "Rebel child. What did she do this time?"

"Nothing. Yet. Actually, I was really impressed with her this morning. But that's the second thing, not the first."

Shawn rolled his eyes. "Oh, boy."

"There's a dance at school tomorrow night. It's a Sadie Hawkins dance."

"A who dance?"

"Sadie Hawkins. C'mon. You remember. When girls get to ask the guys to dance. Janine likes this boy named Jimmy."

Shawn slapped his hand on the table. "Lemme at him!"

Michelle laughed. It was a deep belly laugh. It felt good, especially with what she had been going through. "You can't keep her in a bubble forever!"

"I can try!"

Michelle put her hand over his. "We want her to experience everything life has to offer, and that includes love."

"Maybe when she's 30."

Michelle sighed. "It's a lucky guy to have our beautiful daughter ask him to dance. I'll bet there are many more hoping to be in his shoes. But we have one problem. Janine is grounded for another week."

"That sounds more like a solution than a problem."

"Shawn, she's so upset. She wants more than anything to go to this dance. And Jaimee is all over it, as you can imagine, giving her such a hard time. I have such ambivalent feelings about it. On one hand, a consequence is a consequence. A rule is a rule."

Shawn nodded. "Rules are not meant to be broken."

Michelle continued. "But on the other hand, social relationships are very important to Janine and not feeling included is what got her into trouble in the first place. And is going to the dance really going to turn her into a mass murderer?"

"A mass murderer? What did I miss?"

"Just my mind going off on tangents, like what if we let her go and she gets the idea that she can get away with bad behavior. If we let Janine go to the dance, how do we justify it to Jaimee? And will Janine ever take us seriously again? I don't want this to set a precedent with the other girls when they get into trouble and get grounded that they'll get out of it. And I don't know why we decided on grounding anyways. It's just too hard to enforce."

Shawn reached over to Michelle's shoulder and laid his hand over her as if to stop her from taking off on a brisk run. "Hold on there! This is your specialty, getting all wound up with what if's. Let's just roll it back a bit."

Michelle took a deep breath. She felt the tension drain from her body with his touch.

Shawn said, "First of all, it doesn't matter what Jaimee thinks. She does not tell us how to parent. What we decide on Janine is none of her business and if she doesn't like it, she will just have to live with it. I feel like Janine has taken this grounding thing very seriously and she has been very compliant so far. The other girls will likely have punishments in the future as they are all headstrong young women who like to push the limits. But the punishment needs to fit each and every separate misbehavior so we shouldn't even try to compare this to something we have no idea of in the future."

Michelle said, "Shoot, did someone steal my crystal ball? I thought motherhood came with the ability to see the future, so we can be the perfect parent now and in the future. I missed that article in the parenting magazines."

"One crime at a time, my love. Sometimes I feel like punishments seem to punish the parents more than the child. We came up with this grounding because that's what Ms.Witzell recommended, and she is the expert. Supposedly."

"Yeah, who made her an expert at parenting? I don't even think she has kids."

"Well, education, I suppose. So, my gut is to let her go, but what do you think?"

Michelle shrugged. "Truthfully? I'm her mother and would love her to have the chance to dance with a boy and feel beautiful." She looked down at her hands in front of her. "But.."

"But what?"

She looked up at Shawn. "Well, you know. We are her parents and it's our job to keep her on the straight and narrow path."

Shawn nodded in acknowledgement. "True, but...I'm not telling you what you should think here. I do have an initial opinion, but it's not written in stone, and we always come up with the best plan together. Is keeping her from going to a dance going to really keep her on the straight and narrow path? Is that something we do in one decision or something we try to do every day with her? And you two have really made a connection lately. Do you want to sever that connection?"

Michelle cracked a smile. "Well that brings me to why I was impressed with her this morning. She remembered the dandelion."

Shawn looked puzzled. "Okay, confused again."

Michelle laughed as she pulled the dandelion vase towards Shawn. "These dandelions. There was an important analogy we read in one of the letters, about the dandelion and the beauty of human beings. It was about how each one of these rays is a separate flower which makes this one of the most complex flowers in the universe, and how we are made the same way. So sometimes, when we feel like a simple weed, we are actually beautifully complex."

Shawn leaned back, rolling his chair on its back two legs. "Wow, that's cool."

"You're going to break the chair." Michelle tapped him on the arm. "So, yes, overall, there is so much growth I see. But, that doesn't negate the fact that a consequence is a consequence."

Shawn smiled as he brought his chair back to the floor. "Yes, and missing one consequence could be a mass murderer in the making." He brought his hand up to his chin, stroking it absent-mindedly and gazing up toward the ceiling. "So let's consider this..." He brought his glance back down to Michelle. "How about a tiny detour? She goes to the dance for two hours, and we pick her up early and bring her home. She still feels the burn of not being there all night, but she can have some time to ask this young man to dance. And the grounding continues as is when she arrives home."

Michelle nodded. "So we meet her halfway." Michelle slapped the table like an auctioneer. "Sold!" She jumped up and kissed him. "This is why I keep you around."

Shawn smiled. "Okay, so one crisis solved! Now, what else? Wait, do I need to refill these coffees?"

"Oh, right. There's more. I kind of forgot there for a minute." She filled their cups at the coffee pot before returning to her chair beside Shawn.

Shawn spoke. "Okay, what's next?"

Michelle reached forward and grabbed the shoebox from the other side of the table. "These."

"The letters?"

"Yes. You missed a doozy last night! I was startled out of a nearly sound sleep by all three girls arguing! First Janine, begging to let her go to the dance tomorrow night, and then joined by Jaimee and Jessie, demanding to know why they have not been included in the reading of the letters! Oh, it was fun."

Shawn laughed. "I wish I had been there! But I can't say I didn't see this coming. You can't pull the wool over these sheeps' eyes."

"Believe me, I wish you had been there too! To share the misery. Jaimee pretty much accused me of not trusting her and Jessie, and deliberately keeping them from the letters. And of course Jessie follows suit with anything Jaimee declares. Then the girls nearly got into a knock-down-drag-out fight before I stopped them. What a way to be awakened from a peaceful sleep."

"I'm sure. So, what did you tell them?"

"Well, I bought some time by saying we would talk about it this morning. Then my adrenaline was racing, so as you can imagine I didn't get much sleep."

"I'm sorry, honey. I wish I was there to help you deal with that."

Michelle rested her head on his shoulder. "You have to work. Kids tend to hit their moms with stuff like this anyway. It is what it is. So, this morning I was here waiting for them with the letters, and with these dandelions. I told them we would start looking at the letters after school today, and I had a "door prize" drawing with the prize being these dandelions. Jaimee won the door prize and as you can imagine, was not very impressed."

Shawn glanced at the dandelions. "Yeah, not very impressive if you don't know the meaning behind them."

Michelle picked up one of the dandelions. "No, but then Janine jumped right in and explained why the dandelion is one of the most complex flowers in the universe, and I about burst open with pride!"

"And then Jaimee was impressed?"Ha ha no, of course not. But it was a great segway into the letters. Now I just have to figure out how to introduce them. That's my challenge for the day. Do I have us read through them one at a time together? Do I make an outline of what the letters covered? Do I leave the girls to read them and then talk about them after? I just don't know..."

Shawn gently rubbed Michelle's shoulder. "So, you do realize that this may not have a positive outcome?"

Michelle pulled away from Shawn's hand. "What do you mean?"

Shawn shrugged. "Well, let's face it. You kept a secret from Jaimee and Jessie and shared these letters exclusively with Janine. You experienced some of the confusion and anger the girls had last night, but that may be the tip of the iceberg. I wouldn't be surprised if they are feeling betrayed."

Michelle could feel the heat rising in her body. She felt flush. Bile rose into her throat. She could feel the difference in her voice as she tried to choke the words out. "You know I would never betray my own daughters. I am the one who was betrayed by my sisters, leaving me alone to face this world without them. For no good reason. I wouldn't do anything to make my girls face that."

Shawn shook his head. "And yet here you are. You've been keeping a big secret from them, sharing it only with Janine, and now you decide to share it with all of them."

"Jaimee and Jessie figured it out."

"That just makes it worse."

Michelle stood up and started pacing in the kitchen. "I'm...I have to move. I feel sick." After pacing around the room, she stopped and leaned over with her hands on the table, looking into Shawn's eyes. She held back a tear that was ready to explode onto her cheek. "Is that what you think of me? That I have betrayed our daughters on purpose? Because I have heard none of this before now."

Shawn leaned back a little, trying to escape this aggressive stance. "Hey, there is no judgment here. And, no, I certainly don't think you did this on purpose. There were circumstances. Janine walked in on you. You were going with it. I'm just trying to be objective."

Michelle pulled back, then slumped down into the chair next to her. She felt so weak and feared her body would not hold her up. "I never expected this from who I thought was my biggest supporter."

"I am always your biggest supporter. But looking at it as an outsider, you could have made a different choice to include the other girls. And they knew it. I just want you to be prepared." Shawn reached over and attempted to touch Michelle's hand but she pulled away abruptly.

Michelle stiffened up in her chair. "Yeah, well, I have never seen you as an outsider. Now I see where you're standing. Not on my side, obviously."

Shawn shook his head. "There shouldn't be sides. I was just trying to help."

"My whole life I have been a victim of my family, and myself. I have lived with regrets and heartache. I know my choices may not have been the best, but they are all I could come up with at the time. And now you are preparing me to—what—be rejected by my own daughters?" The tears started to flow down her face. "When will all this end? I don't know how long I am supposed to carry this burden."

Shawn cleared his throat to speak. "I am only pointing out that the outcome may not be perfect. I don't have a crystal ball. Maybe it will work out fine, but you shouldn't bank on that. And I have no judgment of you. But you need to look at this not as a victim, but as someone ready to make amends, and that means being willing to admit that you are human and may not have executed all of this perfectly. And be ready to keep your eye on the goal of strengthening your relationship with the girls."

Michelle just looked down at her clasped hands in front of her. She nodded slowly. The silence created a cold feeling in the room.

Shawn pushed his chair back to stand up. "Well, I guess I will head on up to bed. Why don't you just start with the first letter and then see how it rolls? Maybe the girls can help you figure out how to do this. Let them take the lead. Janine may be a great helper."

Michelle nodded. "I've been thinking lately about everything that has come between my sisters and me. I want our daughters to learn how to be supportive of each other, to stay close. I want more for them."

Shawn stood up and placed his hand on Michelle's shoulder. "I know you do, and I want that for you. I know you'll figure it out." He stifled a yawn. "Do you need me to stay up and help you with this?"

Michelle shook her head. "No, go to bed. There are a few baked eggs left in the oven if you want."

"Baked eggs! Woooo! And on a school day. You really did want to make an impression on them."

"The girls said the same thing." She grabbed the shoebox and stood up. "Anyway, I'm gonna go figure this out. I think I'll go into my studio."

Shawn laughed. "Ahhh." He bowed to his wife. "The all powerful wizard."

"Yeah, you better watch out, my powers could turn deadly!" It came out a little strong, so she laughed curtly. "Give me a damn kiss. Maybe I'll turn you into a prince." She grabbed his shirt and pulled him towards her. With the shoebox still in her hands, there was an awkward distance between them. She stood on tiptoe to reach his lips.

He pulled away. "It doesn't work that way. You are supposed to give me the kiss."

Michelle's heart lurched, but she tried not to show it. "Yeah, well, you are supposed to be a frog."

Shawn croaked. "Ribbit, ribbit..."

They kissed, and Shawn stroked her hair. Michelle forced a smile.

Chapter 22

The sun was shining through the windows as the girls came bounding in through the kitchen door. "Mom?" they called.

"Right here in the studio!" yelled Michelle. She was sitting at her art table. She had chairs set out for each of the girls to sit and join her. "Grab a drink and come on back!" She could hear the girls rummaging through the refrigerator and grabbing their drinks. She loved that sound. This is a good start, she thought.

Within minutes, the girls arrived, carrying their drinks. Realizing she was not breathing, she inhaled deeply. She had been thinking all day about how to talk about the letters and how to include the girls on this journey. She thought about the conversation with Shawn and that horrible word. Betrayal. It was so hard for her to admit that she betrayed her two daughters. She thought about the distance between herself and her sisters Tracy and Lisa, the years of heartache and loneliness, without the support of what should have been the two most important people in her life. And the loss of support and love that she yearned for with her mother. This road she was on had created such a burden as she lived her life without them. With nobody to share her fears with, her tears, her joyful moments, her everyday experiences, thoughts and dreams. She wanted her daughters to trust and love each other. She wanted her daughters to trust and love her. To keep the relationship with them that she lost with her mother. She wished she could pinpoint why her family relationships crumbled. There was nothing she could put her finger on, but whatever it was definitely drove a wedge between them.

Suddenly this task seemed daunting. Was it all too much for her to hope for? Would she find her own answers or open an abyss of pain? The only way to know this was to start this journey. Where does she start? She took another deep breath. From the beginning, she thought. Just share how it all started. She tried to soften her body stance to cover the tightening she felt inside.

Jaimee and Janine chatted easily as they chose a place to sit.

Jessie came over to Michelle to give her a hug. "Hi, Mom!" She wrapped her arms around Michelle's shoulders.

Michelle reached up and patted Jessie's arms. "Hi, honey."

Jessie broke the hug and stepped back. "I'm ready to see the secret letters!"

Michelle's heart lurched. "Great! They were a secret from me, too, until just a short time ago! Have a seat, sweetie."

She took a seat next to her sisters.

Jaimee leaned forward. "Okay, so let's talk about dandelions."

Michelle glanced at Janine, smiled, and then returned her attention to Jaimee. "Not so fast. I know how impressed you were with your beautiful dandelion bouquet, but all in good time. We will start at the beginning."

Jaimee nodded her head. She leaned back in her chair. "Okay, so shoot."

Michelle clasped her hands in front of her. She cleared her throat. This was not going to be easy, she thought. She reached out to her favorite tea mug and took a sip of her tea, hoping it would imbue her with strength.

"Okay, well, this all started after Grandma's funeral. You girls had gone back to school, and I told my sister and brother, your Aunt Amy and Uncle Mike, that I would meet them at the house to go through Grandma's things one last time. It was Monday, and Amy and Mike had to get on the road back to their homes. Amy and I were going through Grandma's closet," she leaned over and picked up the jewelry box from the floor next to her feet and set it on the table. "And we stumbled upon this."

Jaimee and Jessie leaned over the table, reaching out toward the box.

Jaimee whistled. "Wow!"

Jessie rubbed her hands along the top and sides of the box. "What's in it?"

Jaimee reached forward and moved the box a little closer. "Wow, that's old. Is it antique? What's inside?"

Michelle waved her hand in the direction of the box. "Open it."

Jaimee slid her hand along the top of the box to the latch and gently opened the top. "Cool." She reached in and picked up the ruby necklace and bracelet set. She held them in her hands, at the same time looking past them to the other pieces in the jewelry box. "Did all this belong to Grandma?"

Jessie was inching up onto the box. She reached her hand in and grabbed the rhinestone brooch. "Oh, look at this!" she gasped. "It's so beautiful!"

Michelle had a surge of remembering how she felt when she found the jewelry. She felt a small quiver in her shoulders as she tried to hold back the emotion she felt. So many lost memories. She reached over and picked up the pearl earrings, rolling them in her fingers. "Yeah, these are Grandma's."

Janine reached out and put her whole hand in the box and ran the remaining jewelry pieces through her fingers. "Mom, we talked about the jewelry in the box, but we never got back to looking through it!"

Michelle set the pearl earrings back in the box. "It stirred up a lot of emotion in me. I guess I wasn't ready to bring it out." She smiled at Jessie. "I used to wear that brooch, and dress up in my mother's ruby colored shoes and dresses. I pretended I was Dorothy from Kansas, and could click my heels and I would be transported to the Emerald City."

Jessie leaned over the table to get closer to her mom. She held the brooch out. "Really? Like in the Wizard of Oz?"

Michelle nodded. "Yes, indeed."

Jaimee chuckled. "Yeah, but then the flying monkeys intercepted you and, well, here you are...stuck with us!"

Janine said, "We are her flying monkeys."

Michelle laughed. "Except that the flying monkeys actually followed the witch's commands, which you don't."

Jaimee took the brooch from Jessie's hands and turned it over, looking at both sides. "Yeah, that's not happening."

Michelle continued. "Anyway, that was many years ago. I was a child. And now? There is no place I'd rather be than with you girls."

Jessie mimicked Dorothy's voice. "There's no place like home."

Janine lifted up her hands and let the jewelry pieces fall back into the jewelry box. "It's like a treasure chest! What are you gonna do with all this jewelry?"

It was a good question. Michelle was not sure. She had thought about donating it all. Maybe it would be less painful. This was a box of memories that had been hard for her to even look at when she first found it. It was just costume jewelry with the added bonus of negative emotions. But now, seeing the girls enjoying it, she wondered if this could be a positive part of their journey.

Jessie held one of the brooches to her nose. "This one smells like Grandma."

Jaimee nodded, her expression wistful. "I feel like Grandma's here."

Michelle shivered as a chill ran down her spine. Was her mom here with them? "Well, I haven't been sure what to do with it all, but now that I see you girls are enjoying this, maybe we should share. How about each of you pick out a piece to keep for yourself, and let it be a reminder of Grandma's love for you, even if you didn't get to know her very well, and that you have come from a long line of women who loved and worked hard and did their best with whatever they had. And you know, those letters were hidden in this jewelry box, too. So these pieces of jewelry can also symbolize a window into the world of the person who wrote these letters and hid them in this jewelry box."

Janine nodded head. "Dorothy Doe."

Jaimee tilted her head toward her sister. "Dorothy who?"

Janine smiled. "Dorothy Doe. That's what we named the person who wrote the letters. They are kind of like a mystery, and at first we thought, Jane Doe, but then we decided on Dorothy Doe."

"I want this brooch!" Jessie reached forward and waved the brooch in the air.

Michelle laughed. "It's yours!" She glanced at Jaimee. "And how about you, my first born sprout?"

Jaimee rolled the bracelet and necklace in her hands and studied them, and held them up to her neck as if to imagine herself wearing them at a royal ball. "I think I'd like these."

Michelle felt her heart pounding as she watched Jaimee roll the set in her hands. "Funny you should pick that set. Grandma wore that on the day you were baptized." There was no doubt in her mind now that her mom was with them.

Jaimee smiled, laying the bracelet and necklace on the table in front of her and studied them.

Michelle watched as Janine was gently sifting through the jewelry in the box. She picked up piece after piece, holding each one up to the light of day as if they would speak to her. Suddenly her fingers landed on the pair of faux pearl earrings. She held them up, studying them quietly. She held them up to her ears. She stroked them gently. "These."

Michelle smiled. On one hand, she was sad to let those earrings–and the memory–go. Yet she realized that by passing them along, she was not only creating new memories but also preserving the memory of her mother as well. "Excellent choice. They're not real, of course, but they were real to Grandma. She used to wear them every morning while she was getting breakfast ready for me and my sisters growing up. It kind of made her feel transported to a happy place." She looked at Jessie. "Kind of like your brooch did for me!"

The room became silent for a few short moments. The girls were admiring their pieces of jewelry, and Michelle relished the moment to appreciate the changing of the guard of the jewelry, as well as to feel a sting of sadness to let them go. Now the girls own a piece of this story, she thought.

Jaimee broke the silence. "So how did the letters fit into this jewelry box?" She turned the jewelry box around in a circle. "There isn't a lot of extra room in here."

"I'll show you." She closed the latch and turned it upside down. "Look here." She moved the box over in front of Jaimee. She ran her finger along the edge where the letters were hidden. "Feel right here," she instructed.

Jaimee ran her finger along the side of the box and hit the hinge. She stopped and looked up.

Jessie inched forward, leaning close so she could see. "Ooh, what is it?"

"It's a hinge, kind of hidden. You actually have to feel for it." Jaimee looked up at Michelle.

Michelle pointed to the jewelry box. "Open it."

Jaimee slid her finger along the seam and found the tab sticking out. She pulled it out and opened the bottom of the jewelry box. Inside lay several small white envelopes, tightly fitted into the small hidden capsule of the box.

Jessie's eyes grew big. "Oh, cool!"

Jaimee pulled the envelopes out. "These look kinda small."

Michelle reached forward to request the letters from Jaimee. Jaimee handed them to her. "They might be small but they pack a powerful punch." She held the letters in her hands. "Let's start with the first one." She held up the envelope with the number one on it.

Michelle looked around to the three girls. "Who wants to read the first letter?"

"I do, I do!" yelled Jessie, squirming in her seat.

Michelle felt a flash of warmth surging up her body. She tried to push it aside. She reached under her chair and pulled out the shoebox. "I'll keep the ones we are not reading in this shoebox to make it easier to get at them." She flushed and her breathing became short. She could not ignore it. She breathed slowly to steady herself, closing her eyes. It seemed that she was on the precipice of a steep mountainside, and her body was slowly leaning off the edge. Well, here goes, she thought. She handed the first letter to Jessie. "This one is called, 'Why do I cry?'"

"Whoa, that's kind of a heavy title," Jaimee said.

Janine patted Jessie on the back. "Go for it, Jessie."

Jessie opened the rose bordered stationery. She studied the paper, the rose border, the typing, the slight yellowing on the edges. "This looks old and worn out."

Michelle nodded. "Who knows where or when it started out, but it certainly has a few of my tears dried onto it."

Jessie took a deep breath. "Okay, here goes... *I woke up crying again this morning. Please, I would like to know–why do I cry?*"

As Jessie read, Michelle was not hearing the words of the letter. The words in her head were too loud. She was thinking about Jessie as a young girl, reading her first words in a picture book. She was eleven now, a young but maturing woman and yet so innocent at the same time. Now reading about the hard subjects of life and growth. Sadness. The flow of tears. Feeling trapped. Despair. Was it right to have her involved in this? It wasn't right to leave her out. She wondered how she could find a way to help the girls deal with the feelings that would come up through these letters. She tried to bring her attention back to Jessie, listening for ideas in the words.

"*I want to know. Is this sadness? I don't know that I am feeling sad. I feel nothing actually. Is it despair? I have everything I need to survive. I have a family, a home, a bed to lay my head. I have my art. I have food to eat. Maybe if I could figure out why I cry, then I could figure out how to make it stop. And I want to make it stop. How do I make it stop??????*"

Jessie set the letter down on the table.

Jaimee took a long, slow breath. "So, this person is pretty sad. That's heavy." She looked at Michelle. "Is this a real person? Are the letters all like this? And why did they end up in Grandma's jewelry box?"

Michelle felt uneasy. She nodded in acknowledgement. "Yes, it's real. But I don't know anything else. I wish I had all the answers to those questions, Jaimee. I can tell you that these letters have opened some wounds." She paused, her eyes unfocusing on a distant point beyond the room. She jerked herself back to the present. "I can tell you what I believe. I believe this was, or is, a real person. Who, we haven't figured out yet. I thought it was Grandma since they were in her jewelry box. But picking up some clues along the way, I'm not so sure now. I believe these letters, although each one unique, have a theme going through them. What is that theme? I think we are still learning that. But that's the third thing I believe. I believe these letters were meant for me to find. And now for us to read. And they will help us learn and grow together." She handed Jaimee the answer letter. "Here, read the answer."

"Answer?"

"Yes, each letter has an answer."

"Who wrote the answers?"

"I don't know. Don't know who wrote them. Don't know who answered them."

As Jaimee reached out to grab the letter, Janine reached over and put her hand on Jessie's wrist. "Pretty intense, huh? Mom was actually crying when I found her." She glanced at Michelle.

"It's okay. It's okay to cry. That wasn't the only time. But, as we will learn, sometimes tears can be a good thing."

Jaimee opened the letter, cleared her throat and began to read. "*Do not be afraid of the tears. They are yours. Whether wanted or not, they belong to you. They are a symbol of your feelings. Yes, you are a living, feeling person! You are alive! Your tears are a testimonial to this. You have many pent-up feelings that you may or may not recognize, but the universe knows that you cannot keep these feelings locked up inside. You must release them. So the universe begins the flow. At the exact time that it is needed.*" She stopped and let a tear roll down her cheek. Her voice cracked a little as she continued. "*It may be in the middle of the night. In the warmth of a bath. While driving in a car. When you least expect it but need it the most. Trust the universe.*"

Michelle felt a heaviness in her chest. Such simple but complex words. Hearing these a second time was different than the first. This time, the words were infusing into her heart. The words.... beautiful words......like paint on a canvas.

"The universe has got you. The universe will make your tears flow, and the universe will stop them at the right time. All you need to do is let them flow and trust in that which you cannot see. Because it sees you. It is one with you. It protects you. It loves you. It knows your worthiness, your strength. And it serves to restore you. Beginning with the warmth of your tears."

The tear flowing down Jaimee's cheek now dropped onto the table below her. "They are beautiful words, Mom."

"Yes, they are. What do these words tell you?"

Janine started. "That it's okay to cry. That tears can be healing."

Jessie nodded. "And that tears are salty and salt water can be healing. Sometimes it helps wounds heal. When we have a toothache, you have us swish with salt water."

Michelle smiled. Her little scientist. "Yes, that's so right."

Jaimee glanced over at Jessie. "Sometimes our wounds are not just on the outside. Sometimes they are in our hearts."

Michelle smiled. "Yes, and when that happens, we can't imagine that it will ever heal. But somehow it does. So often."

Janine turned to her older sister. "Sometimes it takes more than tears to heal a broken heart."

Jaimee agreed. "Yup, it does. It takes a lot more. Time. Love. Gestures. Words."

Words. Michelle jumped up from her chair. "Oh! I got an idea!"

The girls looked bewildered at each other. Janine asked "Got what?"

"Words! You know your mama is an artist, right?"

The girls laughed.

Jessie rocked back and forth in her chair. "The best!"

"Well, have you ever heard of "Word Art?""

Jessie came to a stop in her chair. "I think we talked about it in your art class. It's art made out of words?"

Michelle nodded in Jessie's direction. "Yes! Well, sort of. There are many definitions of word art, but basically it combines visual art with words. You can use the words to form images, or you can lay words over images, or you can border or outline a picture with text."

Jaimee looked as puzzled as her sisters. "So what does word art have to do with tears?"

Michelle was now reaching under her desk to pull out a fresh canvas and was setting it up on her easel. She turned back towards the girls. "You just said it. Tears are only one way to help with healing, but there are other ways, what did you say? Time?.."

Janine jumped in, "Love!"

Michelle pointed at Janine. "Yes. And gestures. And words." She turned back towards her easel, picked up her pencil and began to draw large strokes onto the canvas. The girls were quiet, looking from one to the other. After what seemed like an eternity, Michelle stepped back and showed her pencil drawing. It revealed the many petals of the dandelion flower.

Jaimee shrugged. "Oh, the dandelion again."

Michelle chuckled. "Yes, the dandelion again. So, we are going to embark on a little project. First, we need to fill in the colors of the dandelion pedals. All three of you can do it. Obviously you need to use yellow, but your shade of yellow can be yours alone. I think many different shades of yellow will make a beautiful bloom.Then we will let it set overnight, and tomorrow we will start placing the text."

Jaimee still looked puzzled. "What kind of text?"

Words. It's word art. As we read the letters, you can be thinking of one word that is meaningful to you to describe the contents of the letter, and you will add that word.

Jessie was now up on her knees on the chair. Any talk of art made her jump with excitement. "Just one word, mama?"

Michelle loved Jessie's enthusiasm. It paralleled Janine's sense of adventure and Jaimee's confidence. "Well, it's your artwork. There are 8 letters and three of you. So one word each letter from each of you would be 24 words. But a dandelion can have as many petals as its creator makes it. So we shall see how this develops. We can always add more petals." She looked at Jaimee and Janine. They seemed to be taking it all in. "Well, shall we dive in? Let's get these petals colored up and then tonight, I'd like you to think about the letter we just read and pick a word to describe how it made you feel."

Jaimee raised her hand as if she were in class at school. Michelle smiled. "Yes, Jaimee?"

"Does it have to be a word? Can it be a symbol, or a picture?"

"It can be anything you make it. So come on over. I'll grab paint and brushes."

Jaimee and Janine pushed their chairs back and stood up, walking over to the easel, while Jessie scooted over the top of the table to get there first. Michelle set out the supplies, and stepped back. There was a slight rumbling in the room as she listened to them discuss which color combinations made the different shades of yellow. 'And we are on our way,' she thought.

Later that evening, with dinner finished and Jaimee and Jessie cleaning the dishes, blaring rock music to give them inspiration, Michelle was feeling tight as a rope with a thousand knots as she and Shawn sat down in the living room with Janine. Michelle was so relieved when Shawn began.

"Janine, your mom and I had a very heartfelt talk this morning about your request to go to the dance tomorrow night." Janine sat up proper in her chair, as if to muster the courage to hear the worst. "And?..."

"And, the deliberation is not bad but not the best either. But we think it is fair."

Janine shrugged, asking for clarification. "Not bad but not the best? What does that mean?"

"It means that you are still grounded and need to finish out the last week of your grounding. But...since this Sadie Hawkins thing appears to be something that doesn't happen very often, we will let you go to the dance for half the time. You can choose, first half or second half. We will be dropping you off and picking you up. That should give you a chance to be with your friends and ask some boys to dance, if I got that right."

Janine flopped her body back onto her chair. "Uggghhhh! Really? Half the dance? I am going to be the laughing stock of the class! That's as bad as saying I can't go at all!"

Michelle's knots were not loosening. She hated confrontation with Janine. Janine could be relentless, and Michelle felt she was sure to lose with every argument. It reminded her of the arguments she had with her sister Lisa growing up. Although Lisa was younger, she always seemed to have the quickest wit and the last word.

Shawn said, "Well, Janine, that could still be arranged. Grounding is grounding, but we want to show you that you have earned enough trust for us to meet you halfway on this." He reached out to put his hand on Michelle's back. Michelle knew when he did this he was showing that they were together on the decision. She could see by Janine's face that she knew it as well.

Janine slumped her shoulders forward and held her head in her hands. "This sucks. I have to tell my friends that I can only stay half the time."

Shawn leaned in to Janine. "Hey, there is a way to do this. First of all nobody notices who shows up in the beginning. When I was in school it was the thing to be fashionably late."

Janine looked up at her father. "Yeah, that was back in the dark ages. They didn't even have school dances at the dawn of time."

Michelle said, "The first half of the dance is always so awkward. I agree with Dad, I would go for the second half. Just show up. It's the second half that people start getting more comfortable and start asking people to dance. And the second half is what people will remember. They won't even remember that you were late."

"And what do I say when they ask me why I am arriving late?"

Shawn answered, "Well, that's up to you. You can make some excuse with your great imagination. But if you ask me, I think you should just be honest with them. They all know by this time that you are grounded. Just be honest. Hey, I'm still grounded but my parents let me come for the second half. Period. It shouldn't need to drag on any more than that."

Michelle reached over and placed her hand on Janine's leg. "Janine, we don't want things to be awkward with your friends but a consequence is a consequence. It's not the end of the world. And I'd really like you to have a chance to ask this Jimmie fellow to dance. Lucky guy, by the way!"

Janine rolled her eyes and whispered, "Mom, not in front of Dad."

The conversation was interrupted by Jaimee and Jessie barreling into the living room and tackling Janine. "Ouch! Stop!" she shouted as they rolled onto the floor.

Michelle stood up. "Okay, everyone upstairs to finish homework and get to bed! Big day tomorrow. You need to get home right after school so we can read letter number two, and then you two girls have the dance to get ready for. And while you're doing that, Jessie and I are going to do some baking! And this weekend will be a letter marathon."

Jessie and Jaimee ran up the stairs.

Michelle watched Janine slowly come to her feet. "Are we okay?"

Janine shrugged. "Not really, but I guess."

Shawn said, "Hmmm. I'll take it!"

Michelle nodded. "Me too. I love you, Janine."

"Yeah, I know." Janine dragged herself up the stairs.

Michelle whispered to Shawn, "I would never tell her this, but did that look a little bit theatrical to you?"

"Oh, absolutely. She's excited."

"But she can't admit it," Michelle said.

"Good God, no. How could any self-respecting teenage girl?"

Michelle laughed. She shouted up the stairs, "Love you all, girls! I'll be up to say good night."

Jaimee peeked down the stairs and made a face at Michelle. "Mom, we are a little old for that. We can put ourselves to bed."

Michelle smiled as the girls started up the steps. "Yes, you can, but I need it for me. Humor me."

Michelle was waiting in the art room when the girls came home from school. They knew right where to come and filed into the back room. Michelle was standing next to the canvas with a beautiful yellow dandelion.

Jessie's eyes opened wide as she began to speak. "Oh, wow, look at the different shades of yellow!"

Janine smiled at the beautiful blossoms. "It looks like a kaleidoscope."

Michelle gazed back at the canvas. "Yeah, it does a little. Did you all think of a word to add to a petal based on yesterday's letter? A word from the letter that struck you, or a feeling that was stirred up?"

Jaimee nodded. "Yes. Can I start? What are we using for these words? Marker, paint, black, other colors?"

Michelle pulled out her palette with several colors of paints. "Well, how would you like to do this? I think it would look cool with either all black words or all different colored words, like a rainbow dandelion." Jessie jumped up and down. "I vote colors!" Jaimee and Janine looked at each other and shrugged. Janine declared, "Colors it is!"

Jaimee walked over to the palette and picked it up. "Mom, I want to use a symbol."

Michelle gestured with her hand toward the palette. "A symbol it is, then."

The room was quiet as Jaimee picked up a small brush and mixed a light blue color, turned to the canvas and drew a teardrop on one of the bottom petals, like it was falling off the end of the petal. Michelle walked over and placed her arm around Jaimee's shoulders. "Is this the teardrop that rolled down your cheek yesterday as you were reading?"

Jaimee nodded. "Yes, and as I thought about it last night, I was glad that I was able to let it fall down my cheek. Some things don't need an explanation; they just need to be."

Michelle nodded in agreement. "Well said, my dear." She gave a tiny squeeze to Jaimee's shoulders. She looked to the other two girls. "Who is next?"

Jessie could hardly contain her excitement. "Me!"

She stepped forward as Jaimee turned to sit down to watch. She used her pointer finger to direct her eyes to gaze at each and every color, then landed on the color purple. "I love purple," she said. She picked up a paintbrush and dipped it into the purple paint. She turned to the canvas and began to print a word. She stepped back as the word popped out of the yellow petal. *Warmth.*

Janine read the word out loud. "Warmth."

Michelle looked at Jessie, "Want to tell us about this word? And by the way, ladies, you don't need to explain anything. You can just write a word, or a symbol," nodding to Jaimee, "and not say anything about it."

Jessie said, "I want to talk about it. The last line said, beginning with the warmth of your tears. And I felt a sensation like having a warm blanket over me and protecting me from the cold. And maybe that's kind of like what tears do. They protect us and help us from the cold of the world."

Michelle smiled. "That is very insightful. And although it's just a word, it gives me a visual of something tangible. Great job." She looked at Janine. "Janine, what have you got for us? "

Janine slowly stood up and traded places with Jessie. "For this one, I would like basic black." She picked up a small brush and dipped it in the black paint. She started to etch out the word *Trust.* She stepped back. Michelle read, "Trust." She looked at Janine.

"Trust in that which you cannot see."

"Trust in what?" asked Jessie.

"Well, I don't know, because I cannot see it!" She looked back at Michelle. "But sometimes you have to just believe that things are gonna be all right. Even if you are sad or lonely in the moment. Tears help us get through those moments, but trust moves us forward."

Michelle just gazed at her beautiful middle child. So insightful, this pain in the butt child. "So true, my dear. Not bad for a rugrat." She playfully ran her fingers through Janine's hair, and stepped back to admire the beginning of the dandelion project. A beautiful start, she thought.

Michelle turned to the other two girls and motioned for them to sit. "Sit down, ladies, and we shall read letter number two." As the girls sat down, she pulled letter number two out of her housecoat pocket. She handed it to Janine. "Janine, do you want to start with today's letter?"

Janine reached out and opened the first paper in the envelope. "Sure." She gazed at the first few lines to familiarize herself with the letter. "Oh, yeah. Here we go. *I am so afraid. All the time. If I knew what it was that I was afraid of, it would help me cope. I mean, sure I know a lot of things that I am afraid of–I am afraid of spiders. Those big, furry gray and black ones. I am afraid of bees, especially the big fat yellowjackets. I am afraid of tripping and falling in front of people. I am afraid of swallowing a bug in my sleep. I am afraid of sleep. I am afraid of falling out of bed. I'm afraid of getting into bed. I always check between the sheets. I am afraid to turn out the lights. I am afraid to close my eyes. I am afraid that when I come face to face with what I fear, it will be a force that I will not be able to overcome. Again."* She set the paper on the table and looked up at Michelle. "I remember this one. There are lots of things to be afraid of."

Michelle nodded. "Yeah, we talked about a few of them. Can you share?"

Janine wrung her hands in front of her. "Well the obvious. Bugs. Spiders. Bees. Closing my eyes and seeing images in the darkness."

Jaimee tightened up a little. "What kind of images?"

"Images of the day. Just rolls around and around in my head. Things I wanted to do but didn't. Mistakes I made, stupid comments that I didn't mean but they just came out. Images of how I wish it all went."

Jaimee nodded in agreement. "Yeah, I have that sometimes. Some nights I lay in bed and wish I could just rewind the day."

Michelle leaned forward in her chair and asked, "You know what?"

Jaimee gazed into Michelle's eyes. "What?"

"I have those nights too. I wish I could do everything perfectly the first time so I wouldn't feel I need the rewind."

Jessie asked, "What would you want to rewind, Mama?"

Michelle glanced over at Jessie. "Oh, Jessie, someday you will experience motherhood and you won't even have to ask that question. A mother questions every move she makes, every conversation she has with her child, every decision that is difficult, that nobody agrees with, every simple choice she makes."

"Why?"

She reached out and touched Jessie's hand. "Because of probably my biggest fear. Losing you." Michelle shrugged. "Raising a family is a hard journey. If I screw it up, then when you go off to college I may never see you again. And that is a consequence I cannot live with. My mother and I lost our relationship; I don't want to lose my daughters. Ever."

Jessie reached over with her free hand to place on Michelle's. "Mom, don't say that. You won't lose us. Ever."

Michelle smiled at Jessie. She wished life was so simple. She wished she could know that she would never lose her daughters, or that her girls would never lose each other. Like her and Lisa and Tracy. But she knew otherwise. She knew personally how wishes and reality can have such contrasting outcomes. "I hope not. Did you hear anything in this letter?"

"Yes! Bees! I hate bees!"

The other two girls murmured the names of other fearful creatures. "Spiders....mice...snakes. Wasps...rats...bats."

Jaimee started chanting, "Lions and tigers and bears, Oh my!" The tension was broken as all three girls laughed out loud.

Michelle chuckled. "Okay, okay. Anything else, Jessie?"

"Well, I might be a little afraid of the dark, too. Maybe nightmares, they are so scary." She paused for a short moment. "The boogie man!"

Jaimee nodded. "Oh, yes, the boogie man. We're all afraid of the boogy man." She turned towards Jessie. You do understand that the boogie man isn't real, right?"

Jessie shrugged. "Yes, I know that, but in the darkness it's hard to remember that."

Janine nodded, "Hey, it's okay. That's why I like a light shining in our room at night. To scare away the boogie man. There's nothing wrong with that." She looked at Michelle.

Michelle tightened up. She knew what was coming.

"Is this a good time to share about your nightmare, Mom?"

Michelle brought her hand back from under Jessie's and rubbed her forehead. Her heart hurt. She felt a lump in her throat. The room was silent. She could feel a tear escape and roll down her cheek.

Jaimee broke the silence. "Mom?"

She looked up at Jaimee. "I'm okay, honey." Her eyes traveled from Jaimee to Janine to Jessie. "I have a fear. A recurring nightmare. Except it isn't a made up fear like the boogie man. It's real. It's a memory that I can't shake." She felt her body become numb as she held back tears.

Janine reached across the table and touched Michelle's arm and caressed her. "It's okay, Mom. Take your time."

The numbness subsided slightly. This was a new sensation. Her daughter was comforting her. It was a little confusing. She had always been the mother. The supporter. The comforter. This clearly felt strange, but somehow it gave her the strength to continue.

"Well, first of all, I have a little bomb to drop on you. Your grandpa was not my biological father. He was my stepdad." She could see the confused faces on her girls. "But that doesn't mean I didn't think of Grandpa as my father; he was very much my real father in my heart. He was a great stepdad. He married Grandma when we were pretty young, so he was always my dad in my eyes."

Jaimee asked the question on everyone's minds. "Where is your biological father?"

Michelle cleared her throat. She reached over to her art station and grabbed her water glass and took a sip. "Well, this is where my nightmare comes in. I am in Aunt Lisa's and my room at Grandma's house. I hear yelling and my mother screaming out and our back door slamming. Grandpa was traveling for work so he wasn't home." She stopped and took another sip of water, then continued on. She just wanted to get through this. "A few minutes later, there were two gunshots. Mom was crying in our kitchen. I heard sirens. I see...a man...being dragged out of the neighbor's yard in handcuffs. I see images of yellow crime scene tape." Tears welled up in her eyes.

Jaimee shook her shoulders as a chill ran down her spine. "How awful! Who was the man being led away in handcuffs?"

Michelle gazed toward Janine.

Janine nodded to Michelle, motioning her to continue.

"My father."

Both Jaimee and Jessie's mouths fell open.

Jaimee continued her questioning. "What? Your father? Your father shot your neighbors? What...why? Did they die? How do you know it was your father?"

Jessie interrupted. "Why would he want to shoot your neighbors?"

Michelle took a deep breath in and let it out. "Jessie, I don't know the answer to that question. I suspect my mother knew, but after that night she clammed up and never spoke of it." She turned to Jaimee. "Yes, they died. I saw my father running out of the house with blood spattered on him, until he was no longer in the light of the porch. The next sight I saw was the police dragging him from the side of the yard and putting him in the police car. I never saw him again, except in these dreams...memories."

"Was he in your life before this night?" asked Jessie.

"Yes, sort of. Lisa and Tracy and I went over to see him every other weekend. It was nothing memorable. We pretty much sat in his apartment and watched TV, played a few games in the backyard. Took naps. Ate sandwiches. I remember missing my mom's cooking and counting the hours until we came home. We didn't really like him. We had Grandpa. We didn't need a good for nothing part time dad. But the courts said we had to go. So we did. And that night, it stopped."

"Where is he now?"

Michelle glared at the wall behind Jaimee. She did not want Jaimee to feel the brunt of the emotion in her eyes, but she could not hide it either. "I don't know and I don't care. Probably in jail. Could be alive or dead. He's dead to me, so I don't care to know."

Jaimee stiffened up and leaned backwards. "Okay." She looked at Janine. "You knew about this?"

Janine turned and sadly nodded her head. "Yes. Mom asked me not to say anything. She wanted to be the one to tell you. I was just as shocked as you are."

Jaimee looked up at Michelle. "You asked her not to say anything to us? Like keeping secrets from Jessie and I? This is a pretty big secret. Why did you feel we didn't qualify for the sharing of this? And what changed that we are able to hear this now?" She turned to Janine. "And you? In what world is it okay to keep secrets like this from your sisters?"

Michelle turned stiff and her body felt cold. It was happening. Her worst fear was coming true. She was about to lose her daughters. She betrayed their trust. They would never forgive her. And now the girls are turning against Janine. She began to tremble. She just wanted to run away.

Janine broke the silence. "Hey, I did not intentionally keep any secret from you. I did the responsible thing. I left it to Mom to tell you when she was ready, and she has. She was processing something very heavy. She needed time to understand what was happening before she could share it. I knew she would share it with you. At the right time. I had to respect that. You would have done the same."

"Yes but if you had shared with us, then we could have supported her together."

Michelle waved her hand. "Hey, hey, I am right here! Janine, thank you. Those are very mature words, and you are right. We have to respect each other, and sometimes that means waiting to tell each other things. It's not the same as never telling someone or keeping secrets. There are nuances here." She looked at Jaimee and then at Jessie. "Janine only did what I asked her to. But she is right. I was processing. I thought I would never share this memory with anyone."

A short silence was broken by Jessie's heavy sigh. "I'm glad you are talking about it now."

Michelle continued. "There are still a lot of questions that are unanswered. Like, why my father shot Mr and Mrs. Brandsen. Why my mother could never talk about it. Whatever happened to my father, which I really don't care, but I guess it would be good to know." She looked into Jaimee's eyes. "Maybe I thought if I had the answers to these questions I could be in a better position to share this with you." She picked up the letter. "This letter triggered us talking about our fears, and lately this nightmare has taken a front seat in my life. I'm not sure why, but it just came out and Janine was there. And it felt good to get it out and share it with someone, but also it opened questions that I cannot answer. So I told her I would share with you when I felt ready. I hoped I would be able to share more fully if I knew more. I am giving you my heartfelt apology for waiting. There was a lot going on. Grandma's death. Janine's brush with the law. And now these letters that seem to leave more questions than answers. And each letter seemed heavier than the last. It was never my intention to leave you out of the loop or betray you. Which is why I am glad we are going through these letters. Because there are lots that we can talk about and I want to share this with you. Do you think you can forgive me?"

Jaimee lowered her eyes to the table. "I don't know what to think. Or to say. I feel kind of paralyzed. This is heavy stuff. I don't understand it."

Janine reached over and placed her hand on Jaimee's arm. "You don't have to understand it. But Mom needs us to be here for her."

Jaimee looked up at Michelle. "Wow, Mom. You have to know that we are always here for you. I wish there was something we could do."

Michelle reached into the envelope and pulled out the answer letter. "There is. We can read the answer letter and learn how to face our fears, whatever they are. It will help me to hear it again." She handed the letter to Jaimee.

Jaimee reached out to grab the paper, opened it and read the answer letter out loud. As she read, images kept popping into Michelle's head. "*Experiencing fear is a part of growth. You are growing, not just in years but in knowledge, in strength, in experience. One of the greatest ways to overcome fear is to develop the strength to face it.* [Loud knock on the door]. *Knowing how to do that can be tricky, but know that in the darkest, most fearful times, you are not alone. You belong to the universe, and the universe is with you. It is the buzzing energy inside your soul that speaks to you and propels you forward.* [Mother screaming]. *It is in your breath, which anchors you in the present moment....So breathe. It is in the practice of positivity in the face of uncertainty. Remember that as you flow positivity out into the world, the universe will help it flow back to you. As you keep others safe from their fears, the universe will keep you safe from your fears."* [Gunshots].

Jaimee stopped. She could see Michelle startle as if something hit her. "You okay, Mom?"

Michelle shook in an attempt to dismiss the images and sounds. "I'm fine. Flow positivity. This is great advice. Keep going."

"Ask the universe to show you the meaning of your fears. Meditate .... Reach out to that which gives you peace and ask it, "How can I face my fear? What am I really afraid of? [Distant sirens]. *Failure? Physical harm? The unknown? How is this fear rooted in my mind?* [Man running] *If the fear is of something real and tangible, I may not be able to change it. But what can I do to change my view and my response to this fear?".* [Images of red].

Bring another into your universe to talk about.... [Handcuffs]. *Plan ways that you can distract yourself from the fear. Know that the universe holds you in the palm of its hands; ....strength and resilience ..... surrounded with love and acceptance, ...* [crime scene tape]... *confidence and perseverance, and most of all, it helps you breathe.* [Sobbing].

Fear wants you to feel alone. As you reach out to your universe, you gain strength, and the hold of fear weakens. No matter what the cause of your fear is, you can overcome and triumph over its hold on you. Do not cower, stand tall!

Jaimee sat the paper down. "Wow, that's a big answer."

Michelle wriggled her fingers as if to bring the present back into her body and mind. She took a sharp breath. "Yes, it is. But so great to know that there are many things we can do to face our fears. Did anyone hear anything interesting?"

Jessie reached out and grabbed the paper from Jaimee's hands. "Yes, I did. Let me find it." She studied the paper.

Michelle waited. She looked around the room. The girls were staring at Jessie.

Jessie furrowed her brow and pursed her lips.

Janine and Jaimee exchanged a glance. Janine caught Michelle's gaze and raised a brow.

Michelle shrugged.

Still, Jessie studied the page.

Jaimee covered her mouth with one hand. Her eyes were laughing.

Janine cleared her throat.

Jessie did not notice.

Michelle held back a snort.

Jessie burst out, "Oh, yes, here it is - Breathe!"

They stayed quiet for a split second, then everyone broke out in laughter. Great, guffawing belly laughs. Jessie joined in from the sheer fun of her sisters and mother's giggles.

They laughed for a full minute, maybe more. Michelle did not know how much time had passed. Michelle took a large, loud breath of air. "All of that, and this is the one thing you came up with?

Jaimee chimed in. " I love it, because sometimes taking a breath is the hardest thing to do, especially when you are afraid."

The girls mellowed down to a chuckle. Janine grabbed the paper from Jessie. "That's a good one, Jessie. Breathe. Might be the most important word in all of that writing. Good job in narrowing it right down to the brass tacks. You may have a future in investigation."

Jessie saluted her.

Janine looked at the paper again. "I remember there was this one phrase that spoke to me." She pointed to a section on the page. "Here. *If the fear is of something real and tangible, I may not be able to change it. But what can I do to change my view and my response to this fear?* Sometimes what we are afraid of turns out to be real." She turned quick to lunge at Jessie. "Like BEES!" Jessie let out a short scream, raising her hand up to protect her. "So what we need to do is learn how we respond to the fear." She touched Jessie gently. "And you know what you should do if you find that bees are buzzing around you?"

"Stay still and calm?"

"Yes, and if one lands on you, just quietly shoo it off and move slowly. How you react determines the bee's response to you."

Michelle nodded. "So, breathe, and respond. Two good words. And I would go as far as to say that breathing can help you change a negative response into a positive response."

Janine nodded her head. "Yup." She winked at Jessie.

Michelle turned the conversation back to Jaimee. "Jaimee, how about you?"

Jaimee reached out and grabbed the paper back. "Well, I like this positive flow thing." She searched the paper. "Here....*the practice of positivity in the face of uncertainty. Remember that as you flow positivity out into the world, the universe will help it flow back to you.*"

Janine nodded in agreement. "Mom, we talked about this. This is the boomerang thing. Like karma."

"Yes, we did, Janine. What you send out comes back to you."

Jaimee added, "So, if what you send out is positive, then positivity can flow back to you. We talked about this in dance class. It's natural to be afraid of failure. Having a winning attitude can make a difference."

"Absolutely!"

Jessie asked, "What about you, Mom?"

Michelle thought for a moment. "Well, since you asked, I like that last paragraph. Let me see this." She reached out for the paper. "*Fear wants you to feel alone. As you reach out to your universe, you gain strength, and the hold of fear weakens.*" I am really feeling this today, and I am so glad I was able to share my memory with you. It was very hard for me to talk about. But... I hope you realize that you girls are my universe. Since sharing this with you, I think the hold of fear has loosened its grip just a little. It really does help to share your burdens with someone you trust. And I trust you. I'm sorry it took so long for me to share this with you." She looked across all of her daughters. " You are all so grown up. I didn't give you credit. I'm sorry. And I am grateful for you." The girls quietly nodded in acknowledgement until Jessie spoke.

"We're proud of you, Mom."

Michelle smiled. The tightness in her body was subsiding. "So, what are our words for today? We might as well close this session how we ended it. With word art."

Each of the three girls shouted their words.

"Breathe!"

"Respond!"

"Positivity!"

"And if you don't mind me adding one, I'd like to add the word 'share.' I am so happy to be able to share with you."

Jessie jumped up. "Sure, Mom! We're a team!" She lifted her hand up for a high five.

Michelle giggled. "Okay, I'll add mine later and leave you while I go get dinner ready. So let's get to work on this, because two of you have a dance to get ready for!"

Jaimee looked at Janine. "You're going to the dance?"

"Yeah, but don't worry. You got your way, at least halfway. I can't go until the second half. Thanks for butting in."

Jaimee grinned with a sly sense of delight. "Oh you are so welcome. That's what sisters are for! Although you shouldn't be going at all, but this is something. What was that word? Karma?"

"Ha ha. Yeah. Whatever."

Michelle shivered from the cool night air as she waited for Jaimee and Janine to exit the auditorium door. So many things were going through her head. Memories of dances from her high school years. Remembering how scary it was for her, wondering if she would be accepted by the popular kids, if she could possibly muster up the nerve to ask a boy to dance, and if she did, would it end with elation or rejection? She remembered, despite the fears, the excitement she felt at all the possibilities of the night. She loved getting dressed up, stepping out of her daily dull existence, and pretending that she was worthy of the love she yearned for. For Michelle, it never ended up as she had hoped. But she always did hope. Each dance, each sports event, was a new chance. She wanted so badly for Jaimee and Janine to find what she couldn't. Here, in the car, waiting in the night for her daughters to appear, she sat expectantly, praying she would hear of that elation in her own daughters. She wanted so much for them to know acceptance and love. She reached under her seat and pulled out a small pair of binoculars to watch as the kids began piling out of the school. She did not want to miss a single moment, and hopefully she could catch a glimpse of that elation to ease her motherly anticipation. As the early departing kids filed out and strolled past the car, she quickly brought the binoculars down so nobody would notice her investigating prowess.

Finally, she saw Jaimee and Janine come strolling out. It was so great to see them together! Michelle and Lisa were never together at school events. They pretended they didn't even know each other. She appreciated that even though these two girls have a lot of disagreements, they were still friends at heart. She raised the binoculars and refocused. She waited and watched as the girls huddled with their friends, giggled and watched the boys as they strutted by. She remembered that feeling. Hoping for that one last chance at making an impression on their friends, and especially the boys. Michelle would have sat there all night to watch this! Maybe she was living vicariously through them, getting a piece of her childhood back. When she saw that the huddle was breaking up, she flicked her headlights on and off so her daughters would know she was there. That was their secret code. She seamlessly slipped the binoculars under her seat as they approached the car.

Jaimee bounded into the front passenger seat while Janine lingered outside the car to talk to a boy who appeared out of the blue. "Hi, Mom!"

"Hi, how was the dance?" As she talked to Jaimee her head was turning to keep her eyes on Janine.

"It was great, Mom. We had so much fun!"

"And who is this talking to Janine?" almost breaking her neck to see the two of them standing outside the car door.

"Well, why don't you get your binoculars out and get a better look?"

Michelle snapped her head back and glared at Jaimee. "What are you talking about?"

Jaimee smiled. "The ones you keep under your seat. Mom, come on. Everybody knows that you sit here and do a peeping Tom thing after our dances. Most of the kids think it's funny. I just think you are so weird."

Michelle chuckled. Caught in the act! "I don't know what you're talking about." She turned to the back seat. "Janine!" She turned back and honked the horn.

Janine opened the door and crawled into the back seat. "Mom, really?"

"Yes, really. Is that Jimmie?"

Janine smiled sheepishly. "Yes."

"Oh, yay! Did you get to ask him to dance?"

"Yes."

"Was it amazing?"

Janine just smiled. Michelle felt her heart leap inside of her. She turned back to face the front, pretending that she couldn't even feel her heart leaping in her chest. "Any chance you might see him again?"

"Well, he knows I'm still grounded until next week. We might get together next weekend."

Okay, Michelle, act cool, she thought. "Oh, that's nice."

She started the short drive home while Jaimee turned to chat with Janine, about all things hopeful, girlish, and boyish...

Chapter 23

I hate this place!

It was Sunday morning, but it was a day like no other. Michelle sat in her art room, wishing the coffee she was sipping would give her the strength to continue on with the letters. Saturday brought a marathon of sorts as she and the girls read through the next three letters. She gazed at the dandelion canvas, and marveled at the sight of the many differently shaded yellow ray flowers with multiple colored words, each one representing the girls' feelings and lessons of each of the letters. There was letter number three, *How Do I Feel Love,* with the words of loved, clean, worthy, deserving, grace, and imagine. And on one small ray flower, the prefix "un", bringing her back to the discussion of turning our feelings of unworthy, undeserving, unclean and unloved into a more positive focus just by removing the prefix "un". Imagining a new mantra. I am worthy. I am deserving. I am clean. I am loved. She remembered the words, *notice when you remove the prefix from these words, what you are left with: Loved...Clean...Worthy...Deserving... These are words that have the power to make you feel again. When you are loved, and clean, and worthy, and deserving, your heart blossoms like a flower and you feel.* These words spoke to Jaimee. She said we should all feel these important words in our life. She really wanted to choose all four of them, and the group decided that this being art, anything goes. Michelle loved watching as the girls each took one and helped Jaimee place her words on the ray flowers, each word in such a different style but unified in their importance.

The word 'grace' was Janine's pick. She really liked the line, *Love is not earned. It is given to you by grace, and you need only accept it.* She talked about how many people feel they have to do something to earn another person's love, but if you need to try to earn another's love, then maybe it wasn't the love you were looking for. Such a grown up thought, Michelle pondered. She thought about the recent occurrence at school, when Janine told them she thought she had to skip school with the popular kids just to belong, even though she knew it was wrong. She wondered if Janine was thinking back on the same experience. Her young Jessie liked the word imagine, because it "makes all things possible." *Imagine what you would feel and be if these words were a description of who you are. Speak of the words you want to be in a daily mantra.* "I am loved. I am clean. I am worthy. I am deserving."

As she gazed upon the painting, she was brought to letter number four, *I Can Never Measure Up.* She studied the words: 'wallflower,' 'dandelion,' 'symphony' and 'bloom.' This was a powerful letter to read. It fully described the dandelion theme that had become so important to them and helped Jaimee and Jessie to hear and contemplate the uniqueness of their being. *Though you may think of it as a common weed, a single dandelion in the midst of a beautiful green field manifests one of the highest forms of beauty in this universe. Each flower head of the dandelion is actually a collection of thousands of small ray flowers. As the head of a dandelion flower opens, each yellow tubular spike is actually a separate flower, a separate creation of the universe.* She remembered how the girls focused back on the canvas and the beautiful dandelion on the painting appearing to come to life with the beautiful words inscribed in it. She thought about Jessie saying, "Wait here!" as she ran outside and moments later came in with four dandelion flowers and handed one to each of them, including Michelle. She loved to watch as they gazed upon one single dandelion bloom with awe. Something they would not have thought of 24 hrs earlier. Jessie chose the word dandelion. Janine shared that she used to feel like a wallflower, but then Jaimee reminded her that she is no wallflower and the world should watch out because it looks like a symphony may be in her future. And bloom was Michelle's word. She reminded the girls that their job is to bloom in this world, and how that looks will be different to each of them. She had asked Jaimee to read that section of the letter again. *You will bloom in all your splendor when it is your time. Do not feel less successful than someone who has achieved their goals. Those are not your goals. Their time is not your time. Your talents need only to be given the time and opportunity to blossom like the dandelion. Do not rush it. But do keep working at it, and have faith that the universe knows the time and the circumstance. It knows the boy you dream of, the recognition you desire, the love you seek, the touch you quench for, and the talent inside of you. Keep developing your true inner beauty and know that your time to shine is near. Just know that your true success will not fit anyone else's definition but yours. Your goals. Your work. Your success.*

Letter number five brought some somber moments. *Don't Touch Me.* This writer had been touched in places that made her hurt and feel uncomfortable. This is abuse. This is not okay. The girls were able to understand the source of their out of the blue discussion a few weeks earlier when Michelle had called that family meeting. This brought some concreteness to that meeting. She could see the seriousness of their thoughts. The facial tension, furred eyebrows, wringing of the hands, squirming in their seats, especially Jessie as this was a subject that had not been in the forefront of her life so far. She was raised in a loving family, safe and secure. But as she was starting to become a young woman, she was becoming more aware of the concepts of violation and specifically sexual harassment and abuse. She was of course learning about these things in school, and in the books she was reading, but now the subject was right in her own personal world. "How do I know who to trust?" she asked.

Michelle remembered saying, "You don't always know. But if you know what you believe in, and what you believe is right, then you will know when someone is a threat to you because they will want you to go against that. You need to always follow that gut feeling of what is right, what feels right, and most importantly, what doesn't feel right. And never be afraid to tell someone close to you. Me, Dad, your sisters, your teacher, anyone you trust that can help you, even if you're not sure of what it is you are experiencing. We can help you figure it out. Because we have all been there in one form or another." She reminded herself of the words the girls had chosen for this part of the painting. 'Safe zone,' 'confused', 'warrior.' Jessie chose the word 'confused.' *I am confused. I'm uncomfortable. And I am too afraid to tell you so...I want to tell somebody but you kept saying not to, and now I don't know what is okay and what is not. All I know is, it doesn't feel okay. And all I can think is, don't touch me. I hold my breath, I close my eyes, but I can still feel you.*

Janine liked the word 'warrior,' because she imagined herself going into battle against a wrong doing. And being victorious over the enemy. *Do not be afraid. You are not the one who wronged. You are the one who WAS wronged. Tell yourself that this was not okay! Tell the world that this is not okay! Never be afraid to tell all who will listen. This is not okay! Stand tall and know that you are so much stronger than this. You are a warrior. You will conquer this enemy!*

Jaimee chose to paint the phrase 'safe zone.' She felt it was important for everyone to know where their safe zone is, who they can reach out to for help. *You do not have to go through this alone! When someone attempts to violate you, get as far away from that perpetrator as you can, and surround yourself with a safe zone.* Michelle felt like she was speaking right to Jessie, being the protector, the second mother that she was to her baby sister. She loved that in Jaimee.

As she finished her morning coffee, Michelle could hear Shawn in the kitchen with the girls as they finished up their late breakfast. She let them all sleep in instead of getting up for church. Yesterday was a pretty emotionally filled day, with the next three letters. Lots of contemplating on where this writer was in her life and how her feelings relate to their lives. She felt pretty good about surviving all of her own emotions for the second time. It actually felt better this second time around, as she could hear even more in the answer letters. She was actually feeling a bit stronger in her resolve to move forward, although at the same time so scared of the unknown and what was still to come.

Letter number Six was the first letter that all three girls would hear together. Michelle had read it prior to her art class on Wednesday. As the girls came barreling in to the art room, Jessie jumped onto the chair, landing on her knees. "Dishes are done! We're ready for the next letter."

Michelle was waiting with letter in hand. "Great! Get off your knees; you're gonna break that chair."

"You always say that and we haven't broken one chair yet."

"And I am going to take a picture of your face when it happens." She scanned the faces of all three girls. "So, how are we feeling about yesterday? We did finish with a pretty heavy subject."

The room was silent for a few heavy moments. Janine broke the barrier. "Yes, it was a heavy subject, but nothing we haven't heard before. I think it just was heavy because we are getting to know Dorothy Doe and it seemed more personal. It was a real live person. I mean, whoever this Dorothy is, she is real and this happened to her. She was touched. It hurt her. She was scared. That is kind of scary."

Jaimee nodded. Yeah, I wish we knew who this was. Not knowing makes me feel a little helpless."

Michelle agreed. "Well, maybe we will find out. Are we good to keep reading?

Jessie reached out for the letter. "Can I read?

Michelle handed it over to Jessie. "Yes, here we go."

Jessie began to read the first letter out loud. Michelle heard only some of the words as she continued to think about this abused child, pondering what happened to her. Did she meet her? Did she know her? Was there any way she could have eased her suffering? *"Please help me escape from this suffering, this sadness, this fear that I live by.....holding me down, keeping me from being able to get up. What is there to get up for, anyways? Not happiness. Not success."* Jessie's lips mouthed a few more lines. She looked up at Michelle. "Who is Carly Simon?"

"An amazing singer, who sang this beautiful song when I was growing up. It's called 'Haven't Got Time for the Pain'. She began to sing the words. "Suffering was the only thing that made me feel I was alive....thought that's just how much it cost to survive in this world..now I haven't got time for the pain...." She hummed a few more bars. "I don't remember all the words. But what was interesting, was this was a song that Aunt Lisa and I would play over and over in our bedroom. So if this was Grandma writing this letter, then it was later in her life and she must have heard us playing it. The words must have resonated with her."

Jaimee, stiffened up. She pointed to the letter. "Grandma? Do you think this was Grandma?"

Michelle shook her head. "No. Well, maybe. I mean, I don't want it to be. But these letters were in her jewelry box."

"So she is a suspect." Janine added.

"Well, I hate that word. Victim would be a better word. But we don't want to make assumptions, which is why we came up with an anonymous name."

Jaimee brought the subject back to the song. "I know Carly Simon's work. She is a timeless singer. I have heard this song. It actually has a happy ending, right? Someone enters her life and infuses it with love."

Michelle smiled. "Yes, you are right. And I hope this writer made it to the end of the song." She looked at Jessie and nodded to signal her to read on.

Jessie went back to the letter. *"Is this my destiny? Do I deserve to be happy after allowing the terrible things that have happened to me? If only for a moment, I dream of escaping to a place of love, of being wanted, of feeling whole, no longer a fragmented, broken soul. Where does this place exist?"* She stopped and looked at Michelle.

"Wow, this person sounds like she is trapped in a prison."

Michelle shook her head. "Perhaps a prison in her mind. I have felt trapped like that at times. Feeling like I have to escape the craziness of the world."

"From us?"

"Oh, no, I mean, yes, this house can get crazy, with three teenage girls, that's for sure! But no, you girls are my reason for living." She paused for a moment in thought. "Sometimes I feel trapped in my mind, with sad thoughts. And I want to escape those thoughts. You probably were too young to remember but a few years back...I went through a deep Depression. There were days I couldn't get out of bed.."

Janine just shook her head.

Michelle continued. "Well, you were only about two. Right after Jessie was born." She looked over at Jessie. "It was nobody's fault. Something chemical that you cannot control. But I felt so trapped right inside my own body that I felt like I was living in a clamshell. I couldn't even go to Uncle Scott's funeral when he passed. Tracy still has not forgiven me for that."

Janine reached out and touched Michelle's arm. "I'm sorry, Mom. So you really know how Dorothy Doe feels. Sometimes I get sad about something and it can feel like I am detached from everyone. It feels lonely."

Michelle put her hand on top of Janine's. "Yes it does. Well, now you know someone who has felt that way and you can share your feelings. You should never feel all alone in times of sadness." She looked to Jessie and Jaimee. "Any of you."

Michelle gently opened the answer letter. "Here, let me read this one to you. Just listen, and tell me what speaks to you."

Suffering is never a destiny. Some experiences make you suffer, yes. These experiences are part of the journey of your life. But you are the conductor of this train. You decide where suffering stops and living your best life begins.

Jessie nodded. "Sometimes I feel like someone else is in charge of my life and I'm too young to change things." Michelle looked up at Jessie and gave a small laugh.

"Sometimes I feel like that except I think I'm too old to change things! That's funny. So, now we know our age has nothing to do with it!" She continued to read.

This is where a good counselor can be instrumental. You cannot move past the suffering until you see it for what it is. You can't run from something until you know what you are running from.

Michelle looked up. "I went to a counselor for a while after my depression. She really helped me to identify things in my life that I may be running from, and most importantly, helped me figure out a reason to get out of bed in the morning. She would say, 'One baby step a day!' I'm glad I had her to talk to."

You need to stop blaming yourself for what has happened to you. You need to identify where it is you want to be in your life and lay a plan to infuse your world with the things or the people that can take you there. That is where you will find escape. What brings a smile to you, even if but for a moment? What brings joy into your life?

She stopped and looked at the girls.

"Well, I can tell you, for me, it's my wonderful family. My husband, my girls. Even when you are fighting with each other, you are bringing me joy to have you in my life."

Janine smiled. "Yeah, my sisters. Even though they can be a pain in the butt, and Jaimee never shares her clothes with me. I guess I wouldn't want to go through life without them. Or you or Dad."

"As I read the questions in this letter, just think about them for a few seconds and then see if you can answer them. "

Think about your interests and what might give you an outlet for your emotions.

Janine thought for a moment. "Hmmm, I love track. I love to run and I always feel a little better after I run." Michelle shook her head in acknowledgement. "You are letting those endorphins kick in. That's why sports are so good for you. Well, you know that. You're smarter than me, but I never said that."

She looked toward Jaimee. "Well, my music and dance is very important to me and helps me cope with any problems in my life. I imagine that I am dancing them away."

Jessie leaned forward to engage. "Cooking is my escape! I love to cook! Especially with you, Mama."

Michelle laughed. "Oh, yes, I know you do love to cook!" Let's read on.

"Consider who in your world you could talk to. Perhaps most importantly, how do you express yourself? Through writing... art... song... physical activity?"

She stopped and waited. Janine pondered, "How do I express myself? Well, I am a good talker!"

Michelle laughed. "Oh yes you are! Better than me! And you are also a good writer, so words come pretty easily for you."

"Yes, I love to write."

"Of course you know for me, I express myself through my art. But your writing is your art. Did you know that? It's how you express yourself."

Janine nodded. "Yeah, I guess I never thought of it as an art."

"As is Jaimee's dance and Jessie's cooking. We need only to see them for what they are and grab ahold of them and they can be our lifelines in the hard times. I have an idea." She reached over to her art table and grabbed a pad of paper and pen. "Let's do something. Let's brainstorm." Michelle led the girls in brainstorming all the things that they love that can help them escape their sadness. As they offered the ideas, she wrote them down in a list. *Dance...music....reading books....poetry....cooking....art....Winnie the Pooh...macaroni and cheese....friends...track...* the list went on and on. They came up with 32 things that they love!

It was fun to bring up positive things in their life. They talked about how these are all the things they can be grateful for in their lives and can remember whenever they feel overwhelmed. She read the final passage of the letter to bring home the answer to escape...

Sometimes it is good to distract yourself from these thoughts of sadness. Other times, it is good to focus on what you are grateful for. You might try journaling or meditation. Pray to the Universe to bring you strength. The Universe brings you so many resources to grab ahold of and bring positivity into your life. Spread that positivity with others and it will flow back to you, surrounding you with that which you have shared.

Janine interrupted, "There's that boomerang thing again!"

Michelle chuckled. *You need only look within your soul to find the escape you desire.*

"The end."

Janine rubbed her eyes. "Wow, that's a lot of advice packed into one letter. But lots of good suggestions."

Michelle nodded. "Wednesday, after reading this, I ran right to my easel and began a painting. I painted sadness, and then I painted joy right over it. It was so healing. I showed it to my class and explained what it represented, and then I had them do a project. I told them to create a piece of art, in any medium, that has two steps. The first step was to show something that scares them or makes them sad. Then I asked them to do another step that shows how they can get through the fear or sadness. It was so healing."

Janine nodded. "Cool." Michelle continued.

Michelle smiled. "Yes. The painting helped me escape from the fear of my nightmare. Even if for just a few hours. And I felt it was important for the kids to learn that they can use art to acknowledge their fears and to find their own escape within their soul."

Jaimee nodded. "It's never too early to start learning. And you are so good with them."

"And through it I discovered one of my students is sad for his mother who is in a difficult relationship with his dad, and she heals through watching a good movie. When she came to pick him up, I invited her to go to that new drive-in with me to watch a sappy movie, and she said yes! She needs a friend, and I think I am going to be that for her. If it wasn't for this letter, I would not have opened my eyes to see her pain."

Janine smiled. "So the answer might not just be looking inside yourself but looking outside as well."

Michelle pointed to Janine. "And you have wisdom beyond your years."

The girls collaborated on their three words, coming up with very insightful ones. Suffering, Escape, and Infuse. Three very important words. A feeling, *suffering*, a desire, *escape*, and an action, *Infuse* all that is good.

Michelle smiled. "Yes. The painting helped me escape from the fear of my nightmare. Even if for just a few hours. And I felt it was important for the kids to learn that they can use art to acknowledge their fears and to find their own escape within their soul."

Jaimee nodded. "It's never too early to start learning. And you are so good with them."

"Thank you Jaimee. I had a good assistant!"

Michelle could feel the tension rising in her body as the girls painted their words on the canvas. Heart pounding. Breaths short and heavy. She found herself wringing her hands. She wasn't sure what was happening, except that this next letter was new to her as well. She had no idea what to expect. How could she support her daughters when she didn't know what support was needed? She reached up and rubbed her face with her hands, hoping to rub the fear away. But it wouldn't leave. She quickly stood up. "Hey, I'll be right back. I need a refill on my coffee. Maybe I'll make some tea. Or something. Not sure what Dad has left for me. I just....I'll be back."

The girls stopped and watched as Michelle swiftly walked into the kitchen. She stopped at the counter and reached up into the cupboard for a coffee cup and set it on the counter. She grabbed the edges of the counter and propped herself against it. She breathed in and out, trying to compose herself. She didn't want the girls to see her this way. Out of control. Fearful. She needed to forge ahead no matter what was awaiting her.

Her thoughts were interrupted as she heard the girls arguing with each other. She ran into the artroom to find Jaimee and Janine shoving each other, Jessie off to the side beginning to cry. She ran over to break up the fight ensuing. "Hey, stop! What is this about?" She separated the two eldest girls. Jessie pointed to the canvas. A long pen mark had been drawn across the painting. "What happened?"

Janine's face became hardened. "I did it! This is a farce! Nobody here is supportive of anyone! It's just all about blame!"

Michelle looked to Jaimee for answers. "What"s going on?"

Jaimee pointed to Janine. "It's her fault that you are having so much to bear. She should have shared this with us. But she wanted all the glory. And now we have to watch you suffer when we could have been dealing with this all along. And now she has destroyed our painting!"

Janine grabbed for the pen that was now lying on the floor. She stood up and reached toward the canvas. "You started this by blaming me for something I had no control over! Here, let me finish this job."

Michelle reached up and stopped Janine, grabbing the pen out of her hands. "Janine, what are you doing?"

Janine turned to Michelle. "Mom, this painting was supposed to be signify us coming together for a common purpose. Nobody is coming together; they are just looking for someone to blame - me!"

Jessie yelled out, "I didn't blame you!"

Michelle put her body between Jaimee and Janine. "Okay, stop this! Both of you. Sit down!" She pointed to the chairs and waited for the girls to reluctantly plop their bodies into the chairs, both crossing their arms in front of each other. "Jaimee, what has brought this on?"

Jaimee looked into Michelle's eyes. "We saw how you retreated into the kitchen. You are clearly overwhelmed with these letters and the thought of reading a new one. If Janine had confided in us, we could have given you more support. It kills us to see you suffering like this."

Janine stood up. "It's killing me too!"

"Sit down, Janine," Michelle turned and directed Janine sternly.

She turned back to Jaimee. "It appears that this journey is affecting all of us, not just myself. I need you to get some composure and realize that Janine has been nothing but supportive of me and of bringing you two into this. She didn't confide in you before because I asked her not to. About that nightmare, I needed time to process. I'm still not there. It's my fault that we didn't include you earlier. About the letters in general, we didn't know if they were even worth sharing. I take full responsibility for that. But you three girls are a team. There is no justification for you to be attacking each other."

She turned back to Janine. "And Janine, destroying the dandelion canvas? Did you see that you made your sister Jessie cry?"

Janine rolled her eyes. "Yep, that's it! I DID IT! It's all my fault! See? It always is!!" Janine screamed at the top of her lungs.

Jaimee and Jessie covered their ears, and then they began to scream.

Michelle was beside herself. All she could do was scream with them.

As suddenly as the screaming started, it stopped. Michelle looked around the table. She looked at the beautiful canvas, now torn. "We began this project to help us come together and support each other with this beautiful art and words. When you attacked the canvas, you attacked your sisters. I will not have this! No, no, no, no!!!" She turned and picked up the canvas and turned it backwards so the art was not showing. "Done. Done with the Dandelion Project. But what else are we done with? Obviously you cannot handle reading the letters so maybe we should be done with them? And what about this family? Are you done with this family? My sisters are done with me. Are you done with me, too? Are you done with each other? We always had a bottom line that love was the tie that bonds through all issues. What has happened to that?"

She began to sob. She couldn't help it.

Jessie started to cry, then Jaimee. Even Janine.

Silence loomed over the room like a black shroud.

Michelle turned to walk away. "I guess we are done with this whole thing."

Jaimee lunged forward and grabbed Michelle's arm. "No, Mom! Don't! We need to continue. I'm sorry."

"Is it me you need to apologize to?"

Jaimee looked at Janine. "I'm sorry, Janine, that I blamed you. It was just so hard to see mom so vulnerable and I didn't know how we could help her."

Janine turned in her chair towards Jaimee and Michelle. "Okay."

Michelle looked down at Janine. "Is that all? Okay? You just destroyed the art project which represented a family journey."

Janine put her head down. "I'm sorry, too. I just lost it, mostly because I was feeling so guilty and you put that into words, Jaimee. It was really me I was trying to hurt." She looked at Jessie, who was still standing cowered in the corner of the art area. "I'm sorry to make you cry, Jessie. I screwed up."

Jaimee reached out and gave Michelle a hug. "We are with you, Mom, 100%." She looked at the other two girls. "Look, enough is enough. Are we ready to support Mom and each other so we can move forward?"

The other two girls nodded. Jessie walked over sheepishly and took a seat.

Jaimee looked at Michelle. "Can we open the next letter?"

Michelle slowly nodded her head. She was not at all sure if this was the right thing to do at this moment, but was there any other direction to move except forward? She reached over to the art supply shelf, opened the shoebox and pulled out envelope number seven. She pulled up a chair to the table. She started reading out loud.

I hate this place! I hate this town. I hate the people in this town. I hate this bed. I hate to crawl into it, because I know the demons will follow me. Even if only in my dreams. I hate these twin beds. I hate sharing my room. Why can't I have a space of my own? These memories will haunt me forever. There is no way to escape them. They follow me up the stairs to this attic space of a bedroom. Drinking, smoking pot, running as fast as I can, will not help me get rid of these demons. I hate the tie dye bedspreads. I hate the matching curtains. I hate all the posters and albums and books and the afghans that grandma made us and painter pants and this stupid stuffed elephant! I am not alone here, but I feel so alone. I have to get out of this place and never look back!

Michelle stopped. She just looked at this letter. She could not believe what she was reading.

"Wait," she whispered with a broken voice. Her hands began to shake. "Oh my God." Chills ran up her spine, up her arms. She could barely breathe. "My mother was an only child. She didn't share a bedroom. And the description of this room – the tie-dye bedspreads and curtains. The posters and albums and afghans that grandma made. The stuffed elephant – this was me and Aunt Lisa's bedroom!"

Janine put her hand on Michelle's arm to help steady her.

"You and Aunt Lisa's bedroom? Are you sure?"

Michelle looked up from the paper. "We shared a room in the attic space at the top of the stairs in that old cape cod house. This was the exact description of our bedroom growing up!" She felt like she was in shock. What could be the explanation? There was only one conclusion to be drawn.

"These were Lisa's letters! She must have been the victim of assault after I went away to college!" She gasped, as the three girls just watched in silence, not knowing what to say or do. "How did I not know this? Lisa said Mom and Harry were dead to her after she left. She had terrible memories that she ran away from and never looked back. No wonder she wanted nothing to do with these letters. Who did this to her? This couldn't have been Grandpa...or could it? Why didn't she let me know? I would have come back from college if I knew!" Tears started to roll down Michelle's cheek.

Jaimee rubbed Michelle's arms gently. "Of course you would have."

Michelle looked back and forth between her daughters. She could feel herself beginning to hyperventilate. She felt hot and cold at the same time. Her hand felt wet, like she could wring them out.

"If these were Lisa's letters, who wrote these answers? Did Mom find them and read them? That would explain them being in her jewelry box. I wonder if Lisa ever saw the answers? She certainly deserved to."

Michelle could feel the tension and rage building inside her body. So many thoughts ran through her mind. "What to do? What to do?" She wondered if she should approach Lisa with this. If this was something she would be willing to share with her if confronted. Or would it drive even more distance between them? "Does she think I deserted her? Is this the reason she spent most of her adult years sabotaging my life? Because I left her to be a victim?" Michelle felt tormented by the many questions, but above all, she knew in her heart that she had to approach Lisa. She had to offer her apologies for not being there for her. For not knowing. This was her sister; she should have just known! There were too many loose ends and feelings that needed to be addressed. She had to make one last trip to Lisa's house. She had to somehow make a connection, right or wrong.

Janine sat in bewilderment. "Mom?" she whispered. "What is going through that head of yours?"

Michelle gazed into Janine's eyes, wanting to speak, wanting to share what was going through her head. But she just sat in silence. Finally, she looked down at the letters. She opened the answer letter and tried to read but could not find a voice. She handed it to Janine. "Here. Can you read this?" Janine took the letter in her hands and began to read.

Hate is a very intense word. There are many things you don't understand right now, and the world lays a path before you. Do you try to hold onto the few moments of happiness that have kept you alive here in this place, or do you run away and never look back? The people or experiences here that gave you sanity may be enough to sustain you, but you have to let them be your support. If you cannot open up to the love that is in your world, then you will be swallowed by your grief. The decision is yours to make. The universe gives you what you need; you don't need to run away. If you choose to try to bury the past, then you risk the chance that you may be running the rest of your life. Because a memory cannot be buried until it is settled. The universe surrounds you with people to love you, experiences to make you smile and laugh, and chances to feel passion in so many forms. But you cannot ever express yourself in this passion until you let go of the chains that hold you back. Destructive behavior is no cure for the demons you try to escape. The only answer is finding the people and things that touch your soul, to open your heart to allow them to bring you joy. For the answer to restoring your soul is found in moments of joy.

Michelle thought about this. She could certainly identify. Yes, she had been running her entire life. She had no idea what from, but she understood this concept. She sometimes hoped that what she was running from would come out in her paintings, but what comes out is usually a tormented soul who does not know what drives these feelings. If these letters were written by Lisa, she was almost jealous, as Lisa then has justification to these inadequate, fearful, lonely, angry, hateful feelings. Michelle found herself more detached than ever before. For many reasons. For not being there for her sister in her time of need. For having these same feelings described in these letters, and yet no tangible reason for them. For the loss of her younger sister, and the love they should have shared all these years. For being afraid to face the world and the opinions that may be rendered about her. But this time was not about her. It was about Lisa, and she needed to make one more trip over to her house to confront her.

Abruptly, she stood. She grabbed the letters out of the shoebox. "I have to go."

Janine stood up with her. "What? What do you mean, you have to go? Where?"

Michelle walked to the kitchen, frantically looking for her purse. "To...Aunt Lisa's. Where is my purse? I always put it in the same spot and it's never there when I reach for it. I swear that thing has a life of its own." She found her purse on the counter and pulled the car keys out of the front pocket.

Janine bolted toward the door with Jaimee and Jessie behind her. "I'm coming with you."

"No, stay here with your sisters. I need to do this myself. Dad is upstairs if you need anything." When she got to the door, she turned to Jaimee. "Can you start dinner? There's.... hamburger....or macaroni... or something. You can figure it out.'

As she started to open the door, Janine called out, "Mom, wait!" She gave Michelle a big strong hug. "I'm in your heart, right here with you."

Jaimee and Jessie both followed. They each gave Michelle a hug and added, "We're with you, Mom. Love you!"

Michelle wiped tears from her eyes. She stepped out the door into the hot afternoon sun.

Michelle felt sick to her stomach as she rang the doorbell. She could hear Prince barking from inside the house, followed by Lisa's footsteps. Lisa looked through the stained glass door and could see that it was Michelle on the other side. She cracked the door open.

"I thought we were clear the last time you were here. I would let you know if I remembered anything, and I haven't."

Michelle held up the collection of letters. "We need to talk. Now."

Lisa looked at the letters in her hand, and said, "Just a minute." She closed the door. Michelle could hear her bring Prince to the basement. After a minute that seemed like an hour, Lisa opened the door. She said nothing. Michelle walked past her and sat down on the stairs leading to the second floor. She just looked at Lisa.

"What?" asked Lisa.

Michelle took a deep breath and let it out, gathering the strength to begin this conversation. She opened the last letter, and began to read. "I hate sharing my room. Why can't I have a space of my own? These memories will haunt me forever. There is no way to escape them. They follow me up the stairs to this attic space of a bedroom. Drinking, smoking pot, running as fast as I can, will not help me get rid of these demons. I hate the tie dye bedspreads. I hate the matching curtains. I hate all the posters and albums and books and the afghans that grandma made us and painter pants and this stupid stuffed elephant!"

Lisa just looked at Michelle. "So?" she asked.

"So. This is our bedroom. Those were our tie-dye sheets. We used to sneak out and smoke pot and drink Boones Farm Wine. That was my stuffed elephant and you hated it."

"Yes, I did. What's your point?"

"My point is," continued Michelle, "that these were not Mom's letters. They were yours."

"What?" gasped Lisa. "Wow, you have gone off the deep end!"

"Well, whose else could they be? Lisa, what happened after I left for college? Who did this to you?"

Lisa was shocked. "Look, I don't know what you are smoking, but I assure you that these were not my letters!"

Michelle pressed on. "It certainly explains a lot. Your attitude toward me all these years. You were violated, and I wasn't there for you. I only wish that you had reached out to me. I feel so helpless. I feel that I let you down. And you took it out on me all these years."

Lisa laughed a little, "Ha, of course, this is so like you! Everything revolves around you. So you think I was abused but it is all about how it affected you. Well, don't flatter yourself. I don't know who wrote the damn letters and I don't care. Are we finished?"

Michelle stood up and moved closer to Lisa. "No, we are not. We need to talk about this. I feel terrible. I wish I could have been there for you. I want to know, who did this to you? I'd like you to share this with me. I feel responsible."

Lisa turned away from Michelle. "Unbelievable," she muttered.

Michelle continued, "Lisa, I need to know. Who did this to you? Was it Harry? Was it a boy at school? Anybody I knew? How did you deal with this? How can I help you now?"

Lisa began to become more agitated. "Mickey, I am telling you I did not write those letters!"

Michelle would not take no for an answer. She worked to keep her voice calm. "Lisa, I am here, reaching out to you. There is nobody else who could have written these letters. You and I were the only ones who were in that bedroom. I want to help. I may not have been there for you when this happened, but I want to help you in any way I can now."

Lisa finally lost her composure and raised her voice." Look, Mickey, I did not write the letters! I found the letters. I did not write them!"

Michelle stopped in her tracks and just looked at Lisa. She then inquired, "What do you mean you found the letters?"

"Just like I said. I found them."

After a long moment of silence, Michelle asked, "If you found the letters, then who wrote them?"

Lisa looked into Michelle's eyes. "You did."

"What?" gasped Michelle. She could not believe what she was hearing.

"You did. You wrote the letters, okay? I found them under your bed after you left for college. I don't know how long you took to write them, but they were yours. I know because that was your rose garden stationery. You wouldn't let anybody use it because that sacred neighbor guy gave it to you."

Michelle stepped back. "Rose garden stationery? I don't remember owning any rose garden stationery. And I couldn't have written these letters. First, I don't remember writing them. And second, I was not sexually assaulted."

Lisa took a deep breath, in and out. "Yes, you were. We both were."

Michelle stared at Lisa.

"Breathe, Mickey."

Michelle breathed.

Lisa continued. "By Dad. We used to go there when we were young. Dad had us take naps together and then he..."

"Stop!" interrupted Michelle. "Stop this! Nothing like that happened! Why are you saying this to me? You want to save yourself from admitting that these were your letters, that's one thing, but to suggest that we were molested by Dad....now, that is going too far! I know he was an asshole and treated mom horribly, but sexually assaulting us?"

"I am not suggesting anything," stated Lisa. "I was there."

Michelle sat back down on the stairs and just held her head in her hands for what seemed like forever. Finally, she looked up at Lisa. "Okay, so just for the sake of a ridiculous argument, let's say I wrote these letters. Michelle paused for several moments, then asked, "What did you do with them when you found them? And who wrote the answers?"

Lisa walked over and sat down next to Michelle. The air was thick and it was hard for Michelle to breathe. Lisa began to speak in a quiet voice. "I wrote the answers."

Michelle just looked at Lisa in disbelief. "What do you mean you wrote the answers?"

"Just like I said. I wrote the answers."

Michelle's voice was barely a whisper. "No."

Lisa ignored her and continued. "I found them under your bed like I said. As I read them, I felt the same shame and loneliness and fears that you described. Remember, I was there. I was in this psychology class in college and was learning about resources that can help the abused person so I read and read and learned as much as I could. And I wanted the answers as much as you did. I thought, if I answered these questions for somebody else, maybe I could heal from them as well."

Michelle paused for several moments, then asked, "And did you?"

Lisa answered, "It's a process."

Michelle stood up, and walked toward the door. "I can't...no." She looked at Lisa and said, "I don't know what to say or what to believe."

Lisa nodded her head as she opened the door, as Michelle walked through.

Chapter 24

Can I really forget?

Michelle drove for what seemed like an eternity. It was an hour to Tracy's house. She had not talked to Tracy since just after her husband's funeral. Michelle had tried to call her to explain why she could not make it, to tell her about the depression that took over her life. She finally gave a cordial forgiveness to Michelle, but there had been no contact since then. The ties had been severed. Lisa had convinced her that Michelle did not care to be there for her on that most difficult day. So now she found herself driving to Tracy's house. She had no idea what type of reception she would receive, if any. She had been there many times earlier on, their children having many play dates while she and Tracy just talked about anything, everything. And though she knew in her heart that Tracy just did not want to further their relationship, this was a visit that needed to happen. She drove into Tracy's driveway and stepped out of the car.

As she looked at the beautiful brick structure, she remembered memories of the past. Their children playing in her pool in the backyard while she and Tracy sat and sipped iced green tea, and spoke of all the worries of the world. Memories of her own wedding with the justice of the peace, when Tracy came and witnessed Michelle's wonderful wedding day. Memories of play dates, mama luncheons, and just plain talking together. As she thought about these memories, Tracy appeared from her front door. "Well, I would for sure say this is an unexpected surprise. "

"Hi," said Michelle timidly. Several moments passed. "Can I talk to you?" she asked.

Tracy at first looked disinterested, but then tears started to roll down Michelle's face. "Come on, girl," she said, motioning for Michelle to come into the house. Tracy led her into the kitchen and put on a pot of coffee.

Michelle sat. She tried to wipe the tears away, but they kept coming.

Tracy started the conversation. "So what's going on?"

Michelle started to speak but wasn't sure what words to use. "I don't know how to even describe what has been happening these past few weeks. But I need to ask you a question." The two women sat in silence for a few moments. "Was I abused by our father?"

Tracy just looked at Michelle, and could feel the tension, the sadness, the thick air of suffering that just lingered between them. Almost pushing against the air, she got up and poured two cups of coffee from the pot that wasn't even finished brewing yet. She sat down and placed a cup in front of Michelle. "Yes," she said. Her voice was flat. "You and Lisa both."

Michelle put her head in her hands and sobbed. She thought back to that first letter and her thoughts of not knowing why she cries. Now she knew. And the second letter of what she was fearful of. Now she knew. And of what she has been trying to run away from all these years. Now she knew. She looked up at Tracy. "And you?"

Tracy shook her head. "No, it didn't happen to me. Maybe because I was older. Maybe because, as I found out much later in life, I was not his child."

Michelle gasped, "What? What do you mean, you were not his child?"

Tracy shrugged, and took a sip of her coffee. "I always suspected there was a distance between us growing up. When he was taking you and Lisa for your visitation, he never seemed to want me there. The times I came he only spent his time with you. He put me in front of the TV most of the time and then disappeared with you two. Later when Mom was alone, after Harry died, I went to see her. She looked at me and said, 'You look so much like your father.' I said that was silly because our father had dark hair and dark eyes and I was blonde with blue eyes. And she said, 'Like I said, you look so much like your father.' And then she changed the subject and I knew that was all she was going to offer."

"So you don't know who your real father was?"

Tracy answered, "No, and I'm dealing with it. There is not much I can do about it unless he comes looking for me."

"I'm sorry, Tracy. And I'm sorry for so many things in my life but mostly for missing Scott's funeral, for the distance that has been put between us. You were my lifeline, my support. If I could have made it that day, I would have. The strength of a chemical depression is so overpowering. I should have been in counseling to help deal with it so that I could at least engage in the one day that you needed me. I have never forgiven myself for that. I did go to a counselor after that, I felt so guilty."

Tracy reached out to Michelle and held her hand. "No, Mickey. I'm sorry. I was so hard on you. You never had a chance to heal, because you didn't even know it had happened. I was unfair to you."

Michelle sobbed. Her heart, shattered into a million pieces by her father, again by Tracy and her mom and Lisa...somehow it had shattered again. How could they do this to me? she thought. Finally she said, "I found these letters in Mom's jewelry box."

Tracy brought her second hand up and clasped Michelle's hand in both of hers. "I know about the letters."

"You do? How do you know about the letters?"

"Mom showed them to me. Lisa found them in a box under her bed after you moved out of the house. Mom was devastated. Lisa tried to explain that she went through it as well, but Mom didn't believe her. She blamed Lisa for the abuse. They had a huge fight. I guess she couldn't handle the fact that it was both of you. She knew it was you, because Mr Brandsen told her. That's why Dad came over that horrible night. Mr Brandsen was going to call the police. Dad had to stop him. She carried the knowledge of your abuse with her all these years. She didn't know what to do. But to hear Lisa was also affected by it, well, she just couldn't handle it and she blamed Lisa. Dad had died in prison years before. You were essentially raised by Harry. He was a very good man, but the damage was done. You had suppressed the memories so she thought best to leave it alone. Lisa never forgot. I think Lisa always struggled with what happened. It tore her first marriage apart, and then she went into counseling. That has helped her move forward, but....she's still hurting."

Michelle reached up and rubbed her forehead, hoping all this information would just pass through and return to the universe. She wiped another tear from her eye. "Lisa never said anything to me. How do you keep a secret like this for so long?"

Tracy shrugged. "I think the two of you being estranged from each other made it easier. I remember her saying to me once that she didn't know who was the lucky one – Lisa for being in counseling and facing the past or you for suppressing it."

Michelle gently pulled her hand back. "Well, the memories may have been suppressed, but the pain has always been there."

"I am sure," acknowledged Tracy. "So where do you go from here?"

"Wow," realized Michelle, "I still have to go on? Because I feel like my life just ended." More tears forced their way down her face. "I feel empty and yet overflowing with sadness at the same time. I don't know. I guess I go home, hug my girls, talk to Shawn and figure out step one."

"And Lisa?" asked Tracy.

"I can't even think about Lisa right now. Too much hurt has come between us. I don't know if we can ever find a path back to each other."

Tracy nodded, then got up and walked over to Michelle and gave her a hug. "And remember, my sister, you do have me. I'm so sorry that I let so much time and distance between us pass. Let's fix that."

"I'd like that, Tracy." Michelle looked at her mug. "I didn't even touch my coffee!"

Tracy chuckled. "Don't worry about that."

"Yeah, I guess in the grand scheme of things, that's pretty small potatoes.

"Microscopic."

She smiled. Looking up, she saw Tracy smiling. It was the first time in years they had smiled together. It felt different this time. More raw. But better.

Tracy touched her arm. "Are you okay to drive?"

Michelle nodded. "Yes, but if I sit in your driveway and just cry don't worry about it. The universe decides when I need a good cry and I feel like it may be speaking to me soon."

Tracy gave a little chuckle and said, "I don't mind. Cry all you need to. Love you, girl."

"Love you, too," Michelle said as she hugged her sister. It was a precious feeling. "I missed this, Trace."

"Me too," Tracy said, her voice breaking.

The two parted reluctantly. Michelle caught Tracy's gaze, soaking in Tracy's tearful smile. She turned and walked toward the door, realizing that she was taking her first step into the rest of her life.

The girls were waiting in the living room with Shawn. They jumped up as Michelle pulled into the driveway. She sat there for what seemed like forever until she could muster the strength to go into the house. The girls all gathered around her. "Mom! Thank God you're home!" Are you okay?" They each took turns giving her a hug. Shawn was the last to hug her. He whispered in her ear, "I talked to Tracy."

She was so relieved that she didn't have to explain it to him. "The girls?"

Shawn squeezed her upper arms. "I thought you'd want to tell them."

Michelle nodded. She gently pulled away from Shawn. "Well, ladies, sorry to keep you waiting so long. Shall we go back into the art room? I have some news to share with you. And I have never needed my daughters like I need you now."

Janine grabbed Michelle's hand. "Yes, and Mom, we have something to share with you." She directed Michelle into the art room, where the dandelion canvas was sitting forward on the easel, but with a change. The dandelion was made more beautiful by streaks of gold popping out of the middle of the bloom. The streaks were textured, and iridescent. They glowed as the light reflected against it.

Michelle gasped. "What is this?"

Janine began to explain. "Do you remember teaching us in one of your classes about Kintsugi, which means "joining with gold"?

Michelle smiled. "Yes, I remember. It's a Japanese art form in which they repair broken pottery with gold, silver or platinum to actually highlight the imperfection and make it even more beautiful. The idea is that when we embrace imperfection, we can create something more beautiful and stronger."

Janine brought Michelle over to the painting. "We used an iridescent paint to create textured gold streaks that shimmer, to make the dandelion really pop."

Michelle began to cry. She couldn't believe she had more tears left in her. "I love it, it's beautiful."

Jessie pointed out three new words. "We added our words from this last letter! Restore, Joy, Passion. We took only the positive words because those are the ones you want to remember."

Michelle laughed with a delight she had not felt for many, many years. "I totally agree!"

Jaimee drew her attention to the center of the painting. "Look real close here, Mom. We used the iridescent paint to drop a small heart in the center. Because love is the tie that bonds through all issues."

Jessie added, "And sometimes we can put the broken pieces back together into something even more beautiful."

Michelle nodded. "Yes." She stood in reverent silence for a moment. The many layers of meaning in what the girls had said, how it applied to them, to the canvas, to Michelle's own heart, washed over her. "I cannot tell you how much this means to me." She took a deep breath. "So, let's have a seat. There is something I need to share with you."

As they all filed into their chairs, Michelle could see Shawn appearing in the doorway. He walked over to her and leaned over, touching her shoulder, and whispered in her ear.

"Can you use some support?"

Michelle smiled and patted the chair next to her. "I will take all the support I can get."

Monday came very quickly. Michelle was emotionally exhausted from the weekend. The girls had finished breakfast and were ready to file out the door for the bus. Jaimee took Michelle by the shoulders. "Are you going to be okay today? Do you need us to stay home with you?"

"Oh, yeah, anything to skip school! You guys get out of here. I am a big girl, and after this weekend, I know I am never alone. I know where my strength comes from. My life begins today. I may take a peek at the last letter today; it can't drop any more destructive bombshells than they already have. But we'll share it together as well when you get home."

"Are you sure, Mom? We don't want you to be alone."

Michelle turned Jaimee around and shuffled Janine and Jessie behind her. "Dad will be home soon! I am not alone! Thank you so much for worrying about me! I'll see you in a few hours!" She closed the door behind the girls as they waved and got onto the bus. She sighed, turned slowly and poured herself a cup of coffee. She sat at the table and just stared forward out the window. Her body fell into a trance, reliving the scene that had unearthed her life just 24 hrs earlier.

It wasn't long before she startled to the creaking of the kitchen door. She shook her head as she brought the current moment forward. As Shawn ushered through, she could feel a swelling of emotion in her body. She hadn't had a chance to talk through the events of the day before with Shawn as he had to go to work. Her muscles were aching from the hours of tossing and turning, trying to chase away the demons of her past. She raised her head to receive a kiss from Shawn as he bended over her body. "How is my beautiful wife?"

Michelle smiled. She motioned for Shawn to sit at the table. She stood up and grabbed a cup of coffee and set it in front of him. "Tired, Sad. In disbelief. Angry." She stopped and thought for another few seconds. "Confused. How about you?"

Shawn received the coffee from Michelle and reached out to caress her arm as she sat down next to him. "I thought about you all night. Wondering what I could possibly do to take this burden away from your heart."

Michelle shrugged. "I don't think that's possible." She stared down into her cup as if the answers were hiding in the coffee.

After a short but uncomfortable silence, she cleared her throat and began to speak. She looked up at Shawn. "I just don't understand. If all this is true as Lisa and Tracy say it is, how could I not have known? Did I block it out? Do people even do that?"

Shawn shook his head. "I don't know. I have never heard of that. But that doesn't mean it couldn't happen."

"All those feelings I have had through these years. My fears, insecurities, depression, my inability to have a relationship with my mother, or my sisters, my inability to love you like you deserve."

Shawn reached for Michelle's hand and squeezed it. "Don't say that. You have loved me more than I deserve. And our beautiful family."

Michelle turned her head slightly and lovingly nodded. "I wouldn't have been able to get through all of this, all these years, without you and those three rugrats." She stopped for a moment in contemplation, and then continued. "And also... maybe without the healing words in those letters. Even if they did come from the one person who I blamed for all my suffering. It's ironic that she is connected to the suffering, as well as the light."

" The light?" Shawn had a confused look on his face.

"Yeah, the white light. Remember the words of the Carly Simon song about suffering from the letters? Well, there were more words worth remembering from that song. The song was Haven't Got Time for The Pain. I know the words by heart. Lisa and I used to sing them together."

"What were the words?"

"Suffering was the only thing that made me feel I was alive.

Thought that's just how much it cost to survive in this world.

Til you showed me how, how to fill my heart with love...

How to open up and drink in all that white light

Pouring down from the heavens...

I haven't got time for the pain..."

Shawn nodded. "And the white light is love? Funny, this white light comes from a very unexpected source, the one who stood by and watched you suffer."

"Yeah." She reached up and rubbed her temple. She just wished all the knots in her head would loosen.

Shawn reached up to rub her shoulders. "You will heal from this. The girls and I will see to it."

Michelle reached her hand up to meet his hand on her shoulder. "That is one thing I am sure of. How it will happen, I'm not sure, but I know I won't be alone. I have the four of you."

"And what about Lisa? And Tracy?"

Michelle sighed. "I think Tracy will be there for me. And I'm looking forward to repairing my relationship with her. Lisa?" She shook her head. "I just can't say right now. I need time to process."

Shawn nodded. "Then time you shall have. What do you think about talking to a counselor to help unravel all the unknowns?"

"And the knowns as well! Yes, I do think I need to start there." She took a deep breath. I just need a minute.."

Shawn stood up and kissed Michelle on the forehead. "Absolutely. I'm gonna head to bed. You know where to find me if you need anything."

Later that afternoon, Michelle sat in her art studio as she contemplated the events of the day before. The letters, the words, the art, the destruction of the art, the healing of the art, the news of her past abuse, the reconciliation with her sister Tracy, the truth about the nightmares, the bombshell about her sister Lisa. The girls would be home soon. As she sat there, she thought, there is no time like the present to read the last letter. There wasn't much to lose at this point. She opened the shoebox and began to read from envelope #8.

Can I really forget? Can I really escape? Can I really start a new life, or will these memories follow me, haunt me, all the days of my life? Will I be a prisoner of this man all the days of my life? Did I allow this to happen? Is it my fault? All I want is to start a new life, where there are no more fears and judgments and loneliness. Is it out there? Will I find what I am looking for? What will be the price to pay? Please tell me, will I ever break these chains that bind me into the submission of being a victim? I want so much to find a new identity, but what happens to the person I was? Please help me wipe the slate clean and let me start my life all over. Help me to forget all that has happened. I am not that person. This did not happen to me. I am not a victim!

Michelle felt a greater sense of this message than any of the ones that came before. This is what she was doing all these years; forgetting what had happened, burying these events, thinking that if she did not acknowledge them, then they would never have existed. But you can only do that for so long, and your soul knows the truth. She opened the answer letter.

Running away would be our natural instinct. If we have been hurt, we can spend a lifetime trying to run and hide from this pain. But that pain hangs on in one form or another. As this pain keeps you a prisoner of the past, it is difficult to be fully alive in the present. You certainly have reason to not want to feel this pain, but feel it you must, so that you can move past it. It will always be there, but it doesn't need to be in the forefront of your life. You need to let the memory exist, but then tell it where it needs to be, which is not running your world, your life, your relationships, your emotions. So the answer to your question is, no, you can not really forget. Nor do you want to. You want to remember the lessons you have learned. You want to know what it is that you will never allow to happen to you or anyone you love ever again. You want to know that you can live a normal life, that you can experience happiness again, and most importantly, that you deserve happiness. You want to know what makes you move past the pain and share that with others who are suffering their own pain. You want to remember that this experience gave you a purpose in life. You want to always remember that you are not defined by what happens to you. You want to teach others the meaning of the word no. Don't run from the memories of your past. If you can face the memories of the past and know them for what they are, then you can truly be open to the blessings of the future.

Michelle contemplated this for a long time. She thought about all the letters and the messages of hope. Her relationship with Lisa. Those younger years. No matter how hard she tried, she still could not remember any details; she knew she would need some professional help to assist her in dealing with this. She owed it to herself and her family.

She got up and walked down to the basement, to the very back set of shelves. Reaching high above her head, she took down a box. There she found her high school yearbook. She smiled as she opened it. She had some good memories of that time. She started reading the notes and signatures from the other students. She turned the page, and became frozen in her tracks. Stuck in her yearbook was a single piece of stationery paper; it had an antique edging that resembled the vines of a rose bush, cream colored, with a slightly wrinkled appearance. "I remember this paper now," she thought. She stood up and went into the kitchen and opened the phone book and dialed a number.

"Hello?" she began. "I would like to make an appointment to see a counselor......yes.....possible sexual abuse in my past........."

Epilogue

Since I found one last piece of stationery in my yearbook, it is fitting that I should use it for this final letter. This one does not need an answer. I have spoken to Tracy and confirmed what I still was not 100% sure of when I walked out your door. I feel I need to follow up with you and find some closure to all of this, although I am not quite sure of what to say. There are a few things I know, so I guess I will start with that.

I know that we have had a very rocky road as sisters. Even when we lived together growing up, although we had some good times in between, there was always some animosity between us. Maybe it goes back to the abuse we shared but could not speak of. This may have been increased by my not reaching out to you after I left for college. Many years have passed, and we never seemed to get over the fragmentation of our relationship. You have hurt me very much over the years, making me feel that you were turning our family against me, whether you intended to or not. For these reasons, I am sure that we will not mend our relationship this very minute, and I suspect it may never mend. We will leave the future of us up to "the universe". If it is meant to be, then we will find a way. I hope that I can find enough healing to be open to it when that time comes.

Having said that, there is one other thing I know, and it must be said. Your words have changed my life. They were healing for me in so many ways, and the plain truth is, they are beginning to make me a better person, a better mother, a better wife, and a better friend. For this I will be truly grateful. I know I need to go to a counselor and face these demons that I had apparently suppressed all these years. I promise you that I will do this. I will work *through this. You have given me the confidence I need to move forward and to get the help I need. I hope that these beautiful, healing words you wrote have helped you as well.*

Like the dandelion in my letters, I have come to discover a little more of the complex being that I am and that I strive to be. I make a promise to both you and to myself that my journey begins here, and as the dandelion blooms, so my life begins.

Mickey

Endnotes

1. Neil Diamond, "I am...I said." 1971. Geffen Records.

2. Tony Romeo, "I Think I Love You." 1970. Universal Music Group. Originally recorded for the Partridge Family and sung by David Cassidy.

About the Author

I have been writing words of inspiration for many years—words that come straight from the heart. My life has been shaped by walking alongside others through struggle and hope. I've spent 45 years as a nurse, comforting patients and families through their hardest moments. I've mothered a beautiful girl into womanhood, the caregiver of a mother with dementia, and the guardian of my autistic brother. I've fought breast cancer alongside my sister. While my battle ended, my sister's continues with what is now metastatic cancer. She continues to inspire me with her tenacity and strength. I've known the heartbreak of divorce, the weight of financial hardship, and the quiet strength it takes to keep going. Today I live with my partner Steve on the beautiful Northern California coast.

Through it all, I've come to believe in the power of everyday miracles—the small, sacred moments that move us forward. Writing has always been my way of reaching out to others, offering encouragement and light to those who need to know they're not alone. Whatever you're going through, I want you to know: there is always hope.